The Right Side

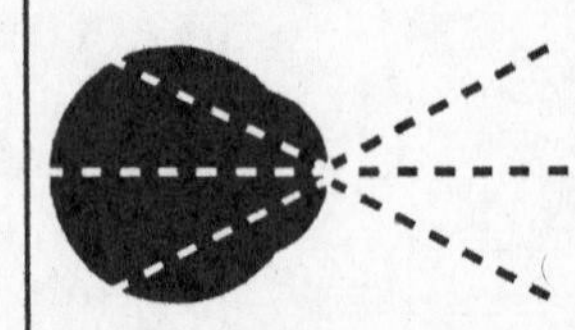

The Right Side

Spencer Quinn

THORNDIKE PRESS

A part of Gale, Cengage Learning

GALE
CENGAGE Learning

Farmington Hills, Mich • San Francisco • New York • Waterville, Maine
Meriden, Conn • Mason, Ohio • Chicago

Thorndike Press, a part of Gale, Cengage Learning.

Thorndike Press® Large Print Core.
The text of this Large Print edition is unabridged.
Other aspects of the book may vary from the original edition.
Set in 16 pt. Plantin.

LIBRARY OF CONGRESS CATALOGING-IN-PUBLICATION DATA

Names: Quinn, Spencer, author.
Title: The right side / by Spencer Quinn.
Description: Large print edition. | Waterville, Maine : Thorndike Press, a part of Gale, a Cengage Company, 2017. | Series: Thorndike Press large print core
Identifiers: LCCN 2017022866 | ISBN 9781432839642 (hardcover) | ISBN 1432839640 (hardcover)
Subjects: LCSH: Large type books. | BISAC: FICTION / Mystery & Detective / General. | FICTION / Suspense. | FICTION / General. | GSAFD: Mystery fiction. | Suspense fiction.
Classification: LCC PS3617.U584 R54 2017b | DDC 813/.6—dc23
LC record available at https://lccn.loc.gov/2017022866

Published in 2017 by arrangement with Atria Books, an imprint of Simon & Schuster, Inc.

Printed in Mexico
1 2 3 4 5 6 7 21 20 19 18 17

For Josh, Angie, and Cassie

CHAPTER ONE

"Just want to make sure I've got your name right." The man — Machado, read the tag hung around his neck — swiveled sideways to check his laptop. The chair made a squeaky sound, intolerable to the woman sitting on the other side of the desk. It sparked a headache in the spot where her headaches got sparked these days, a headache that then blossomed like an explosion in slow motion, so slow you might have thought it would peter out, or be easily stopped. She knew better.

Machado — Dr. Ernest Machado, Psychiatric Services, according to the name tag — squinted at the screen. "Still getting used to these darn progressives," he said, tapping his glasses.

"Poor you," she said.

Dr. Machado shot her a speedy glance, returned to the screen, nudged his glasses a little higher up on his nose.

That glance? Furtive, she thought. Or had she said it aloud, called him furtive to his face? A toss-up, and she really didn't give a shit.

"LeAnne Hogan?" he said.

"Yes."

"LeAnne all one word?"

"Yes."

"But with the *A* capped?"

"That a problem?"

"Oh, no, no, no. You should see some of the names we get here." Dr. Machado tapped at the keyboard, then squeaked back around to face her. She thought of killing him with her bare hands, but it was only one of so many thoughts in her head at that moment, scarcely noticeable.

He gazed at her in the new off-center way people used on her now. "How about we begin by you telling me why you're here? Can I get you water or something? Coffee?"

"Why I'm here?"

"Your understanding of why you're here."

She shrugged. "I was sent," she said. "Referred."

"Right, of course, but . . . but in a larger sense, LeAnne."

"A larger sense? Isn't it part of the protocol?"

Dr. Machado made a note on a desk pad.

It looked like one of those prescription pads. She was on Paxil, prednisone, penicillin, and Percocet, and those weren't even all of the *P*s.

"Right again," said Dr. Machado. "But what is it you'd like to accomplish? That's what I'm getting at. If we know your goals, we can help you reach them."

She nodded. "Coffee. With milk and lots of sugar."

Dr. Machado blinked. He rose and went to a Mr. Coffee in the corner.

"At least two packets. Three's better."

Initial Evaluation for Post-Traumatic Stress Disorder:
Premilitary History:

1: Describe family structure and environment where raised (identify constellation of family members and quality of relationships):

"You got the craziest laugh in the whole goddamn world," Daddy said.

Which only made LeAnne laugh harder.

"What's so funny?"

"Everything!" She took a couple of short, quick steps, then ran off a series of cartwheels, ending with a twist and a two-footed landing, stuck like totally, easy as pie.

"Whoa. Where'd you learn that?"

"Gymnastics!"

"Yeah?" Daddy reached into the truck, took the .22 off the rack. "Here," he said. "Take Little P. I got the cooler."

Little P, short for Little Protector, was what Daddy called the .22. Daddy was big on protection: "It's what we do in this family going way, way back. All the way to the Civil War, both sides." LeAnne took Little P from him, checked the safety — numero uno first goddamn thing every time, like he'd told her — then held it in the proper way, by both hands and with the muzzle pointing down at a forty-five-degree angle, which was how she'd learned degrees, resulting in an A-plus on the class participation half of her Exploring Science grade. Then she and her daddy walked up a long slope where some big saguaros grew, Daddy carrying the cooler. There were bullet holes in a few of those saguaros, always at the tops where the heads would be, if saguaros had heads, but she and Daddy were blameless.

"What the hell is wrong with some people?" he said.

"Does it hurt the saguaros?"

"What do think? Look at them. Those

holes seem right to you?"

"No. But I meant does it give them pain?"

Daddy inclined his head toward her. He had the best face you'd ever want to see, a big rough face with watchful eyes that shone when things were going well, like now, out in the desert. "Good question," he said.

They walked on, reached the top of the slope, sat down. Daddy lifted the cooler lid, cracked open a cold one. The other side of the slope was very steep and rocky, all the way down to a dry wash with two cottonwoods growing along the near bank. An old rusted-out car shell was parked between the cottonwoods, if you could say parked about such a wheel-less ruin. But that was how it looked to LeAnne, like someone had been out driving and ended up parking in a shady spot on some long ago nice day for a spin.

"Nineteen-forty-seven Buick Roadmaster. My uncle Rodney had one, if I remember right."

"Who's Uncle Rodney?"

"Great uncle."

"What's great about him?"

"Christ. Just means . . . forget what it means. Doesn't matter. A hopeless juicer. Went boots up when I was just a kid, younger than you. Roadmaster was long departed by then. I only know from old photos."

"Can I see them?"

Daddy shook his head. "All gone."

"In the fire?"

"Yup."

Daddy tossed the empty into the cooler, helped himself to another cold one, and handed her one of those gingerbread men with mint-green eyes that Mom baked and LeAnne loved. The fire was a big deal in family history, burning down the house Daddy had grown up in, outside of Flagstaff, and killing his parents, meaning LeAnne's grandparents. Daddy was overseas at the time, just getting started in the service, and hadn't even met Mom yet, meaning this was way before LeAnne was born, so she'd never known that set of grandparents. For different reasons, she didn't know the other set, either.

"Okay," Daddy said, taking a nice sip. "Enough chitchat. Let's see what you can do."

"Just sitting like this?"

"Why not?" Daddy gestured down at the 1947 Buick Roadmaster. "Right side taillight still intact?"

"What's intact?"

"Unbroken."

LeAnne peered down. She had very sharp

eyesight, according to Dr. Ralpundi, who did the preseason examinations for all the sports teams — 20/15 in her left eye, even better in her right. "Yeah."

"Break it."

The right, of course, was her shooting eye, although she kept the left open, Daddy-style. "How else are you gonna know when someone comes after you outta left field?" Which never failed to get her laughing, like suddenly baseball was turning up in your life.

LeAnne raised Little P. "Let the weapon find the target," Daddy always said. Also pretty funny, to LeAnne's way of thinking. Because how could it do that on its own? The weapon was just a thing. But she'd learned early on that it turned out to be kind of true. She peered through the sight with her right eye, not looking at the distant taillight at all, just at the space inside the little *V,* let out every puff of her breath, stopped time, and in the moment before time would start up again, she pulled the trigger, *pulling* not being the right word. Pulling was too strong. This was more like the force you'd use to press the thingamijig at the top of a ballpoint pen to make the tip stick out.

Crack. But not a loud crack. This was only

a .22, after all. Neither was there much in the way of recoil, just the slightest of kicks, like a baby in the mommy's tummy. Then came the soundless shattering of the taillight, and tiny red shards went flying in the sunshine. Real tiny, like solid blood drops. Weapon finds target.

"Yup," Daddy said.

Then it got very quiet, middle-of-the-desert quiet mixed in with that quiet that comes when the shooting stops. "Maybe it's the same one," LeAnne said.

"Huh?"

"Great uncle Rodney's nineteen-forty-seven Buick Roadmaster."

"Where'd you get a notion like that?"

"Don't be mad."

"I'm not mad. Why'd I be mad? I'm just saying where'd you get the goddamn notion?"

"It popped up in my mind."

He looked down at her again. Then he rumpled her hair. "Got a head of hair on you."

"Mom says there's nothing to be done with it."

"She does, does she?"

"A rat's nest."

"That what she calls it?"

"Uh-huh."

Daddy turned away, drained the cold one, tossed it in the cooler, and was reaching for another when he paused. "Gimme that thing," he said.

LeAnne clicked the safety into place, handed him the .22.

"Maybe that is Rodney's old Roadmaster, after all," he said.

"Really, Daddy?" She came close to jumping up and down.

"Better odds than the lottery. Lottery's like millions to one. But the Roadmaster? Think about it. How many forty-seven's got sold in Arizona? A few thousand?"

"So the odds would be a few thousand to one? Is that how you figure out odds?"

Daddy didn't answer. Instead, he stepped close to the edge of the ridge and yelled, "Hey, Rodney! Heads up!" And then, holding the .22 kind of casually, like Little P was only a toy, he took a series of shots, so quick it was almost like automatic fire, and a line of holes appeared all along the side of the Roadmaster, so perfectly and evenly spaced that they might have been part of the design.

"Here you go," Dr. Machado said.

"Huh?" said LeAnne. She hadn't seen his approach — he'd come out of left field;

actually, right. She took the coffee, didn't say thanks — seemed like too much effort, plus who was this asshole anyway? And why was she here? She took a sip.

"Enough sugar?" he said.

What was that supposed to mean? She foresaw a hot and splashy ending to this interview. If that was what it was.

"Play any baseball?" she said.

"I'm sorry?"

"You. Baseball. Did you play?"

"No. Why do you ask?"

LeAnne shrugged. Then came silence — not that anyplace in the hospital was ever silent, or even close — while Dr. Machado sat back down on the other side of the desk. He looked at her. She looked at a framed photo on the wall behind him: Dr. Machado, smiling in a polo shirt, with wife and two little boys, all smiling, all in polo shirts. She considered asking him if he'd played any polo.

"How about we begin at the beginning?" Dr. Machado said.

She turned to him.

"With your early life — father and mother, where you grew up, et cetera."

She kept herself from saying, *Let's begin with et cetera* but offered nothing in its stead.

Dr. Machado riffled though some papers. His fingernails were in great shape, salon quality. She didn't want to think about hers, so she didn't. Kept her mind far distant from her fingernails, especially the two that were still growing back in.

"I see here that your father was also military. Master Sergeant Rex Hogan, Green Berets." Dr. Machado looked up. "Tell me about him."

"There's not much to tell," LeAnne said.

"Checking the dates here, he seems to have left the army when you were . . . what? Eight or nine? What sort of work did he do after that?"

"Doesn't it say?"

Dr. Machado nodded. "But it's always nice to confirm the written data."

LeAnne had no interest in that.

"Can you describe your relationship with him?" Dr. Machado went on. "Or would you prefer to start somewhere else, with your mother, for example?"

LeAnne rose. "I'd prefer to go back to my room. I have a headache."

Dr. Machado placed his hands flat on the desk. "Sorry to hear that. We'll reschedule. Would you like me to get someone to help you?"

"Help me?"

"Escort you back."

"To where?"

"Your room."

He said it like: Where else? Yeah, she got that, got it good. She kept an eye — ha! — on his hands, flat on the desk: Yes, a complete asshole. Soft, soft hands. They reminded her, the way opposites sometimes will, of those hands that had appeared so suddenly out from under a burqa.

"I don't need any help," LeAnne said.

Chapter Two

LeAnne had the bed by the window. Marci, her roommate, had the bed by the opposite wall. She was lying in it when LeAnne got back, under the covers and facing away. All LeAnne could see of Marci was her hair, growing out now, the brown roots longer than the blond ends, and the topmost tip of a tattoo on her shoulder, the letters AX and a sort of mushroomy thing which LeAnne knew to be a champagne cork in midair, the full inscription being TO THE MAX.

"Who's Max?" LeAnne said.

"It wasn't funny the first time," said Marci, tugging the covers up higher.

LeAnne looked out the window. In the middle distance was some sort of ring road. She tracked an ambulance that turned off, came closer, and got blocked from view by the lower part of the building, jutting out. Small trees lining the entranceway that just yesterday had their branches bare were now sprouting tiny pink blossoms.

"The cherry blossoms are out."

"Whoop-dee-fuckin'-doo," said Marci.

LeAnne sat on her own bed. She wasn't at all sleepy, but crawling in anyway seemed like a good idea. Someone knocked on the door.

"Yeah?" said LeAnne.

A woman with a big, cheery voice called in. "Ocular prosthetics!"

LeAnne said nothing. After a moment or two, the door half opened and the woman stuck her head in the room. "Hi, there, LeAnne. Sorry it took so long. I —" She noticed Marci, lowered her voice. "Oops. Is she sleeping?"

"No," said Marci, the sound muffled by her pillow.

"Oh, good then," the woman said. She produced a small plastic box. "The challenge was reproducing your shade of blue. What an absolutely stunning color, reminds me of bluebonnet season down in Texas. Ever seen the bluebonnets, LeAnne?"

"No."

"Something to look forward to then," the woman said. She stepped into the room, leaving the door open behind her. LeAnne hated that. In the past, she'd never had any strong policy on doors. Now she wanted them closed at all times.

"What's going on?" she said.

"Again, sorry for the delay. But it's really like I said — all because of the color match. We ended up going out of network to an actual artist — in Brooklyn, New York, I believe. All possible because of a generous civilian grant. I think you'll be pleased with the results." She held up the box.

"What's in there?"

"The three I thought were the best. I just couldn't make up my mind, and why not leave the decision to you, after all."

LeAnne got the feeling she'd had dealings with this woman before. She searched her mind and came up empty.

"Three?" she said.

"Did you want to see more? He made up over a dozen in all."

"Eyes?" said LeAnne.

The expression on the woman's face changed, slightly and briefly, revealing something less friendly. LeAnne preferred her this way, but the woman's other self quickly retook control. "Prosthetic eyes, yes," the woman said. "I'm here for the fitting, although, of course, they'll fit, no problem, since all the prep work's in place."

LeAnne thought about that. "Did that happen in Germany?"

"Germany?"

"The prep work. At Landstuhl."

"Oh, no, that was here. But it's not at all uncommon for those details to get muddled. I apologize if I'm going too fast." Maybe the woman saw something on LeAnne's face. For whatever reason, she looked away. "That is, if I'm not explaining properly."

"No," LeAnne said. "You're explaining just fine. I get it. I get the whole picture. And the thing is," she went on, her voice starting to rise, "I've decided."

"But . . . but you haven't seen them yet," the woman said. "Wouldn't it be —"

"I've decided," LeAnne interrupted, although maybe it was her voice taking over the decision-making controls, and her voice wanted to take it to — yes, TO THE MAX. "I've decided that I don't want any of this fucking bluebonnet shit." She lashed out at that little plastic box, but the woman proved to be very quick, almost like she'd known what was coming, and snatched the box away. That — and the realization of how slow she was now, she who could pluck those goddamn Afghan flies right out of midair — made LeAnne even madder. She ripped off her patch and flung it with all her might, not at the woman, not at anything in particular, simply away. The patch flew through the open doorway and into the hall.

An orderly — if that was what the big guy in the green outfit was — glanced in. With a guy of that size you went right for the neck. LeAnne's hands knew just how to do it. They stiffened into the correct positions.

"Any problems?" the orderly said.

"None whatsoever," said the woman.

He handed her the patch and went away. Just before passing from sight, he took in where the patch had been, real quick, yeah, furtive — there was furtive again — but LeAnne didn't miss it. Not pretty enough for you, big guy?

The woman placed the patch and the plastic box on LeAnne's rolling tray table. "I'll just leave this here, so you can make the choice at your convenience." She went to the door. "Most folks end up preferring the prosthetic to the patch. They're so remarkably lifelike nowadays. But it's entirely up to you." And out.

"Lifelike," LeAnne said. "You hear that shit?"

Marci still lay the way she'd been lying, tucked in deep and tight, face to the wall. "Who didn't?"

"What's your problem?"

"No problem," Marci said.

Which was bullshit. Marci had problems,

all right, although nowhere near as many as . . . as whatever her name was, the roommate before. Or was she getting the roommate before mixed up with the roommate in Germany? Had there even been a German roommate? She searched her memory for something German, found only a wastebasket full of bloody bandages. And some blood that had leaked out of the bottom of the wastebasket and pooled on a black-and-white-squared floor. Kind of the cherry on top of the memory, in reverse. But here in Bethesda the cherry blossoms were gearing up once more.

"Ignorant bastards," LeAnne said.

"The prosthetics people?" Marci said, rolling onto her back and sitting up.

LeAnne had actually been talking about the cherry blossoms, but to say so would be an out-and-out admission of craziness. "Nothing," she said. "I don't know what I'm talking about."

Marci gave her a funny look. Was it just because she wasn't wearing the patch? LeAnne didn't know. And could you even blame Marci for that? Meanwhile, Marci pushed the covers aside and swung her legs over the edge of the bed. Over the edge for one, but not the other, which came to a lumpy, thickly dressed end a few inches above where the knee would have been. She reached for her crutches, leaning against the wall by the head of the bed, grabbing one, no problem, but knocking the other to the floor. It clattered around for what seemed like an impossibly long and noisy time. By now LeAnne had some expertise in these matters and knew not to help her. She kept her mouth shut and looked no place until Marci got everything squared away. Marci stood up with a grunt, leaning on the crutches.

"PT?" LeAnne said.

Marci nodded and made her way out of the room.

"You were right about the cherry blossoms," LeAnne called after her.

Marci, now in the hall, paused. LeAnne sensed that Marci had a notion to give her the finger just then, but with the crutches it was all too complicated. Marci moved on. In the hospital you got to see those who had lots of crutching experience and those who did not. Marci was still a newbie. LeAnne closed the door.

Theirs was a good room, not big, but it had its own bathroom. LeAnne went to the sink, splashed cold water on her face, and looked in the mirror. *Christ, help me.*

■ ■ ■ ■

"Nothing to do with talent," Mr. Iglesias said. Mr. Iglesias had been LeAnne's gymnastics coach forever, starting when she was two years old. He was a little guy with big muscles and a bouncy walk, wore a thick gold cross around his neck, and always switched to Spanish when he was really pleased with how she or any of the girls had done. "LeAnne's got tons of talent, plus she's a quick learner and a hard worker. The problem is . . . well, look at her."

"What about her?" said Mom and Daddy, not looking at LeAnne but keeping their eyes on Mr. Iglesias. This was outside the high school after the central Arizona club championships. LeAnne had placed eighth overall. She'd been fourth the year before. Kind of a strange moment, Mom and Daddy saying the same thing at the same time. By now, halfway through ninth grade, Mom and Daddy were divorced, Daddy living in the old house, Mom in Scottsdale, and LeAnne going back and forth but mostly living with Daddy, on account of Alex, Mom's new husband, already had three kids of his own, and there were no more bedrooms. LeAnne was cool with that.

She didn't much care for Alex — he was hardly a man at all, compared to Daddy — and the three kids were the spoiled rich kind who lived to shop and spent most of their time indoors.

"I wish you'd stop with this rich business," Mom said. "Alex is a partner in a suburban accounting office. That's not rich." But Mom now looked rich, had rich-style hair and rich-style skin — especially her forehead, smooth as polished stone — although she still drove the same minivan and had kept her dental hygienist job.

"That right there, hanging on to the job," Daddy said, one night when he'd maybe had too many, "tells me she's gonna come crawling back someday. Good luck with that."

"Daddy. Please."

Unpleasant, but not derailing. LeAnne had no complaints. She still got on fine with both her parents, separately, had lots of friends, and was very busy with school, practices, meets. One small thing: her mom no longer baked those gingerbread men LeAnne liked, gingerbread men with mint-green eyes. Sometimes she missed them.

"Eleven's the cutoff point," said Tasha, her best friend on the team. "If your parents get divorced before you're eleven, that can be bad. After that the circuits in your brain are harder and all the upset really doesn't penetrate."

"Yeah?" said LeAnne, who'd been twelve at the time of the split. "Where'd you hear that?"

"I didn't hear it. I read it. In fact, I researched the whole subject."

"Your parents are getting divorced?"

"No. Well, who knows, right?"

Which started LeAnne laughing, even though the joke was hard to explain. Tasha joined in. LeAnne's laugh was like that, a party invite, according to Tasha. As the laughter faded, Tasha said, "I looked it up on account of you, naturally."

"Yeah?"

"Got your back," Tasha said.

They'd bumped fists, Tasha punching up and LeAnne down, Tasha still so small. In all their competition over the years, Tasha only beat LeAnne in LeAnne's very last meet, that statewide club championship held at the high school, Tasha coming third.

"What about her?" Mr. Iglesias repeated, looking surprised. "Well, she's grown quite a bit in the past year. You must've noticed."

"So what?" Daddy said. "She's in great shape."

"And," Mom said, "she —"

"I'll handle this, if you don't mind," Daddy said.

LeAnne backed away a little. Over on the other side of the parking lot, Tasha was getting big hugs from her parents, neither of them much bigger than Tasha. Tasha's mom was bouncing on her tiptoes, like she was barely stopping herself from jumping up and down. LeAnne smiled.

"Whoa," said Mr. Iglesias, raising his hand palm up. "Of course, she's in great shape — the strongest girl who's ever come through the program. That's not the point. The point is she's . . . well, she's grown so much this year, hair under five ten at last measurement. Look around. How many five-foot-ten gymnasts do you see performing at the top level?"

The answer was none, a fact LeAnne had been trying not to face for some time. Because: What comes after that? She loved gymnastics, but not as a hobby. It was more like she wanted to go pro, even though there was no going pro in gymnastics, with the exception of one woman sometimes getting on the Wheaties box in Olympic years.

"Well," said Mom, "isn't there always a first time?"

Normally, a comment like that, especially

from Mom, would trigger some sarcastic expression on Daddy's face, but now he said, "Right. There's always a first time. That's basic."

"Can't deny it," said Mr. Iglesias. "Tell you what. No reason to rush into anything. Take time to think things over. But while you're thinking, here's an idea you might want to add to the mix." He took a rolled-up magazine from his back pocket and opened it to a two-page spread.

"What's this?" Daddy said.

"Last year's top three finishers," said Mr. Iglesias. "NCAA national women's pole vault. Notice anything?"

They all nodded, Mom, Daddy, LeAnne. It was pretty obvious.

"Same size, same body type," said Mr. Iglesias. "Plus LeAnne's got upper-body strength off the charts, runs like a deer, and has the timing and body control you only get from gymnastics." He handed LeAnne the magazine. "Pole vault," he said, and patted her shoulder. "You're gonna kill."

The plastic box was lined in velvet and had three small compartments, as though made for dividing up jewelry: rings, necklaces, earrings. Like jewelry, what lay inside was brightly colored and shiny, and, also like jewelry, totally decorative.

"My jewelry box," LeAnne said aloud, looking into the mirror again. Looking with her left eye, never her best, although still better than 20/20. So, no complaints on that score. But here was the problem with having just the one. With two eyes, the unknown snuck up on you from behind your back. With only the one, the unknown covered more ground, opening up new firing angles from the side. Three dark quadrants: she felt the thinness of her margin of safety at all times. Except when she was asleep. In her dreams she saw the way she used to, all her nightmares on the wide screen.

Tears welled up in her left eye. Why say left eye? Just plain fucking eye! And tears: that was despicable. LeAnne gave her head a furious shake, removed a glossy little booklet from the box, opened it: Instructions.

LeAnne read the instructions twice, absorbing nothing. There were also visuals, featuring a pretty woman who looked to be about LeAnne's age, resembled her in some ways — blue-eyed (also left only), dark-haired, clear-skinned. Clear-skinned in the model's case also included the surroundings of the right eye, which was far from true in LeAnne's case. Once she'd seen a picture of a crater on the moon, a dark pit with what looked like silvery rays branching out from it across the lunar surface, like frozen runoff from an impact. LeAnne's runoff rays — forehead, temple, cheek — were red, not silver, but all the nurses said that the redness would fade, especially if she used an aloe-based cream not supplied by the VA but easily found on the internet.

She closed the plastic box and put on the patch. It was nice and big.

CHAPTER THREE

Her mouth was dry. And the insides of her nose, and her sinuses, and her whole head: dry, dry, dry. This ugly desert did that, although the beautiful one back home did not. But like all deserts, it was good for carrying sound. She could hear the faraway pounding of 155s and hoped to God they were hitting something that counted in the plus column. God was on the side of . . . something or other. She tried to remember, and while that was going on, the barrage came much closer, like she was in the target zone. LeAnne opened her eyes.

Eye.

It all came back to her, in a rush, a flood, a locomotive off the rails. "Fuck." Would she have to endure this every time she woke up for the rest of her goddamn life? Why couldn't she hold on to the memory every night, spare herself from the daily rewounding? What was wrong with her? She realized that someone was knocking on the door. She glanced over at Marci's bed. Empty. Also, the room was full of the kind of light you didn't see first thing in the morning.

"Who's there?"

"Stallings," said a man. "Captain Gerald, G-2."

LeAnne took her water bottle from the bedside table and drained it. She remembered where God was: on the side of the big battalions. Meaning her mind wasn't totally fried. She sat up.

"May I come in?"

She searched around for the patch, which had slipped off during her sleep, found it under the pillow, got it in place.

"If you're looking for Marci, she's not here."

The door opened and in came a soft-faced man in blue, two silver bars on his lapel. He looked her way, then came to attention and saluted, which was very weird, captains not routinely initiating salutes with sergeants, to say nothing of sergeants out of uniform, in fact in pajamas.

"No," he said, lowering his hand to his side, "I'm looking for you."

LeAnne wondered about returning his salute. She was still in the service, although not on active duty — unless she'd missed something. That thought — her missing something — made her laugh.

Captain Stallings smiled. "Let me in on the joke," he said.

"I wish," said LeAnne.

Stallings's smile wavered a bit but didn't completely fade. "I'm glad to see you in good . . . in relatively good spirits."

"Do I know you?"

"No, ma'am."

"We haven't met before? Because my memory's not the sharpest these days."

"This is our very first get-together, right here and now."

LeAnne gazed at Stallings, wondered where she was going with this. "Then," she said, her mind snatching at bits from the stream of conversation, "how can you say anything about my spirits?"

And still, his smile did not quite vanish. "I can't. My mistake. But I am interested in how you're doing, no mistake about that." He glanced at the footstool under the rolling tray table. "Mind if I sit down?"

LeAnne shrugged.

Captain Stallings pulled up the stool and sat down with his briefcase, supple brown leather with brass fittings, on his lap.

"G-2?" LeAnne said.

"That's right."

"Meaning intelligence."
"Correct."
"What do you want?"
"We'll get to that," Stallings said. "As long as you're feeling up to it." He had a soft voice to go along with that soft face, kind of refreshing considering the scarcity of soft voices in her line of work. But his eyes weren't soft. Not hard, either, more like watchful. "Are you in pain?" he said.
"Nope."
"Glad to hear that. Do, um, they have you on a lot of medication?"
"Nope."
He nodded in an agreeable way, his eyes growing more watchful at the same time. She'd had just about enough of him.
"We're trying to get a handle on the events of January seventeenth," Stallings said.
January seventeenth? And today was . . . ?
"The date of that last mission," Stallings said. "Your last mission." He checked the screen of his phone. "Designated Operation Midnight Special, I believe. If you don't want to talk about it, just say."
"That's not it," LeAnne said. "But since I don't remember a thing, what can I tell you?" That closed the door on that, good and hard! LeAnne enjoyed a moment of triumph. After it passed — so quickly — all

she wanted to do was crawl back into the bed, way down deep.

"Understood," said Stallings. "Where did that designation come from, by the way?"

What was this? He hadn't noticed that the door was closed, good and hard? If that was the best intelligence could do, they were fucked. Which she already knew.

"In other words," Stallings went on, "who chose it?"

Watchful eyes, beyond doubt. "Captain Cray," she said. She kept her voice perfectly steady, or just about.

"The mission commander?"

LeAnne nodded, a perfectly businesslike type of nod.

"Did it have any particular meaning, Midnight Special?"

"Not that I know of."

"I like it," Stallings said.

"You like the name of the operation?"

"I do." He put his phone away. "How about we backtrack to the last memory you have of that night?"

"I told you — I don't remember anything."

"Understood," said Stallings again. The word had to mean something different to him, because he pressed on. "How about the ride into the target area — do you have any recollection of that?"

"Full moon," LeAnne said.

"Yeah?" Stallings opened the briefcase, rummaged around inside, leafed through some printouts. "First time that's come up."

"What are you saying?"

"It's a bit of a surprise, that's all. No mention of it in any of the reports or interviews."

"You don't believe me?"

"Not a question of belief. It's a checkable fact." He took out his phone, busied himself with it for a moment or two, then nodded. "Rose at 7:43 p.m. local time, January seventeenth, set at 2:19 the following morning." Stallings pulled the stool in a bit closer. "Full moon. What else?"

"I don't like a full moon."

"Why is that?"

"On a mission," she said, possibly snapping at him. "I don't like a full moon on a mission — might as well go in with a marching band." But what really bothered her was how he'd moved in closer. Just an inch or two, but she felt his presence way more strongly and wanted him gone. Meanwhile, he was nodding in an affirmative and supportive sort of way that she found maddening.

"I didn't," LeAnne corrected herself. "I didn't like a full moon on a mission."

"Understood. Did you share that thought with the commanding officer?"

"It doesn't work that way."

"No? How does it work?"

"Have you been in combat?"

"I have not."

Silence fell, a hospital-type silence meaning murmurs, beeps, distant sirens. LeAnne remembered another full moon and how she'd pole vaulted under its light, all by herself, a night of practice where her left wrist had suddenly figured out how to get involved, opening the door to the big time.

No trace of Captain Stallings's smile remained. LeAnne felt like she was getting somewhere. Did that make sense? She thought so.

"I'd like to show you some pictures," he said. "See if you can ID any of these subjects."

LeAnne shrugged.

Stallings reached into the briefcase again and withdrew a wad of five-by-seven photos that he held up for her inspection one at a time. First came a bunch of Afghan men, some in tribal outfits, a few dressed western-style, and one or two in Afghan army camos.

"No," said LeAnne. "No, no, no, no, and no."

"Sure about this one?"

"Yeah. Why?"

"Just double-checking." Stallings started to return the photo to the stack. LeAnne grabbed his wrist. A bony wrist and cold, meaning she was hot. His eyes opened wide, like he was shocked. For a moment, she was in touch with her old strength.

"I want another look."

"No problem. No problem at all." He wriggled free of her grip. She let him. Her old strength receded, or maybe departed. She tried to feel it somewhere inside her and could not. "You all right?" said Stallings.

"Yes."

"Looked like you were uncomfortable there for a sec."

"I was not."

She studied the photo. There was an otherness shared by all Afghan men that you had to get past if you were going to accomplish anything over there or simply tell them apart. This otherness was strongest when they were having their pictures taken or confronting western women. It pretty much disappeared when they smiled, which hadn't happened often in LeAnne's experience.

The man in the photo was not smiling. He wore a President Karzai–style karakul hat, a lamb's fur hat, as she'd learned from her studies, made from aborted fetuses. Why not, if they were dead anyway? But it had bothered her when she'd found out and it bothered her now. Did everything have to get used? Could nothing be spared? The man himself had a narrow face, prominent ears, and deep-set eyes, dark and highly intelligent, like he was the one doing the examining.

"Change your mind?" Stallings said.

"No," said LeAnne. "Never seen him before. Who is he?"

"Name's Gulab Yar-Muhammad. At least, that's the name we've got. Yar-Muhammad means 'friend of Muhammad,' which could be real — not at all an uncommon surname over there — or could be just sending a message. A *nom de guerre,* if you're familiar with the expression."

Her gaze slid down from the photo over to his wrist, slightly reddened from her grip. That was good.

"We have information that may tie him to the events of that night, January seventeenth."

"What kind of information?"

"Sorry, some of those details are classified."

"What the fuck? I have clearance."

"Unfortunately," Stallings said, his eyes zeroing in on the patch, no doubt about it, "we're in kind of a gray area on that score. But," he went on, possibly seeing some change in her expression, "how about we let the lawyers squabble over the pros and cons?"

LeAnne lost the thread. Stallings went on and on about Gulab Yar-Muhammad, things he may or may not have done, people he may or may not have known. LeAnne made a few slight movements of her left hand, movements that made no sense unless you knew she was holding a pole. Her wrist still remembered, still had the goods, still knew how to get her that extra inch or two of height that meant winning instead of coming second. Oh, to be vaulting under a full moon! She could feel a daydream about that waiting in the wings. Actually more of a night dream: it lurked behind her right eye socket, where night prevailed. That hit her pretty hard: now she had night inside her, twenty-four seven.

"Getting a bit tired?" Stallings said. She focused on him. He was looking at her with concern.

"Nope."

He extended his hand, like he was going to pat her knee but then thought better of it. "Let's continue another time. More info to come, in any case. Just want you to check out one more of these." He produced another five-by-seven from the stack.

"That's Katie."

"Katie?"

"Of course, it's Katie. My terp. You must have known that."

He nodded. "Just confirming. Tell me about her."

"What do you want to know?"

LeAnne took another look at the photo. Katie — her real name was Khatena, but everyone, meaning all the Americans, called her Katie — was gazing dead ahead, her eyes blank, and none of her funny side apparent, although her physical beauty still was. She was a tiny woman and feisty, always whipping off her burqa first thing when they were inside a dwelling with just the women and kids. Outside, in the presence of men having some kind of confab, she would comment in English from behind the veil, her voice cheery, her accent that of a British TV newscaster: "Imbecile. Blockhead. Dunces all." In those moments, LeAnne knew winning was both possible and very distant.

"Did something happen to her?" LeAnne said. "They told me she was okay. And she wasn't on the list."

"Nothing happened to her. For which she owes you big time. No matter what."

"No matter what? I don't get it."

Captain Stallings put the photos away, zipped up his briefcase. "We're in the early stages here. I hope to have more for you in a few days." He rose. "Meanwhile, just concentrate on getting better."

"But what are you saying about Katie?"

He smiled. "More to come."

After he left, she got up, rummaged through a drawer, found the list. When had she gotten it? Here? Landstuhl? Before? Who had given it to her? Why? LeAnne could answer none of those questions. She checked the list. Katie wasn't on it. There were six names, in alphabetical order, five Afghans and one American — Cray, Captain Jamie R., age thirty. Cause of death: *hostile — explosives.* Her mistakes, numbers one and two, meeting up.

Marci came back to the room, not on crutches. Instead, she wore an artificial leg, black and silver, very sleek and high-tech-looking.

"Wow," LeAnne said. "Is that the kind for running real fast?"

"Fuckin' better be," Marci said. She

stumped over to her bed and sat down, her lips pursing.

"It hurts?"

"Like a son of a bitch, but that goes away, supposedly." She gazed down at her feet, real and not, but both now shod in bright red sneakers.

"You got new sneaks?"

"Free. Good to know there's free shit in this life, LeAnne. Things are looking up."

LeAnne went over to Marci's bed, sat beside her. She put her arm around Marci's shoulder. They looked at Marci's new leg together.

"It's kind of beautiful in a way," LeAnne said. "I mean that."

"Some men find them sexy. At least, according to the PT lady."

"I believe it."

Marci nodded. "Nothing about men surprises me anymore."

LeAnne laughed. Marci joined in. Hey! Leanne thought. Is my laugh still a party invite? She stopped at once.

Chapter Four

"Want to go outside?" Marci said sometime in the next day or two.

"What for?" said LeAnne.

"I'm supposed to walk around. You can criticize my technique."

"What's wrong with walking inside?"

"Inside the hospital? Where do you want me to start?"

"I . . ." LeAnne tried to remember the last time she was outside, meaning outside and conscious.

"What's with all the thinking?" Marci said. "Yes or no."

"Yes."

They put on robes over their pajamas, took an elevator down to the lobby, and stepped out into a warm spring day. Warm and sunny. LeAnne had always loved being in the sun, but now the glare was unbearable even though she wasn't looking in the direction of the sun or anywhere close. She squinted her left eye almost shut. It did no good. She was feeling the glare on the other side.

"Something wrong?" Marci said.

"Be right back."

"Huh?"

LeAnne turned around, reentered the hospital. The glare faded, but real slowly, like it didn't want to go. She found the gift shop and charged a pair of cheap sunglasses to her room, the oversized kind of sunglasses you get from the eye doctor after he's given you the drops but you still need to drive home. In the mirror behind the cash register she saw that the sunglasses covered the whole patch and maybe one third of the scarring. What she needed were still bigger sunglasses, like . . . like a veil. The thought made her sick. She almost puked right there, almost puked all over the cashier's sensible black Oxfords.

Back outside, Marci was sitting on a bench under one of those cherry trees. LeAnne sat beside her, the glare pretty much gone. Because Marci had taken the spot by the right-hand armrest, LeAnne was forced into having her on the blind side. This was a first, a first she should have seen coming. She almost circled around a few times like a dog in search of the exact right spot to settle.

She felt a slight movement on Marci's part, maybe glancing over at her.

"Going Hollywood?" Marci said.

That was a good one.

"Actually," Marci said, "you remind me of that actress, what's her name."

In the distance LeAnne saw — but how much distance? She realized she had no way of knowing. It was like watching the world through some early version of a new technology, before the updates.

"Give me some help here," Marci said.

"Help? What's wrong?" LeAnne turned to her, which meant twisting far around to get her eye in play.

Marci looked a bit alarmed. "Hey. Nothing. Just trying to remember the name of that actress you look like."

"I don't look like any goddamn actress." LeAnne faced away from her, shifted a few inches down the bench.

"Cruella De Vil," Marci said. "Although come to think of it, she was a character, not an actress."

By then LeAnne was barely listening. She was watching what she'd spotted in the distance, a high school track team out for a training run. LeAnne counted them — she'd developed the habit in her job of pinning down exact numbers in groups. In the dwelling in that compound the night of January seventeenth, for example, there'd been sixteen people, including her and Katie, plus two chickens. There were four-teen runners on the track team, boys and girls, pretty much in all the possible human colors, a few of the kids effortless looking and talented, but each and every one with-out worldly cares, which was the beauty of long runs if you were doing them right. Le-Anne knew high school track.

"Potential pole vaulter, huh?" said Mr. Adel-son. Mr. Adelson was the track coach at Fremont High. He'd been a shot-putter in his own track days, had the thickest wrists LeAnne had ever seen.

"I hope so, Coach," she said.

"Tony Iglesias seems to think you've got potential, for what that's worth," said Mr. Adelson. "What do you think of him?"

What was this? One coach was asking what she thought about another coach?

"Come on," Mr. Adelson said. "Gotta have opinions in this life. Unless you'd rather be a sheep."

This was new, and couldn't be right. On the other hand, LeAnne didn't want to be a sheep. "He's great!" she said.

"Didn't say to go overboard," Mr. Adelson said. "Reminds me — how are you with falling?"

"Falling?" Or had he said "failing?" He had a funny accent, like he was from somewhere else, somewhere back east like Boston or Philly.

"Exactly. The body in uncontrolled motion from up to down and landing hard."

"I've fallen off the beam like a million times, Coach. I guess I'm used to it."

"A million times?" Mr. Adelson took a crumpled envelope from the pocket of his sweats, smoothed it out, checked some scribbling on the back. "Then how come you won all those championships?"

"I never won any of the big ones."

"Because of falling?"

"Well, no, sir. Just someone else being better that day. There are so many little things in gymnastics."

"So all this falling went on in practice."

LeAnne had never thought of it that way.

"Okay," said Mr. Adelson. He nodded his head a few times. "Okay, okay. And how are you at push-ups?"

"Mr. Iglesias loves push-ups."

"Loves doing them himself?"

"It's possible," LeAnne said. "But I've never seen him."

"Ha!" Mr. Adelson made a very loud

noise, part laugh, part bark, startling her. "All right, then," he said. "Let's see a demonstration."

"Of push-ups?"

"What else are we talking about?"

"Here?"

"Floor not clean enough for you?"

LeAnne got down on the floor. A dull green linoleum floor, and actually not that clean.

"Talking real push-ups now," said Mr. Adelson. "From the toes."

"Are there other kinds?" LeAnne said, facedown on the floor, ready to go.

She did a hundred, could have done a few more before the effort started to show, but Mr. Adelson stopped her. "Enough. Enough already. You're hurting me."

A fountain stood in a little grouping of cherry trees. It wasn't running, but there was water in the basin, with cherry blossoms floating on top.

"I'm supposed to be walking," Marci said. "But I don't feel like it. Know what I feel like? Getting wasted."

Getting wasted? LeAnne hadn't done much of that in her life. The night of the senior prom, where the track kids always ended up on a houseboat on Lake Pleasant;

once down in the Florida Keys, also on a boat, but this one very fast; and the last day of her first weekend leave in Qatar, where she and the other CSTs had gotten off the base with its three-beer minimum and checked out a rooftop hotel bar in town, robed Saudi businessmen on one side of the dance floor and American soldiers in T-shirts and jeans on the other. And that was it.

"How would we do that, exactly?" LeAnne said.

"Get wasted? We'd need booze."

They looked past the *U*-shaped entrance to the hospital and out to the road, the high school runners now gone.

"Any chance there's a liquor store down that road?" LeAnne said.

"Even if there is, so what?" said Marci. "No way in hell I can walk there."

A breeze sprang up. A tight little squadron of cherry blossoms took flight, wafting down into the basin of the fountain.

"How about we train for it?" said LeAnne.

"Huh?"

"Today we'll try to get to that fountain and back. Tomorrow we'll add a little more."

"You sound kind of perky all of a sudden. I think I prefer your real self."

They rose and made their way toward the

fountain. LeAnne moved around, getting Marci on her left side.

"How you doing?" she said.

"My knee wants to bend," Marci said. "But it's fuckin' gone. How stupid is that?"

LeAnne dropped back, studied Marci's stride. "Maybe reach out more with the new foot."

"Fuck you." But Marci seemed to be reaching out more with her left foot, seemed to be lurching a bit less. Her breathing grew louder, and after a few minutes they took a break on another bench, almost at the fountain, LeAnne keeping Marci on her left. That had to be the MO from now till forever: everything on the left.

"I'm getting all these wicked thoughts," Marci said after a while.

"Like?"

Marci took a deep breath. When she let it out, LeAnne heard a sort of thrumming, like a muffled baby rattle. A strange sound, and new to her. Was her sense of hearing stepping up in some sort of compensatory way? Maybe a whole auditory world was about to open up to her. That thought got pushed aside by the memory of her first look in the mirror after the bandages came off, the memory rising up without warning, like a tsunami, overcoming anything the least positive.

"Like I wish it was someone else," Marci said. "Someone else and not me that it happened to."

"What's so bad about that?" said LeAnne.

"How about if it's someone specific?"

LeAnne said nothing.

"Makes one hell of a difference, huh?"

"I'd have to know more," LeAnne said. "This was in Iraq?"

"For Christ sake! Where else? I told you I was in Iraq, told you the very first day."

LeAnne turned on her. "Amp it down, little lady," she said. That led to a pause, kind of grim. LeAnne got a bit of a grip, lowered her voice. "I don't know what you're talking about."

Marci shot her a quick glance and turned away. "You're one scary motherfucker, you know that?" LeAnne gazed through her oversized sunglasses at the cherry blossoms floating in the fountain. "I told you I was in Iraq," Marci went on, her voice also lower. "You told me you were in Afghanistan. The first day."

"What first day?"

"Monday. The first day you came to the room."

"What's today?"

"Thursday. But I'm talking about the

Monday before."

LeAnne thought that over.

"Thursday was always my favorite day of the week," Marci said. And then, after a silence, "Want to know why?"

"Sure."

"Because you're getting jazzed for Saturday night, making plans, looking forward to everything. Which is usually better than what actually happens, but that's okay, too. By the time the next Thursday rolled around, I was all set to be jazzed again." She put both hands under her leg, where the prosthetic part met the stump, lifted up, and shifted its position a little. "The someone specific is Eddie Mears," Marci said. "He was on the drive schedule, but he got the shits. I filled in. But who doesn't get the shits? It's a hellhole."

"Iraq?"

"And probably Afghanistan, too, but Iraq's all I know firsthand. It's like hell is down below, but sometimes it pops up through the ground. That's Iraq. Like the IED's the perfect symbol of the whole goddamn situation. Which is what did me in."

"Motor transport?"

"Correct. Deuces, back and forth on the Baghdad Airport Road. It gets swept all the time. But . . ." Marci raised her hands, let them drop slowly to her sides. "Who doesn't get the shits? Tell me."

LeAnne rose. "Break's over," she said, extending her hand and helping Marci up. "Let's go."

They set off for the fountain.

Chapter Five

"Hey, Champ," said Coach Adelson. "Been looking all over for you."

LeAnne, trying to maneuver her pole through the school bus door so she could get it safely laid down the center aisle before the rest of the team straggled up, turned to him. He was with a tall woman LeAnne didn't know.

"Like you to meet a former high-jump star of mine, from back in my California days. Say hi to Gina Torrelli. She knew me when I had a full head of hair."

"Hi," said LeAnne.

"Pleasure to meet you," said Gina Torrelli. "Congratulations. That was some performance."

"Thanks," said LeAnne. Spring of sophomore year, second to last meet of the season. She'd cleared thirteen one, a personal best. The winning trophy was sticking out of the back pocket of her sweats.

"Gina here is an assistant track coach at West Point," Coach Adelson said. "Familiar with West Point, LeAnne?"

"Yes, sir."

"I was telling Gina about your family's military connections. Your dad's a Green Beret, I believe?"

"He was, yes."

"And your grandfather served as well?"

"In Vietnam."

"Neither of them as commissioned officers?"

"That's right."

Coach Adelson glanced at Gina. "Is college in your plans, LeAnne?" Gina said.

"Yes."

"Have you ever considered a military career yourself?"

"Not really. I haven't thought that much about any careers."

"Care to do a little thinking now?" Gina said.

"I'll get that pole," said Coach Adelson. He grabbed it from LeAnne, grunted his way up the steps, made bumping and crashing sounds inside the bus.

Gina rolled her eyes. "He hasn't changed a bit, except for the hair, which was actually way too full, just between you and me. Not that we'd want him to change much, would we?"

"Um, no," LeAnne said, although some of the kids on the team didn't like Coach Adelson, especially when he tried to relate to them by saying "bro" and "dude," and other stuff like that.

"The coaches get older, but the kids on the teams are always the same age," Gina said. "That's the dilemma."

LeAnne nodded. Had Gina just read the questions forming vaguely in her mind and tidied them up a little bit? All at once and for the first time, LeAnne could see herself in college. She wanted to go, came very close to wanting to go at that very moment!

"But not your problem, LeAnne." Gina smiled. LeAnne took her first good look at Gina, a real college coach. Hard to tell her age: thirty-five? Forty? Adult faces were tricky. But one thing LeAnne had noticed on many of them was a kind of wariness. Gina's didn't have that. Maybe that was what made it nice to look at, even though it wasn't a beautiful face, or even pretty.

"Any idea where that thirteen-one would put you on my team this year?" Gina said.

LeAnne shook her head.

"You'd be second. I've got a junior who's hit thirteen-three twice and thirteen-two a bunch of times."

"Thirteen-three?" LeAnne said. "Wow."

Gina looked like she was about to laugh a happy sort of laugh, but if so, she kept it inside. "She's five years older than you, don't forget. Who knows what you'll be clearing by then, if you stick with it."

"Oh, I'm sticking with it," LeAnne said. Any other possibility had never occurred to her.

"Why?"

"I love the pole vault," LeAnne said.

"What do you love about it?"

LeAnne had never considered that question. What did she love about the pole vault? "The feel, I guess."

"Tell me about that."

This wasn't easy.

"Take your time," Gina said. No more bumping and crashing sounds came from inside the bus. Was Mr. Adelson eavesdropping?

"Well," said LeAnne, "in English the other day we were learning about three-act plays. And I wondered if the pole vault was like that. First, there's the setup — that's the run. Then there's the complication — getting all the moves down so the pole bends just right. And after that's the resolution — when you let go and fly." Gina was watching her closely. "Is . . . Is that the kind of thing you mean?" LeAnne said. "Or something else?"

"Good enough," Gina said. "I've seen your transcript, by the way. Your grades are in our zone, and if your SAT tracks your PSAT when you take it next year, then it will be, too. What I'm saying is that you have a real good shot of getting into West Point, if that's of interest to you. Bear in mind that you'll be on the radar of other schools. And I'm sure some of them will be offering scholarships, although there's no saying how big. What I can tell you is that West Point is a completely free ride, with the condition of five years of active service duty and three on reserve after graduation. Paid service as an officer, I should add. But you have to understand you're making a commitment."

LeAnne nodded.

"You said you haven't given any thought to a career, but you must have a general notion or two."

"Not really. But I . . ." LeAnne stopped herself, afraid of sounding silly and immature.

"Go on."

"I don't want to be behind a desk."

Uh-oh. Immature for certain — she could see that on Gina's face. Just then from inside the bus came Mr. Adelson's booming voice. "Tell her about your goddamn — your family's military tradition."

LeAnne felt her face turning red, but then Gina rolled her eyes again, and the embarrassment went away.

"Uh," she said, almost in a whisper, "didn't Coach already mention that?"

"Multiple times," said Gina. She spoke up nice and loud. "He's not the reticent type." Then she lowered her voice and looked LeAnne right in the eyes. "But I'd like to hear what the military tradition means to you."

At that moment, the team started showing up, everyone munching on snacks, guzzling sodas, fooling around. "My dad says our family's all about protection."

"What does he mean by that?"

LeAnne knew exactly what he meant, from hearing it so often: *The average American's a pig in shit, too stupid to even realize the wolf's at the door. Got to look out for them, even if they don't fucking deserve it.* She said, "Someone needs to keep the peace." Then a brand-new thought struck her and she threw it in, too, feeling strangely grown-up all of a sudden. "Peace doesn't keep itself."

Gina's eyebrows rose. "Your father says that? Peace doesn't keep itself?"

"Sort of," LeAnne said.

■ ■ ■ ■

Two more practice sessions went by before LeAnne and Marci reached the fountain. It still wasn't running, and the water in the basin was scummy. They sat on the edge, as far away as they could from the only other occupant, a whiskery old guy drinking from a paper bag.

"We made it," LeAnne said.

Marci, gazing at the old guy, wasn't listening.

"We made it to the fountain," LeAnne said. "Step one."

"Hey!" Marci called to the old guy. "You!"

The old guy turned to them, slow and reluctant. Then he got more interested, checking out Marci's prosthesis, LeAnne's oversized shades, the prosthesis again.

"Yeah, you," Marci said. "Speak English?"

"Uh-huh."

"What's in the bag?"

"Huh?" he said, making a feeble attempt to conceal the paper bag under one arm.

"You heard me," Marci said. "What you got in the bag?"

"You cops or somethin'?"

"Do we look like cops?"

He examined them again, prosthesis and

shades one more time, but after that more comprehensively. "You're in PJs. Cops wouldn't be wearing PJs."

"PJs?" said Marci. "What are you? Five years old?"

LeAnne looked down at herself, saw that she was indeed wearing pajamas. Plus flip-flops. Her toenails were broken and dirty. She tried to think what she possessed in the way of clothes, remembered the MultiCams and body armor she'd been wearing in that moonlit compound — Katie dressed the same way, with the addition of a head scarf — and got no further.

The old man drew himself up, as if offended. "I'll be fifty-six come June."

"You don't look it," Marci said.

"He looks way older," said LeAnne.

"That's what I meant."

Had the old man caught this bit of byplay? He didn't seem to have; LeAnne neither knew nor cared.

"Happy future birthday," Marci called over to him. "We'd like to drink a toast."

The old man shoved the paper bag deeper into his armpit.

"But not with whatever swill you've got. How far to the nearest liquor store?"

"From here, you mean?"

"Fucking Christ," Marci said. "No, from

the moon."

"From the . . ." His mouth, mostly toothless, opened and closed.

LeAnne rose and went over to him, moving more quickly than she had in some time. He shrank back, but way too slow. She snatched the paper bag from him, took out the bottle.

"That's rightfully mine," the old man said. "You got no probable cause."

"Zip it. Think we're not going to pay you?" LeAnne patted the pocket of her pajamas shirt. "Got any money, Marci?"

"But it's swill," the old man said. "You don't want no part of swill."

"What kind of swill is it?" Marci said.

LeAnne held up the bottle for closer examination of the label. For some reason, the lettering was still unclear. She took off her oversized sunglasses in order to see better, completely forgetting what those sunglasses were for. The old man scuttled back as far as he could without falling into the fountain. LeAnne jammed those fucking sunglasses back on her face and came real close to giving the old man a little push. If he'd been just a bit younger and a bit less decrepit, she would have.

Instead, she stepped away from him. "I think it's liqueur," she told Marci. "The writing's in German or something."

"Hell with that," Marci said. She held up a twenty-dollar bill. "C'mere."

"Me?" said the old man.

"Fucking hell," said Marci.

The man went over to her, almost like a sleepwalker, his gaze locked on the money.

"Where's the nearest liquor store?" Marci said.

He pointed toward the road.

"How long's the walk?"

"Um. In time, or, or —"

"Yeah, time."

He shrugged. "Five minutes?"

Marci handed him the twenty. "Pint of vodka. Bring it back — unopened. You get to keep the change and on top of that we'll give back your swill. How's that for a deal?"

"Good," said the old man. "It's a good deal."

"Then move."

He went off, leaving his odor behind.

"Smell that?" LeAnne said.

"What?"

"He stinks."

Marci sniffed the air. "I don't smell anything. Like actually nothing. Goddamn IED took my sense of smell away."

"How would that work?" LeAnne said.

"Calling me a liar?"

"No."

They sat on the edge of the basin. Time passed. "Maybe he got run over," Marci said.

"First optimistic thing you've said today."

Marci laughed. LeAnne passed her the old man's liqueur. Marci rubbed off the old man's cooties on her pajamas sleeve, drank, and passed the bottle back.

"What's it taste like?"

"My aunt's apple brown betty," Marci said.

"She a good cook?"

"Yeah."

LeAnne took a sip, then a real hit. "A great cook," she said. Did it taste like apple brown betty, or pears, or what? It could have tasted like turnips. LeAnne had no idea. But it was exactly what she needed.

"Want to tell her yourself?" Marci said.

"Tell your aunt? On the phone?"

"I was thinking in person. And stop hogging that bottle."

LeAnne handed it back. "In person?"

"You could come for a visit. Meaning after we get our walking papers out of this joint."

"A visit where?"

"Home. Where I come from. Ever been to Washington, state of?"

"Nope." LeAnne took the bottle, helped

herself to more. "You married?"

"Twice so far. But not at present. You?"

"Never been married."

"Got a boyfriend?"

"Not at present."

"But you must have had some. Like plenty."

"Why?"

"Because — don't bite my head off again — because you look like that actress, and if I wasn't so scrambled up I'd remember the name."

"Let's cut out the bullshit," LeAnne said.

For a second or two, Marci looked angry. Then she said again, "You're hogging the bottle."

They drank. A bird flew down and sipped from the scummy water. A nice buzz started up in LeAnne's head. The controls of the missing eye switched on, wanting to see. This was a very strange sensation — like she was going to see out of that socket any second now — a strange sensation in which LeAnne lost herself. When she came out of it, Marci was saying, "Whaddya think's worse? No leg or no eye?"

LeAnne turned to her real slow. Toppling Marci into the water seemed like a very good idea at that point. Then she was struck by something in Marci's expression, impossible for her to define although friendliness was part of it, and she let go of the idea, sparing Marci as she'd spared the old man. But didn't someone have to pay?

"Say again?" she said.

"Leg or eye — which is worse?"

LeAnne thought it over. "I don't know. But it's checkable."

"Huh?"

"There'll be different disability payment amounts. I'll ask Machado the next time I see him."

"Who's Machado?"

"Shrink," said LeAnne. "They don't have you seeing a shrink?"

"Nope."

"How come me and not you?"

"You must be crazy. I must be sane."

LeAnne laughed. "Where in Washington, state of?" she said.

"The boonies. A nothing little town called Bellville. Rains all the time. Hubby numero uno loved the rain. And me."

"And he loved you? Or you loved the rain, too?"

"Both. But I fucked it up. Numero dos was just what he looked like — a great big mistake."

"I can't picture him from that."

"You don't want to," Marci said. "I'd like

a do-over on that decision — let's leave it there."

"My high school coach always said morons make the same mistake twice and smart people make new ones."

"Yeah?" said Marci. "What sport?

"Pole vault."

"Were you any good?"

"Not bad," LeAnne said. "Play any sports yourself?"

"I wrestled."

"Against boys?"

"All the fucking time."

"We're a couple of jocks."

"Whoop-dee-shit," said Marci.

A silence fell over them, finally broken when another bird squawked and flew down, attacking the first one and taking over the water rights.

"Any children from these marriages?" Le-Anne said.

"One." Marci turned to her. "Funny — she was just on my mind this very second. Mia's her name."

"Nice."

"She's a great kid. But what's her future if something happens to me? That's my biggest worry."

"You'll have to come up with another one."

"Huh?"

"Because something's already happened to you, for fuck sake. And you're still on your feet."

There was a long pause, and then Marci said, "Foot."

"I stand corrected," said LeAnne.

Marci laughed. "You're lots of fun, you know that? How about some music?"

"Sure," LeAnne said, expecting Marci to produce some sort of music player. Instead, Marci simply opened her mouth and sang "Rip This Joint" from start to finish in a strong, on-key voice that chilled LeAnne all over.

Chapter Six

"Which is worse?" LeAnne said, entering Dr. Machado's office. "Leg or eye?"

But Dr. Machado wasn't there. LeAnne checked the clock on the wall. Zero nine thirty on the nose. Didn't he know you showed up on time in the army? Then it occurred to her that Dr. Machado might be a civilian; in fact, it was probable. How in hell was a civilian supposed to help her? The right move now was to get out of there and never come back, but just to be contrary, she headed toward his desk instead. She had years and years of contrary stored up inside her, like a smoldering mound just waiting for a blast of oxygen.

LeAnne checked out Dr. Machado's desk, a wooden desk topped with a sheet of glass, and under that glass more photos of him and his polo shirt family. A dog appeared in one of the photos, a short-haired brown dog lying on a pile of leaves. LeAnne had never been interested in dogs. Once when she was little, she'd come upon a dog eating its own shit. Didn't there have to be something wrong with a being that did that? She'd carried that conclusion with her ever since. Now, for no reason, she studied the short-haired brown dog, trying to get a handle on what it was like: personality, character, disposition. She got nowhere. Maybe this dog had nothing inside that was worthy of those labels. Maybe no dog did. LeAnne wasn't particularly interested in the question. That didn't stop her — *go, you contrary girl!* — from raising the sheet of glass, taking possession of the dog photo, and slipping it into the pocket of her jeans. Some clothes had shown up in her room the day before, or the day before that, nice new clothes in her size, including these jeans. They'd made her feel nice and new for several minutes.

LeAnne slid open Dr. Machado's top drawer, found a Hershey bar first thing, already open. Chocolate was one of those things — like ice cream, potato chips, cake — that LeAnne just didn't eat, going all the way back to gymnastics. She peeled back the foil, broke off two squares and popped them into her mouth. Next she came upon Dr. Machado's appointment book. She leafed through to today, found herself inked in at zero nine thirty. Good to see her memory confirmed. She was locked in, with the program, ready and able. Beside her name he'd written *reference conv. with mom?*

Reference conv. with mom? To his question mark she mentally added one of her own. "Conv." would be what? For that matter, what about "reference?" Was he using it as a noun or a verb? Could it even be used as both? LeAnne was sure she'd known the answer to that once, known it stone cold. Nouns, verbs, adjectives, adverbs. What else? Prepositions. And she was pretty sure there were others, but they refused to come to her. Or maybe they tried but couldn't get past the rubble piles in her brain. LeAnne broke off another Hershey square or two, sat down in Dr. Machado's chair. He turned out to like it on the high side. Was he short? LeAnne hadn't noticed. She released the lever, lowered the seat an inch or so, then switched on Dr. Machado's laptop.

Password protected — but on a civilian machine. LeAnne tried *password, 123456, Machado, DocMachado, shrinkster,* all with no result. She thought about throwing the laptop out the window, was actually on her feet when she realized that Dr. Machado's window was the kind that didn't open. She was going over the pros and cons of hurling the laptop right through the glass — no cons so far — when the answer hit her. LeAnne took the photo from her pocket, flipped it over, and found more of Dr. Machado's handwriting: *Bruno on Thanksgiving Morning.* She typed *Bruno* in the enter password box.

"Ta-da."

After that it was no trouble at all to locate the folder marked "Patients." The patients were listed alphabetically, Hogan coming between Hilliard and Hopper. LeAnne opened her folder.

Inside were three files: "Military Record," "Notes," and "Conv. with mom." She clicked on "Conv. with mom."

Down in the dock at the bottom of the screen an icon jumped. That was followed by a ringing phone — the kind of ring you hear when you're calling someone — and then the phone got picked up and LeAnne's mother said, "Hello?"

LeAnne hadn't seen her mother in a few years — she knew she could pin it down precisely if given more time — and hadn't spoken to her since a Skype call last Thanksgiving or maybe the Thanksgiving before, but of course she knew her mother's voice. The sound of it made her cry. What the hell was wrong with her? There was no reason for goddamn tears, yet here they were, not just from her eye, but also from under the patch on the other side, even though those tears ducts were obliterated. Weren't they? Hadn't some doc in Germany said so? LeAnne couldn't remember. She pounded her fist on Dr. Machado's desk.

"May I speak to Donna Marsh? This is Doctor Machado calling from Walter Reed National Military Medical Center."

"This is her. Is it about LeAnne?"

"Yes. Your daughter, according to our records. Can you confirm that?"

"Confirm that she's my daughter? Of course. Is she there?"

"In the hospital, yes. Not in this room at the moment."

"Why . . . why did you want to confirm that she's my daughter?"

"Just routine."

"She's not . . . not denying it, is she?"

"No. Not at all. Why do you ask?"

"No reason. Never mind. Is she all right?"

"I'm afraid I'm not at liberty to discuss patient health without a signed consent form, but I can tell you that her physical health is good."

"Good? How can it be good? She lost an eye."

"Um. Can you tell me your source on that?"

"My source? Are you saying it's not true?"

"No, no, nothing like that. It's true. Unfortunately. I'm just wondering how you know."

"You're unaware of the fact that I saw her at Landstuhl?"

"Landstuhl?"

"It's the military hospital in Germany."

"I realize that, but —"

"I flew there the moment I heard. This was in January. I can supply the exact dates if you give me a moment or two."

"That won't be necessary."

At that point, LeAnne got breathless and missed some of what came next. When she recovered, her mother was speaking.

"Doctor . . . Machado, was it?"

"Correct."

"Have you spoken to LeAnne?"

"I have."

"And she didn't mention my visit?"

"No."

"And there's nothing about it in your records?"

"I'm afraid not. But don't feel bad. It's a confusing situation."

"I'm not feeling bad, Doctor. At least not for myself. I am feeling bad for her."

"Understood. I'd like to hear more about this Landstuhl visit of yours."

"Why?"

"Well, the more data I can accrue, the more I'll be able to help."

"Help LeAnne?"

"Correct. That's the job description."

Pause. "The doctors at Landstuhl told me there might be some scarring."

"They were unfortunately right."

"How bad is it?"

"Mostly peripheral, I would say."

"Peripheral? What does that mean?"

"Circumferential, more or less."

"Excuse me?"

"Around the eye, in essence. Above, below, to the sides, temple, that sort of thing. I haven't actually seen the scarring, not in toto."

"You haven't seen the scarring? What kind of doctor are you?"

"On account of her eye patch, which is on the large side. But I'm afraid I can tell you that the plastic surgeon is of the opinion that only minimal amelioration is possible in this case. As for my specialty, I'm a psychiatrist. And it's in that capacity that I'm calling you, in fact. But before we get to what I was going to discuss, I'd appreciate more details of your Landstuhl visit."

"More? Like what?"

"Anything that comes to mind, really. What was her mood? What sort of things were discussed? Did she speak of any plans?"

"Mood? Plans? They were fighting to save her life."

"So, ah, there was no discussion of her future?"

Now, in the background, another man spoke. LeAnne hadn't heard his voice in years; the tone had not improved. This was Alex Marsh, suburban accountant and husband number two.

"Donna? We're running late."

"Just a sec. Please. Doctor Machado, have you and LeAnne been discussing her future?"

"Just approaching the topic, Ms. Marsh. Around the edges, kind of thing."

"Can she have a career in the army with only one eye?"

"I don't see how."

"Then what future does she have? The army's her life."

"Uh, isn't that a bit unusual?"

"What's so unusual about the army being her life? Don't lots of people feel that way about their jobs?"

"Undeniably."

"Donna?" Alex's voice was still in the background, but louder now.

"So what are you saying? A woman and the army — that's the unusual part?"

"I didn't mean to . . . no, nothing like that. I'm only trying to —"

"You're a civilian, aren't you?"

"I don't see what difference that makes. I'm only trying to help your daughter. It's part of the protocol to see what kind of support system is in place or can be put in place. According to what I've seen, her father —"

"Never mind her father. And what about the shrapnel or whatever it was?"

"Shrapnel?"

"You don't know about that, either? There's a piece of metal in her brain, too dangerous to remove. They were going to reevaluate when they got her to Walter Reed."

"Hmm."

"Donna!"

"I have to go, Dr. Machado. Good-bye."

"What would be a convenient time for me to call again?"

Click.

LeAnne was dripping sweat. There were actual drops on the glass cover on Dr. Machado's desk. Also the glass had a star-shaped crack in it that either she hadn't noticed before, or . . . or something else, some other reason. But that wasn't important, not compared to two things. One: she had no memory of her mother at Landstuhl, and hardly any memories of Landstuhl at all, possibly none. Two: LeAnne couldn't think of two. She tried and tried, but what happened was her eye got tired. She closed it, and in the darkness heard her father's voice: "The smarts you get from your mom. The rest is me, God help you." Her father's voice after he'd downed a few cold ones, to be accurate.

She opened her eye, took in once more the polo-shirted Machados. The future had come up in *conv. with mom.* Those Machados were all about the future. LeAnne rose and left Dr. Machado's office, taking the rest of his Hershey bar with her. That was a promising start.

"Apparently the army's my life," she said as she entered their room, hers and Marci's. But Marci wasn't there. The prosthetic leg lay on her bed. LeAnne sat down beside it. "What about you, Marci? Is the army your life, too?" LeAnne moved the prosthetic leg aside and lay down on Marci's bed. "What does minimal amelioration mean to you,

Marci?" She curled up and dropped down into dreamland.

Sometime later — the room at its darkest and quietest, so it had to be night — she felt Marci crawling in beside her. LeAnne was lying on her side, face to the wall. Marci lay on her back, her arm barely touching LeAnne. Then Marci rolled on her side, and they lay like spoons. The feeling of Marci against her was warm and nice. Sometime later, Marci put her hand on LeAnne's shoulder and rolled her over — not particularly gently — so they were face-to-face.

"I brought you some chocolate," LeAnne said.

"Is that what we're calling it?" Marci kissed her on the mouth. LeAnne kissed her back with everything she had in her, not a whole hell of a lot at that point.

Later that night, she remembered point two: she had shrapnel in her brain.

"Marci?"

No answer. Marci slept a deep sleep, and in that sleep seemed to radiate some sort of power. LeAnne held onto her. During the night, point two slipped out of her mind; point one came and went.

"So," said Ms. Spears, teacher of AP English, "let's take a look at the imagery in these lines — 'Time held me green and dying / Though I sang in my chains like the sea.' Who wants to start us off?"

Haskell started them off, even though he'd been accepted early to UC Berkeley and no longer needed to impress anybody at Fremont High; he just couldn't help himself.

"Firstly," he said, "there's personification. Time is personified."

"As what?" said Ms. Spears. "What's the correlative?"

"Well," said Haskell, "I guess as someone with hands."

"Hands?" said Ms. Spears.

Uh-oh, LeAnne thought. Hands? When "chains" was right there in the next line? She'd been in more classes with Haskell in the last four years than she could even remember. Was he losing it at last? Ms. Spears turned toward the class, looking for somebody to get things on track. Before that could happen, someone in the visitor parking lot, right outside the window, leaned on a car horn and didn't stop.

"Good grief," said Ms. Spears, going to the window. She looked out. "LeAnne? I think it's your dad." Pretty much all the faculty at Fremont High knew LeAnne's dad by sight — he hadn't missed a track meet in four years. LeAnne went to the window. There he was, parked in the nearest row, battered hood of his pickup facing the school, oily smoke rising from the tailpipe. He saw her at once and jumped out of the cab, waving a thick packet. The pickup rolled forward and came to a gentle stop against the curb. Her dad ran toward her, grinning and shouting, his words inaudible, his long, uncut, graying hair streaming behind him. LeAnne saw that the packet was in fact a large envelope. Her eyesight was so good she could even make out the crest in the top left corner, with its eagle and helmet — the golden helmet of Pallas Athena. She was in.

Not long after that, probably less than a minute, her dad was actually inside Ms. Spears's classroom, hugging LeAnne, tears on his face. An unprecedented situation, but LeAnne was very popular, and it was the spring of senior year. Everyone clapped. "Proudest moment of my life!" LeAnne's dad said, way too loudly and way too often, pumping his big, scarred fist at the ceiling. On a whim, he gave Ms. Spears a hug, too. LeAnne could see she didn't like it.

Ryan had a Corvette, blue and white, the colors of Fremont High. He and LeAnne sat in it the following Saturday night, parked outside her father's house. Her house, too, of course, but not for much longer. By this time, they were no longer in the predivorce house, had moved twice since then: first when Daddy took the trucking job, and second when he lost it. This latest house was a double-wide, but they didn't think of it as a trailer since it couldn't be towed, certainly not with the add-ons Daddy had built, like a sort of step-down den off the living room and a room he called the lanai off the back. At the moment he was in the den, impassive profile visible in flickering blue TV light.

"Kind of weird, huh?" Ryan said.

LeAnne knew just what he meant. That was one of the many good things about her and Ryan. Right now he was thinking about these last few weeks of high school, somehow made even stranger by the fact that their futures were set.

"No pressure?" she said.

"Exactly!" He took her hand. "I didn't even realize that was what I was feeling — no pressure." He let out a huge long breath.

"Again," she said. He let out another huge long breath. This time she joined in. A two-person-sized bubble of love came down over them, not real or material, of course, except for the fact she could feel it.

LeAnne and Ryan sat there for a while, did some kissing and other stuff. But not much of the other stuff, not with her father in view, even if he wasn't looking their way and couldn't have seen them in any case, the night so dark here out beyond the last developments. But development was coming this way, Daddy said, and when it did, they'd sell their lot and make a killing. Inside the den, he raised a bottle to his lips.

"I checked the mileage," Ryan said. "Hanover to West Point. Guess how far."

"Four hundred miles?"

"Only two sixty. Things are closer together back east."

"That can't be."

"It is. You'll see."

"I wish we were there already."

Ryan followed her gaze, which was directed at the flickering blue profile. "He'll be all right."

Chapter Seven

In the summers, LeAnne worked for Hidden Canyon Trails, a small desert tour company owned by Mr. Adelson's wife, Bernice. Bernice conducted the tours. LeAnne booked the reservations, ran the gift shop, gassed the ATVs, and showed the tourists their two pets, a javelina named Bruce and a diamondback named Willis. Bruce lived in a shady pen, ate anything available, and bristled at the sight of all humans except for LeAnne, who could actually pat him. Willis lived inside an escape-proof wire-mesh cage constructed by Mr. Adelson around an old and very big barrel cactus that somehow hung on to its flowers, the rare pink kind, all the way to the Fourth of July. Willis was not the original Willis, or the Willis after that, both escapees, but a far larger and more active Willis who actually exposed his fangs to the tourists, and was therefore "worth every penny," as

Bernice said, although Willis had cost her nothing since he'd been caught by LeAnne one evening in the ATV shed.

One day, that summer before West Point, LeAnne's dad drove up while she was alone in the office, reinstalling some new software that had been misinstalled by Mr. Adelson the night before. The office was in an old ranch house Bernice had bought during the housing bust, at the end of a two-mile dirt road with state land all around. LeAnne heard the pickup and went out on the porch, an old-fashioned Western porch decorated with trophy horns. Her dad was in the front seat of the pickup, fumbling with some papers. The dust raised by the pickup hung in the still, hot air, and didn't seem to be dissipating at all, one of those strange desert sights.

He stepped outside, clutching the papers in one hand, and saw her.

"Hey, there!" He kicked the door closed behind his back, not noticing an empty beer can that rolled off the seat and fell on the ground.

"Hi, Dad. What are you doing out here?"

"Where does it say a father can't visit his daughter?"

"There's a UN resolution."

"Don't get me started on those peckerheads." He glanced around. "Where is everybody?"

"Still out on the tour. What's up, Dad?"

"Just want to go over a few things." He walked onto the porch, the floorboards creaking under his weight. Her dad had very broad shoulders and a deep chest, and for a long time he'd maintained a *V*-shaped upper body, but now the middle part of him had broadened, too. He sat on the porch rocker, patted the footstool. LeAnne sat down.

Her dad rocked back and forth for a few moments. "Nothing like a rocker."

"Why don't you get one?"

"Too late," he said.

"Too late to buy a rocker? We could pick one up at a garage sale. How about next weekend?"

He shook his head. "Naw," he said. "Next weekend's no good."

"The weekend after that, then."

"Time's past for rockers. Time just keeps . . . what's the point of even saying it?"

"Saying what?"

Across the yard, over in Willis's cage, LeAnne caught a slight slithering movement. Snakes were supposed to lie quiet during the heat of the day, preserving moisture, but Willis had his own ideas. Her dad stopped rocking. He gazed in the direction of the dust cloud, still hanging in the air.

"You'll be gone real soon," he said.

"Not gone. Just gone away to school. That's different."

He turned to her and smiled. Her dad had a beautiful smile; she'd almost forgotten. "You're not coming back," he said. The beautiful smile didn't lose its shape in the slightest but somehow now looked confused, a confused kind of beauty that made her feel bad inside.

"Come on, Dad. We get two weeks at Christmas. I already checked."

He said nothing, showed no sign he'd even heard. What was this about? She remembered he'd applied for work at a golf course — which had turned out to be the one where Ryan's father played, a fact she'd kept to herself. Maybe he'd gotten turned down. But why? Her dad was a hard worker, and he could fix anything with a motor in it. She glanced at the papers he'd brought, now held loose in one of his big hands. Had the golf course sent him a bunch of complicated forms to fill out? And now he was embarrassed to ask for help?

"Dad?" she said. "Is this about the golf course?"

The smile, confused or not, vanished at once. "Golf course? What fuckin' golf course?"

"Wasn't it Desert Springs? The one on the way up to Cave Creek?"

"That's enough about golf. You know what golf is? A sign of our weakness, nothing more, nothing less. Think the Muslims are playing golf? Think they're lining up putts in Afghanistan?"

LeAnne laughed. "That's silly, Dad."

For a moment, he looked like he was about to blow. But then he gave his head a hard shake, like he was unscrambling things inside, and he laughed, too. "That goddamn laugh of yours," he said. He reached out with his free hand, patted her knee. "By the time you get your commission, the pansies in charge'll have us out of that cesspool, one potential worry off the table."

"What cesspool?"

"Afghanistan. They'll teach you about tactical retreats at the Point — tactical retreats that are goddamn routs in disguise. That's what this country's all about now."

"You don't believe that."

"And what's more," he said, raising a finger, "you don't have to do this."

"Do what?"

"Go to the Point. You got other offers —

UCLA, Rice, Vanderbilt."

"None of them are full rides, Dad. But the main thing is I want to go to the academy. I thought you wanted that, too. Don't you?"

Her dad's eyes seemed to mist over a bit. He narrowed them down to fierce slits. "They don't deserve you, that's all."

She half rose, gave him a quick kiss on the cheek. He dabbed at his eyes with his sleeve, then got busy with the papers.

"Damn paperwork," he said. "You'd think you could make up your will in one or two sentences, but no."

"Your will?"

"Irresponsible not to have one at my age."

"But you're still young!"

"Ha ha."

"Comparatively."

He shook his head. "Cut the bullshit. The point is everything I've got goes to you. Not a hell of a lot, as you know, but not nothin' either, on account of this here." He handed her some stapled-together sheets of paper.

LeAnne leafed through. "Insurance?"

"Exactly right. Life insurance policy I took out the day you were born, using my share of the settlement. A goodly part, in any case."

"Settlement? I don't understand."

"From the fire."

"The fire? But that happened long before I was born."

"So? I still had the money, or at least some. What matters is I locked it in, and you're the sole beneficiary." He leaned over, jabbed his finger at some clause on the page.

LeAnne handed back the papers. "Well, that's very . . . nice of you, Dad. But it's all theoretical."

"What's with you and all the fancy words?"

She shrugged.

"Aren't you even gonna ask the amount? The payoff on the policy?"

"Nope."

"You're a hard-ass, you know that? I'm gonna tell you anyway."

LeAnne covered her ears, the most anti-hard-ass move she could think of.

The worst thing about Willis was that his food had to be alive. Bernice handled the feedings, which took place just before closing time every third afternoon and involved small rodents. LeAnne made herself watch the whole performance her first summer on the job, once and once only. On one of those third afternoons, not long after the life insurance visit, LeAnne was sweeping the porch and Bernice, wearing rubber gloves, was on a stepladder, lowering some sort of rat down into Willis's cage, when a squad car from the sheriff's department drove up, parking near the cage. Two uniformed deputies got out and looked around. That distracted Bernice, who took her eyes off Willis, coiled down below and making plans.

"Bernice!" LeAnne shouted. Bernice jerked away, letting go of the rat. Willis's head shot up to where Bernice's hand had just been, fangs flashing in the sunlight.

"Nice try, Willis," Bernice said, climbing down off the stepladder and stripping off the rubber gloves like nothing had happened. She walked toward the deputies, giving her hair, sprayed into a hard sort of helmet, a pat or two.

"Can I help you?"

"That a rattler in there?" said one of the deputies.

"Perfectly legal," Bernice said. "What can I do for you?"

"Looking for a LeAnne Hogan," said the other deputy.

"What's this about?" Bernice said.

LeAnne stepped off the porch. "I'm LeAnne."

The deputies approached her. "Daughter

of Rex Hogan of 2241 Lost Hills Road?"

"Yes."

"Best if you're sitting down for this."

"What? Tell me."

Bernice was now at LeAnne's side.

"We're sorry to inform you that your father was killed in a wreck up in Wickenburg at approximately two forty-five this afternoon."

"No." Everything solid inside LeAnne, mostly meaning her foundation, weakened at that moment. "No. Please no." The hot, late-afternoon sun seemed to turn liquid and spill across the sky. "No." She had no idea at what volume she was speaking, or even if she was producing any sound at all.

"Afraid so." The rims of the deputies' hats shaded their eyes from view. "He was dead on arrival at St. Joe's."

"No." The hot liquid sky blazed down, but LeAnne iced up inside.

Bernice gripped her arm. "What kind of wreck?" she said.

"Not good."

"What does that mean?"

"There was a strong smell of alcohol in the cab of the deceased's vehicle. In ideal driving conditions, according to eyewitnesses, the vehicle swerved directly into a bridge abutment, just south of the county line."

LeAnne almost toppled over. Bernice, a very small woman, kept her on her feet.

The day after that came the results of the blood alcohol test: 0.39, the legal limit being 0.08. She looked up blood alcohol level 0.39, learned that it could be deadly just by itself, no driving involved; which would have been better. LeAnne wrote two letters, one to West Point withdrawing her application, the other to Gina Torrelli thanking her for everything, taking care that no tears stained them. Two days later she buried her father, then drove to the nearest recruiting office and enlisted in the army.

LeAnne awoke, found herself alone in Marci's bed, the prosthetic leg pressing uncomfortably against her side. She sat up, checked the time on the wall clock, forgot it, and checked it again.

"Marci?" she said, making no sense in the empty room. "Marci?"

Silence; that hospital silence of beeps and murmurs and distant sirens on the move. LeAnne rose, with a plan in mind to go down or up to PT, wherever it was, and find Marci. Then came a knock on the door.

"What?" LeAnne said.

"LeAnne? Are you decent?"

She felt her face. Her goddamn patch had slipped off again, the way it always seemed to when she slept. She turned to the bed and was rummaging through the covers when she heard hard-soled footsteps in the room.

"Afternoon, Sergeant. I didn't wake you, did I?"

LeAnne turned very slowly, more than a reluctant movement, actually one she had to force. Then she just stood there, not knowing what to do. Normally a salute would start things off, this being her commanding officer, Major Ladarius Sands, and he was in uniform, but she was not and would never be. She kept her hands at her sides. Meanwhile, he had a good long look at her face, his own showing no reaction whatever. Then he took off his hat, came forward, and gave her a hug, a warm, tight, brotherly hug.

"So good to see you," he said, patting her back. "Especially looking how you do, way, way better than the last time."

"The last time?" LeAnne gazed into the hall. A nurse came to the door, glanced into the room, went away.

"The last time I saw you." The major gave her another pat or two. LeAnne tried to remember the last time she'd seen him. In the chow line just before that last mission, a mission he hadn't been on because of some quirk of scheduling she no longer remembered. But not the point. The point was that at that hour, that night, she'd still looked like her old self. Therefore . . . therefore he'd seen her since? She had no memory of that.

The major stepped back but still held on to her upper arms. "Everyone says hi and how much they miss you," he said. "All the guys, and the CST team. Here's a card, signed by everybody." He reached into an inside pocket of his jacket and handed her an envelope. She took the envelope but made no move to open it. "And here's something else," he said, "which I'm honored and proud to present."

He gave her a small box, the size earrings might come in. She made no move to open it, either.

"To tell you the truth," he went on, "never more honored and never more proud."

LeAnne opened the box. Inside was a ribbon with red, white, and blue stripes, and on the end of that ribbon hung the Bronze Star. She looked up at him. The expression in his eyes was indeed one of pride, mixed in with a kind of sorrow as well. LeAnne couldn't bear the thought of him feeling sorry for her, and was thinking of giving the Bronze Star back to him, when she suddenly pictured herself saying to Marci, "I almost gave it back to him." Just to see Marci's reaction. So she didn't return the Bronze Star, instead simply said, "Thank you."

"No," said the major. "Thank you."

The nurse appeared at the door again. "May I come in? Just for a moment?"

LeAnne shrugged. The nurse came in, walked quickly by them, picked up Marci's prosthetic leg, and headed for the door.

"Hey," LeAnne said. "Where are you going with that?"

The nurse stopped and turned.

"Are you taking it to Marci? I can do it, if you want. Where is she?"

"No one told you?"

"No one told me what?"

The nurse took a quick, deep breath. "Marci threw a blood clot in her lung. It all happened so fast. There was nothing we could do."

"What are you saying?"

Chapter Eight

"Is that how you hold your girlfriend?" LeAnne said.

"Sorry, ma'am?" said the pimply recruit lying at her feet.

"Am I a commissioned officer, Dracut?" Dracut had been in her life for less than five minutes and because he was prone, his tag couldn't be seen, but she'd already memorized his name. She always learned the names, first thing.

"Uh, I'm not sure, ma'am."

"Look at my arm."

"Yes, ma'am."

"What do you see?"

"Stripes, ma'am."

"How many?"

"Three, ma'am."

"Meaning?"

"Sorry, ma'am?"

She heard smothered laughter from down the line. "Cruz. Give me twenty."

Cruz started doing push-ups.

"Those are pathetic, Cruz. They count as minuses. So now you owe me twenty-three."

Cruz did twenty-three push-ups, a bit less pathetic, but not much, his soft middle touching down first every time.

"Dracut?"

"Ma'am?"

"Christ Almighty, Dracut. What's the meaning of three stripes?"

"Sergeant, ma'am?"

"So what do you call me?"

"Sergeant?"

"Very good, Dracut. Also very slow. How does slow stack up against the enemy, Dracut?" All the prone bodies seemed to change a little bit, like they'd felt something inside.

"Not good, ma— sergeant?"

"Worse than that, Dracut. Real fuckin' bad." She let that hang for a moment or two. "Back to your girlfriend. Is that how you hold her?"

"I don't have a girlfriend, Sergeant."

"But let's say by some miracle you did. Is that how you'd hold her? Crushing the life out of her?"

"No, Sergeant."

"Then why hold your weapon like that, Dracut? Hold it nice and it'll be nice back."

Dracut relaxed his grip slightly on the M16.

"Steady," she commanded. "Breathe in. Hold. Squeeze."

Dracut fired a round. The silhouette, distance one hundred meters, went unscathed. Not just the circle at the center, meaning the actual target, but the whole thing. A snicker came from down the line. Without looking that way, LeAnne said, "That'll be twenty, Ferguson."

"Wasn't me, Sergeant!"

"Thirty."

LeAnne turned back to Dracut. "Do you know how to hold your breath gently, Dracut? So your face doesn't go that disgusting shade of purple?"

"I think so, Sergeant."

"Is anyone asking you to think?"

"No, Sergeant."

"Then don't think. Just hold your breath gently."

"Yes, Sergeant." He held his breath gently.

"And don't pull that goddamn trigger ever again. Squeeze doesn't mean pull. Look it up. Squeeze is the way you'd press the thing at the top of a pen to get the point out. Ever used a pen, Dracut?"

"Yes, Sergeant."

"It's just like that. I ever see you pull a

trigger again, I'll have Ferguson bite your finger off." She glanced at Ferguson, still doing push-ups, all of them crappy. "Isn't that right, Ferguson?"

"Yes, Sergeant," he said.

"You constipated, Ferguson?"

"No, Sergeant."

"You sound constipated. How many's that?"

"Twenty-six, Sergeant."

"Those last two are minuses, Ferguson. Add 'em on."

"Yes, Sergeant."

"Dracut."

"Yes, Sergeant."

"Steady. Breathe. Hold. Squeeze."

Dracut fired the weapon. This time he hit the very edge of the silhouette, bottom left-hand corner. The class checked Dracut's target through their scopes.

"A flesh wound at best," LeAnne said. "Maybe it'll get infected."

"Sergeant?" called a voice from the far end of the line, the only female voice in the class. "You can see that without a scope? Where Dracut hit, I mean?"

"You doubting me, Haynesworth? Give me twenty-five."

Then, from behind: "Excuse me, Sergeant."

LeAnne turned, found herself facing the range officer. Standing beside him was a woman wearing silver eagles on her epaulettes, the highest-ranking woman she'd seen in person so far in her career. She saluted.

"Sergeant Hogan, like you to meet Colonel Bright."

"Ma'am," said LeAnne. She shook hands with Colonel Bright. Colonel Bright's hand seemed to be the exact size and shape of her own, plus she squeezed pretty hard. LeAnne squeezed pretty hard right back.

"I apologize for interrupting your class," the colonel said. "Which seems to be going well." The recruits lay prone, unsure, gaping. LeAnne hoped to God none of them shot themselves while her back was turned. "But," the colonel went on, "I'd like a few moments of your time."

"Recruits," she said. "Safeties on." She heard a click or two, knelt to examine the nearest weapon, the stock shiny with newbie sweat. "See where it says 'Semi'?' Switch it to 'Safe.' " A sweaty, grimy finger made the right move. That was followed by *click, click, click* down the line.

"Your record is outstanding," Colonel Bright said.

"Thank you, ma'am," said LeAnne.

They sat in a corner at the back of a Burger King near the base, LeAnne still in the MultiCams she'd worn on the range, the colonel in dress blues.

"For a, quote, 'non-combatant,' end quote, you've seen a hell of a lot of combat. The situation's a joke, of course — once you're in a combat zone, you're in combat. But still — you've been a model for what's coming. And while we're at it, I'd be interested in more details about that suicide bomber episode south of Herat. You were with the Fifth Infantry? Bob Keefer is an old friend of mine."

"As far as I know, those details are still classified," LeAnne said.

The colonel's lips, glistening with hot pink lipstick, and quite a lot of it — turned down. "Meaning you're not going to discuss it?"

"I'd never want to be in a position of refusing a direct order, ma'am."

Colonel Bright laughed. "Bob warned me about you." She took out a nicely bound leather notebook, glanced at a page or two. "End result, you saved the life of some tribal muckety-muck by not missing a detail that everybody else missed. That the gist of it? Just nod."

LeAnne nodded.

"What do you think about those tribal muckety-mucks in general?"

"That's not really my assignment," LeAnne said.

"First, I'm not so sure about that whole compartmentalized way of dealing," said Colonel Bright, dipping a French fry into a pool of ketchup and popping it into her mouth. "Second, if everything goes the way I think it will, those questions are going to be very much on your plate."

LeAnne thought about the tribal leaders question. "They mistake restraint for weakness," she said.

"Agreed. So what do we do about that?"

"On the ground, ma'am?"

"On the ground. For example, we could go on-purpose crazy once in a while, shoot up some folks just to make a statement."

LeAnne had seen something like that a couple of times, bad scenes that no one talked about after. But had they worked? Not that she could tell. "Better to show them that we're the ones who don't go crazy, no matter what," she said.

"How do we do that?"

"I don't know."

"Take a swing at it. No penalty for wrong answers. Hell, maybe they're all wrong."

All answers ending up wrong: that was something LeAnne, now with three tours behind her, and a trunk full of bloody and stinking memories best left unopened, had begun to fear. Meanwhile, the colonel was waiting. There had to be a reason for the question, had to be a reason for this whole meeting. LeAnne searched her mind for something to say, came up with only this: "Show them what we're really like," she said, "but take no shit." Better to have kept her mouth shut? LeAnne was pretty sure of that until she saw Colonel Bright open her leather-bound notebook and take out a pen.

The colonel spoke what she was writing, the way people do sometimes, drawing out the words. "Show — them — what we're rea—lly like, but take — no — shit." She closed the notebook and sipped from her coffee cup, gazing at LeAnne over the rim. "If you're worried I'll pass that off as my own, don't be."

"I wasn't," LeAnne said. "And you're welcome to it, ma'am."

"Oh, I'm going to use it all right, but with attribution." Colonel Bright glanced at LeAnne's burger, untouched. "Eat."

LeAnne took a bite. The colonel watched her chew. That reminded LeAnne of her mother, otherwise unlike Colonel Bright in every way she could think of.

"I understand you're not planning to re-up," the colonel said.

"No, ma'am." LeAnne had eight weeks of service left, all of them to be spent here, stateside, instructing recruits on the range.

"Hate the army?"

"No, ma'am, not all."

"Have some grievances?"

"No."

"Bored?"

"No."

"Then what?"

LeAnne put down her burger. "It's just that I've thought of something I'd like to do next and I'm kind of excited to be doing it."

"Mind sharing?"

"Well, it's not anything earthshaking," LeAnne said. "I want to start a military-style summer camp for girls, ages ten to twelve or so. Living in tents, cooking outdoors, hiking, rope climbing, building stuff, martial arts . . . that kind of thing." She watched the colonel's face for some reaction, saw none.

"What kind of girls?"

"Any who want to come."

"Including inner-city ones?"

"For sure."

"How are inner-city girls gonna pay?"

"That's something I have to work on."

"And what about setup costs?"

"I've got some money saved. Plus a small inheritance."

Something unmilitary appeared for a moment in the colonel's eyes, and in that moment they weren't a colonel and a sergeant, but just two people contemplating an idea. Then the colonel nodded. Her expression returned to normal, and they were back in the army.

"Hate curveballs, and you've thrown me one," Colonel Bright said. "But it's a hell of a concept, and you're just the right person. Can't help you with the money, not directly, and I suspect any direct link — or any link at all, really — to the military isn't the way to go. But I've got contacts who I'm pretty goddamn sure will be useful on the fund-raising side, and I'm going to start lining them up no matter what happens from here on in."

"What happens from here on in?" LeAnne said. "I don't understand."

"Meaning whatever you say to a proposal I'm about to make," said the colonel. "Yes or no, I'll still back this camp of yours. Understood?"

"Yes, ma'am."

"Got a name for it, by the way?"

"I'm not sure."

"Out with it."

LeAnne felt herself blushing, a strange sensation for her, but she couldn't help it, the feeling rising up in her also being strange: a mixture of shyness and pride. "Roadmaster," she said.

"Roadmaster Camp or Camp Roadmaster?"

"Camp Roadmaster."

"I'm with you." The colonel rubbed her hands together, as though heating things up. "Back to the agenda — ever heard of CST?"

"No ma'am."

"Not a surprise. We're still new. Stands for Cultural Support Team. Special Ops finally realized that those nighttime raids of theirs, hunting bad guys in the Afghan boonies, yield at best fifty percent of the potential intel. Any idea why that might be?"

"Because the Afghan women won't talk to them."

Colonel Bright sat back. "You've already thought about this?"

"Some," said LeAnne.

"So the idea of attaching highly trained and combat-capable female troops to Special Ops makes sense to you?"

"Yes, ma'am."

"It's a one-year commitment," the colonel said. "That includes two months at Fort Bragg for selection and training and the rest for deployment. Someone like you won't have any trouble getting selected. Hell, you could probably train most of the trainers — all male at the moment, which pisses me off like you wouldn't believe. With me so far?"

LeAnne nodded.

"Like the idea?"

"Yes, ma'am."

"Any questions?"

"Does combat-capable mean official combatant?"

"No." The colonel smiled one of those conspiratorial smiles, like they were a couple of mafiosi planning some heist. "Not officially official, at least not yet. But that's just politics. The CSTs will be fully armed, identical to the men. What else?"

"I don't like the name," LeAnne said.

"Cultural Support Team? Just politics, again. I hate it, too. But we've got to think big picture, you and me."

In the parking lot, Colonel Bright's driver got out of the car and came toward the door, tapped on the glass. The colonel rose, held out her hand. "Just tell me you'll consider it. No pressure."

LeAnne didn't feel any pressure. She said yes on the spot, not because of pressure, not because Colonel Bright was higher in rank, not because of all the colonel's flattery. It was simply that the job needed to be done and she could do it.

They shook hands again, and again LeAnne felt the similarity in hand size, hand strength, and power; although now the colonel's palm had dampened a bit. As she watched the colonel's car drive off, LeAnne suddenly pictured the cover of a brochure for Camp Roadmaster: a pigtailed girl in shorts and a T-shirt climbing up a rope toward a golden sky. That was when she realized she'd had enough of the army. Not that she didn't still love it. She did. But she'd seen enough blood and guts, literal blood and literal guts. She'd come to her limit, meaning that this CST gig would have to be played out in overtime.

Chapter Nine

Initial Evaluation for Post-Traumatic Stress Disorder:
Military History:

9. Combat wounds sustained (describe):

"If you don't put a lid on it this second, we'll be forced to sedate you," the nurse said, her voice rising.

LeAnne herself was already at full volume and had been for some time. She stood in front of the nurses' station, screaming her head off. "What did you do to her? What the fuck did you do to her?" Just those two sentences, over and over, her brain on fire. Meanwhile, she was surrounded by nurses, doctors, orderlies, with her former commanding officer, Major Sands, pushed out to the periphery, his mouth open and her Bronze Star in one hand.

"This is your last warning."

"Just try it. Go right ahead." LeAnne raised Marci's prosthetic leg as a weapon, ready to use it on anyone who came one step nearer, and was just realizing she did not in fact have the prosthetic leg, was weaponless and empty-handed, when she sensed movement on her blind side. She started to turn in the that direction, felt a sharp jab in her right arm, just below the shoulder. Then all the faces around the nurses' station melted into funhouse shapes.

She awoke.

Eye.

LeAnne rolled onto her side and took her bearings, task one when you were in the field. She was not in the field, just back in her bed, meaning her bed in the room at Walter Reed that she'd shared with Marci, but no longer would. LeAnne had always had a compass in her head — getting a compass in the head of every girl who came to Camp Roadmaster was high on her list of bullet points — except at that moment she had no idea where east was. Did it matter? Camp Roadmaster, the brochure with its bullet points, the girls: all scratched. Hey, Marci, she wanted to say, where the fuck is east?

No Marci. Her gaze went to Marci's empty bed. What was this? Marci, sleeping on her side, back turned to the room, her favorite sleeping position? Could it be? Hadn't there been some sort of scene about Marci's demise? Only a nightmare, was that it? In which case the scene, noisy and nasty, hadn't happened in real life? How far back did the nightmare go? All the way to before? Meaning before that big hairy hand emerged through the folds of the burqa? Of course not. Much too much to ask. LeAnne had seen enough of the world — oh, brother — to know that. But if the nightmare began with Marci alive, and therefore still alive in the right now, that would be good enough.

"Marci?"

The woman in the bed turned over. Not Marci. This was a black woman with her hair in neat cornrows. Her skin was smooth and flawless, her features delicate. She looked like a kid. Nothing but her head was visible; the rest of her a series of lumps beneath the covers.

"Excuse me?" the woman said. She had a small, high voice: looked like a kid and sounded like a kid.

"I was looking for . . . nothing. Doesn't matter."

"Are you LeAnne?"

"Yeah."
"Dr. Machado wants you to call him as soon as you wake up."
"That hasn't happened yet."
"Excuse me?"
"Forget it." The woman was looking at her funny. "Fucking shit." LeAnne felt around under her pillow, found the patch, put it on. "Was Machado in here?"
The woman nodded.
"You know him?"
The woman shook her head.
"Was he wearing a polo shirt?"
"No. A white coat."
"Did he mention stolen chocolate?"
"He just said he wanted you to get in touch."
"We all have our little wants, don't we?"
The woman took that in, like it had deep meaning. Then her perfect face started to crumple. With an effort of will, an effort LeAnne could feel from across the room, the woman got her face back to normal. As for her own face, LeAnne wanted to punch it. What she didn't want was to see what was under those covers, not now, not ever. She threw back her own covers and got out of bed.
"Where's all my shit?"
"Maybe in the closet?"

The closet. LeAnne had been living in this room for . . . she actually didn't know how long. But in all that time, she'd never once thought to look in the closet. The truth was she might not have even noticed its existence. She was pitiful.

"What happened to my goddamn compass?"

"I don't know," the woman said. "Mine got blown up."

LeAnne looked at her and nodded. Then she went to the closet and opened the door.

"My stuff's on the right," the woman said.

LeAnne checked out the left side. Two uniforms — MultiCams and dress blues — hung on the rail. On the floor was her camo duffel. She squatted down, opened it, checked the contents: jeans, sweats, two bras, two pairs of panties, socks — all new — plus boots, dopp kit, wallet. She looked in the wallet: driver's license, red no-fee passport, bank card, four twenties, a ten, two fives.

Good to go. LeAnne stripped off her pajamas, got dressed, pulled the boots out of her duffel. The smell of goats hit her right away. She did not want to wear those boots, but there was no choice. She bent to put them on and noticed two bright red sneakers at the back of the closet. Marci's sneaks?

Yes. She tried them on. The fit was perfect. LeAnne shouldered her duffel, kicked her boots to the back of the closet, left the uniforms on the rail. She closed the closet door, trapping Afghanistan in there, like a tiny battlefield.

What else? She moved to the rolling table beside her bed. The box from the ocular prosthetics lady lay on the table; beside it, a small paper cup with three pills inside. She swallowed the pills.

"For the road."

And stuck the ocular box in her duffel.

"You going somewhere?" said the woman in Marci's bed.

"Yup."

"Any, like, message, you want me to pass on?"

"Not a goddamn thing." Did her words seem to leave a harsh after-sound hanging in the room? What kind of good-bye was that, especially since this woman had to be a sister in arms? LeAnne went over to her and touched the top of her head, very lightly. The woman looked scared. Now was the moment for saying something positive, but nothing came to her, not even the feeblest encouraging word.

On her way out, LeAnne spotted something on the floor. She bent to examine it:

the photo of Bruno, Dr. Machado's little brown dog, that she'd acquired somehow. LeAnne left it there.

LeAnne headed down the hall toward the elevators, meaning she had to pass the nurses' station on the way. But so what? Who was going to stop her? She pushed on and was just reaching the station when an elevator opened and out stepped a man in uniform, a man she thought she might know. Soft face, two silver bars on his lapel, brown briefcase with brass fittings in hand. All that added up to someone she knew, all right, but the name, and what he was about, wouldn't come. LeAnne wheeled around before he could look her way and walked quickly back down the hall to a door marked Stairs. She shouldered it open and charged down, flight after flight, almost losing her balance several times on account of her half-screen vision, but finally banging through the G door at the bottom. LeAnne crossed a broad, busy lobby, whirled through a revolving door, and stepped outside. The glare was terrible. She fumbled around for her oversized sunglasses, found them perched on top of her head, and put them on.

Two taxis sat idling by the curb. LeAnne

got into the nearest one, shoving her duffel in first.

The driver glanced at her in the rearview mirror. "Where to?"

"Phoenix."

"What number?"

"Huh?"

"Phoenix Drive? Other side of one eighty-seven? What number?"

"The bus station, then."

"The bus station? Like for out of town? No bus station on Phoenix. I could take you to the station in Silver Spring, you want out of town."

"Yeah," LeAnne said. "Out."

The taxi pulled away. LeAnne took one glance back, saw the soft-faced captain hurrying outside. He looked this way and that, spotted the taxi. She faced front.

"Step on it. I'm late."

"Not allowed to exceed the speed limit."

"Pussy."

No more was said. LeAnne felt watched from behind. The taxi merged onto a busy street, made a couple of turns. LeAnne took a deep breath. It came back to her: Captain Stallings, G-2, the man with the photos, of which she remembered two: Katie; and Gulab Yar-Muhammad, the man with the deep-set, examining eyes. The driver hunched over the wheel and didn't look at her again.

LeAnne took a window seat on the left-hand side of the bus, perfect for left-eyed viewing, but stormy weather moved in from the west and state after state went by pretty much unseen. She napped; she had headaches; she ate chocolate, refreshing her supply at every pit stop and washing it down with chocolate milk. She kept her oversized sunglasses on at all times and had no seatmates until a stop in Cookeville, Tennessee, or possibly Kentucky.

"This seat taken?"

LeAnne turned, had to twist practically all the way around to get this person in her field of view. A smiling man, dressed in clean, pressed clothes, freshly shaved, short hair wet with rain. She shrugged. He took the aisle seat. The bus pulled away from wherever they were. Raindrops slid horizontally across the glass and pelted the roof hard, like gunshots. She felt the man shift in his seat, sensed that he was looking down at the floor on her side, where her feet, shod in Marci's red sneaks, rested on the duffel.

"You in the army?" he said.

LeAnne nodded, facing straight ahead.

"Thank you for your service."

She didn't respond. The bus rolled on.

The sliding raindrops sped up and the overhead barrage grew louder. LeAnne tried to sleep, knew that sleep was the best answer at this moment, but she was way too wound up. She twisted around to the man.

"What would you know?"

He blinked. "About the army? Nothing. Sorry if I've offended. I only —"

"Don't want to hear it," LeAnne said.

She turned away, but not before noticing the Bible, open on his lap. Was he some kind of missionary? Fuck all missions. Sleep came soon after that. When she awoke, it was night and the aisle seat was empty. She felt better. Partly it was the rain. Somehow she needed rain. At the next pit stop, after stocking up on chocolate and chocolate milk, she stood outside the bus, her face tilted up to the downpour. She took off her sunglasses and her patch and luxuriated.

"Hey, let's go," the driver called through the open door. "Don't have all —" He got a better view of her — most likely in passing headlight beams — and cut himself off. LeAnne put on her sopping patch and her misty sunglasses and climbed back on the bus, just about soaked through herself. She shivered all night.

LeAnne awoke in a fog, a double fog, in her

head and outside the window. The bus, smelling of cooped-up mammals after a long night, was stopped, but stopped where? Getting her bearings first thing was step one. Impossible: the bus was cocooned in charcoal gray. LeAnne heard the front door squeak open, heard soft footsteps coming down the rubber-padded aisle.

"Is this seat taken?"

She twisted around to get this new person in view, maybe grunting with annoyance at the same time. A woman stood in the aisle, her form dim in the charcoal-gray light.

"Sorry if I woke you," the woman said.

There was something about her, something not good. LeAnne took off her sunglasses and things brightened up. That took away all doubt. This newcomer, this woman who wanted to occupy the seat right beside her, was wearing a burqa, the full kind, with only a slit for the eyes. LeAnne grabbed her duffel, wrenched it loose, bolted up, shoved her way past the woman, knocking her aside — or even down to the floor — and strode, almost running, to the front of the bus. The door was closing.

"Sorry," the driver said. "Stop's over."

"Open the door."

"I can do that, but then we'll leave without you."

"Open the fucking door."

The door opened. LeAnne jumped off, not taking the time to use the steps. She hurried away from the bus. The bus hurried away from her.

LeAnne got her bearings. She stood in foggy flatland, a row of gas pumps on one side, a low, square building on the other, with a neon sign on the roof: Okeydokey's Easy On Easy Off. She hitched her duffle higher on her shoulder, fumbled for her sunglasses, again finding them on her head, again getting them back in place, and entered Okeydokey's.

There was no one inside except a big Native American man behind the counter. LeAnne scooped up a few Hershey bars and went over to him. He had two long braids, black and gleaming, the best sight LeAnne had come across in a long time. She handed him the Hershey bars. His gaze moved to the duffel.

"Just coming back?" he said.

LeAnne sensed a trick question and kept her mouth shut.

"Back home from overseas?" the man said.

"Yeah. Overseas."

"Iraq? I did a tour in Iraq."

"Yeah. Iraq. Iraq, Afghanistan, Germany, Maryland."

"Maryland?"

"Bethesda's in Maryland."

He seemed to think that over. "True enough." He handed back the Hershey bars. "No charge."

What the hell was he up to? LeAnne peered at him through the big dark left lens of her sunglasses. "Yeah?" she said.

"Yeah."

Now was the time for saying thanks, but LeAnne just couldn't get the word out. She nodded and tucked the Hershey bars in her pocket.

"You from here?" he said.

"Here?"

"Okemah."

"What's Okemah?"

He smiled. "This town. Okemah, Oklahoma. Saw you get off the bus. No one gets off at this stop except they live here."

"What's it like?" LeAnne said.

"To live here?" He shrugged. "Depends on you, pretty much."

She turned, looked out the windows. The fog was starting to lift, peeling away from strip malls, empty lots, and I-40 in the distance, a headlight stream and a taillight stream flowing in opposite directions.

"I want to buy a car," LeAnne said.

"What kind of car?"

"Rolls-Royce."

He laughed. "Good you got your sense of humor. When I came back . . ." He took a deep breath and shook his head.

"I'm a fuckin' laugh riot," LeAnne said.

He backed away a step, tilted his head slightly, as though trying to get a fix on a position. "You serious about a car? My uncle runs a used-car lot."

"Is he honest?"

"For military, yeah, he'll be honest. Within reason."

Chapter Ten

"This Honda over here I can let you have for thirty-seven fifty," said the uncle.

"What about if I pay cash?"

"At my place everybody pays cash. Thirty-seven fifty."

LeAnne walked around the Honda. Her last car — sold before she deployed to Afghanistan — had been a very cool Mini, British racing green, six-speed manual, the biggest engine they had. She'd practically flown that baby, jitterbugging through traffic like she was in a video game. This sun-bleached beige Honda sat in the corner of the uncle's lot like sitting was what it liked to do and did best. In its favor it had no deep dents, only a few dings here and there, plus the tires matched and had plenty of tread left.

"What's the mileage?"

"Hundred twenty, give or take." The uncle was a little guy, half the size of his nephew but had the same gleaming black hair. "My nephew says you were in Iraq."

"A few years ago."

"He didn't come back the same as how he left."

LeAnne grunted. He stared at her, a stare she'd seen a few times now, when people tried to see through her sunglasses. Which she knew was impossible on account of the darkness of the lenses; all anyone saw would be their own gawking selves. She got down on the pavement, peered under the car, spotted no oil stains. When she rose, a headache started up behind where her right eye used to be. Why all these goddamn headaches? LeAnne had been about to offer three grand, but now she only wanted to be done with this. "I'll write you a check."

"Got an ATM here. For actual currency of the Union, I'll knock off two hundred."

LeAnne began disliking this little uncle. She didn't want to dicker; she wanted to go. "The daily limit's . . ." She couldn't remember. "Five hundred." Only a guess but it sounded right.

"Call the bank."

Call the bank? She felt her hands curling into fists. A horrible deterioration of this little back and forth was somewhere in the cards.

"They'll usually extend," the uncle said. "Use my phone, if you want."

LeAnne realized she didn't have a phone. Where was it? Left behind at Walter Reed, or Landstuhl, or on the hard, dried-out ground of that village of hovels? In that case, it would have been sold and resold and re-resold, or repurposed as a bomb igniter, or some other bad shit.

"That's what happens over there — even the shit turns to shit."

"Uh, at your bank?" said the uncle.

Had she spoken aloud? LeAnne turned away, got a grip. "Nothing," she said. "I'll call the bank."

LeAnne had had an account at a small community bank in Columbia, South Carolina, since Fort Jackson days. They approved a cash withdrawal of $3,500, leaving her with a balance of $11,090. She traded the cash for the keys to the Honda and hit the road.

Here was one plan: drive back and forth across the country until some better idea cropped up. Why not? She'd always loved driving, starting out as one of those babies whose fussing could always be stopped with a car ride. But right away, headed west on I-40, a problem, and so obvious: driving with only one eye, while possible, was not easy, forcing her across the line separating play from work. On interstates, LeAnne had always driven the passing lane, eighty plus, which now felt too fast. Seventy was about right, or even a bit less. But seventy in the passing lane meant cars zipping by on the right, each one a kind of shock, looming suddenly out of the dead quadrant. LeAnne steered her way into the right-hand lane, taking her spot among the old and the timid. It occurred to her that she'd forgotten to take the Honda for a test drive, kind of basic. She glanced at herself in the rearview mirror, saw someone she didn't know and didn't want to know.

What went on in the hearts of these women? "They are just like you and me," Katie always said, "except for different circumstances."

At the moment — waiting for the ceremonial opening of the Afghan and American Women's Friendship Weaving Co-Op — the women looked happy. There were thirty-five of them — LeAnne counted twice — plus Katie and her, crowded into the still not quite completed twelve-hundred-square-foot cinder block space, funded by some program at the embassy in Kabul. They wore robes and scarves, but their faces were uncovered and the mood was one of vacation. Beautiful rugs on the walls, newly built looms on the floor, plates of baklava and pistachio fudge: optimism was in the air, and LeAnne hadn't felt much of it on this posting. She heard motorized vehicles pulling up outside and moved to the door. The women covered their faces; Katie put on her head scarf; LeAnne, wearing a standard-issue multicam patrol cap, counted the women one last time.

The door opened and in came three Afghan men, a lead muckety-muck in pantaloons and embroidered shirt with a blue blazer, and two followers in traditional dress. The muckety-muck raised his hand in greeting and began to speak. The women rearranged themselves into neat and attentive rows, messing up LeAnne's count.

"Would you like me to translate for you?" Katie whispered.

"Sure, that would be —"

What was this? A tall woman in the second row was wearing boots? Boots, in fact, similar in color and style to the ones LeAnne was wearing, except bigger, sticking out from under her robe? All the other women whose feet she could see were wearing leather sandals or woven slippers; and on the petite side, each and every pair.

"Well," Katie was saying, "first he's praising Allah for his kindness in . . ."

LeAnne had tuned out. She was moving away from the door, around one of the new looms, toward the woman in the boots. A tall woman, the tallest in the room, and she wore a niqab of the most concealing kind, a rectangle of netting covering even the eyes. The woman seemed to turn her head slightly in LeAnne's direction, but it was hard to tell and her eyes could not be read.

"Hey," LeAnne said. "You."

Yes, the woman was looking at her now, beyond doubt.

"Hands, please. Show me your hands."

The woman did nothing; maybe not quite nothing — it was possible she tensed up, but hard to tell because of the burqa.

LeAnne slid her M9 from its holster. "Hands! Hands up where I can see them! Yad! Yad!" *Yad* being the Arabic for hand, the Pashto word not coming to her when she needed it.

The woman backed up, backed up in a powerful sort of way, her hands not in view. From the rows of women came uneasy stirring, like penguins in a rookery.

LeAnne raised the weapon and sighted. "I'll blow you away! Hands up! Yad! Yad!"

The muckety-muck fell silent. Fearful murmurs started up and spread across the floor, growing in volume, on their way to screams.

"Hands up!"

There was movement under the tall woman's burqa, the movement of hands. But hands did not appear. Instead they were doing other things, out of sight. That was that. LeAnne let loose a controlled pair. The woman toppled over and lay still, blood seeping through the burqa on the left side of her chest — a breastless chest, the woman turning out to be a man with four pounds of C-4 loaded in a suicide belt around his waist.

The muckety-muck had given LeAnne her pick of the rugs hanging on the walls of the Afghan and American Women's Friendship Weaving Co-Op. Later, through Katie, LeAnne had found out that the rug wasn't his to give, and sent it back, a six-by-nine rug with a border of finely detailed purple flowers. The women had quickly lost their enthusiasm for the co-op, and it closed within months. She never learned what was in their hearts.

LeAnne made two big mistakes in her military career, the first a secret now guaranteed never to get out, the second known to everybody, both coming late in the game. As she drove through Oklahoma, a scene that hadn't happened in real life played and replayed in her mind, a scene that ended with her saying no to Colonel Bright. Each time, she pounded the wheel, trying to get the scene that should have been to stop, trying to flip her mind to something else, but it wouldn't flip. *Thank you, Colonel, but no. I've done enough. My plans are set.* She tormented herself with that scene for miles and miles, before noticing a grandmotherly type looking down at her from the passenger seat of a passing eighteen-wheeler, peering down at LeAnne pounding the wheel until it shook. Now she was getting spied on? LeAnne gave the grandmotherly type the finger and got the finger right back. For a single red-hot moment, she considered a quick leftward swerve, just to let that grandmotherly type — and anyone else who wanted a piece of her — know what sort of person they were dealing with.

Not long after that, her eye got too weary to go on. LeAnne took an exit, loaded up on chocolate bars and chocolate milk, plus a couple of bacon burgers for protein. It was probably the first time she'd even uttered "bacon burgers" in her life. She sat in a parking lot — chocolate bars, chocolate milk, and burgers on the passenger seat — and fell asleep.

Fraternization can kill. LeAnne had heard someone say that all the way back in basic, but it was one of many things she'd innately known already. She'd never had a military boyfriend of any rank, or even come close, never given out the slightest vibe and never responded to one. Never even come close, up until that last posting. And did something expressed only on leave count as fraternization? Maybe LeAnne fooled herself a bit on that, although the code did not. She'd checked.

LeAnne had three boyfriends after Ryan: the first a whitewater rafting guide on the Ocoee River, a relationship that hadn't survived her Iraqi posting; the second a charter boat captain in Islamorada, which had an ending similar to the first, Afghanistan substituting for Iraq; and Jamie.

"Captain Cray," said Major Ladarius, "like you to meet Sergeant LeAnne Hogan, who's been running our CST program here in Herat province. She's the brains of the outfit."

Jamie Cray was about LeAnne's height, had similar coloring, and even the same sort of broad-shouldered build, although much more exaggerated in the male version. LeAnne saluted him.

"Sir," she said.

"Nice to meet you," said Jamie. "I've heard good things about CST."

"I wasn't just referencing CST," the major said. "She's the brains, period."

"I'll bear that in mind, sir."

"You do that," said the major.

Later she learned that Jamie had graduated from the same West Point class she would have been in, a fact she kept to herself. She also kept the feelings he aroused in her to herself, and he did the same with how he felt about her. Nothing untoward, verbal, physical, or noticeable in any way ever passed between them, not in the Afghan theater. But they both knew.

"Cork blew off," Jamie said.

"One way of putting it," said LeAnne.

"I meant about you and me — the pent-up things inside."

"Sure you did."

He laughed and rolled her off him. She let herself be rolled. This was in LeAnne's room, night two — the last night — of a three-day leave in Qatar, her second, and the last leave she'd have before going home and mustering out. They weren't staying in the same hotel — officers usually stayed at the Hilton, enlisted personnel at the Ramada — and had spent no time together out in the open, but he'd knocked on her door at 2:00 a.m. on the first night. She'd known who it was just from the knock, even though she'd never heard his knock before. LeAnne had opened right up and after that things had happened fast, except for those that were better when they happened slow. He'd left before dawn.

Now, night two, same MO in the cards, meaning late arrival and early departure, the whole world — huge and violent, as they both knew as well as anybody — shrank down to just them.

"I'm going to be exhausted when we get back," Jamie said.

"Boo hoo."

He shook his head. "How come you're so tough?"

"I'm not tough."

"Right. That's one thing I love about you." The debut of that word coming up between them. "But it wasn't the first."

"No?"

"Your eyes — that was first. Like, so beautiful and not missing a trick at the same time. Second was your butt."

"I believe that part."

Which was the part he smacked. She smacked his, maybe harder. That led to other things, despite his exhaustion. Then, way too soon, he was pulling on his pants and headed for the door. He turned to her.

"So what are we going to do?" he said.

"What do you want to do?"

"Be together."

"You know that's impossible."

"Impossible now, but you're out in three months."

"So? You've got a year left. And aren't you re-upping?"

"I was going to. Now it's not what I want."

"What do you want?"

"I told you already. Six letters. Starts with *L* and ends with *E*."

"Lassie."

"How come you're so tough?"

"Does every time you say that mean we're going to do the spanking thing again?"

He laughed and went out, closing the door.

"Either way, I'm in," LeAnne said to the empty room. Two empty bottles of Negra Modelo — his favorite beer — stood together on the coffee table.

Chapter Eleven

LeAnne awoke.

Eye.

She was slumped sideways against the door of her Honda. Behind her empty socket she felt a strange new pressure, the pressure of something being stuck, like the metal lid on a jam jar, and someone very strong was trying to twist it off. Her daddy had been a champ at that, never once failing to open anything capped or lidded, and could also crush improbable things with his bare hands, coconuts, for example.

LeAnne sat up. Nighttime in a parking lot, a single sodium lamp leaving it mostly dark. She took off her sunglasses and saw that things were brighter than she'd supposed. Brighter meaning more depressing, the opposite of what you might expect: deserted parking lot, scraps blowing across the pavement, low bushes at the boundaries, all hung with scraps. Plus she saw now that the seats and floor coverings of the Honda were worn and ratty; also there were smells she didn't like. She gathered up the chocolate bars, chocolate milk containers, and bacon burgers, carried them across the lot and dumped them in a trash barrel. It turned out to be full to the brim, even overfull, topped like a muffin with trash. Her trash bounced off all the other trash and made a big mess on the ground. LeAnne got into the car. It still smelled bad. She sniffed her armpits.

"Fuck."

LeAnne hit the road. Her expectation was that after a day of practice, she'd be more like her old motoring self, back in the passing lane. The truth was she'd gotten worse. Everybody — even the old and the timid — was now going too fast. It wasn't just on account of her eye straining to carry the whole load by itself. Her brain, too, was part of the problem, so slow to process all the movement around her. And that stuck metal lid thing going on behind her . . . what would you call it? Crater? Yes, exactly, like a bomb crater. Where had she been headed with this? She'd lost the thread. But then a new idea came and settled her down: she was simply overtired. There was nothing wrong with her brain, and the fact that she seemed to be sweating profusely was also not a problem, most likely due to . . . to something or other. Meds, perhaps? Was she even on any meds? Yes, since the nurses brought little paper cups full of pills twice a day; no, since she'd left all that behind. Wasn't cold turkey the only way to really quit anything? Where had she heard that? The details eluded her, but not the big picture, which was all about being overtired — had to be way worse than simply tired. LeAnne resolved never to sleep in the car again, to find a motel by eighteen hundred hours at the latest every day of the trip and bed down in a real bed. There: a plan. Knowing she had one sent a little surge of optimism through her body. She pulled out of the slowpoke lane and passed an ancient lady with her hair in curlers and a cigarette sticking out the side of her mouth. And as she passed the ancient lady, LeAnne twisted around and called to her: "Thank you for your service." The ancient lady, eyes on the road, didn't see her and, with the windows rolled up in both cars, could not have heard her. No matter: saying those words was enough. They weren't ironic or sarcastic; LeAnne meant them from the bottom of her heart.

Not too long after that, she decided to

make another plan, namely about what to do when she got home, meaning home to Phoenix, even though she hadn't lived there in ten years. She actually owned a condo near Fort Bragg, leased at the moment to an administrator on the base. When was that lease up? Soon, right? Hadn't she timed it to coincide with her return, which would have been in . . . what? A month or two? She tried to organize time past and future in her mind, and was getting nowhere when she decided some music would be nice. LeAnne jabbed the radio's on button. No tunes, no sound of any kind. She jabbed it again and again, harder and harder, until there was broken plastic all over the floor. But her mood soon recovered and, following Marci's example, she started making her own music. She sang "That's When Your Heartaches Begin," "Redneck Woman," "Mamas Don't Let Your Babies Grow Up to Be Cowboys." LeAnne and Jamie both liked country music, one of many little grace notes they had in common.

"Hey, Sarge," said Corporal Crannack, squeezed in next to her in the backseat of the Humvee, "how come all these people eat shit? Wouldn't you expect at least one or two good ones, like just from the odds?"

"What people are you talking about, Luke?" LeAnne said. She felt the front of her helmet, made sure the night-vision goggles were mounted in place.

Corporal Crannack pointed to a bundled-up group standing around a trash-can fire by the side of the road, a pock-marked mudbrick wall behind them. The flames turned their faces red. LeAnne watched to see if any of them reached for a cell phone; none did. "These fuckin' rag-heads, Sarge."

"Language, Corporal," said Jamie from the front seat.

"Sorry, sir. These fuckin' citizens."

Everyone — the driver, LeAnne, Crannack, and Jamie last — started laughing.

"They don't all eat shit," LeAnne said. "Some do, some don't. Just like us."

"Name one that don't," said Corporal Crannack.

"There's plenty, but how about Katie, for starters?" LeAnne could see her in the back of the RSOV, point vehicle in their convoy of five. She was sitting straight and still, and very small next to Lieutenant Skoll beside her. The moon, full and bright, made Katie look like she was made of stone. Way too bright, in LeAnne's opinion, so bright the night-vision goggles would be nothing but useless baggage on this mission. Then a burned-out sedan suddenly appeared on the roadside, and she changed her mind about the NODs, and gave them another quick touch.

"Katie's not one of them," Corporal Crannack said.

"No?" said LeAnne. "She prays five times a day."

"I've never seen her."

"The women don't pray in front of men."

"So you can't see them with their asses up in the air? I'll take American women every time."

"The feeling's not mutual," LeAnne said.

More laughter. They left the town and rolled on through the too-bright night. Jamie handed out diagrams of the target area, a five-building walled compound three hundred yards behind an abandoned gas station. LeAnne had already gone over all the visuals three times. She closed her eyes, re-created the diagram in her mind, then checked to make sure she was right. Around then was when she found herself staring at the back of Jamie's neck. Her mind wandered, wandered all the way out of Afghanistan and to a vision of her, Camp Roadmaster, Jamie. That wasn't like her at all. She gave her head a quick shake, got herself back in order.

"Sir?" she said. "Could we have a look at that photo one more time?"

"Photo of the bad guy, Sergeant? Here you go."

Jamie passed the photo over his shoulder, his head not turning in her direction. LeAnne angled it toward the window — a glassless window at the moment, still awaiting replacement after a rollover — to better catch the moonlight. The bad guy, wearing jeans and a leather jacket, was entering a market stall, his face turned toward the camera in a way that struck her as sudden and alert. But she might have been wrong: the shadow of the stall's tin roof fell across his eyes and forehead; the lower, better-lit half of his face was kind of pudgy, not a look you often saw in Afghan men.

"Name of Wakil Razaq Salam," Jamie said. "Graduate of some tech school in Pakistan. He travels around the country teaching IED construction."

"Fuck him with a cactus," said Corporal Crannack. "Any chance he's actually going to be in the target area, sir?"

"According to intel."

"Is intel meaning Lieutenant Skoll? Sir?"

LeAnne glanced at the RSOV up ahead. Lieutenant Skoll had his back to her, of course, but she was pretty sure from how he ducked his head that he was snacking on something, most likely the Jolly Ranchers some of the team carried for giving out to village children.

"Lieutenant Skoll is the Humint officer attached to this unit, Corporal. Any problem with that?"

"No, sir. No problems. Have no problems, make no problems — that's the Crannack family motto."

"I like it," Jamie said.

"My momma made it up, sir."

"Sounds like an interesting lady."

"Oh, yeah. She did some stand-up back in the day."

"No shit."

"Like in comedy clubs, mostly in the Midwest. She had a routine about the invention of the dildo. Wanna hear it, sir?"

"All in good time, Corporal."

"Is that positive or negative, sir?"

"Can you explain to him, Sergeant?" Jamie said.

"It means after we're done with this mission," LeAnne said.

"Midnight Special, correct?" the corporal said.

"Correct," said LeAnne.

"Cool name. Like a ginormous fuckin'

freight train, barrelin' through to hell and gone." He pounded his right fist into his left palm. "Bam!"

LeAnne took another look at the photo of the IED teacher, Wakil Razaq Salam. His jeans were frayed at the cuffs, but in a fashionable way, forming a sort of fringe around the tops of his combat-style boots. She passed the photo to Corporal Crannack, lowered her NODs, scanned the road ahead. The abandoned gas station appeared, a squat dark square in a flat and featureless plain, all even bleaker than normal in night-vision green. From above came an approaching *whap-whap-whap,* and then another: air support moving in, right on schedule.

"Bam!" said Corporal Crannack, one more time. The back of Jamie's neck stiffened, just a bit, like he was having an unpleasant or unwelcome thought. LeAnne made a mental note to ask him about it the next time they were alone. Not here, but in Qatar, or Germany, or even back home. The driver cut the lights. All the drivers in the convoy cut their lights, excepting the driver of the Afghan army transport behind them, but finally he did, too. Teamwork was possible and not everyone ate shit. LeAnne felt a little surge of optimism. They were good to go.

"Miss? Miss?" *Rap rap, rap, rap.* "Hey, miss — you all right?" *Rap rap.*

Eye.

LeAnne pulled herself up and out from a horrible mess of dreams, pulled herself up, out, and into a world that was just as bad, a world that was all about head pain and head pressure, the pressure that comes from a giant trying to twist off a stuck lid behind your crater.

"Miss?" *Rap rap:* knuckles on a window. "You okay in there?"

LeAnne saw nothing but glare. She felt around for the sunglasses, piecing together the facts of the situation. Like fact one: she was slumped across the front seat of her car. Fact two: she smelled real bad. And other facts, all negative. Her hand closed on the sunglasses. She jammed them on, discovering in the same motion that her patch was gone. She sat up, faced the driver's-side window. A man in uniform stood outside. She turned the key, slid down the window.

"What service are you in?" she said.

"Excuse me?"

"I don't recognize the —"

"The what?"

By that time, LeAnne had taken in a few

more details. She was parked off to the side of a two-lane blacktop road in flat, dry country, no other vehicles in sight except for a black cruiser angled in front of her. The shield on the door read: New Mexico State Police.

"Nothing," LeAnne said. "I was about to say uniform, but now I won't. I'm all right. Fine. Good."

"You been drinking?"

"Nope."

"What about drugs?"

"Too many to count." She had a thought. "Although actually I've left all that behind."

"You're off drugs?"

"Left them all at Walter Reed. My . . . departure could have been organized better."

"You're talking about the military hospital?"

"Correct."

"You a vet?"

"Coming home." She gazed past him.

"From overseas?"

"Afghanistan. Desert, but not like this. There are good deserts and bad."

"Where's home?"

A tough question. LeAnne attacked the problem, but right away her mind wanted to go somewhere else. "It's possible I made a mistake, Officer."

"What kind of mistake?"

"I'd better not say."

The trooper nodded. "I'll need some ID."

"What if I tell you the mistake? The possible mistake. It's about Katie."

"License and registration."

Possibility one involved opening the door real fast with the goal of knocking him aside or even down, followed by a quick exit and the application of a chokehold before he recovered his balance. Possibility two was much simpler: a direct punch to his windpipe, right through the open window. She went back and forth.

"License and registration, please."

LeAnne, still making up her mind, found both in the glove box. She handed them over. He returned to the cruiser and started running the documents through his system. LeAnne fished around in the glove box some more, just in case her 9 millimeter was in there. No luck. Where was it? She searched her memory.

"You are a marksman," Katie said. "Or would markswoman be the word? Marksperson?"

"No clue," LeAnne said. They were drinking sodas back at the base, the night after the ceremonial opening of the Afghan and American Women's Friendship Weaving Co-Op.

"It will render my job more complex."

"Oh? How so?"

"But no worries. All within the job description, mate."

"Katie? How does me being a sharpshooter — which I'm not, by the way — make your job more complex?"

"I hope I have not perturbed you."

"Nope," LeAnne said. "But we're a team, so I have to know."

Katie nodded. "It's about the attitude of the women. In their eyes, you CSTs can never be the enemy, even though you're soldiers. Why not? Because you are women first. But what you did today was manly in their eyes. So the situation is complicated now. Do you see?"

"I'll bake cookies the next time."

Katie laughed. "I wish I was an American woman."

"You do?"

"Sometimes." Katie poured more coffee for the two of them. She stirred sugar into her paper cup, watched the coffee swirl around. "I'm curious about one detail."

"What's that?"

"How did you know the bomber was a man?"

"Simple," said LeAnne. "All the women wore sandals or slippers. He was wearing these huge shitkickers."

"Shitkickers?" Katie laughed. "A new one on me. It doesn't sound British. American most likely, perhaps with rural origins. Meaning combat boots, I take it?"

"Just big boots in general."

"I'll add that to my vocab," Katie said.

Chapter Twelve

Crunch crunch: the sound of shitkickers on a gravel roadside. LeAnne awoke instantly, searched frantically for a weapon.

"Okay, LeAnne, you're all set."

What was this? She swung around to her left. The trooper was at the window. He seemed to be handing her something. For a moment she was confused; then she caught up and took her license and registration.

"You can go," the trooper said. "But no more naps by the side of the road. Never know who could happen along. It's not safe." He tapped the roof, a tap like a gunshot to her ears, coming out of nowhere. She winced and ducked, but he was already on his way back to the cruiser and didn't see. He hitched up his gun belt, swung inside, and then just sat there.

LeAnne started the Honda, pulled onto the road. He followed her for a mile or so, then turned onto an intersecting road, also two-lane blacktop, also deserted. LeAnne kept going, now on her own, watching for some sign to tell her where she was, but no signs appeared. She checked her watch, found she wasn't wearing one, tried the clock on the dash instead. Zero eight thirty-five. Given that and the direction of the shadows, she realized she was pointed east. Eastbound in New Mexico: that was wrong. She slowed down — maybe not quite enough — and spun around in a U-ey, fishtailing, but not wildly, and not a problem since her dad had taught her how to gently steer a fishtailing car way back when she was ten or eleven, and got herself pointed the opposite way. It was all about not fighting the fish, instead just playing it until things settled down.

"Thanks, Dad!" she said, adding after ten or twenty or thirty miles or so, "I sang in my chains like the sea." Although possibly not aloud. She checked the dashboard clock. Zero eight thirty-five. What had it been before? Zero eight-oh-five? Zero eight fifteen? One or the other. She memorized zero eight thirty-five and drove until she got tired. Then she pulled off to the side of the road and went to sleep. The lid twister in her head relaxed his grip a little. That was nice. And so was the air. She felt and breathed the air in her sleep, nice western air, until it changed for the worst.

The wind blew across the village, picking up the smell of sanitation practices from another time. The coalition team came in on the run, boxing the village in from three directions, the Afghans from the north, airborne from the south, and LeAnne and the rest of the special forces from the west, cutting off access to the track that led to the abandoned gas station and the only road out. Dogs didn't bark because there were no dogs. Neither were there sentries, meaning the villagers believed they had no enemies, which was unlikely, or they were simply incompetent, also unlikely, or it was something else, which turned out often to be the case on this deployment. Soon from the south side came some shouting and a thud or two, and after that, figures in loose-fitting clothes got herded by figures in form-fitting clothes, the moonlight sometimes reflected in a pair of eyes and always shining on the breath clouds that rose from every mouth and melted in the sky.

The women and children were all in one mudbrick house, white-washed inside with a dark-red woven rug on the floor and rug-covered benches lining three walls. The only light came from a smoky kerosene lantern hanging from a ceiling hook. LeAnne stood in the doorway, weapon in hand but not raised, with Katie, unarmed, waiting slightly behind her.

"How many you got, Sarge?" Corporal Crannack called from outside.

Too many for such a small space: that was the answer. "Ten women, three kids, at least one baby," LeAnne called back.

"Supposed to be eleven women."

"We got ten. Go back and confirm, Corporal."

"On my way, Sarge."

LeAnne didn't wait for confirmation. A female overcount could be bad; there was nothing to be feared from an undercount. She stepped forward and took off her helmet, the kind of thing no soldier would dream of doing in a situation like this, but essential to the CST purpose. She shook out her hair — just long enough to be shaken out — and smiled.

"I'm an American soldier," she said, "here to keep you and the children safe. Okay, Katie."

Katie moved up beside her and repeated the message in Pashto. The women unveiled themselves, all except for two in the back.

LeAnne's weapon rose an inch or two,

almost by itself. "Katie? What's going on?"

Katie pointed her finger at the two women who had kept their veils in place. She spoke to them in a tone that sounded harsh, irritated, and somehow upper class. The woman on the left bowed her head and replied in a low, hushed voice.

"She says that they have horrible scars, too shameful for a visitor to see."

"No go," LeAnne said. "I have to see."

Katie spoke again, louder than before and with angry gestures. The woman on the left slowly lowered her veil. After the briefest glance, LeAnne couldn't look again. The woman's face was an acid ruin, nothing normal except for one dark eye. Where the other eye should have been there was just a hole, kind of like a crater. Meanwhile, the other veiled woman had begun to whimper in a strange and desolate falsetto, terrified and terrifying at the same time. They both wore long burqas, but they didn't quite cover their feet. LeAnne moved a step or two closer so she could check their footwear. Woven slippers on both of them; no combat boots.

"Forget it," LeAnne said.

"Forget what?"

"She can keep her veil on." LeAnne raised her voice, although there was no reason for getting mad at Katie. Katie said something to the woman. She bowed her head and kept her veil in place. The woman with the ruined face spoke, just a whisper.

"Can that one put her veil back in place?" Katie said.

LeAnne nodded. It was cold in this house, maybe not even fifty degrees, but she was sweating inside her uniform. She scanned the faces of the other women, some old, some young. The youngest woman, perhaps twenty, wore a hint of green eye shadow. If there was intel to be gained about Wakil Razaq Salam or anything else, it would come from her, meaning this party had to be broken into smaller groups.

"Tell them I've got treats for the kids," LeAnne said.

One of the kids — a sturdy-looking boy, ten or eleven — knew the word *treat* and started forward before Katie opened her mouth. The very oldest woman reached out and grabbed his shoulder, yelling something at him, but he shrugged her off.

"That the grandma?"

"Oh, no, the mom for sure," Katie said.

"Should I give him something or not?"

"The kids love those Jolly Ranchers."

"But what about the mom?"

"Pah," said Katie.

The boy, runny-nosed — all the kids had runny noses — wore ragged trousers and a sweat shirt with "Hollywood High School" across the chest, a baggy sweatshirt with a pouch in front. He had his hands inside, the coldness in these village dwellings probably why all the kids had runny noses. LeAnne slung the M4 over her shoulder, muzzle down, and fished in her pockets for Jolly Ranchers. The boy stepped up and stopped in front of her.

"Here you go," LeAnne said, "three Jolly Ranchers plus a Tootsie Roll for good luck." She held out the candy, but the boy made no move to take it. He was muttering something and not looking her in the eyes, his gaze directed inward. Was there something wrong with him?

"What's he saying, Katie?"

No response.

"Katie?"

LeAnne glanced to the side, didn't see Katie. She looked out the open doorway, spotted silhouettes on the run, maybe twenty yards off, headed her way. Jamie was in the lead — she knew how he moved — with Corporal Crannack right behind.

"Sergeant!" he called. "You all right?"

"Yes, sir."

"We're shutting this down. Let's go."

"Yes, sir."

At that moment, turning back to the room, she saw Katie, crouched outside against the mudbrick wall. "Katie? What's wrong?"

"Be right there."

LeAnne faced the room. She still had the candy in one hand and the boy in the sweatshirt still stood before her. "Here. Take it."

The boy made no move to take the candy. LeAnne shot a quick look past him. The women were still, silent, tense, like spectators at some gripping performance. Then a horrible shudder passed through the boy and he began to sob.

LeAnne bent down. "Hey, buddy, what's the matter?"

He looked up at her, his eyes streaming. She reached out to pat his head, comfort him in some way, but just as she did there was a furious shout from the far end of the room, where the two scarred women stood. The boy backed up and then his hands emerged from the pouch, not empty. Instead, they held a snub-nosed pistol: a little weapon, but it seemed big in the boy's hands.

The boy's action and LeAnne's reaction were almost simultaneous. He was still tilting up the barrel of the pistol, tilting it up toward her face, when she knocked it away with the back of her hand. The pistol went off and pinwheeled across the room. A woman screamed. The boy fell against LeAnne, knocking the M4 loose and trapping it under his motionless body.

"Sergeant?" Jamie called, now much closer, maybe right outside the door.

LeAnne rose, tugging at the strap on her weapon, trying to free it. All the women dropped down and lay prone, all except the second scarred woman, the one who hadn't shown her face. A hand emerged from under her burqa, a hairy hand, a big hand, a man's hand. And in that hand: an M67 fragmentation grenade, US Army issue. Thumb on the safety lever, pin already pulled.

"Sergeant?"

"Down, Jamie, down!"

The man in the burqa threw the grenade. It flew right past LeAnne's head — she felt its tiny breeze — and out the door. Then came the blast, followed by cries and moans from outside and wild screaming from within. LeAnne wrenched the M4 out from under the boy, wheeled around. The man in the burqa was in throwing position, had another grenade all set. He let it go. Le-

Anne shot him right in the forehead, dead center. The second-last image she absorbed was the tiny red hole she'd made. The very last image was the fringed hems of the jeans he wore under the burqa, exposed as he toppled over. There was no time for anything else on account of the M67's detonation delay being only four seconds.

A sign passed by: Welcome to Arizona. LeAnne, on a winding two-laner all by herself, sagebrush covered hills to the north, rocky plain to the south, slowed down, backed up, got out, and took a closer look at the sign. A very old sign in a bygone style, faded by the sun and pitted by wind-driven sand, with a tall pine on the left, a saguaro cactus on the right, and a distant mesa in the middle. There was also a bullet hole through the middle of the triangle in the first *A*. LeAnne gazed at the sign until she felt herself being transported into it, entering this old and bygone Arizona like a kid into a storybook. She got a little dizzy, staggered back, almost fainted. LeAnne put her head between her knees, took a few deep breaths. Much better, except for getting a whiff of her own smell. But it was good to be home.

She drove on and came to a small town, her mood rising for the first time since . . .

when? Something or other with Marci? The good mood topped out right there, but it didn't sink back down very far. LeAnne realized she was hungry. When had she last eaten? No data input on that. She removed her sunglasses, took a very quick glance in the mirror. Cheekbones at last, but not in a good way. There was nothing whatsoever good about her face now.

She passed an Indian souvenir shop, closed, and an RV campground, deserted, and came to a high school, just a single low brick building with Go Red Buffaloes on a portable sign out front. Beyond the school lay a grassless baseball diamond, and after that an oval track. Inside the oval was a jumping pit. Two girls stood at the top of the runway, one stretching, the other making little movements with a pole. LeAnne stopped the car.

The track was cinder with weeds growing through and no markings. The girl with the pole started her run-up. They had the bar at eight feet two, which LeAnne could tell just from looking. The girl, a bit on the heavy side, wasn't fast and barely got her lead leg into position on time, but the plant was clean. The pole, too soft for her, bent beyond the optimal launch angle, and there were problems with her grip and her trailing leg. Up she rose, the twist rushed, her chest skimming the bar. It quivered but stayed in place. LeAnne clapped her hands softly.

"This seems not very possible," Katie said.

"How do you mean?" said LeAnne setting up the equipment that had finally arrived, after weeks of messaging, paperwork, bureaucracy, obstruction.

Katie stood watching, arms folded across her chest, and made no move to help. Manual labor was beneath her, as though she were some sort of aristocrat, which was how LeAnne had come to see her.

"We are not ready."

"For Christ sake," LeAnne said, dragging the landing pads into position, just so. "Why not?"

"I wish you wouldn't say Christ like that. It mocks your religion."

"I'm not religious," LeAnne said.

"Neither am I, but all the same."

"You're not religious? You pray five times a day."

"And that makes me religious?"

LeAnne looked up at her. Katie wore a short, form-fitting suede coat and a crimson silk head scarf that looked expensive, like something from Paris. Behind her stood the school, small, dun-colored, none of its right angles quite right, and in the distance rose bare dun-colored mountains. The crimson stood out, almost like a flag. "Well, yeah," LeAnne said, "doesn't it?"

"How can you ask such a thing?" Katie said. "But right there is the proof, if you like. We are not ready."

"I don't get it."

"Because to reach this sort of . . . play" — Katie gestured at the equipment: the two standards, the bar, the mats, the box, the pole — "you must pass through a long history."

"Why make it such a big deal?" LeAnne said. "It's just the pole vault."

"Plus," said Katie, counting on her leather-gloved fingers, "baseball, football, basketball, two — at least — kinds of hockey, lacrossticks —"

"Lacrosse."

"— and who knows what else? Water skiing, snow skiing, boards for this and that — it is endless."

"Your point?"

"My point? We are talking about girls. Afghan girls."

Which was when the school door opened and six girls came out. They looked to be about twelve or thirteen, all dressed alike in loose-fitting ankle-length black dresses and long white head scarves. The girls approached LeAnne's improvised pole vault pit, doubt and shyness reflected in every movement.

LeAnne turned to them and smiled. "Hi, kids."

They looked up at her, their eyes checking out her uniform, her sidearm, her hair — worn in modified dreads at that time, courtesy of a rifleman in Captain Cray's company who'd worked at a salon in civilian life.

Katie snapped at them in Pashto.

"Hello," the girls said, tackling the word in several ways.

Katie snapped at them again.

"Hello, Sergeant Hogan."

"Katie? How about they just call me LeAnne?"

Katie blew air between her lips, one of her many ways of showing disdain. "Very well," she said, and passed the request on to the girls.

"LeAnne," they said. They tried it out a few more times, then lapsed into a bit of giggling.

"And what are your names?" LeAnne said.

Before Katie could translate, one of the

girls spoke up on her own. "Wrashmin," she said.

"Nice to meet you, Wrashmin."

The rest of them followed up, LeAnne matching the face to every name: Laila, Durkhani, Hila, Muska, Laila.

"Two Lailas?" LeAnne said.

The girls laughed. "Two Lailas," they said. "Two." They all held up their right hands, two fingers raised. Those fingers — still unworn, childlike — made a surprise impression on LeAnne.

"Not so different from LeAnne," she said. "Laila, LeAnne."

The girls thought that over. Meanwhile, Katie was checking her watch. "Recess is twenty minutes, start to finish. Any plans to proceed to the actual pole vaulting?"

LeAnne picked up the pole, a short pole, eleven feet, and soft, and walked to the top of the imaginary runway.

"All right, kids, it's like this." In exaggerated slo-mo running steps, she moved toward the bar, counting her steps. "And right here we plant the pole in the box like so, hands up high, and driving off the back leg, then into the swing, and up, up, up, and over." She turned to the girls. "Got all that? I know it's complicated. Just feel the pole in the beginning, let it do the work."

"You want me to tell them that?" said Katie. "To feel the pole?"

"Why not?"

"It sounds touchy-feely."

"Where'd you learn an expression like that?"

"I am an interpreter," Katie said. She spoke to the girls, an impatient-sounding flow in which LeAnne was pretty sure she heard the words "touchy-feely." Then the taller of the Lailas asked a question.

"She wants to know if you'll show us a real vault."

"It's been a long time," LeAnne said; in fact, more than a decade.

"But isn't it like riding a bicycle?"

"No."

"Although in truth I myself have never been riding on a bicycle."

"We'll have to do something about that," LeAnne said. She set the bar at nine feet — a laughable height, but she hadn't vaulted in ten years, and she was wearing combat boots — and walked up the runway. She took a deep breath, rose up on her toes, and said, "Always run tall, kids." Then she took off, and with that silly little pole and in her clunky boots, she soared over the bar, clearing it by so much it stunned her.

"Oh my goodness," said Katie. And all the

girls started clapping.

"Well, enough of that," LeAnne said. "But right there's the fun of it." She moved the bar down to four feet, handed the pole to the taller Laila, walked her to the starting position, showed her the grips, slo-moed her down the runway and into the plant, behind her all the time, holding the pole with her. "Okay, Laila, all set?"

The girl nodded, just a little scared nod.

"Let's see what you can do."

Laila went to the top of the runway. She took a deep breath, rose up on her toes, raised the pole, and started running. The deep breath and rising up part was perfect, and then came a messy series of mistakes, and LeAnne was preparing for total failure, but somehow the pole got planted perfectly square in the back of the box, and it bent and launched Laila up and over the bar, her appearance in that voluminous black dress and streaming white scarf more like that of a soaring fish or dolphin than a human.

The girls cheered and so did LeAnne. It was actually one of the happiest moments of her life. She turned to Katie. "What were you saying about history?" she said.

But Katie didn't hear. She was gazing at a rooftop beyond the schoolyard wall and across the street, her face dark and frowning. A man in traditional dress stood watching from the rooftop. At that distance, his face was just a smudge. All LeAnne could really make out were his prominent ears.

"Katie? Something wrong?"

She shook her head, then checked her watch again. "Recess is over."

CHAPTER THIRTEEN

LeAnne opened her . . .

Eye.

The two girls were gone, the oval track and jumping pit deserted. High above, a hawk was drifting on an air current. Somehow the sight reminded her of Jamie, and at that moment she heard his voice, as clear as if he were sitting with her, over on the blind side where she couldn't see him anyway.

Cork blew off.

"One way of putting it," she said aloud. Then it was Jamie's turn to speak, but he did not. Was he searching for the exact right words?

"Don't worry," she said. "Say anything. Anything at all will do."

But Jamie was silent. So strange, to have been granted that brief prequel in Qatar, a prequel to a future that was not going to happen, two nights of living life . . . TO THE MAX, for sure. She thought of the popping cork tattooed on the back of Marci's shoulder. The pop of a champagne cork: a jolly little explosion.

"There are explosions, and then there are explosions, Jamie."

The hawk began spiraling up and up, until it was nothing but a black dot in the blue. LeAnne turned the key.

In the next town, she stopped at a drugstore and bought a family-size bottle of ibuprofen. LeAnne took four to get things started, swallowing them dry in the parking lot. Across the street, she spotted a bar called Rooster Red's. A carved rooster, red combed and pissed off, hung over the entrance. When had she last had a drink? With Marci. She glanced down at her red shoes, got the feeling that she was somehow not living up to them, and therefore failing Marci. "Fuck you, Marci," she said in a low voice, to herself alone, although a woman in curlers emerging from a car a dozen spaces away seemed to be listening.

LeAnne gave her a look and the nosy bitch turned away. If Marci were with her, she'd have snapped out some nasty and funny remark, making everything right, and then they'd have sauntered into Rooster Red's and downed a couple. Red shoes and

Rooster Red's: life was full of clues and messages. You had to pay attention. She hadn't known Marci long, but she'd known Marci deep. They'd been comrades, not while they'd been in arms, more like comrades out of arms. Red was the clue, and comrades was the message. LeAnne crossed the street and walked into Rooster Red's.

It was dark inside Rooster Red's, long bar on the left, a few tables on the right, the décor all about wagon wheels and steer horns. A man wearing a Stetson occupied a spot halfway down the bar, and an old couple sat at one of the tables. LeAnne took the very last seat at the bar, meaning the entrance was on her left and nobody could be on her right — a comfortable situation, like having the higher ground. The bartender — middle-aged, his face dominated by bushy sideburns, although it was the kind of face that could have been dominated by just about anything — came over.

"Hi, there," he said, "what can I getcha?"

"Beer," she said. "Beer and a shot. And ice. Ice in a glass."

"Any special kind of beer?"

"Negra Modelo."

"Negra Modelo, shot, ice, glass — coming up."

He moved off. LeAnne saw herself in the

mirror behind the bar. She was mostly oversized dark sunglasses, messy hair, a streak of dirt on her chin. Cruella De Vil on a bad day.

"Here you go," said the bartender, sliding things into place. "Anything else I can do you for?"

Go away. Stop being an asshole. "Napkin," LeAnne said.

He laid a napkin on the bar and withdrew. She wrapped a few ice cubes in the napkin, held it to her head — where a weird thing was going on inside, like metal getting sheared, real slow — and drank the shot. It turned into a small fire that flowed in and woke her up. The head pain started backing off. She washed down two or three more ibuprofens with beer to get that head pain on the run. Negra Modelo: a beer she'd never heard of before Qatar and now her fave for life.

"Again," she said.

The bartender, in conversation with the Stetson-wearing customer down the bar, turned to her. "Another round?"

"Bingo."

He served her another shot and another Negra Modelo. "More ice?"

"Sounds like a plan."

He brought another glass of ice cubes.

"Run you a tab?"

"Yup."

"I'll need a credit card."

She handed over her Army MWR MasterCard.

"You in the military?"

"A comrade out of arms," LeAnne said.

He laughed, changing the shape of those bushy sideburns. "Meanin' on leave, huh? Shoulda told me — we got a ten percent discount for active military. I'll make it retroactive." He ran the card and returned it, also laying a small folded towel on the bar. By that time, the second shot was a goner and LeAnne was working on Negra Modelo numero dos. The head pain was almost beyond detection, lid twisting or metal shearing or whatever the fuck went on beneath the crater easing up. LeAnne was struck by two realizations. First, she understood what the towel was for, namely drying her hair, wet from the melting ice. Second . . . second was something that had evaded her back at Walter Reed, but now she had it. Number two turned out to be . . . turned out to be . . . it slipped it away again. *Damn little varmint.* The trick would be to keep drinking until her mind reached autopilot and then would do all the remembering on its own. Another round or two and she'd be there. Sounded like a plan!

LeAnne unfolded the towel and patted her hair dry. She shook it out in the free and confident manner of good-lookin' gals everywhere. Of course, she knew the real actress she reminded people of — she'd been hearing it since her late teenage years — but she wouldn't voice the name to herself. She downed the rest of her beer and took another look at her image in the mirror. Her face was dark and gloomy, so different from what she was feeling inside.

LeAnne took off the sunglasses. Hey! Not so bad. Even kind of distinguished and piratical with the patch, or was that only for men? And the scars, which had invaded so much of the right side of her face, didn't seem so ugly. Were they more like interesting features? Or was all this because of the dim lighting down here in the dimmest part of Rooster Red's?

LeAnne pocketed the sunglasses. Then she patted the bar, a wooden bar with a worn, homey feel. "Again."

■ ■ ■ ■

Initial Evaluation for Post-Traumatic Stress Disorder:
Mental Status:

4. Suicidal or Homicidal Thoughts, Ideations or Plans or Intent:

LeAnne's image in the mirror behind the bar at Rooster Red's in a southern Arizona town whose name she hadn't noted was starting to look like its old self when the front door opened and someone came in. LeAnne didn't bother looking. She was happy to be all by herself at the far end of the bar, working on a Negra Modelo — no more shots for her, feeling plenty good already, thank you very much! — and a bowl of mixed snacks: pretzel sticks, peanuts, and little Chex-like squares with a taste she couldn't identify. She ate them first, and moved on to the peanuts, saving the pretzels for last. But just when she was almost there at the pure pretzel stage, the bartender refilled her bowl with the whole mixture! And it might not have been the first time! She didn't get mad — you'd have to be crazy to get mad at something like that — and just started all over on the Chex-like squares.

Meanwhile, she was aware that the newcomer had taken a stool somewhere between her and the Stetson wearer. She had real good situational awareness: it was in all her evaluations. As long as whoever it was stayed in his or her own space, they were cool. No need for LeAnne to even glance that way. She sipped her Negra Modelo, kept busy on the Chex-like squares — she was kind of hungry today. When was her last real meal? She was trying to remember that when she felt someone's gaze on her face; the left side, in profile.

Then he — the someone turning out to be a he — spoke. "What the heck are those things, anyway?"

LeAnne turned very slightly in his direction, maybe fifteen degrees, no more. From the sound of his voice, she might have expected some sort of good ol' boy, or a desert cowboy wannabe, but he turned out to be something else, an urban type, most likely: clean-shaven, short-haired, dressed in a button-down shirt, jeans, and loafers, about her own age. LeAnne remembered the dirt streak on her chin and wiped it off on the back of her hand.

"These?" she said, holding up one of the

Chex-like snacks.

"I can't figure them out at all. And I'm in the business."

"The snack business?"

"Well, no. Broader than that. I'm in restaurant supplies."

"Sounds . . . normal."

The man smiled a puzzled smile but friendly. LeAnne could see he was the friendly type, at ease with people. "Normal how?" he said.

"Blessedly normal."

"Depends where you're coming from, I guess," he said. "There's nothing normal about the restaurant business, in my experience, except for failure, usually sooner rather than later."

"So why are you in it?" LeAnne said. All of a sudden she was her old sharp self. Was ordering one more shot a good idea? Why not? She'd been a sharpshooter practically her whole life. LeAnne came close to laughing out loud.

"The restaurant business isn't the same thing as the restaurant supply business," the friendly man was saying.

The bartender, loading glasses into the underbar dishwasher, snickered. The corner of a paper napkin on the counter fluttered in his snickery breeze.

"Meaning," the friendly man went on, "the more failures, the more start-ups. And start-ups like to start all over with their own visions."

"I got it the first time," LeAnne said. Yes, her old sharp self for sure. And maybe a touch of Marci-like snappishness as a new add-on. What a crazy idea: she could be better than before! And take Marci along for the ride!

His smile wavered. He sipped his beer. "And you?"

"What about me?"

"What do you do, if I'm not being too pushy? Name's Kevin, by the way." He shifted closer, settling two stools away, and extended his hand.

That set LeAnne up for a tough choice. She could either shake hands — right hands, of course — which involved turning far enough to face him, leading to the big reveal; or not shake hands, which would be uncalled-for rude. There was also the possibility of first putting on the sunglasses and then shaking hands, but that was just weird. LeAnne turned and shook his hand, a small hand for a man and cool to the touch.

"LeAnne," she said.

"Nice to meet you, LeAnne." His gaze went directly to the patch and fucked-up flesh that couldn't quite be covered by the patch, despite its size, almost cartoonish. But the next moment he was back to just looking at her in general, meaning maybe the damage was invisible in the murky depths of Rooster Red's. "What are you drinking?"

"I'm good," LeAnne said.

He glanced at the bottle in front of her, called to bartender. "A Negra Modelo for LeAnne, here." He downed what was left in his glass, tapped it on the bar. "And a refill for me."

The drinks came. Kevin held out his glass for clinking. LeAnne clinked it. She caught a whiff of his smell, slightly lemony, kind of nice. Plus he looked kind of nice, and his manners were kind of nice. Then, from out of nowhere, came a real bad thought: she herself most likely did not smell kind of nice. In fact, there was no way she could smell nice. When was her last shower?

"So," Kevin said, "you were about to tell me what you did. Or not."

Good fuckin' question. LeAnne gulped down a big hit of Negra Modelo. It had no effect, certainly not on the cave-ins happening under her mood. "I'm . . . between things at the moment."

"Cool," said Kevin. His nodded toward

the patch. "I had to wear one of those when I was a kid myself."

"What are you talking about?"

The bartender, entering orders on a touch screen by the beer taps, seemed to stiffen. LeAnne was aware of that, but had no idea why.

"The, uh, eyepatch," Kevin said, gesturing toward it with his glass. "For lazy eye. I wore it on the good eye so that —"

"Huh? You're saying I have lazy eye?"

His head moved straight back a few inches like he was avoiding a punch, which was where LeAnne got the idea of what could come next. "No, no," he said. "I was saying *I* had a lazy eye, not that —"

"Stop it with the fuckin' lazy eyes," said LeAnne, now on her feet.

"Whoa!" Kevin said, raising a hand palm up in the stop sign. LeAnne was in no mood for anybody to raise a hand to her, even if you couldn't really count this as raising a hand. "There's no call for any —"

She batted his hand away, good and hard. "Don't order me around."

"Order you around? I wasn't ordering you around. Geez. All I —"

"And don't fuckin' mention lazy eyes again." LeAnne stepped toward him, ripped off her patch, and leaned in close. "This look like a lazy eye to you?"

"Oh my God," said Kevin, shrinking back. At that point, his nostrils quivered slightly and he made a bit of a face, smelling her for sure. LeAnne placed both her hands on his chest and pushed, not even that hard, but he was already shrinking away and now hit the stool and tumbled backward right over it, falling hard to the floor.

"Hey!" said the bartender. "What the hell do you think you're doing?"

"Back the fuck off," LeAnne told him.

Instead the bartender reached behind the bar, came up with a baseball bat. LeAnne grabbed her Negra Modelo by the neck, smashed it on the edge of the bar, brandished what was left. He, too, shrank back, lowering the bat.

"Get some help," he said.

LeAnne dropped the broken-off bottle and walked out of Rooster Red's. If only she had a weapon! She'd shoot up the whole town. LeAnne took a few more steps and reached the Honda, where it suddenly hit her that shooting up whole towns was the kind of thing the Wakil Razaq Salams of the world aspired to. She bent over and puked her stomach empty.

Later that day, LeAnne checked into a

motel outside an old mining town, about half a mile beyond the last heap of bright orange tailings. The motel was empty except for an old woman in the office, who barely looked up from her screen. She gave LeAnne a military discount — based on the credit card and without being asked — and a key to the best room, which had a kiva fireplace.

First thing, LeAnne took a shower, long and hot, washing her hair and scrubbing her body once, twice, and again. Then she brought all her clothes into the stall and washed them. She wrung them out, hung everything that would fit on the shower rail, spreading the rest — jeans, hoodie, two T-shirts — on the floor. After that she lit a fire, and sat in front of it, wrapped in a blanket. Outside the wind blew, a cold, mile-high-type wind, whistling and moaning. It was good to be alone, with lots of time to organize her thoughts. Her initial thought: it was horrible to be alone.

Thought two was all about Jamie: What had he wanted? *I told you already. Six letters. Starts with L and ends with E.* Had anyone ever said anything better than that to her? And what had she given in return? LeAnne gazed into the shifting flames of the fire. Were they mocking her? Did they seem to be engaged in a hostile and contemptuous dance? Why would that be? Not too hard to figure out: she'd failed Jamie, gotten him killed on account of her stupidity or incompetence, or exaggerated self-regard, or some other bad quality. That was the reward for his love: he was dead and gone forever. So was there any reason she deserved to live? The flames had the answer to that one, a great big dancing negative.

For the first time in her life, LeAnne considered voluntary ways out. You could make an exhibition of your inner self, by hanging, for example, or settling into a hot bath and slitting your wrists. She didn't want to make an exhibition of herself. ODing on something or other seemed cowardly to her. How about driving off a lonely road at ninety miles an hour, straight into a boulder? She must have fallen asleep, they'd all say, what a tragedy. Nothing queasy-making about it, nothing guilt-inducing or too painful for friends and family to contemplate. Call this Plan A, the kind of pain accommodated by normal human contemplation.

LeAnne went on to Plans B, C, D, and more, but none topped Plan A. Ninety mph plus boulder: call it a family tradition. The flames died down, still dancing their nasty dance, but smaller and smaller. LeAnne lay down on the floor in the best room of the motel beyond the last heap of bright orange tailings and pulled the blanket tight around her. You had to face facts in this life.

Next morning LeAnne stopped in at the office to return her key. The woman wasn't there, but a landline phone sat on the counter. LeAnne tried to remember the last time she'd seen her own phone and could not. All the way back in Afghanistan? Very possible. But so what? Who was she going to call? Who was there to talk to? She picked up the woman's phone, called Walter Reed, was put through to Dr. Machado's office.

"Hi, this is Dr. Machado. Sorry I'm not here to take your call right now. Please leave a short message after the beep."

Beep.

"Dr. Machado? Um, if you're there, I'd . . . like you to . . . I'd . . ."

It was one of those bad connections where you hear an echo of your own voice. LeAnne heard her own voice, maybe not loud and clear, but loud and clear enough. She sounded pathetic. Pathetic and pitiful, useless and helpless. And now a fucking beggar on top of it, begging for she didn't even know what. Not so long ago — hardly any time at all, really — she'd been a leader of men.

She said no more, just hung up, leaving the room key on the counter. Then she hit the road. The speedometer readings went from zero to 140.

Chapter Fourteen

No boulders appeared. What a crazy development! When couldn't you find boulders in the desert, and if not a boulder, how about a cliff face, or even a cottonwood tree? But no. LeAnne laughed at herself, at first just on the inside, then out loud.

"Can't even goddamn —" she began, but then — this was on Highway 79, closing in on the Valley — she heard a scary high-RPM buzz from right above. She wrenched the wheel to the side, jammed on the brakes, came to a fishtailing stop ten or twenty yards off the road, then threw herself on the floor, hands clasped behind her head, mouth pressed into the dirty rubber mat. After that came sounds pretty close to whimpering. The *buzz buzz buzz* seemed to circle above her before receding. LeAnne rose and got out of the car. She saw a helicopter, altitude maybe three thousand feet, range close to a mile, moving north.

Close enough to be identifiable: a Little Bird, easy to tell from its chubby, egglike shape.

"One of ours," she said. But who else would be in our airspace? So what was there to be afraid of? LeAnne's mind stopped being afraid. Her body kept shaking and sweating a little while longer. Also she'd pissed herself. She stood by the side of the road, hands on hips. An eighteen-wheeler blew by and the driver checked her out and leaned on his air horn, a horrible noise that didn't scare her, just made her mad. She waved her fist and shouted something at him, smothered by the air horn.

In the bathroom of a gas station south of Florence, she cleaned herself up and changed into her freshly washed jeans from the night before. What was the point of having freshly washed jeans on hand if you'd be dead before wearing them? And how set on suicide was someone who whimpered at the sound of passing helicopters? Was she a coward? Or did she simply want to live more than to die?

Someone knocked on the door.

"Be right out," LeAnne said.

"Hurry!"

"Did it, uh, work this time?" Ryan said. "I

tried not to hurry."

Yes, it had worked, beyond doubt. LeAnne, gazing at the ceiling in her bedroom, which was on the sunny side of the double-wide — the double-wide now hers alone — had a very strange thought: was sex a form of work? She rolled over and there was Ryan, sharing her pillow, a casually anxious expression on his face.

She smiled, more like she just relaxed into a smile, as though smiling would be her default look, now and forever.

"Yeah?" he said.

She nodded a tiny nod.

"Oh. Good. Nice." He laughed at himself, then got a look in his eyes that meant some little joke was on the way. "Good job," he said.

Yes: a form of work! LeAnne laughed, a laugh that suddenly threatened to turn into tears.

"Hey. It wasn't that funny."

A lock of his hair fell over one eye. She brushed it aside.

"And did it work for you?" she said.

You hardly ever saw boys blush, but Ryan's cheeks pinkened a little bit. "Yeah," he said. "Like it's kind of obvious, right? For guys, I mean."

"I know that," LeAnne said. "I knew that.

I guess I meant . . . damn, who knows what I meant?" She poked him between the eyes, very gently.

Ryan withdrew his head an inch or two. This was after her dad's wake. How much after? LeAnne didn't really know — those days went by in a fog of pain, remembrance, and useless wishes — but there were still leftover deviled eggs in the fridge. LeAnne had had very little sexual experience. This was the fourth time with Ryan, and the first successful attempt, if you could put it that way. Why now? And was it too soon after her father's death? Were there unwritten rules about that? She wondered what Daddy would have had to say on the subject and shied away from that real quick.

Fourth time with Ryan and fifth overall, including one single episode after a meet the year before with a visiting track star who'd shown an amazing lack of endurance for a distance runner, although she'd only been struck by that fun asymmetry weeks after the event. Right after the event, she'd gotten the feeling he never wanted to see her again, and it was totally mutual. The next week she'd placed fourth, the first time she hadn't been top three in any competition for her whole high school career. But in between vaults, the Saturday of the week after that, she'd glanced out from the infield, watched the progress of the boys' ten thousand meters on the oval track, and realized that the lead runner was this former — what would you call him? Certainly not lover. More like one-night stand. She'd kept her eye on her former one-night stand, gliding round and round, and not long before the finish line, tape already held up for him to burst through in triumph, he'd finally glanced her way. And stumbled on his very next step! Which had led to his getting passed and nipped at the post, nipped at the post being a favorite expression of Mr. Adelson. LeAnne felt a very odd arousal, faint but definitely there. Less than a minute later was when she cleared 13' 2″ for the first time and got back to her winning ways.

"You're talking," Ryan said, "about another . . . sort of level? Did it work on another sort of level? Is that what you mean?"

She nodded, this time not that tiny nod, but more emphatic.

Ryan didn't say anything. He closed his eyes, kept them closed for longer than a normal blink, opened them up. Then he reached out, wrapped his arm around the back of her neck, and pulled her in. LeAnne took that for a yes. So that the next day, when he said something about how much he was looking forward to September and the start of their college lives, she had the confidence to tell him she'd changed her plans.

"Huh? Where are you going? You can still take one of those other offers? Even this late?" While she was figuring out how to put what was coming next, he saw something in her eyes and sensed bad news. "Not UCLA?" he said. Which was about as distant from Dartmouth as you could get.

LeAnne shook her head. "I enlisted."

"Enlisted? Enlisted in what?"

"The United States Army."

"Right. West Point's the army."

"Not West Point. The regular army."

"Like . . . a shortcut or something? You're an officer right away?"

"You can't enlist as an officer, Ry."

"But . . . but — so it's like being just an ordinary . . . private?"

"Exactly. At first I'll be an ordinary private, second class, actually. If I make it through basic, that is. It starts September nineteenth. I report to Fort Jackson."

Ryan steered the Corvette over to the side of the road and stopped. "What the fuck? You're not going to college? This is a joke, right? A joke about throwing your life away?"

It was no joke. LeAnne folded her arms across her chest.

"Jesus, what's wrong with you?" Ryan's eyes shifted, like he was working on his own answer to the question. He raised his hands, palms up. "Okay, okay. Sorry. My fault. Of course, you're upset. Upset isn't even the word, doesn't do justice to all the shit — all the horrible things that happened. But is that when to make decisions? When you're upset and not thinking clearly?"

"When you're upset is just when you have to think clearly," LeAnne said.

"Huh? Who told you that? That asshole Adelson? Why do you buy into his guru act?"

"It wasn't him."

"Then who?"

"Nobody. I'm capable of having my own ideas."

"Yeah? This one sucks."

LeAnne reached for the door handle.

"Wait. Stop." Ryan licked his lips and started over. He had beautifully shaped lips. She loved kissing them. At that moment she took an inner step or two toward giving in, changing her mind, doing whatever he wanted. "I'm pretty sure I get what's going on here, LeAnne. But you can't make it right, what happened. No one can. And besides, it's not your job."

"I know all that," LeAnne said. "I'm doing it for me. I want to get started."

"With what?"

"With what I want to do. The army."

"For fuck sake — West Point's the army, and you get a great degree, and after you're out, there's this whole network waiting for you."

"Yeah, but I'm ready now."

Ry gave her a long look, somehow seemed to recede, like a falling tide. "You can't make a dead person's life turn out right." He drove back onto the road.

"I had a very disturbing phone call from Melanie Fraser," LeAnne's mother said.

"Ryan's mom?"

"Correct."

"You know her?"

"I do not. At least, I did not."

A waiter appeared. They were in a nice restaurant in Scottsdale; it had taken LeAnne almost two hours to get there from her end of the Valley.

"Welcome, Ms. Marsh," the waiter said. "The usual for you?"

"Thank you, Jason. And I'd like you to

meet my daughter — my oldest daughter — LeAnne."

"Ah. Hi, there," said Jason, handing her a menu.

"Hi," LeAnne said.

"I know you like shrimp," her mother said. "The shrimp diablo here is excellent."

"I'm afraid we don't have it today," said Jason.

Which was just as well: LeAnne had gotten sick on spoiled shrimp on a class trip down to Nogales the year before — her history teacher wanted her students to see the wall — and no longer cared for shrimp. She ended up ordering a BLT. As Jason headed for the kitchen, her mother leaned forward and said, "Do you like this place? Alex is a part owner."

"Meaning you're a part owner, too?"

Her mother gazed at her. "In a manner of speaking, I suppose." The crow's-feet at the corners of her mother's eyes had grown and deepened in the years after the divorce, as had the single groove between them, but her presentation — hair, clothes, jewelry, all that — had only gotten better. As for what was going on in her mind, LeAnne didn't know. Her mother had surprised her at the funeral by crying quite a bit. At the time, LeAnne had thought it was because Alex hadn't come with her; now she wasn't sure.

At the moment, her mother was far from tears. "Be that as it may," she said. "I'm here to discuss this alarming piece of news. Please tell me it isn't true."

What's alarming about it? That was one response. *I'm nineteen and it's my decision and mine alone.* That was another. LeAnne went with, "I can see why it might seem a little sudden. But I'm very happy with the decision. I'm ready to move on."

"Whatever are you talking about? Going to West Point is moving on." Her mother tapped the rim of her water glass with the crimson tip of her fingernail. "You can't do someone else's penance."

"I know that."

"And even if you could, it's not your responsibility."

"I know that, too."

"Then what is it? What's it really about?"

"I want to . . . to be in the world. To do something in the world."

"What does that even mean?"

"The world out there, where big things are happening. Not the school world."

"What makes you think you're ready?"

LeAnne sat back. She started to fold her arms across her chest. Was that a habit she was slipping into? She put her hands in her lap instead. The readiness question was a tough one, but totally fair, deserving of her best answer. *The smarts you get from your mom. The rest is me, God help you.*

"That's the question, Mom. Maybe I'm not. It's going to be a big challenge. But I'll never know if I don't try."

"That doesn't sound very convincing. Lots of people say they love a challenge, but very few do, in my experience."

"I don't care about all those others," Le-Anne said.

"Why would you? You're pigheaded, just like —" Her mother stopped herself. Le-Anne folded her arms across her chest, couldn't stop herself this time. "And that? What you're doing right now? He used to do that all the time. It drove me crazy."

"That doesn't mean I —"

Her mother's voice rose. "Want to know what I think? Undoubtedly not. In fact, beyond a shadow of a doubt, since you didn't consult me. But here goes anyway. This is all psychological." She held up her hand. "And I'm not talking about some pie-in-the-sky notion to make up for your father's wretched . . . for him. I'm talking about me."

"You?"

"But yes. You're doing this to get back at me."

"What the hell? That's crazy!"

Her mother's face reddened. Something about the tonal change made her look like an angry cartoon of herself. "Exactly how he said you'd react."

"Oh, so this is coming from Alex?"

"Where do you get the right to patronize him? Alex is an extremely successful man, not just compared to . . . an extremely successful man, let's leave it at that. And do you know why? It's because he understands what makes people tick."

"Well, he doesn't know what makes me tick," LeAnne said. "And I couldn't care less what he thinks." Her mother's face got even redder. There was no turning this conversation around, not that LeAnne could see. She rose. "Also, I have nothing to get back at you for. Thanks for lunch."

"Wait a minute."

But LeAnne did not. She walked out of the restaurant and drove back to her double-wide on the far side of the Valley. Another long ride, and she was all done with the shaking at about the halfway point.

LeAnne and Ryan got together a few more times before he left for freshman orientation, but what had worked for them on the fourth attempt did not work again. She framed a photo Bernice had taken in the desert and gave it to him as a going-away present. In the photo was a two-armed saguaro cactus that seemed to be lurching across a ridge. Bernice had entitled it *One Too Many.* At the bottom, LeAnne almost wrote, "To Ry with all my love," changing it to "Lots of love, LeAnne" when she had a last-second vision of Dartmouth girls checking out the funny picture.

Ryan's good-bye letter arrived in her first week at basic training. She happened to be the only female in her group, and the drill sergeant in charge of hand-to-hand combat paid lip service and lip service only to the concept of women in the army. LeAnne cried silently into her pillow that night, partly because of what they had sort of had, partly because she could tell just from how he expressed himself in the letter that Ry was already turning into someone else, partly because she was alone. The next morning the drill sergeant selected her for the pugil stick demonstration. There had been a pair of pugil sticks lying around when LeAnne was a kid, and she and her dad had fooled around with them some. She remembered a move he'd taught her: "Two quick fakes with the left end of the stick —

first one looks like a fake, second looks for real, but it ain't. Then kaboom with the right."

The drill sergeant didn't bother with the headgear. He got faked out left and then kaboomed right: on the point of the chin, and hard enough to make his eyes go foggy, hard enough to shake loose a new thought or two. The difference between school and real life was suddenly as clear as could be in LeAnne's mind. She was on the right track.

Chapter Fifteen

The sun was low and silvery, the sky a metallic color instead of blue, by the time LeAnne had worked her way through the metro area plus the endless developments on the other side, and finally reached Lost Hills Road. Nothing had changed. Lost Hills Road was part of a development that had been subdivided but never built on back when she lived there with her dad, and would not be built on until a really big housing bubble came along. But her dad had bought the half acre lot at 2241 and now it was hers. She drove past the spot where she and Ryan had sat in his Corvette discussing drive times between Hanover, New Hampshire, and West Point, and coasted up the driveway, hard-packed dirt now pretty much indistinguishable from the surrounding desert, and stopped where the double-wide had stood. A double-wide that she'd always thought too big to move, plus there was the lanai her dad had built — how would movers handle a rambling offshoot like that? — but it had all been handled quite easily after some trailer reselling company bought it, a deposit landing in her account at the community bank near Fort Jackson. But Fort Jackson wasn't home, and neither was her condo near Fort Bragg, leased to the perky little payroll administrator and her perky little boyfriend. This, 2241 Lost Hills Road in a community still to come, was home. She got out of the car and just stood there. The wind rose and made her eye watery, despite the protection of the sunglasses, bluing everything she saw into a kind of mirage. She liked that. It was very quiet here at home. She liked that, too.

That night LeAnne slept in the Honda. The next morning, she drove to a camping supply store in Surprise and bought a tent, a sleeping bag, a fold-up stool, a portable camp toilet, a portable camp shower, and a tool kit, loaded them into the trunk, and got behind the wheel. Then she climbed out, went back inside, and bought a long-handled spade. She got behind the wheel again, climbed out again, went inside again, and bought a watch.

"That be all?" said the clerk, maybe making a joke at her expense.

There were two ways to go. LeAnne chose the peaceable route. "I've got other fish to fry," she told him.

"Huh?"

LeAnne went home, found the cap over the water line coming up from the ground, pried it off with a screwdriver, connected the shower intake pipe, set up the tent, and was good to go by fourteen hundred hours. After that she tried out the shower — cold, but she'd had many far colder showers. Le-Anne got herself good and clean under a huge western sky. Then she dressed, took some ibuprofen, four or possibly five, climbed into the car. She checked herself in the mirror, adjusting the patch strap and straightening the sunglasses, and went job hunting.

Job hunting was overstating things. LeAnne had only worked one job before the army, and worked it successfully, so this was merely a matter of letting them know she was back and available. At fifteen hundred forty-three minutes — nice to have a watch again; LeAnne made a mental note to buy a compass of the kind that attached to the steering wheel — she drove into the parking lot at Hidden Canyon Trails. The sign was newly painted, as was the office exterior, formerly white, now red and yellow, plus the shady pen where Bruce the javelina had lived was gone, as was Willis the diamond-back's wire-mesh cage, but otherwise things looked the same. LeAnne checked herself in the rearview, straightened the sunglasses, always going crooked in the wrong way, meaning slanting low on the right side, and walked toward the office. The big barrel cactus out front was in bloom. LeAnne sniffed the pink blossoms, smelled nothing. She went inside.

A girl stood behind the counter, chewing gum and folding brochures, a tall, strongly built girl, maybe fifteen or sixteen, with a tan face and dirty-blond ponytail.

"Hi, there," LeAnne said. But then she realized the door hadn't quite closed behind her. She turned back, got that taken care of, started again. "Hi, there."

The girl was watching her. "Can I help you?"

"Yeah," said LeAnne, then got sidetracked again, this time by the sound of the girl's voice, older than fifteen or sixteen. "How old are you?"

"How old am I? Twenty-two. Why?"

"Doesn't matter." But why did she look so young? "You look kind of young for your age, that's all."

"Um, what can I do for you?" The girl — the woman — slid the stack of brochures to the side, like she was keeping them safe.

"I'd like to see Bernice," LeAnne said. "Is she here?"

"Who's Bernice?"

"Mrs. Adelson. Bernice Adelson. The owner."

The woman cracked her gum. "There's no one here of that name."

"Huh?"

"The name of Bernice. There's no Bernice, and the owner is Mr. Nasrallah."

The door opened and a man entered. He wore a floppy hat, cargo pants, a safari-type shirt. The man smiled and said, "My ears are red."

"I'm sorry?" said the woman behind the counter.

But LeAnne got it. "You're Nasrallah?" she said.

"That's right. What can I do for you?"

A smiley, friendly type, with gentle eyes, but LeAnne saw through all that immediately. "What kind of name is Nasrallah?"

The smile wavered, but only a little, and his eyes didn't lose that gentle look, although they did seem more alert. "An American name," he said.

A smart-ass. LeAnne could deal with

smart-asses, also knew what it felt like to have America in the blood, but was that the point of this visit? No. This visit was all about . . . all about . . .

"She's asking for someone named Bernice," said the woman. "Bernice Adelson."

"May I ask why?" said Nasrallah.

"It's none of your business," LeAnne said, "but she owns this place no matter what anyone says. I know because I worked here."

"Ah," said Nasrallah. "Well, the truth of the matter is that I'm the owner. I bought it from Bernice six years ago. A lovely person."

"Bernice doesn't own it anymore?"

"I'm afraid not. Was there anything special you wanted to discuss with her?"

"Yeah," said LeAnne, right back in gear. "A job."

"A job here?" Nasrallah said.

"Where else?"

The room went silent. LeAnne had no idea what that was about. Was it possible they doubted that she knew her stuff? "I can do everything there is to do here," she said. "Lead the tours, run the shop, tweak the website, maintain the ATVs, you name it."

"Actually," said Mr. Nasrallah, "I sold off the ATVs — not ecologically sound, in my opinion. All our touring is on foot now, and the consumer response has been very positive."

"Check us out on Yelp," said the woman.

LeAnne turned to her. Inside she was . . . it was hard to describe everything that was going on inside. She remembered Marci's words about Iraq: *It's like hell is down below, but sometimes it pops up through the ground.* That was the description she was looking for. She had Iraq inside her. That thought, or realization, and the add-on that quickly came with it — namely that she was nurturing some sort of Iraq in her womb — took all her strength from her at once. She sagged down onto the floor of Hidden Canyon Trails and sat there, her arms around her knees.

"Oh, dear, are you all right?" Nasrallah said. The woman hurried out from behind the counter with a bottle of water. They fussed over her for a minute or two until she felt more like herself, not her old, real self, but this new version, damaged and inferior. Hands reached out to help her up. She ignored them and rose on her own.

"I'm fine," LeAnne said. "Don't ask."

Then came an awkward moment or two, the three of them just standing around. LeAnne wasn't sure about the cause of their awkwardness; hers was all about finding the best way to make Nasrallah give her the job.

"Uh, did you have a good relationship with Bernice?" Nasrallah said.

"And with Mr. Adelson. He was my high school track coach."

"What a character!" said Nasrallah. The door opened and in strode some hikers, sweaty and happy; seven of them, by LeAnne's count. Nasrallah gave them a quick wave, turned back to LeAnne. "Thanks for dropping by."

LeAnne tried to think of some way to get this interview back on the right track, or at least prolong it, but failed. She made her way through the hikers, like some sort of fish going the wrong way, and out to the Honda. LeAnne got in, closed the door, and finally came up with something. She tried it out. "Is it the patch, Mr. Nasrallah? Don't let it scare you." She sat for a bit, listening to the internal echo of that, and added, "Even though it scares me. It scares the shit out of me, Mr. Nasrallah." Was that better? Worse? At least worth a shot? LeAnne approached the question from all possible angles, and then, at the top of her lungs, screamed, "Give me my fucking job!"

LeAnne drove for a while, took her mind off things. She considered serenading herself again Marci-style with some country music, but the energy wasn't there. When had she ever wanted for energy? Plus she was suddenly thirsty, not just a little thirsty but desperate for water. Somehow the desert air — which she'd always loved — had changed its relationship with her, was no longer on her side; more like that other desert air, so distant now but with her every single goddamn day. On a fancy street in one of those West Valley towns, where she was driving en route to who knows where, she spotted a sidewalk café bound to sell bottled water. LeAnne parked in one of those diagonal slots, got out, stepped up onto the sidewalk, and —

But no. In fact, she hadn't seen the small dog leashed to a bike rack down there on her lower right. Of course, the lower right — wasn't that how things worked, from now on until she finally found the nerve to . . . whoa! She was getting ahead of herself. At the moment she was tripping over the leash, losing her balance, and falling hard on the sidewalk.

She blurted some sort of loud and guttural noise on impact, a noise followed by the clatter of her sunglasses across the poured concrete and the furious yipping of the dog. LeAnne rolled over, her mind in two places, one about recovering the sunglasses with all possible speed, the other about kicking the dog, good and hard. Then, as she picked herself up, a man appeared in front of her, holding out the sunglasses.

"Ma'am?"

LeAnne grabbed them out of his hand and jammed them onto her face, real fast, maybe before he had a chance to notice all the defects. "When is it fucking enough?" she said.

"Uh, excuse me," said this do-gooder, a man slightly taller than her, well-dressed, well-groomed, possibly handsome. "I mean no, uh . . ." His eyebrows rose. "LeAnne?"

LeAnne stepped back, tried to bring his face into some sort of clear view. The lips were beautiful.

"It's me," said the man. "Ryan. Ryan Fraser."

Before she could even start dealing with that, a little boy jumped up from a seat at a sidewalk café, ran by, and scooped up the yipping dog.

"Daddy! Daddy! She stepped on Lew!"

"Oh, I'm sure it was an accident, Caleb. Besides this is an old friend. So good to see you, LeAnne — this is my son, Caleb. Caleb say hi to Ms. Hogan — if it's still Ms.

Hogan — you'll have to bring me up to speed." Ryan flashed her a big smile. Meanwhile, Caleb was glaring up at her and stroking Lew, which seemed to have no effect on the yipping. In short, a kind of madhouse, a madhouse closing in on her in every dimension.

LeAnne glared right back at the boy, forgetting that no glare could be seen through the sunglasses. "I did not step on your stupid dog."

That shocked him — LeAnne could see it on his innocent little kid face: *no kid gloves when real life comes knocking, little man.*

Ryan laughed a bit uncertainly, as if some joke had misfired. Then his hand was on her shoulder, and he was moving her toward one of the outside tables of the sidewalk café. "No harm done," he said. "Come on over here, LeAnne, and meet the rest of my family."

Now she was standing by a corner table, white-clothed with heavy-looking silverware, nice china, flowers in a vase.

"Everybody, please say hi to LeAnne Hogan. LeAnne, my wife, Dana. And these are my other kids . . ." A boy and a girl, who Ryan named, names LeAnne missed. But did she give a shit? No. The point was how beautiful, happy, and rich they all were, just livin' the dream — a dream made possible, it hit her at that moment, by others toiling in a nightmare down below.

Dana smiled, an unforced genuine smile, impossible to dislike. "So nice to meet you, LeAnne. Even though I've always been a bit jealous."

"Jealous?" LeAnne peered down at her. Was this some track meet rival? LeAnne didn't recognize her.

"On account of you were Ry's first love. But all is forgiven! Won't you join us?" Dana pushed a chair toward her.

"Great idea," Ry said. "Something to drink? Dessert? The sorbets here are homemade — the kids are addicted."

LeAnne stood by the empty chair. Silver bowls were at every place, bearing little sorbet balls, green, orange, white. There was also a basket of brownies and cookies. The smells were powerful and good, and LeAnne couldn't remember when she'd last eaten, but she couldn't imagine sitting down. She couldn't even imagine standing there, with these people and in this place, although she was actually doing just that.

Ryan patted the empty chair. "So what are you up to these days? Are you back here full time? I think my mom ran into your mom a few years ago, but I don't remember much in the way of details."

In the center of the madhouse, LeAnne thought of something funny to say, and said it: "Me neither."

Ryan laughed, and Dana, too.

Leave 'em laughing: wasn't that a show business cliché? Maybe you could live your life taking all cues from show business clichés. She'd have to make a list, tape it to the dashboard. For now, she grabbed a handful of brownies and cookies and walked away.

"LeAnne?"

There was more laughter, increasingly uncertain as the odds on this being some sort of humor grew longer, but still audible until she got in the car and drove off, one hand on the wheel, the other fumbling desserts into her mouth. They turned bone dry right away and she spat them out.

Back at 2241 Lost Hills Road, she found someone there, meaning on her property. Or at least someone's car: a small black sedan with a bar code strip on the rear window, meaning it was a rental — one of those practical little things LeAnne had learned from her charter boat captain boyfriend in Islamorada who had a headful of information like that. A funny guy, and he'd begged her — "I'm begging you, baby" — to leave the army and marry him.

LeAnne got off that what-if detour before it started. She parked beside the black sedan and stepped out of her car. At the same time, the flap of her tent opened and out came a soft-faced man in army blues, two silver bars on his lapels.

"What the hell are you doing in my home?" she said.

"Hello, LeAnne," he said. "No offense. I was just seeing if you were in."

He moved aside, left to right, making him hard to track. An army captain who somehow knew her name, also knew how to find her. Plus there was something familiar about him.

"Are you all right?" he said. "Looks like you've lost some weight."

She gazed at him, her left eye just not getting it done on its lonesome.

"Stallings, G-2," he said. "We met at Walter Reed, but I wouldn't blame you for not remembering, what with the recent trau— what with the medication, and all."

"I remember," she said, mental fragments reassembling just in time. "Why are you here? And how did you find me?"

"That second part's not too interesting," Stallings said. "Just routine." Which was when the meaning of G-2 — intel — came to her. "But as for why I'm here," Stallings went on, "two reasons. Well, three actually, including checking on your welfare. How are you doing?"

"Fine."

"Glad to hear that. Dr. Machado was somewhat concerned when he tried to return your call and had a confusing — had no success. He asks that you please try again, with whatever you wanted to discuss."

LeAnne waved all that aside with the back of her hand. There was nothing she wanted to discuss with Dr. Machado, now, then, forever.

"He's also concerned, bringing us to point two — in fact, the medical staff as a whole is concerned that you seem to have left all your pills behind."

"Tell them to worry about something else."

Stallings nodded. "I've put some medications in the tent, together with dosage info and VA contact numbers in the Phoenix area, and some things you left behind."

LeAnne shrugged.

"As for the tent itself — and this whole setup, very resourceful, by the way — I was wondering how long you planned to stay here."

"Why is it any business of yours? Am I on active duty?"

"Pending a final determination, technically yes, I suppose. The thing is — coming to the final point — I'd like to be able to reach you. I gather you don't currently have a phone."

"So?"

"So maybe," he said, pulling a red phone from his pocket, "you'd consider accepting this. I'll only call when it's important."

LeAnne made no move to take the red phone. The lid twister or metal shearer or whatever the hell was in her head suddenly awoke and started making up for lost time. She thought about the medications waiting in the tent.

"And when I say important, I'm not just referring to me, or G-2, or the army in general," Stallings said. "I'm meaning important to you, too."

"I don't know what the hell you're talking about."

"Then why don't I take you to dinner — name the place, anywhere you want — and I'll try to explain."

LeAnne tried to picture a restaurant dinner with this or any other man and could not. Actually, that was not quite true — her mind was all set to drift down to Islamorada. But hadn't the charter boat captain gotten married sometime in the past few years? And if not, what was she bringing to the table, his or any man's?

"I'm not hungry," she said.

"Fair enough," said Stallings. "I'll take a rain check. But before I go, I'd like to pick your brain a bit on the subject of your terp."

"Katie?" She wouldn't have minded seeing Katie at that moment. Katie could always crack her up with that sarcastic BBC-style English commentary, flowing from behind her veil while all the meat-headed men were fucking things up. *Oh, indubitably, good sir.*

Stallings smiled, which was the only time that soft face of his seemed to harden.

"Something funny?"

What the hell? He was some kind of mind reader? "Katie," LeAnne said. "Katie can be pretty funny."

"Oh?" he said. "How?"

"Hard to explain," LeAnne said.

"Try."

Stallings was starting to bother her. He was maybe an inch or so taller than she was, but narrow-shouldered and thin-chested, at least compared to many men she knew.

"Please," he said. "I'm just asking you to help me do my duty."

"Your duty is to find out how Katie's funny?"

"It can be a strange job sometimes."

Was there a slight catch in his voice when he said that? Some person was inside those army blues, maybe struggling with the fit? LeAnne had seen plenty of that in her military career, but she couldn't relate personally.

"I don't know if other Afghan women are like Katie," LeAnne said. "In fact, I doubt it. She had this Brit accent she could do, and a whole Brit kind of sarcasm."

"What was she sarcastic about?"

"You know — all the bullshit."

"Such as?"

"The way the men are."

"The Afghan men?"

"Yeah."

"So you don't think she respected them?"

"I know she didn't."

"But on every level?" Stallings said.

"Huh? What are you getting at?"

"The possibility that she wanted you to think she didn't respect them."

"Why would she want me to think that? And it's not even her to begin with."

"What's not even her?"

"That kind of twisted shit. Katie's straight up."

"Making fun of people in a language they don't understand doesn't sound straight up to me," Stallings said.

A wind rose, coming out of the west and rippling the tent fabric, in a strange sort of way, like . . . like someone was moving around in there. At that moment, she knew one thing for sure: Stallings couldn't be trusted. LeAnne brushed past him — actually knocking him off balance, worth it right there — and barged into her tent, ready to do harm and do it . . . TO THE MAX.

But there was no one in the tent. Nothing had changed, except for the addition of a shopping bag lying by her backpack. She picked it up, looked inside, saw pill bottles, an envelope or two, and a small leather case. LeAnne opened the case. Her Bronze Star was inside. She'd forgotten all about it.

"Just the meds and some things you left behind," Stallings called from the other side of the entrance flap. "In case you wanted them."

LeAnne went outside. He turned out to be standing very close to the entrance flap, so she almost bumped into him. She didn't back away.

"What do you want from me?" she said.

Stallings took her right hand in both of his, his movements slow and gentle, as though dealing with a wild animal. LeAnne liked that label, resolved to make it a keeper in her heart.

"Don't you want to understand what happened?" he said.

"There's nothing to understand," she said, withdrawing her hand. "I fucked up."

Stallings shook his head. "If you did, that would be fine with me — make a tidy parcel. But I've found out enough already to doubt this can be hung on you."

"You're hanging it on Katie?"

"I haven't ruled that out. Can you?"

"How would I do that?"

"Explain her whereabouts when that grenade detonated. She was supposed to be by your side for the duration of every mission. That's straight from the job description."

"You're asking me to think back?"

He nodded, just a slight, soft-faced nod.

In her mind, she started down that road, caught dark and bloody glimpses, and shut it down. "Nope," she said. "I don't remember a thing."

Stallings gazed at her. In disbelief? The opposite? LeAnne didn't give a shit. Now was the time for him to go. First, of course, he'd hand her his card, or some other professional move like that, all about sticking her in his web.

Instead, he said, "I won't bother you again." And headed for his little black sedan.

LeAnne went into the tent and lay down. A car door opened and closed. Then it opened and closed again, sounding different the second time, a lower sort of thump, so maybe not the same car. That didn't make much sense, but the point was she'd never heard so acutely in her life — checkmark on the plus side, but all on its lonesome; the negative checkmarks went on for pages. After the thumps came the sound of an engine firing and Stallings driving off. The wind blew against the tent, causing all kinds of movement, like the tent was a life form. An image rose up through all the dark and bloody glimpses in her mind: the fringed hems of a pair of jeans, and two feet in woven slippers. She began to shake and couldn't stop. After way too much of that, she finally remembered the meds in the shopping bag. LeAnne fumbled around with the pill bottles, took some of this and a little of that.

Chapter Sixteen

Next morning, LeAnne felt for a few minutes like pretty much nothing at all, and then she graduated to not so good, fairly bad, and finally worse than before, meaning before her pill mini-binge or maxi-binge, or whatever it had been. She opened the tent, let in some light — a terrible glare she endured while getting her patch and sunglasses in place — and rummaged around until she'd gathered up all the pill bottles. Suicide was on the table, for sure, but not that way. She was — correction: she had been — a warrior, and no one was taking that away from her.

LeAnne went outside, walked to a brambly strip at the rear of the property, opened the bottles, and tossed them all away, the pills bright tiny projectiles in the sky and then gone. After that she turned on her outdoor shower, first just standing there with her mouth turned up, drinking the cold water, and then letting it drum down on her head and body. The blood started flowing. An idea came to her, all about warriors needing weapons. She remembered the Little Protector. What had happened to it?

LeAnne was in the tent, almost dressed, when she heard a car approaching. "Stallings, you shithead," she said, and stepped outside, buckling her belt, now loose even in the last hole.

It wasn't Stallings. Instead this was a woman in a shiny new Range Rover. She drove up the hard-packed driveway, maneuvered carefully around a small pothole, and came to a stop near the Honda. The woman climbed out, a middle-aged woman dressed in cream-colored slacks and a yellow blouse, fat pearls around her neck, tastefully applied makeup, short light blond hair in that sort of boyish cut that turns out to be very feminine on the right sort of woman. And this was definitely the right sort of woman. It wasn't until she'd advanced a few steps that LeAnne recognized her own mother.

Her mother came closer. The skin on her face was so smooth, unwrinkled, unmarred; not even any — what were those grooves at the side of the eye? Crow's-feet: that was it. She'd managed to get rid of the crow's-feet? Here was aging gracefully, a state of being you heard about but didn't often see. At the same time, something was wrong. LeAnne could see it in her mother's eyes and their changing expressions: shock, horror, pain. It was around then that LeAnne realized she wasn't wearing the sunglasses or the patch.

"Oh, darling," her mother said, and took a quicker step or two but then caught a heel on rough ground and stumbled, almost falling, almost losing her grip on a plastic bag she was carrying. She recovered and kept coming, her arms slowly unfolding, like some sort of embrace was in the plans. What the hell was the point of that, especially with her mother's gaze locked on the right side of LeAnne's face, all fucked up and out there for inspection? But no counterplan occurred to her, so she just stood there. Then her mother was right in front of her, throwing her arms around her, the plastic bag bumping against LeAnne's back, and embracing her, holding her tight. "Oh, my darling girl."

LeAnne let herself be embraced but kept her own arms by her sides. Her mother's tears dampened LeAnne's shoulders. "You're so thin, LeAnne. Much, much too thin."

"You're wrong," LeAnne said.

"Oh, no, you are," her mother said. "So, so thin, just like your friend said."

"What friend?"

"That nice officer — Stallings, I think his name was. He said you were just a wraith. At least when I saw you in Germany you weren't so very thin."

LeAnne remembered *conv. with mom*, fumbled through her mind for the details. "You came to Landstuhl?"

Her mother nodded. "Don't worry. They prepared me for . . . for memory issues."

Memory issues. No doubt about that. Wasn't there something she'd been trying and trying to recall? Yes, number two, that was it. But what was number two? LeAnne caught a whiff of hot steel, came no closer than that.

"Do you smell anything?" she said.

"Maybe these," her mother said, taking a box from her plastic bag and holding it out. "You asked for them in Germany."

LeAnne made no move to open the box. She pictured an explosion getting triggered the instant she raised the lid, crazy maybe, but so what? Crazy things happened in real life, and plenty of them.

Her mother ended up raising the lid. No explosion. Inside were neat rows of the baking specialty from long ago: those gingerbread men with the mint-green eyes. At that point LeAnne started crying, not sobbing or bursting into tears, just slow and steady like it would never stop. They stepped into each other's arms, the gingerbread men falling free and breaking to pieces on the hard desert floor, and clung together for what seemed like a very long time.

They sat in the tent, LeAnne on the sleeping bag, her mom on the camp stool. LeAnne put on the patch but kept the sunglasses in her lap. Indoors with the sunglasses was just too dark and narrow, and besides what was she hiding now? Her mom had seen what there was to see.

"Mr. Stallings believes you should go back to Walter Reed," her mom said.

"So he can watch my every move?"

"Why would he want to do that? And as it happens, I'd already booked a flight for next Tuesday."

"Booked what flight?"

"To come see you."

"Sorry to mess up your plans."

"I didn't mean it that way. I meant —"

"It doesn't matter," LeAnne said. "I'm never going back there."

"But I got the impression your treatment's not finished. Mr. Stallings said —"

"Don't want to hear about him."

"Whatever you say. In fact, this will be much better."

"Anything's better than the hospital."

"I'm talking about what's happening next."

"Which is?"

"You're coming to live with me, of course. With me and Alex — we've already discussed it, it's all set. All the kids — the other kids are out and on their own now, don't know if you're aware of that — so you've got your pick of bedrooms."

Her pick of bedrooms: the one she wanted was Marci's.

"What's funny?"

"Nothing," LeAnne said.

Her mom glanced around the tent. "Um, at the risk of mentioning Mr. Stallings one more —"

"Captain, for Christ sake."

"— sorry, Captain Stallings one more time, he said that you'd been supplied with . . . ocular prosthetics is the term he used, I believe."

"So?"

"Can I see them?"

"Why would you want to do that?"

"Because that's what moms do."

"Like trying on prom dresses?"

Her mom rose, came over, kissed the top of LeAnne's head. "Yes, like that."

There was a long silence, nothing happening except LeAnne's mom bent over her. Her smell was glorious and unattainable, like the flowers at a celebrity wedding. Despite that, LeAnne said, "The plastic case in the backpack."

Mom moved to the backpack, fished inside, drew out the plastic case. LeAnne twisted around for a better view of Mom opening it up.

"Oh, my," Mom said. "I didn't realize there was a choice." She held the case closer to the light coming through the open tent flap and gazed at the contents. The meaning of that old saying about not knowing whether to laugh or cry became clear forever when LeAnne saw the expression on Mom's face: the look of a certain type of woman who knows all the ropes when it comes to high-end shopping. "I think the middle one, don't you?" She brought the case over to LeAnne so they could study the contents together.

The contents: three fake blue eyes, each nestled in a velvety little compartment. Mom pointed to the middle compartment, her fingernail immaculate, the color a muted ivory. "Sky blue is a much too general description. Your eyes, for example, are the blue of the winter skies we get here, and just after dawn if you want to nitpick."

"Eye," LeAnne said.

"Excuse me?"

"I don't have eyes, plural. That's the whole point."

"I'm sorry, dear. I didn't mean to offend you. I'm just so nervous, that's all."

"You are?"

"Why, of course," Mom said. She didn't look up. A tear fell and landed in the box, but on the velvet, not the objects. "Oh, dear."

"Hand me the instructions," LeAnne said. "But I don't see the point."

"Don't you still want to look your best?"

"Oh, Mom, Jesus fucking Christ!"

Mom looked up. "And if not that, then how about so people don't feel sorry for you, at least as a starting point? Give yourself a fighting chance — that kind of approach."

The smarts you get from your mom.

"Well?" said her mom.

"Did you think Dad was stupid?" LeAnne said.

"What a question!"

"Is that why you broke up? Fundamentally, I mean."

"He most certainly was not stupid," Mom said.

"Compared to Alex," LeAnne said.

Mom flinched, just a bit. "What's the point of getting into this? People are smart in different ways, as I'm sure you know."

"How was Dad smart?"

Mom laughed. "Like that, right there. What you just did."

"Okay, I give up."

Mom laughed again. This time LeAnne came close to joining in. Then they went outside into the good light, laid the plastic case on the hood of the Range Rover, and went over the instructions together. "Clear enough?" Mom said after a bit.

"Yeah." LeAnne reached for the middle eye.

"Whoa," said Mom. She felt in the pocket of her slacks, took out a thin pack of wipes. They both cleaned their hands, took the eye from its velvet-lined compartment; and together fitted the eye into its place in LeAnne's socket. Mom stepped back.

"How does it feel?"

"I don't know. A little funny."

"You'll get used to it," Mom said. She tilted her head. "One thing I can tell you — it looks great. You'd hardly even notice."

Mom reached into the car, got a mirror

from her purse, and handed it to LeAnne. LeAnne took a look at her new self.

"Well?"

LeAnne tried to examine this new self objectively. The lid twister woke up from what was a pretty long slumber for him. "I don't know," she said.

"It's a step, LeAnne." If there was any impatience in Mom's tone when she said that, it was very slight. "Now let's pack up and get going."

"Where?"

"Where? My place. Mine and Alex's. And yours, too, as long as you need."

Want would have been better, LeAnne thought. Who was going to be the judge of need, to blow the whistle when time was up? But she didn't get into any of that. Instead, she said, "You're sure he's all right with this?"

"Alex?"

"Yes, Alex."

"No worries there," Mom said. "He considers it his patriotic duty."

The wind rose suddenly, almost blew the plastic case off the hood of the Range Rover before Mom clamped a hand on it.

"Tell you what," LeAnne said, her voice remarkably steady, at least to her ears. "This will take me some time, breaking down everything, the shower, et cetera. I'll be along in a bit."

"But we've moved. You wouldn't even know where to go."

"Tell me."

Mom wrote out directions. It was pretty simple. "And here's my number in case you need it."

"I don't have a phone."

"We'll have to do something about that. See you for dinner?"

Then with a kiss on the cheek and a cautious three-point turn, her mom was gone. She left the mirror behind, and also her impossible smell, which lingered in the air for some moments before the wind took it away.

"I'm not hungry," LeAnne said. She closed her eye — her good eye — testing out the new one for any miraculous attributes. The world went blank. Strictly for show, her ocular prosthetic, differing from Marci's prosthetic leg, which was actually useful. This new eye was just another kind of patch. LeAnne patted her pockets in search of the real one. No patch. Her mom had taken it.

The wind picked up. LeAnne stood on her land, examined her . . . what would you call it? A campsite? That was it. She liked her little campsite. How long could she keep living here? With her mother around, the answer was: not very. But living at her mother's place, every single day bumping up against Alex's patriotic duty? No way. So what was the answer? She could get in the car, put the pedal to the floor, and find peace. No other solution occurred to her. LeAnne took another look at herself in the mirror. The fake eye did not look so bad. But the scars did look bad, and even worse was what the mirror couldn't show, meaning behind the surface. LeAnne got down on her knees. The wind was now blowing strong enough to raise dust off the desert floor; the sky around her turned garish.

LeAnne had never prayed. What was the point? Asking for help from a being that might or might not exist? And if the being did exist, how about stepping in before the desperate pleas were necessary, Mr. or Ms. Being? She wasn't smart enough to answer these questions, or even find a place to begin. Down on the ground, she noticed pieces of broken gingerbread men. She picked up the remnants — arms, legs, and a head or two with those mint-green eyes — and ate them, realizing she was hungry after all. The taste was much drier than she remembered.

LeAnne was picking a mint-green eye out of a gingerbread face when she heard a loud flap, like a clapping sound, and the wind lifted the tent and its pegs right out of the ground and sent it bounding and rolling like tumbleweed. That snapped her out of a bad inner place and got her moving. She was at her best when moving, something obvious she should have realized long ago.

LeAnne chased after the tent, corralled it, jammed it into the Honda. Then she raced around, gathering up all the scattered things — backpack, sleeping bag, clothing, pill bottles, Bronze Star, loose sheets of paper — scuttling back and forth at 2241 Lost Hills Road. All of the stuff she threw into the car, and climbed in herself, huffing and puffing, heart racing, sweat dripping down her chin. What was going on? Some moments passed before LeAnne realized that for the first time in her life she was out of shape.

She sorted through the papers. They seemed to have fallen from the manila envelope Captain Stallings had brought; things she'd left behind at Walter Reed. One by one she smoothed the pages and replaced them in the envelope. The very last sheet was a printout entitled: Getting to Know

Your Xion-3 Prosthetic Leg. On the front were instructions and diagrams. The back of the printout was blank, except for some handwriting, round, neat, childlike:

1. Strengthen hip flexors.
2. Life fucking goes on.
3. Get LeAnne to visit when I'm back "home."

LeAnne went over those listed items again and again, searching for meanings behind meanings, and finding lots — starting with the prosthetic leg, even more useful than she'd thought. Did prayer work? Maybe it was the down-on-your-knees part that did the trick, and all the blather was irrelevant. But whatever she'd been praying for, the answer was Marci.

Chapter Seventeen

The boonies. A nothing little town called Bellville. Rains all the time.

Rolling hills, orchards, some sheep, some cattle, and it was at least drizzling when LeAnne passed a sign: Bellville 10 miles, Canada 22. Had Marci said anything about nearness to Canada? LeAnne had no desire to be in any sort of foreign country, not even one that she'd heard resembled her own.

She stopped for gas at a crossroads in a one-light town, checking herself in the rearview mirror before filling up. The fake eye looked worst on dim days like this, unable to reflect any sparkle, and, of course, also unable to produce it from within. But nothing sparkling was going on inside her in the first place. There was nothing fake about the face in that respect, a kind of face you actually saw too much of in life, the face of someone who was beat.

"But," said LeAnne, getting out of the car,

"I've never had cheekbones like this."

An older woman at the opposite pump heard her and glanced across. This older woman was plain and unadorned, in no way like LeAnne's mom, but it was then that she realized she hadn't told her mom she wasn't coming to dinner after all, would not be moving in. And when was that? Yesterday? The day before?

"Fuck."

"No need for language like that, young lady," said the woman at the opposite pump, her gaze shifting to the right side of LeAnne's face.

"You the queen of the boonies?" she said.

"Excuse me?" said the old lady.

LeAnne decided to be the mature one and let it go. She went into the gas station, passing a man on the way out, a man with a case of beer under one arm and a roll of duct tape dangling from his hand, only interesting on account of his build — similar to her Daddy in his younger years, except way, way bigger. Other than that, no resemblance: Daddy's face had been of the craggy type; this man's face was round, almost babyish, with a wave of jet-black hair slanting over his forehead. He didn't look at her and she only looked at him because he went by on her left.

At the counter, LeAnne bought a prepaid cell phone, plus a bottle of vodka on second thought. Outside she drove away from the pumps, parked on the back side of the station, found the directions her mom had written; directions and phone number.

"Hello?"

"Mom?"

"I thought you didn't have a phone."

"Now I do. I guess I messed . . ." LeAnne ran out of words. She gazed at the steering wheel compass she'd picked up somewhere or other, the needle pointing right back at her. "What day is it?"

"I'm sorry?"

"Today. What's the day?"

"Tuesday."

"Okay, thanks. Good to know. Mom?"

"Yes?"

"I just couldn't do it."

"Because I said Alex considered it his patriotic duty? That's why, isn't it?"

"So?"

"So? Some remarks are meant to be taken in a lighthearted way. There's such a thing as being too thin-skinned."

"Meaning I'm the bad guy."

"Damn it, LeAnne. I didn't say that."

"It said itself."

"What does that mean? You've got to find

a way to move on."

"Too thin-skinned? The hell with you."

"I'll ignore that. And moving on means treating people with respect."

"Fuck that."

"I'll ignore that, too. But you could have at least let me know you weren't coming. Didn't you stop and think for at least a moment that I'd be worried? Whereabouts in Oregon are you?"

"Oregon?"

"Weren't you there yesterday?"

"What are you talking about? Does it say Oregon on your screen?"

"Um, yes. Well, no. It doesn't say anything."

"Huh?"

"Nothing. It's a bad connection."

"I was in Oregon yesterday." Or had it been the day before, or the one before that? But certainly not today. "What the fuck is going on?"

"Nothing is going on. And I'd be very grateful if you wouldn't speak to me like that."

"You and the queen of the boonies."

"I don't understand."

LeAnne said nothing. She heard her mom taking a deep breath.

"Please come back. If living here is out of

the question, we can make some other arrangement."

"I'll make my own arrangements."

There was a long silence. Then her mom said, "Suit yourself."

LeAnne left the gas station, headed for Bellville, the compass now pointing directly away from her. That was where she wanted any kind of pointing: away from her. On an empty stretch of road, she lowered the window and tossed her prepaid cell phone into a ditch.

A long curve on a rising grade, and at the top LeAnne got her first look at Bellville. The town lay in a valley where two rivers met at about a forty-five-degree angle, one wide and dull gray, the other much smaller and bright blue. Right about where the last of the blueness got swallowed by the dull gray, a bridge spanned the water, connecting both sides of the town, one part rising into eastern hills, the other spreading onto western flats before petering into farmland. She spotted two church spires, a big open space set up for baseball, football, and track, which had to be the high school, and a mill of some kind with a tall chimney, rising higher than the spires and sending up a thick column of smoke, which merged with the mist that hung over the whole town. Then the rain really started coming down, blotting out everything she'd just seen. Maybe that was enough, right there. LeAnne actually thought of turning around and . . . and then what? She took her foot off the brake and coasted down into Bellville, the windshield wipers whipping back and forth at their fastest, a wild motion that gave her a creepy feeling that found its place among all the fucked-up feelings already in her head.

The road leveled out, turned into East Main Street, the main drag. The downtown took up two or three blocks and then came a small residential neighborhood of modest houses and after that a sign reading Canada 16 Miles. LeAnne slowed down, and as she did, spotted a motel set back from the road in a grove of budding trees: Shady Grove Motel and Cabins, Flat-Screen TV, Free Wi-Fi, Reasonable Rates. The rain stopped, not instantly but just about. She pulled in.

"I can give you a room for fifty-nine ninety-five," said the woman behind the counter in the office; a short, round woman wearing a Bellville High School baseball cap. The woman's eyes were on her face, but they showed no reaction at all to what she saw.

"Okay," said LeAnne, handing over her credit card.

The woman glanced at it. "Military? For military I can do you a cabin for the same price."

"Okay," LeAnne said, although she'd forgotten the quote.

"How long you gonna be staying?"

LeAnne picked a number. "Two."

"Two nights?"

"Yeah."

"Cabin six." The woman handed her a key. "My name's Dot, anything you need. Follow the path. Plug in the icebox if you plan on using it."

LeAnne left the office, followed a white crushed-stone path through the trees, past several simple wooden cabins, none looking occupied, to number six, like the other cabins except that it backed on to a pond. A nice, round pond, surface area of maybe one half acre, with a pair of ducks sitting motionless on the far side, tall evergreens lining the banks. This had to be one of the most peaceful spots she'd ever been in. There was a lot to be said for drowning: no violence, no mess, and it could have been an accident. LeAnne unlocked the door to number six and entered.

Cabin six had a damp, foresty smell

inside. She was fine with that. She was also fine with pine walls; and the linoleum floor, covered here and there with woven scatter rugs picturing moose, bears, wolves; and the little bathroom with a stall shower and fishing and hunting magazines on the toilet cistern; and the desk, an old schoolhouse desk with an inkwell hole and a flashlight in the drawer; and the bed, a double bed with a headboard that had a carved cameo of leaping fish, and a gingham spread. LeAnne kicked off Marci's red sneaks and lay down. The red sneaks were back home. That couldn't be bad. In fact: mission accomplished.

She closed her eye. Actually, they both closed; the right eyelid had survived and now it seemed to remember the program on its own. Had there been an eyelid discussion in Germany? Was there something else about titanium posts? LeAnne got no further with any of that. She felt around. Yes, her right eyelid was down, and in place for sleeping. Out on the pond, one of the ducks quacked, not a harsh cartoon-duck quack, but something softer, welcoming, beckoning.

LeAnne slept, first soundly and then not. A dream started up, she and Daddy building a birdhouse, then nailing it to a tree.

Without warning, that changed to Wakil Razaq Salam hammering nails into Daddy's chest. Then came more and more bad things, lots of shouting and screaming and shooting and slashing and the barking of a dog, and LeAnne awoke.

She was soaked in sweat, her body almost stuck to the gingham bedspread. Her heart was beating like a little drum machine turned up all the way. She'd never felt so afraid. A dog barked, not loudly, but close by. The dog was real? What else was real? The dreams stirred deep inside her, trying to draw her back down or simply letting her know they were there, patiently waiting.

LeAnne got up, stripped off her wet clothes, went into the bathroom, and took a long shower, first cold, then hot, and finally lukewarm. Her pulse and breathing returned to normal. The dark parts of her mind went blank.

There was a small four-paned window in the shower stall at head level. LeAnne wiped away the steam from one of the squares and looked out. She had a good view of the pond. The ducks were gone, but on the near bank, maybe fifty feet from the cabin — although she couldn't be confident when it came to distance estimation, not anymore — a dog was prowling around. This dog was big and black, with a huge, square head, smallish ears, and a powerful way of walking. Not a cute dog like — what was the name of Ryan's dog? Lew? — cute if you liked dogs — but . . . LeAnne forgot where she was going, spent time trying to recall the name of Dr. Machado's dog. She could picture it — short-haired, brown — but the name wouldn't come. Did it mean anything that very late in the game she had dogs in the picture? How could it? How were you expected to know even one goddamn thing for absolute sure? She made a mental note to get a weapon, ASAP.

LeAnne rubbed away the steam again. The big dog was still out there, now in the water at the edge of the pond, pawing away at the bank. Mud tore loose in big clumps and plopped into the water. What was he after? Once she'd seen a human femur, just lying by the side of a hilly track in Kunduz Province.

The dog paused, one huge paw raised, and then dipped his head toward the bank, momentarily hidden from view. Next he scrambled up from the pond — actually more like a bound — and shook himself off, water spraying everywhere, coppery in what looked like late afternoon light. But meanwhile, he had something in his mouth. Le-

Anne leaned closer to the glass, her left eye almost touching it. The something in the dog's mouth was large, oval, off-white: a duck egg. A duck egg! The bastard had driven off the parents with his barking and he was about to —

LeAnne pounded on the glass. The dog heard, looked her way immediately, that one paw still raised in the air. LeAnne bolted from the shower and ran outside.

"No, goddamn it! Put that down!"

The dog turned its great head toward her, and in one jerking motion swallowed the egg, yoke running down his chin. LeAnne bent down, grabbed a stone, and flung it at him. She missed, although not by much, the stone sailing over his head and splashing down in the pond. The dog wheeled around immediately and leaped into the pond, swimming — and with amazing speed — toward the center of the spreading circles where the stone had fallen. Then he dove down, out of sight. LeAnne just stood there, naked and dripping, outside the door to cabin six.

The dog popped up to the surface, muzzle first. The stone was in his mouth. He swam to the edge of the pond, lurched out, came flying toward her, his speed and power and otherness terrifying. LeAnne backed quickly into the cabin and slammed the door.

Standing just on the inside, she heard him breathing a foot or two away. Then came a soft thud: the stone landing on the welcome mat. Then more breathing, followed by a soft *pad-pad-pad* as the dog trotted away. LeAnne went looking for the bottle of vodka.

Chapter Eighteen

And before she knew it, she was right back down in a hellhole of bad dreams. The only way out was waking up, a fact known in one small part of her mind, but that part was not in control. She thrashed around, heard screams of agony, and watched live people she knew ripped to pieces, and the blood washed all over her, clotting her hair and soaking her whole body. Finally, she banged her elbow hard on the headboard and woke up, soaked not in blood but in sweat. She leaned over the edge of the bed, vomited on the floor, rose, and in rising put her hands on the gingham spread, put them right into a vodka-smelling puddle of previous vomit.

This could not go on.

LeAnne walked to the door, opened it, and went outside. A dark, moonless night, which was a good thing: she did not like moonlight on a mission. Might as well go in with a marching band. Someone had said that, probably long ago. She listened, heard no music of any kind, no traffic, no wind in the trees, nothing. The pond was the big feature of this night, somehow glowing faintly as though a dim, pearly light were shining way down deep. LeAnne climbed over the bank and stepped into the pond, up to her knees.

This pond was perfection. The water had to be cold at this time of year, but LeAnne didn't feel its temperature at all, just the wetness. It was comforting. She'd been so thirsty and now she had all the water she would ever need. From the outside, bravery, of which she'd seen plenty, could look spectacular. It wasn't like that on the inside. On the inside it was simply making up your mind to do something no matter what and then never thinking about it again. LeAnne's mind was made up. She shut down all thinking and took another step, imposing her will on life.

Shutting off thought didn't mean you weren't aware. LeAnne was aware: of the wetness, of the soles of her feet on the bottom, thick, gritty mud squishing through her toes, of the pearly light. The bottom dropped quickly away and then she was buoyant. She turned on her back, floated on the surface. No moon, but there were stars, not bright, maybe on account of mist she couldn't see. To those stars, she was dead already. The truth was she was dead already, period. The stars were right. She rolled over and swam a few strokes. LeAnne was not much better than an average swimmer, had never worked on her technique, but she'd always enjoyed the feeling of moving in the water — and, of course, the feeling of movement in general. She stopped swimming at once and lay on the surface, facedown. Tonight was not about enjoyment. The lid twister or metal shearer or whatever he was relaxed his grip at last and let her go.

How this was done: you jackknifed into a little duck dive — those poor ducks when they saw what was happening to their baby and could do nothing about it! — and kicked down to the bottom where you clung to a rock or a log or simply dug your hands into the mud and held on for all you were worth, and then . . . that was it. A done deal, mission accomplished. LeAnne did a little duck dive, cut through the still surface, and swam down toward the source of the pearly light. She shut down everything inside, everything unrelated to this one last physical task of finding an anchor and hanging on.

Despite the pearly light, things got darker the deeper she went in the pond. By the time her hand touched bottom — sandy, weedy bottom — she couldn't see a damn thing. The water at the bottom of the pond was much warmer than the water above. That had to be a good sign, even a good sign of what was to come on the other side, if one existed. Things were starting to go her way. LeAnne felt around and almost immediately encountered something thick, woven, slimy. A rope? Yes. Her hands moved along it, came to a metal ring to which the rope seemed to be knotted. The metal ring was in turn attached to a large metal hunk, thick and triangular. An anchor? Yes, an actual anchor stuck on the bottom and just when she needed it, as though plans had been made long ago and now she was finally showing up. *What kept you?* LeAnne kicked her way down until she lay flat on the bottom. She got a good, strong grip on the anchor with both hands and made ready to let all the air out of her lungs, which would by reflex lead to . . . what it would lead to. That was that. She had made her own arrangements. And in those final moments it occurred to her that Daddy, too, had made his own arrangements. She was following him to the very last step. So, at the very end, she understood her life as never before. That had to be a blessing. She was at peace.

LeAnne told herself: on three. In her mind, she counted down: one, two —

But that was where the countdown came to an end. From out of nowhere — more accurately, from directly above — something sharp and mighty and alive clamped down on her right arm, just below the elbow. Then with a quick twisting motion of enormous raw power, this mighty living thing yanked her loose, jerked her away from the anchor and off the bottom — like her grip meant nothing — and up.

LeAnne felt the kicking of strong, hairy legs against her; thick blunt claws scraped her skin. She screamed, and that, not one last exhale, led to the desired end, meaning the inhalation of pond water. But at just about the same moment, she broke the surface, back into the world of air, where she gasped and sputtered and coughed up water, and breathed. Meanwhile, the mighty being still had her by the arm and was propelling her across the pond toward the cabin side. By starlight she saw the big square head of the mighty being, cutting through the water. It was the dog.

The dog swam LeAnne to the edge of the pond and then dragged her up the bank.

Then he finally let go and gave himself a good shake, spraying water all over her. That was when LeAnne, lying in the grass and sucking in air, saw that he was in fact a she.

The dog came closer, stood beside LeAnne. Then she lowered her head toward LeAnne's side and prodded her with her warm, wet muzzle. The message couldn't have been clearer: *Get up.*

But LeAnne was too weak to get up. And did she even want to? What she wanted to do, and had almost pulled off before this dog had interfered, was to . . .

"What the fuck?" she said, the first time she'd addressed a dog in her life. "Where do you get off messing with me?"

LeAnne glared at the dog. The dog gazed back at her, not glaring, just alert.

"Go away, for Christ sake."

The dog didn't budge. Instead it — or she? Did dogs get called he and she or were they its? LeAnne had no idea. All she knew was that the dog had started emitting a series of low rumbly barks. Bark, pause, bark, pause, bark. Same basic message as the muzzle prod, except now more like, *Get up, goddamn it.*

LeAnne rolled over and sat up. Cold now and starting to shake, she — who'd been able to spring erect in one easy motion practically all her life — found herself unable to rise. The dog — seeming to grasp the problem, which, of course, was impossible — moved in closer. LeAnne placed her hands on the dog's neck and pulled herself up. Then she made her way unsteadily, even staggering once or twice, back to cabin six. The door was open. She went inside and tried to close the door before the dog could get in, but the dog was already in. There was no more she could do. Her will was weak and her ability to impose it weaker. She shut the door, got in the bed, trying to avoid the pukey parts, pulled the covers around her, and lay there trembling.

Then came a thump. A long time went by before she realized what that was: the stone she'd thrown at the dog, now being dropped on the floor. The dog had brought it back after their first encounter, depositing it outside, evidently not quite a satisfactory conclusion. Now the stone was properly inside. The dog liked to play the game right.

LeAnne opened her eyes.

The events of the night before came back to her in bits and pieces, but she didn't know whether to trust them, didn't know what to believe, not until she twisted around and saw the dog, lying with its — with her back to the door, eyes closed, massive chest rising and falling. It had all really happened, meaning this was the first day of . . . of a sort of afterlife, as if she'd reached the other side after all.

Soft, gray daylight entered through the windows. It was raining outside, not hard. LeAnne took a good look at the dog. She was short-haired, pure black with no hint of other markings — not even a few nonblack hairs anywhere on her body — and powerfully built, with that deep chest and a broad back. Her tail was thick and short, slightly too long to be called stubby. Her eyes were wide apart, her ears small and round, her neck without tags or collar. There was nothing soft about her expression, not even in sleep.

LeAnne swung her legs over the side — she remembered Marci doing that exact same thing at Walter Reed, except one-leggedly — and stood up. The dog was awake and on her feet immediately.

"Why?" LeAnne said. "What do you want?"

The stone lay on the linoleum floor between them. The dog moved to it, lowered her head and gave the stone a nudge in LeAnne's direction.

"This is all about fetch? You need me for

a fetch partner?"

The dog just stood there, giving no indication of anything. Weren't their tails a guide to dog mood and behavior? This dog's tail was sticking out straight back, completely motionless.

"Do you want to go outside? Is that it?"

The short thick tail didn't move. Slowly and with exaggerated enunciation, LeAnne repeated the word "outside" several times, figuring that if dogs were capable of recognizing a few words, *outside* would probably be one of them. But nothing. The dog gazed at LeAnne. She gazed at the dog. The dog's eyes were as unreadable as shiny little coals. LeAnne had never taken a good long look at the eyes of any dog before this. She did now. Unreadable for sure, at least by her, but something was going on in that big square head.

LeAnne moved past the dog, went to the door, held it open. "Come on."

The dog sat.

" 'Come on' means 'sit'?"

No reaction from the dog. LeAnne walked into the bathroom, closed the door, took a hot shower, felt a little bit alive. She checked her fake eye in the mirror. Its color did match, almost exactly, but the expression was dead. That was one way of seeing it.

But could the fake eye also be seen, like the dog's eyes, as unreadable? Was it possible to find a plus side to all this? LeAnne ran her hands through her hair, tried to think, found the thinking parts pretty much still shut down. But there was a strange, new feeling inside her head, or maybe more like a non-feeling. An ache that had been there for weeks or months — she wasn't even sure how long — and to which she had become accustomed as though it were just another part of herself, seemed to be gone. This ache had been a background ache, much milder that what the lid twister could do, although he, too, was inactive at the moment. LeAnne's gaze wandered, took in the prominence of her collarbone and ribs; the bruises on her arm where the dog had gripped her, although the skin hadn't been broken; and, of course, the scars on her face, more silvery than red today, maybe on account of the soft, gray light.

LeAnne opened the bathroom door. The dog, waiting directly on the other side, brushed past her and lowered her head into the toilet. Then came lapping sounds, although "lapping" was much too gentle to describe what was going on, namely a frantic slurping up of every drop of water in the toilet basin. All done drinking, the dog turned toward LeAnne, water dripping off her chin, and barked another of those low barks.

"Time to go home?" LeAnne said. "Is that it?"

She got dressed and opened the front door again, took a step toward the outside. The dog beat her to it, squeezing through first but hardly knocking into her at all, which LeAnne couldn't have done much about, the squeezing through happening on her blind side.

"Okay," LeAnne said. "We're out. Where's home? Go home."

The dog sat.

"What do you want? A great big thank you or some shit like that?"

No reaction.

"What am I doing?" LeAnne said, continuing silently: *Talking to a dog? Like I'm expecting conversation?* She raised her voice. "Go! Scat!" LeAnne made backhanded waving gestures. The dog sat.

LeAnne turned and started up the white crushed-stone path toward the office. The dog was at her side immediately, again to her right, meaning LeAnne had to twist around to see her. LeAnne tried ignoring the dog. She walked through the light rain; it felt good on her face.

She — more like they, because the dog was still glued to her side — came to the office. LeAnne turned to the dog. "Stay. Or sit. Both. Sit and stay. Just don't fucking move, all right?"

The dog remained standing, possibly even standing with a certain rigidity. LeAnne opened the office door, felt the dog instantly squeezing by her and entering first.

The short round woman — Dot? Dolly? — looked up from behind her desk and smiled a big smile, a genuine kind indicating happy surprise.

"I didn't know you had a dog! Hi there, beautiful. What's her name?"

Chapter Nineteen

"I don't have a dog," LeAnne said. "I've never had a dog. It's — she's a stray, just showed up. No tags, no collar."

"Well, well." The woman opened a drawer and rose. "I may have a little something you'll like, beautiful." She took a dog biscuit from the drawer and came closer. "Got some Rottweiler in you, huh? And maybe a pinch of Malinois, plus an X factor or two. Want to sit for Mama Dot?"

The dog did not sit, by this time no surprise to LeAnne. Dot looked a bit surprised but in no way discouraged. She knew dogs; that was pretty clear. She raised the biscuit and waved it around a bit. "Got your attention now? Sit."

The dog did not sit but growled instead and shifted slightly, bumping right up against LeAnne.

"My goodness," said Dot, taking a backward step. "We don't mean that, do we?"

Hair rose on the back of the dog's neck and she growled again.

Dot turned to LeAnne and frowned, her grandmotherly face changing into something closer to judgmental aunt. "What's bothering her?"

"I have no idea," LeAnne said. "I don't know anything about dogs — but you seem to."

Dot's frown lines deepened, and for the first time her gaze went to the bad side of LeAnne's face. "It just so happens I've had dogs all my life. In fact, I'm still grieving poor Dottalita." She nodded toward a framed photo of a dog hanging on the wall, about the size of Lew, but fluffy.

"Uh, sorry," LeAnne said. "When did she . . ."

"Cross the rainbow bridge? Six years ago come June. The second."

LeAnne wondered if dog lovers shared some special form of insanity. Meanwhile, this nameless dog seemed to be pressing harder against her. LeAnne pressed back, trying to push the dog away. That didn't work. And for the first time in their relationship — slated to end very soon — the dog was wagging her tail.

"You don't recognize her, do you?" LeAnne said.

"Never laid eyes on her."

"So what are we going to do?"

"About what?" Dot said.

"This dog. Should we just let her go? Maybe she'll head for home, wherever home is."

"Maybe. But suppose someone drove out from Seattle and just dumped her from a car? Happens all the time."

"How about calling the police?"

"They'd just take her to the shelter."

"Where is it?"

Dot pointed up the road, toward Canada. "Two miles, thataway."

"I'll do it."

"Your call, I guess," said Dot. "But you might want to factor in that it's not a no-kill shelter."

"Meaning what?"

"Meaning if someone doesn't take her after a set amount of time, it's curtains."

"How long a set period of time?"

"Seven days, as I recall."

"Christ," said LeAnne. She didn't want to think about this problem, or this dog. If anything, she wanted to think about . . . well, herself, supposing she had to think at all. She glanced at the goddamn dog, which, if human, would probably be of the opinion that she was owed big time for last night's lifesaving performance, when in fact she'd fucked up everything. The truth was it hadn't been so easy for LeAnne to do what she'd done, and she wasn't sure she could do it again, probably not anytime soon.

"Maybe she'll get lucky," LeAnne said.

"At the shelter?" said Dot.

"Yeah."

"This dog?" Dot shook her head. "Cute puppies are what get lucky at the shelter. What you have here is not a cute puppy."

"I don't have anything here. She's not mine. Why don't you take her?"

"Me?" said Dot.

"You've had dogs all your life — you said so yourself."

"But I told you — I'm still grieving."

"I don't get the connection."

"Because you're clearly not a dog person."

"I admitted that," LeAnne said.

Perhaps she'd raised her voice. In any case, Dot took another step back. *With our voices alone we could drive Dot right through the wall, this fucking dog and I.*

"Any dog person," Dot said, "knows that it's a huge mistake to welcome in a new one before the end of the grieving process."

"And when would that be?" LeAnne said. "Six years seems like a long time."

"Come June. The second. And since

when, no offense, do you get the right to set the limit on who feels what?" Maybe Dot saw some changed expression on LeAnne's face at that moment. She added, "I don't mean you, personally. I mean anyone."

So no one had a right to set limits on another's feelings? That was all too complicated for LeAnne this particular morning, or maybe at any time in her life, even before her head got messed up, inside and out. All she knew was that she didn't really want to fight with this woman, was not in the mood for fighting at all. Although that could change.

"All right, no reason you have to step up," LeAnne said. "I'll take her to the shelter, check it out."

"Your call."

"You said that already. And I specifically said check it out, no more than that."

Dot gave her a long look. Her expression changed back from judgmental aunt to grandmotherly. "Thank you for your service."

"Huh?"

"Your military service."

"I get it," LeAnne said. "But why now?"

"I'm just glad we have tough people like you defending our country, that's all."

LeAnne felt her face going red; she turned

away to hide any show like that. "Come on," she told the dog in a voice that sounded harsh and impatient and mean, even in her own ears. And why the fuck not? Why shouldn't she be harsh and impatient and mean? It didn't seem to bother the dog, who followed at once, managing with a half-bound to once again beat LeAnne through the doorway, immediately maneuvering around to her blind side.

"What the hell is wrong with you?"

The dog pressed up against her as they headed back down the path, way too hard to be anything but aggressive.

"Don't you even know where the fuck you're going? To the slaughter." LeAnne suddenly remembered the long-ago AP English class with Ms. Spears: *Time held me green and dying / Though I sang in my chains like the sea.* She felt sick to her stomach and might have vomited there and then, but she had nothing left to vomit.

LeAnne opened the rear door of the Honda and was about to say, "Get in," but before she could the dog leaped past her onto the backseat, where she scrambled immediately into a sitting position, facing front and alert.

"Expecting something? Or you just like cars? Or what?"

LeAnne drove out of Shady Grove and turned right on the main highway. She'd driven maybe a couple of hundred feet when with no warning the dog bolted over from the back and into the shotgun seat, again quickly sitting up straight, eyes on the road. The sudden movement startled LeAnne, and she came close to taking a good shot with her elbow or even her fist. But something stopped her.

"Don't you ever do that again," she said, which was stupid and unnecessary, this being their last drive.

Five minutes later they came to the shelter. Can-Am Animal Care and Control read the sign on the front of the building, a peeling-painted structure about the size of a two-car garage, with a flat roof extending over one side to cover an adjoining caged area. LeAnne got out of the car. Two dogs lay on their sides in the cage, not close together. Their eyes were on her, but they didn't bark or get up.

LeAnne opened the passenger door. "Let's go."

The dog remained motionless, sitting tall, eyes straight ahead.

"Ride's over. We're done."

No response. LeAnne tapped the roof of the car.

"Move it."

The dog did not move. Meanwhile, the door to Can-Am Animal Care and Control opened with a high-pitched squeak of hinges that aroused the background ache in LeAnne's head, not gone after all. The noisemaker was a bearded man in stained overalls, lighting a cigarette. He tossed away the match and noticed her.

"Help you?" he said.

LeAnne was not in the mood for bearded men. "I've got a stray."

The man took a deep drag on his cigarette, let the smoke curl slowly from his nostrils. He checked out the dog through LeAnne's windshield. "Bring it in."

"It's a she," LeAnne said. And then to the dog. "Out. Now." She used her command voice, the one that scared the shit out of new recruits. The dog did not react at all.

"The balky type, huh?" said the man, coming closer. His beard was the untrimmed kind, nicotine-stained in places.

"I wouldn't know about that," LeAnne said. "I don't know anything about this dog — or any dog." The man was giving her a squint-eyed look, like he doubted her word, so LeAnne added, "She just turned up last night — no collar, no tags."

The man said: "What the hell happened

to you?"

"What did you say?"

The man motioned with his bearded chin. "Like, your face. You in a car wreck or something?"

This man, that remark, the beard — all of it together started to uncap something in LeAnne that could only act in ways that were once and for all. She wheeled on the man — her height, broader, but also paunchy and out of shape — and focused on his neck, totally unprotected, with a prominent Adam's apple ripe for crushing, stiffened her hands, and —

And that was when the dog rose and sort of ambled out of the car, moving around LeAnne and standing on her blind side, facing the man. For some reason, this development knocked LeAnne off the track she was barreling down, and she got that inner cap back in place.

"What happened to me is none of your goddamn business," she said.

LeAnne knew a lot of tough men, so many that maybe she'd forgotten they weren't all like that. In fact, most were probably like this guy, who now looked alarmed, raised both hands in surrender position, cigarette ash falling on his pouter pigeon chest, and said, "Whoa! Sorry — no offense."

LeAnne laughed in his face. The sound of her laughter — or possibly something else, or simply nothing — made the dog start growling. LeAnne turned on her. "Shut up."

The dog went silent at once.

The man, who'd retreated a step or two, said, "Look, lady, I gotta be honest with you. Nobody's gonna take a dog like yours."

"She's not mine. How many times do —"

"A dog like this one, excuse me. We can keep her here for five days, but —"

"Five? I heard seven."

"All right, seven, for all the difference it'll make."

"Aren't there farms around here, ranches?" LeAnne said. "She could guard, herd sheep, that kind of thing."

The man shook his head. "Takes a trained animal to do that. This ain't a trained animal, never will be. We're not lookin' at a puppy here. What's more, I'd say she got herself a little twisted inside, probably from coming up rough."

"What are you talking about?"

He made that chin-pointing motion again, this time at the dog. "Check out the tail."

LeAnne looked at the dog's tail. Thick but not long, as she'd noticed already, although too long to be called stubby. At the moment the dog had it raised high, the first time Le-

Anne had seen it that way. "What about it?" she said.

"Tail like that's not natural."

"You mean it's been cropped?"

"Some folks do crop the tail, but on account of what you might call esthetic preference. This ain't that."

"I don't get it." *And don't fucking point with your chin one more goddamn time.*

But he did. "A cropped tail is way shorter. This is more like somebody got pissed off and swung an ax. See how ragged the end is? Cropping's more surgical." He shot a very quick glance at LeAnne's face, looked away.

"Someone cut off her tail with an ax?"

"Or an act of that nature. It happens, and not only out here in the country, neither."

By now the dog had stopped growling and just stood there. She might have been in a trance. "What about we just let her go?" LeAnne said.

"How would that work, exactly?"

LeAnne shrugged. "I drive off. You go back inside."

"No can do," the man said. "Speakin' just for me. I get paid to do a job, do it right. You do what you have to do."

"She stays here," LeAnne said.

"Gotcha," said the man. He ground the

cigarette under his boot heel, rubbed his hands together. "First things first, let's see if she's got a chip in her — chances about one in a thousand, I'd say." He took a device the size of a TV remote from an overalls pocket and approached the dog. The dog went stiff, muscles bunching in her back, and bared her teeth; the incisors seemed shockingly long to LeAnne.

"Probably reacting to scanning sounds we can't hear," the man said, taking another step. "Not gonna hurt you, big girl."

The dog snarled.

"Maybe she'll let you do it," the man said.

"Why?"

"Can't hurt to try."

"Can't hurt you."

"Heh heh." The man handed her the scanner. "Run it over her back."

LeAnne moved in with the scanner. The dog stopped snarling, stopped showing her teeth. LeAnne ran it back and forth.

"No dice, like I thought," the man said. "Let's go inside, get her in the cage, take care of the paperwork. She'll follow you."

LeAnne and the man headed toward the shelter door. The dog did not follow.

"Hey," LeAnne called to her. "Come on."

The dog sat.

"Wait here," the man said. He went inside,

came out with a long metal pole that had a knob at one end and a cable loop at the other. A strange-looking thing until LeAnne realized that "noose" was more accurate than "loop." The man approached the dog indirectly, like he was headed someplace else, and then with surprising speed spun around and thrust the pole forward, sliding the noose around the dog's neck. The dog jerked back right away, but the man did something with the knob on his end of the pole and the noose tightened.

The dog hated that — the first clear emotion LeAnne had seen in those shiny-coal eyes. She twisted around, tried to run, tried to attack the man, tried to pull herself free — and almost did, actually dragging him partway across the parking lot. He stumbled, lost his balance, fell to one knee but did not lose the pole. From down on the ground he yanked on it with what looked like all his strength, a vicious expression now on his hairy face, an expression that had nothing to do with a professional on the job. The dog let out a sound LeAnne had never heard before, a sort of howl with the power of a roar. The man twisted the pole hard to one side and the cable sank into the dog's neck, choking the sound down to one miserable last yelp.

The next thing LeAnne knew she had the man by the shoulders. She shook him so hard his head snapped back, and screamed, "Stop!" over and over at the top of her lungs.

Chapter Twenty

Is this your dog? was in big letters at the top of the flyer Dot printed up. Then came a photo of the dog, and under that Dot had written, *Large black female mix, no tags. Found in Bellville, east side. Call* — and following a bit of a dispute, Dot had added her own number.

"Why not yours?" she'd said.

"Don't have a phone," LeAnne had told her.

"How come?"

"I just don't."

"Thought I heard one ringing in your car just a few minutes ago."

LeAnne glanced through the Shady Grove office window at the Honda parked outside. The dog sat in the front passenger seat, eyes straight ahead. For a moment, LeAnne couldn't remember what she'd done with the prepaid cell phone, but then she recovered a mental image of it arcing down into a roadside ditch. "Not possible."

"Okeydoke," Dot said. "We'll put my number, but you're gonna have to make all the arrangements."

"I'll make the arrangements," LeAnne said.

She took the flyers, got into the car, and sat there for a minute or so, feeling a bit dizzy. The dog took no notice of her, continued gazing straight ahead in a very alert way.

"I threw the stone *at* you, you stupid fuck. It had nothing to do with fetch."

Initial Evaluation for Post-Traumatic Stress Disorder:
Post-Military Psychosocial Adjustment:

5. Degree and quality of social relationships:

LeAnne pulled out of the Shady Grove lot. She drove around Bellville, stapling fliers to telephone poles, a bulletin board outside a supermarket, where the only space was beside a Missing Child poster, and another one outside the police station where the Missing Child poster thing happened again. The same missing child? LeAnne hadn't really noticed the photo on the first one.

The Missing Child poster outside the police station showed a smiling girl, eight or nine, with pigtails and a combination of baby teeth, adult teeth, and no teeth.

LeAnne got back in the car. The dog didn't look at her but did open her mouth wide. A yawn? Did dogs yawn? Or was it something else, some signal a dog person would know how to read?

"Hungry, maybe?"

The dog closed her mouth, went on gazing straight ahead. LeAnne drove back to the supermarket, bought various kinds of dog food, a dog bowl, a dog collar, a dog leash, and some food for herself. Back in cabin six they ate, LeAnne a sandwich of cold cuts and then another, when she realized how hungry she was, and the dog two bowls of kibble, a bowl of some sort of moist canned stuff, and a bone-shaped biscuit.

"That's got to be enough, right?"

The dog licked the bowl a few times, then went into the bathroom and slurped the toilet dry.

"Remind me to get you a water bowl," LeAnne said. She lay down on the bed. "Jesus Christ, listen to me. I've lost my mind." She fell asleep in seconds, woke up with a start, remembering how she'd left the bedding, all puke-stained, saw that it had been changed — meaning Dot had changed it — and went back to sleep.

A radio played German music. LeAnne knew it was German because she kept hearing the word *liebe.* "Liebe" was German for love. A stream of unintelligible lyrics flowed by and then would come a liebe, and back to incomprehension. While she waited for the next liebe there was nothing to do but gaze at the wastebasket in the corner, overflowing with bloody bandages, or possibly towels, with more blood that had leaked out of the bottom of the wastebasket and pooled on the black-and-white squared floor. She would have preferred some other view, but didn't seem able to move her head, like maybe it liked that view and had decided to overrule her.

Meanwhile, a man was asking annoying questions.

"How's the pain?"

"Huh?"

He spoke more clearly. "How is the pain?"

"You tell me."

"That we can't do, I'm afraid. Remember the pain scale we talked about?"

"No."

"With zero as no pain at all, a day at the

beach, and ten as the worst, unbearable."

"Like crucifixion."

"Well, yes. Um, is that where you are?"

"No."

"So where are you, one to ten?"

"Minus."

"Minus?"

"What I said."

"Meaning less than no pain?"

"Uh-huh."

"I'm not sure I —"

A woman interrupted. "Doctor? There's a visitor outside. Can I show her in?"

"What visitor?"

"Her mother."

"Did you hear that, LeAnne? Your mother's here to see you. How about we get you comfortable and —"

"Are you crazy? Don't let her fucking see me like this! Are you crazy? Are you crazy?"

LeAnne rolled over, her head getting sheared in half — and there was the dog, lying on the bed beside her. The coal-black eyes were open, seemed to be watching her intently. LeAnne calmed down a little. She just lay there. So did the dog.

"I feel so goddamn . . ." LeAnne couldn't find the words.

The dog went on staring at her.

"Go get me a glass of water and some ibuprofen." No reaction from the dog, of course. "If you could do shit like that I might change my mind." LeAnne turned onto her back, closed her eye. The fake eye closed along with it. She wasn't blind. You couldn't even call her half blind, not with one eye working perfectly. Meaning not that bad, get a fucking grip. That bad was Jamie, for example, dead.

"Better be careful," she said. "I'll get you killed, too."

Somewhere outside a phone rang and rang.

Something felt good. It was moist and warm and nubby, kind of like a hot towelette they gave you sometimes on a long flight or at a Chinese restaurant. Except it wasn't hot. She awoke with a start. The dog was licking the side of her face; the bad side.

LeAnne sat up, scrambled off the bed. "What the fuck?"

The dog opened her mouth wide, maybe doing the yawn thing again, this time a satisfied kind of yawn. Then she wriggled around a bit, like she was getting more comfortable.

"Try that again and so help me . . ." Then came an urge that had to do with axes. "Oh,

God." Things were going on in her head that weren't her. That was the scariest part of all this. LeAnne went into the bathroom, intending to wash off where the dog had licked, but forgot about that when she caught sight of herself in the mirror. What had become of her body? So bony, so skinny, like all her strength was gone. She hadn't contained the damage and how could you even start regrouping until the damage was contained? Wakil Razaq Salam was still destroying her. He was dead but somehow winning, and she was losing.

Was she a loser? Had she been a loser her whole goddamn life and not known it? Losing was unacceptable, the only exception being those times when you'd put up your very best fight. LeAnne got dressed — jeans, T-shirt, Marci's red sneaks. "We're going for a run," she said. The dog jumped off the bed and trotted to the door. "You know 'run,' huh?" The dog rose up, got a paw on the doorknob. "Don't even think about it. And you're wearing the leash."

The dog remained in position, on her hind legs, front paw on the doorknob. LeAnne went into the kitchen, got the collar and leash off the counter, returned to the front door.

"No bullshit about this."

The dog slid down from the door, trotted over, and sat in front of LeAnne.

"Collar first," she said, ripping off the price tag, draping the collar over the dog's neck — so thick and strong — and buckling it underneath. She was testing the snugness when the dog suddenly leaned in and licked LeAnne's face again; again on the bad side, meaning she didn't see it coming.

"Fucking hell!" LeAnne backhanded the dog across the side of her head, good and hard. "What did I tell you?"

She felt an inner surge of adrenaline, her body readying for some sort of attack. Nothing like that happened. The dog continued to sit before LeAnne, the coal-black eyes on her but expressionless, at least as far as LeAnne could tell.

"Okay," LeAnne said, her voice thickening, as from a clogged throat, "we're good then." She clipped the leash to the collar and opened the door. The dog squeezed through first. By then LeAnne was already wishing that the dog had attacked her; well, maybe not attacked, but at least barked or growled.

A dirt track began at the end of the white crushed-stone path and continued past the end of the pond and into some woods. The dog wouldn't walk beside LeAnne, stayed out in front as far as she could, straining on the leash. LeAnne knew there was a command for getting dogs to walk at your side, but she couldn't think of it and didn't really care. Why was it important? *Just don't lick my fucking face.*

The track rose up a gentle slope and from the top continued straight and level for as far as LeAnne could see, orchards of blossoming trees on both sides. A light rain started to fall, felt good on her skin. LeAnne dropped the leash. "Let's see what we can do."

She started running. LeAnne was a good runner. Pole vaulters had to be fast, as she'd told those Afghan girls. Or maybe she hadn't told them, merely had the thought. There'd been six of them. She could see every face, but not a single name would come to her. LeAnne tried to get past her frustration by picking up the pace and found she could not pick up the pace. She was huffing and puffing from practically the very first step, and also developed a stitch in her side, which she couldn't even identify at first, never having had one. Meanwhile, no dog. LeAnne glanced back. The dog sat where LeAnne had left her.

"Come on, for Christ sake — what's

wrong with you?"

The dog turned in the other direction and ran off, trailing the leash.

"Fine! Suit yourself!"

LeAnne put her head down and kept going. She was a goddamn good runner, in fact, had once run the Soldier Half Marathon at Fort Benning in 1:42. So what was happening now? The stitch got worse; she couldn't catch her breath, had nothing in her legs; legs that all at once gave up completely and stopped even trying. Stopped even trying? That was shameful. LeAnne dropped down on the ground and started in on push-ups, just to show her goddamn legs what her arms could do. Give me twenty-five! Give me thirty! That one counts negative! More!

LeAnne did three push-ups, the last one unacceptable by any standard.

She stayed where she was, lying facedown on the dirt track. The rain was falling harder. Her T-shirt clung to her bony back. She was losing, no doubt about that. She was still losing the war in Afghanistan. Maybe some politician would happen along and save her.

Then came the warm, moist, nubbly feeling on her face. The dog was back on the scene, appearing silently from wherever she'd gone, and once again licking the bad side. This time LeAnne didn't stop her.

She got to her feet. Now the dog was just standing there, rain puddling around them. The leash, still connected to the dog's collar, lay on the ground. The dog snapped it up between her teeth and came closer, swinging her head back and forth, brandishing the leash, giving orders. There was no other interpretation possible.

"I had a drill sergeant a lot like you," LeAnne said. She took the leash, and they continued on the long straightaway. "Except not nearly so good looking."

Very soon, the dog had had enough of walking side by side and bounded ahead, straining at the leash. LeAnne tried running again. The dog helped, partly by pulling her along, but after what must have been a few hundred yards — meaning much farther than her first attempt — LeAnne began to suspect there was more than that to this little resurgence. Something the dog had deep inside was making its way down the leash and sharing itself with her. How was that possible? Did life run on some sort of magic rules that she'd missed the whole time? All LeAnne knew was that strength from the dog had passed into her own legs, and although she didn't come close to running the way she used to run — and this performance wasn't even respectable — she was doing better. LeAnne almost reached the end of the straightaway before she had to stop. The dog didn't get the message and, tearing the leash right from her hand, kept going.

LeAnne bent over, hands on her knees, getting her breath back. The rain fell harder, matting down her hair, running in her eyes. Her eyes: that was funny, to think of them now as a pair. But the rain was running into her eyes, making them feel good, both of them. She straightened up, looked around for the dog, spotted her trotting through a cemetery abutting an orchard beside the track.

"Hey! Come here."

The dog, maybe one hundred yards away, stopped running immediately, turned in LeAnne's direction.

"Come."

The dog didn't move, just stood there watching her.

"I don't understand you."

LeAnne left the track and entered the cemetery, an unfenced cemetery with no clear boundaries. The dog trotted away, in an unconcerned sort of disobedience. Le-

Anne made her way through gravestones, old and eroded at first and then newer, a hodgepodge of shapes and sizes, some flat, some vertical, most unattended although here and there lay dried-up bouquets. A few rows ahead she spotted a small clean white stone with fresh flowers at its base. LeAnne walked over to it. The flowers were roses, pink and white, wrapped in plastic. The bouquet leaned against a round bronze marker sticking out of the ground on one side of the grave stone, with a US star in the center and around it the stamped words Iraq War Veteran. On the other side of the stone stood a small American flag, maybe two feet high, drooping in the rain.

The name on the stone itself was Cpl. Marci Cummings. Then came Marci's dates, an engraved rose, and this: *Daughter, Mother, Patriot. She gave all.*

The dog came over from wherever she'd been, sniffed around, and began digging into the wet grass a foot or two from Marci's stone.

"Don't do that," LeAnne said, not loudly.

The dog stopped at once, one paw still in the air.

"I won't hit you again," LeAnne said. "That's a promise."

Chapter Twenty-One

Back in cabin six at Shady Grove, LeAnne found a steel mixing bowl in a kitchen cupboard, repurposed it as a water bowl, and set it beside the dog. The dog ignored it so completely LeAnne wasn't even sure she'd noticed the bowl or smelled the water, which had to be one of her abilities, didn't it?

"Water. Nice and fresh. Drink."

The dog turned and moved out of the kitchen. LeAnne heard the sound of her claws *tack-tack-tack*ing into the bedroom and beyond. Then came frantic slurps from the toilet, on and on, the franticness increasing.

LeAnne left the cabin, checking that the door was closed firmly behind her, and walked up to the office. Dot was folding towels by a laundry basket.

"Thanks for . . . for changing the bedding."

"You're welcome," Dot said in a matter-of-fact voice, no detectable overtones of disapproval or curiosity. "Anything I can help you with?"

"Yeah," LeAnne said. And then for some reason couldn't remember what it was. That led to a strange silence. Dot kept folding towels. LeAnne picked up a whiff of fabric softener. "I'd like to buy some flowers."

"Flowers you can pick yourself in these parts — lots of buttercups out right now, other side of the pond."

"I was thinking of roses," LeAnne said, now fully back on track.

"Roses," said Dot, in a tone that seemed to savor the very idea. "For roses you could try the supermarket." She folded another towel, laid it in the basket. Her hands looked older than the rest of her, veined and liver-spotted. "Planning to stay for long? No problem if you are — it's just that I had a customer asking about number six for the weekend."

"What day is it?"

Dot's eyes shifted toward the bad side of LeAnne's face for some small fraction of a second. "Thursday."

"I guess it depends," LeAnne said.

"On what?"

"On what?" LeAnne's voice started amp-ing itself up, but this time — maybe for the first time in a long while, she heard it herself, and amped it back down. "The dog. Any calls come in?"

"Claiming the pooch? Not a one."

"Then I'll be staying, unless you can think of some other solution."

"Such as?"

"Maybe you know someone who wants a dog."

Dot shook her head.

LeAnne turned to leave, paused. "Is this the kind of town where everybody knows everybody?"

"Not really. We're bigger than that. So maybe there could be a prospect — I'm just saying among the folks in my circle there's none."

"Do you know a family named Cummings?"

"Nope. Have you got a lead?"

"This is something else. What about Marci Cummings? Corporal Marci Cummings?"

"Uh-uh."

"She's from here," LeAnne said.

"A friend of yours?"

"She died."

Dot stopped in mid-fold. "Was this recently?"

"Yes."

"Wait a minute." Dot went to her desk, fished around through the wastebasket, came up with a crumpled newspaper, the local giveaway kind that was mostly about coupons. She returned to LeAnne, flipping through the pages. "Here we go, the *Bellville Bell,* last week's edition."

LeAnne took the paper, and at the bottom of an inner page saw a blurry photo of Marci in uniform, complete with black beret, looking tough and serious. Beneath it was an article she and Dot read together, Dot on her tiptoes, peering over LeAnne's shoulder.

> Funeral services will be held today at 11 a.m. at McCutcheon's Funeral Home in the Woods for US Army Corporal Marci Cummings of Bellville. Corporal Cummings, 31, died at Walter Reed National Military Medical Center in Bethesda, MD, of wounds suffered in Iraq. She was a graduate of Bellville High School, where she was the first female to ever join the wrestling team, winning numerous matches in her varsity career. Corporal Cummings is survived by her mother, Coreen, and daughter, Mia, both of Bellville.

"The wrestling part rings a bell, now that I think on it," Dot said. "It made a bit of a stir at the time."

"That sounds right," LeAnne said.

"I happen to know the pastor at the McCutcheon's Funeral Home," said Dot. "Supposing you wanted to look up the mom, for example."

Looking up the mom? Was that the purpose of the trip?

1. Strengthen hip flexors.
2. Life fucking goes on.
3. Get LeAnne to visit when I'm back "home."

Yes: time to look up the mom.

First, she had to go back to cabin six to check on the dog. This was a lot like being on duty. The dog was standing directly on the other side of the door, her food bowl in her mouth.

"For Christ sake — didn't we just do that?"

The dog pressed the bowl against LeAnne's hip.

"I get it."

LeAnne poured kibble into the bowl. The tinny sounds of the kibble chunks plinking into the bowl made her feel hungry herself, like some mixed-up signal was going on. They ended up eating together, LeAnne at the kitchen table with a ham and cheese sandwich, the dog on her right, head lowered over the bowl in a single-minded way.

"Why are you always on that side?" LeAnne said.

The dog made munching noises.

LeAnne rose, stretched, and came very close to going into the bedroom and lying down. What was wrong with her? She could ruck march for twenty miles in broken country and carry on afterward as though she'd spent the day at a desk. *Shape up! Demand more from your stupid, lazy self!*

LeAnne walked out of cabin six. Licking-the-bowl sounds followed her outside, right through the walls. She'd almost reached the car when there was a tremendous thud inside the cabin. LeAnne turned back. Another thud, this time actually bending the door. LeAnne opened it. The dog was winding up to do it again.

"Get in the goddamn car."

The dog ambled peacefully out of the cabin, trotted over to the front passenger door, and stood there, calm and patient.

"You're not fooling anybody."

■ ■ ■ ■

LeAnne followed the map Dot had drawn for her: back into town, across the bridge to the flat side, and into a neighborhood of simple, one-story houses on small lots, a kind of neighborhood she'd often seen near military bases, where people were just getting by. She came to Apple Street, turned left, stopped in front of 136, a small *L*-shaped house with the foot of the *L* for the garage, and a willow tree with a swing hanging from a thick horizontal branch about fifteen feet up. A police cruiser sat in the driveway; Sheriff's Department read the badge on the door. The dog began to pant. LeAnne parked on the other side of the street, leaned over, and cracked the dog's window open a few inches. Not the dog's window, for God's sake. Her window. This was her car.

"Don't get used to anything."

The door to 136 Apple Street, which fronted the driveway, opened and a uniformed cop came out. The dog began barking furiously and tried to stick her head out the window.

"Knock it off!"

The cop glanced over, got in the cruiser,

and drove off. The dog kept barking until the cruiser was out of sight, then slowly lowered the volume down to a sort of harrumphing.

"You're staying in the car. You're shutting up. You're being good." LeAnne got out, crossed the street, and knocked on the door at 136. She glanced back. The dog had stuffed pretty much her whole muzzle, and one eye and one ear, through the gap in the opened window; slobber slid down the glass. "What the hell do you —"

LeAnne heard footsteps on the other side of the door. It opened and a woman looked out. The woman was an older, smaller, less pretty version of Marci; the voluptuous mouth was identical. Her eyes — hazel like Marci's, but maybe not so intelligent — looked tense and worried.

"Hello," LeAnne said. "I —"

The woman's eyebrows rose. "LeAnne, wasn't it?"

LeAnne stepped back. "I'm LeAnne, but —"

"You don't remember me? I'm Marci's mom."

"Right, but —"

"I met you when I came to visit. Visit Marci at Walter Reed."

LeAnne shook her head, not denying what

Marci's mom was saying, just simply in confusion. She was still losing, and worse than she'd thought.

"Well, it must have been the meds," Marci's mom went on. "If you've come for the service — and how nice of you — I'm afraid you missed it." Marci's mom covered her mouth with both hands. "But . . . but maybe you don't know that she . . ."

"I know," LeAnne said.

Marci's mom reached out, took one of LeAnne's hands in both of hers. "Thank you for coming anyway. And it's good to see you looking so so much better." She gave LeAnne a close look. "Did they . . . save the eye after all? I must have misunderstood."

"It's a fake."

"Which one?" said Marci's mom, her gaze steadily on the fake. "I can hardly tell."

"It doesn't matter," LeAnne said. "I just want to say I'm sorry about Marci."

"Thank you. Thank you. My name's Coreen, which you probably don't remember, either. Well, certainly not, now that I think, if you don't recall the visit. My mind's not at its best these days. But please come in." And she drew LeAnne inside the house, closing the door behind her. A dog barked, very distant, so not her dog, nothing to worry about. *Her* dog? Christ. No fucking way. LeAnne took her place on a window seat in a little sunroom at the back of the house.

"We tend to gravitate to this room," Coreen said, filling two glasses with iced tea from a can. "It was always Marci's favorite, so full of light."

At the moment, it was dark and shadowy. Rain fell steadily outside, making puddles in a small lawn that was mostly dirt, bordered on three sides by a fence; a weathered wooden fence that had a bicycle leaning against it. Streamers dangled from the handle grips.

"So, um, forgive me if I sound stupid," Coreen said, pulling up a footstool. "All these things, one after another. But am I right in thinking you and Marci didn't know each other before Walter Reed?"

"You are."

"You weren't in that horrible IE whatever it was attack?"

"IED," LeAnne said. "I was not."

Coreen raised her glass, took a sip of tea. "What kind of people would do something like that? On top of all the horror, it's just so . . . careless. Suppose a child stepped on it?"

Careless was exactly the word. They just didn't care. Or maybe they cared so much about something else that all the other normal cares shrank down to nothing. "I don't know the answers," LeAnne said. But at that exact same moment she remembered the names that went with the faces of the six pole-vaulting girls: Wrashmin, Durkhani, Hila, Muska, plus the two Lailas. Then came the kind of horrible possibility that could only occur to two types of people: those that would dream it up and those who would try to stop them before it happened — the "it" being planting IEDs under the padded safety mats in the pole vault landing pit.

"A dumb question, I apologize," Coreen was saying. "And Marci would have been peeved with me. I can just hear her — 'I knew the risks, Ma.' She was proud to serve. I have to admit it was quite an adjustment for me — not the women in the military part per se, but the combat zone aspect."

LeAnne tried to absorb that, but her mind was preoccupied with a vision of the man with prominent ears, watching the pole-vaulting lesson from a rooftop. She glanced around the room, her gaze landing on a photo on the wall behind Coreen — Marci, maybe from ten or twelve years before, on her wedding day: strapless white dress, kind of low cut for a wedding dress, and somehow all the more lovely for that. The groom was looking at her in adoration — no other word for it. He seemed even younger than she was, about Marci's height, slim, and kind of homely faced in a way that somehow got more and more pleasing the longer she gazed at his image.

"That's Harvey," said Coreen, twisting around. "Her first husband."

Hubby numero uno loved the rain. And me.

"She mentioned him."

"Marci was the love of his life. He's been such a huge help."

"How do you mean?"

"The funeral arrangements. All the paperwork. Getting her . . . her poor body back home." Coreen had a tissue tucked under her sleeve. She took it out and dabbed at her eyes. "Did Marci tell you he'd never remarried?"

LeAnne shook her head. "She didn't tell me a whole lot about her past."

"No, that wouldn't be her," Coreen said. "But she spoke highly of you."

"She did? When was this?"

"During my visit. I only stayed two days — had a lot on my plate back here, which turned out not to be the half of it — and the doctor said — promised me! — that she was going to be fine and ambulatory in no time. You were in the room for that conference, as I recollect." Coreen gazed at her. Whatever she saw — confusion, annoyance, anger — made her look away. "Maybe you were asleep. The point is I wasn't there for her at the very most critical time. And what good did I do here?" Coreen clasped her hands together, lowered her head, kind of folding herself up small.

LeAnne rose, went closer, thought about touching Coreen's shoulder. "What could you have done? It happened in a hospital."

"I'm sorry," Coreen said. "And with you coming all this way." She looked up — surprised and maybe a little frightened to find LeAnne so near. "Marci said you're a hero."

"Far fucking — far from it," said LeAnne, stepping back. "Thanks for seeing me." She stepped back some more. "I won't keep you any longer."

Coreen dabbed at her eyes again. "Oh, please don't go. I'll stop embarrassing myself, I swear."

"You're not embarrassing yourself."

"It's just nice to see someone who was with Marci." Coreen smiled, a wavering, unhappy smile that didn't stick. "A roommate, after all. Tell me some of the things you talked about. Please, stay awhile."

LeAnne sat back down on the window seat. "Nothing, really. We pretty much just joked around."

"Really? Joked? That makes me happy to hear. That sense of humor of hers — so sharp."

"For sure," LeAnne said. Her gaze went again to the wedding photo. "How come they broke up?"

"Her and Harvey?" Coreen shook her head. "Marci . . . made a misjudgment. She was so young. Usually it's the woman who's more mature at that age, but not in this case. Did . . . she talk about her regrets? I only ask because she always put on a stoical face for me."

I fucked it up. "Regrets?" LeAnne said. "I don't know. She seemed pretty stoical to me, too. Wasn't that her?"

"On the outside, yes," said Coreen. "And maybe, over the years, on the inside too, more and more — especially after she got going in the military, and all. But deep down she was a very passionate person."

"Yes," LeAnne said.

"That's what got her into trouble."

"What kind of trouble?"

"Poor Marci. She fell for one of those macho men."

"This was her second husband?"

"Did she tell you about him?"

Numero dos was just what he looked like — a great big mistake. "Not really. Just the fact of his existence, more or less."

"It didn't last long, but long enough to —" A phone buzzed. Coreen whipped it out of a skirt pocket, held it to her ear with both hands. "Yes? . . ." Her face fell. "Just that the sheriff was here. But no news . . . thanks." She clicked off, repocketed the phone, looked up at LeAnne. "How much are we expected to bear, all at once?"

"What are you talking about?" LeAnne said.

"That was Harvey, actually. He's been out with a search party since before dawn — and he's not even the father."

"Is someone missing?"

"Mia."

"Who's Mia?"

"You don't know about Mia?"

"How the hell would I?" LeAnne's voice got loose and rose up. But maybe she should have known. Hadn't Marci mentioned that name? But in what context? LeAnne tried to remember, found nothing in her memory but the feel of Marci's kiss. "How would I?" she said, this time much more quietly.

"Mia's Marci's daughter," Coreen said. "She's been gone since the night of the funeral. Of course, you'd have no way of knowing — I'm so mixed up, I don't even —"

"Marci's daughter?" Facts stirred down deep in LeAnne's mind, like they were digging themselves up from under the ground.

Coreen pointed to a photo on the side wall, LeAnne's blind side, which was why she'd missed it. In the photo, Marci and a girl of eight or so were standing by the willow tree swing in Coreen's front yard, laughing their heads off. The girl had pigtails but more of her baby teeth than she'd had when the picture on the Missing Child poster was taken.

Chapter Twenty-Two

"I don't even know where to begin," Coreen said. "There's just been so many . . . what would you call them? Events? Anyway, how do you put them in order?" She picked up her tea. The liquid trembled in the glass.

Meanwhile, the bad side of LeAnne's face was suddenly very hot. She rubbed it with her hand. The feel of her hand was icy on her face, like the meeting of two different people.

"Maybe with the custody situation?" Coreen said, taking a sip. "That was a big event, for sure."

"The second husband was the father of the girl?" LeAnne said.

Coreen nodded. "Mia was four when they divorced, but the marriage was over long before then, certainly for Marci. She got full custody, not hard to do considering the abuse that went on."

"Abuse of Marci or Mia?"

"Marci. He — I wouldn't use the word *love* because I don't think he's capable of it — but he never harmed Mia."

"You're talking about physical abuse?"

"I'm afraid so. There were three incidents. Marci was too shocked the first time to really know what to do. The second time she warned him. The third time — this was out in an old hunting cabin of his family's, always too much boozing in a place like that — she left. Why are you shaking your head like that?"

Shaking her head? LeAnne had been unaware. She stopped at once, tried to figure out why she'd been doing it. "Because, um . . . because I can't see Marci taking any abuse from anyone. Not even once."

"Marci wasn't quite as tough then. This was before the army. But . . . but it wasn't only that. This might be a strange comment about my own daughter. Maybe I should just say she was head over heels and leave it at that."

"I'm not following you."

"Or that she was wild about him, another way of putting it. Wild sexually — there, I've said it. She had his name tattooed on her back before she'd actually left Harvey, if you can believe a thing like that. She —"

"What was the name?"

"Excuse me?"

"On her back."

"Max. Max Skelly, but she just did the Max part. And she made a sort of funny pun about it, but I didn't see the humor, especially since Marci had always said she'd never get a tattoo of any kind."

"To the Max," LeAnne said.

"You've seen it, then?"

"Yes."

"Did Marci say anything about it?"

It wasn't funny the first time. "No," LeAnne said. "Not that I understood. Why didn't she have it removed?"

"That's expensive," Coreen said.

"There must have been more to it than that."

Coreen nodded. "I brought it up once, gingerly, you might say. She told me she wasn't about to Photoshop her own life. I'm actually not sure I ever quite understood what she meant, to this day."

LeAnne had never admired Marci more than at that moment. She gazed down at her feet, meaning down at the red shoes. "How did the army come into her life?"

"Another big event," Coreen said. "Marci couldn't find any sort of decent-paying work, so she enlisted when Mia was old enough for kindergarten. I took care of Mia during basic training and a few other times like that, but mostly they lived together wherever Marci was based. Until she got posted overseas. Then I had Mia again."

"Who took care of her when you went to Walter Reed? Or . . . or did you bring her with you?" Meaning, LeAnne thought, have I seen Mia before? Had there been something familiar about the face on that Missing Child poster? She was back in the rubble pile section of her brain.

"That was one of the very first questions the sheriff asked me," Coreen said. "The answer is that my sister drove up from Boise and stayed here with Mia. All Mia really knew was that her mom was recovering from being hurt and would be home soon. I never got to the part about the . . . the nature of the injury, and so forth."

"Because you wanted to consult Marci first?"

Coreen looked up. "Are you an officer in the army?"

"I'm not in the army."

"I meant when you were."

"Negative."

"I didn't mean to offend you," Coreen said. "It's just that you're very smart."

"Enlisted soldiers can be as smart as

anybody else. Marci herself, for example."

"Oh, she was smart, for sure. But in a different way from you."

LeAnne wasn't interested in pursuing that line of talk. The truth was that intelligence didn't rank at the top of human characteristics that mattered to her, not even close. "What did Marci say when you had that conversation?"

"About her poor leg?"

LeAnne nodded, just the slightest nod. She didn't dare speak: that little phrase — *poor leg* — had uncapped a flood inside her, and the instant she spoke, her voice was going to crack and tears would flow and she'd be making a hideous spectacle of herself.

"I'm sorry to tell you we didn't get around to it," Coreen said. "The Walter Reed visit didn't . . . didn't go well. I kept putting my foot in it, no matter what I tried. Whatever I said only seemed to set her off, make things worse instead of better. Why couldn't I have done better? And now Mia's up and gone — up and gone while in my care."

Inside LeAnne the flood receded. "Up and gone?" she said.

"Sometime during the night after the funeral. I lay down with her at bedtime so she wouldn't be alone — poor kid has nightmares at the best of times — and didn't go to my own room until she was asleep. In the morning her window was open and she was gone. Tell me what kind of a mother and grandmother I am, for not doing better?"

LeAnne had no idea. Maybe Coreen was right and she should have done better. Maybe it was an impossible situation. This was all so complicated. LeAnne latched on to one little fact before it disappeared. "She has nightmares?"

Coreen, maybe about to burst into tears, pulled herself together and nodded. "Not every night. She's basically a happy kid, by day. But she's also very imaginative, and I think that combined with her mother being away — away and in danger . . ." Coreen went silent.

"What kind of nightmares?" LeAnne said.

"She never remembers in the morning. But sometimes in her sleep I hear her sort of . . ." The tears came flowing now, unstoppable. ". . . sort of crying, 'Mommy, Mommy.' " Coreen lowered her head and sobbed and sobbed, making awful cawing sounds, unbearable to LeAnne. But LeAnne did not go over, did not consider touching her shoulder. That hadn't helped the first time. What the hell was she supposed to do? She was trying to think of some practical response, when she heard scratching on the window behind her. She swung around and there was the dog, looking like a maniac, if dogs could be maniacs.

LeAnne stood up quickly. "Be right back." Coreen showed no sign of hearing her. LeAnne ran through the house to the front door, flung it open. Somehow the dog was there and waiting. At the sight of LeAnne, she sprang forward, as though to leap into LeAnne's arms, as a much smaller dog might do.

LeAnne came very close to catching the dog. For a moment, she had the big animal in her arms, but she staggered and lost her grip, her old strength just not there, plus the dog was wet and slippery. The dog hit the ground running — not a figure of speech: her legs were actually making bounding motions in midair — and raced into the house.

LeAnne fell against the door jamb, recovered her balance, and took off after the dog, through the living room and down the hall that led to the sunroom at the back of the house, where the sobbing seemed to have quieted down to crying and sniffling. The dog darted through the first open doorway she came to. LeAnne followed her through and slammed the door behind her.

They were in a kid's room — kid-type paintings on the walls, a soccer trophy or two, dollhouse in the corner — LeAnne with her back to the door and the dog darting around, her strange tail wagging.

"What the hell are you doing?"

The dog paid her no attention.

"You want to go to the shelter? Really? Think about it."

The dog went to the bed, snatched something off the pillow.

"Put that down."

LeAnne saw what was in the dog's mouth: a small stuffed animal, in fact, a dog. "I said put it down."

Instead, the dog shook her head back and forth in a very forceful way. LeAnne strode over to the bed and tried to grab the toy. The dog shifted away. LeAnne took hold of the collar. The dog didn't like that, started growling.

"Growl at me and you're done."

They exchanged a furious look. The dog stopped growling.

"Now give me that toy."

LeAnne seized on to one end of the stuffed dog — white, with round black eyes. The dog clamped her jaws shut and would not let go. One of the toy's black eyes came loose and fell to the floor. LeAnne took the dog by the collar and marched her out of the room. The dog did not resist, actually began walking down the hall and out of the house, but started up a new struggle at the door, all about trying to get around to LeAnne's right and LeAnne not letting her.

"Hey, there."

A voice came from the blind side. LeAnne whipped around, saw a man in a full suit of yellow rain gear coming the other way, and in that whipping-around motion, she lost her grip on the collar. The dog bolted away immediately, the toy dog flapping in her mouth.

"Fucking shit!" LeAnne glared at the man.

The man looked taken aback, although with the rain hood obscuring his face it was hard to tell. "Oh, sorry," he said. "I didn't mean to scare you."

"Scare me?" Who was this asshole? "Scare me?" By now the dog was trying to barge through a hedge several houses away on the other side of the street. LeAnne raised her voice. "Come here! Come here this second!"

The dog disappeared through the hedge, actually taking out a large portion of it.

"Wow!" said the man in the rain gear. He, too, raised his voice, a baritone, not unpleasing. "Here —" He glanced at LeAnne. "What's his name?"

"Her name. She's a she. And she has no name."

"No name?"

"What's your point?"

"No point. Might make it easier to call her, that's all." He raised his voice again. "Here, nice doggie. Come on back."

The dog did not appear. The man stuck his thumb and index finger in his mouth and whistled, maybe the loudest, shrillest human whistle LeAnne had ever heard. It split her head like a cleaver. She wanted to kill him, and was turning in his direction, all set to do she didn't even know what, when the dog popped into view far down the street, looking their way and standing in what might have been a questioning posture, head tilted to one side.

"Hey, come on back," the man said, not even very loudly. Without hesitation, the dog came charging down the street, her speed astonishing. She skidded to a stop on the wet pavement and sat at the man's feet, the toy dog still in her mouth.

"Who's a good girl?" the man said, squatting down and petting the top of the dog's big, square head. His hood fell back and LeAnne got her first good look at him. He had a homely face, although up close the only homely part was the nose, and even it wasn't so bad. He'd gotten better looking with age, if Marci's wedding photo could be trusted: this was Harvey. Meanwhile, he was talking to the dog. "How about Goody? You like that name?"

"For Christ sake," LeAnne said.

Harvey glanced up at her. "Isn't she a beauty? Did you just get her?" And at that moment he caught sight of her bad side; there was an almost imperceptible change in the expression of his eyes, vanishing at birth.

"Why do you ask that?"

He smiled. His teeth were on the small side, but white and even. "Just that you haven't given her a name yet." He rose and held out his hand. "I'm Harvey Wald."

"LeAnne Hogan." She shook his hand and added. "I know who you are."

"Yeah?" he said.

"Marci's first husband."

He looked past her to Coreen's house. "You were a friend of hers?"

LeAnne nodded.

He came real close to checking her face again; she could feel the hidden back-and-forth inside him. "From the military?"

"Correct."

"What a horrible thing," Harvey said. "I don't know the words."

They were in agreement on that. LeAnne kept silent. The rain fell harder.

"Not that I really even understand what happened to Marci," Harvey went on. "Meaning the whole story. Coreen's been a bit all over the place, not that I blame her. In fact, I was on my way to sit with her for a while — care to join me?"

"I already sat with her," LeAnne said.

"I hear you," said Harvey. "She's in a bad way. And the situation we've got now, on top of everything."

"You mean Mia? I don't get that part at all."

"It's baffling," Harvey said, pulling up his hood. "How about we get out of the rain?"

"I thought you liked the rain."

"Who told you that?"

LeAnne shrugged.

"Marci?"

She shrugged again.

"Your conversational style reminds me a bit of her," Harvey said.

"We can sit in my car," said LeAnne.

They sat in the Honda, LeAnne and Harvey in front, the dog in the back, stretched out and fast asleep, the toy dog beside her. Raindrops hit the hood and bounced, and the car steamed up inside.

"She was driving M35s on the Baghdad Airport Road, and she hit an IED," LeAnne said. "They just couldn't keep it clear back then. It's supposed to be better now."

"I know the IED part," Harvey said. "But she survived that."

"Not the way I see it."

"I meant she got home, or at least stateside. Did they make some kind of mistake at the hospital?"

"I don't know. All I remember . . ." LeAnne couldn't recall the facts of Marci's death, or how she'd learned of it. Marci's kiss was still out front, blocking the rest.

There was a long silence. She felt Harvey's gaze. He was in the passenger seat, and she sat behind the wheel. "You were there? At Walter Reed?"

"That's how I know Marci. Didn't I explain that already?"

More silence. Then he said, "The lousiest thing you can do is say, oh, if only I'd done this or that, she'd be all right. Beating yourself up but at the same time making it about you, if you see what I mean. Of course, I'm not talking about you personally."

"You're talking about you personally."

Harvey nodded. Then he tapped his fingers softly on the dashboard. Something about the contrast between the worn, scuffed plastic and his skin, so healthy and alive, caught her attention. "So," he said, "unless I'm misunderstanding, you only knew Marci in the hospital?"

"Correct."

"But you've come all this way."

"What are you saying?"

"Nothing. I'm just thinking out loud."

"Ever been in the military?" LeAnne said.

"No."

"What you're missing is how fast you get to know people in war."

"And the hospital is part of the war?"

"Christ," LeAnne said. "Isn't that obvious?"

"Probably should have been," Harvey said. "I don't know anything about war."

"Keep it that way," LeAnne said. "What do you do?"

"I'm a schoolteacher. That's how I got to know Mia. Mia was — she is in my class this year."

He began describing the time sequence — Marci's enlistment, she and Mia moving away to Fort Lewis, Marci getting the call-up, Mia coming back to live with Coreen — but LeAnne couldn't hold it together in her head. With Marci's whole backstory scattered all over the place, she tried to focus on what was absolutely central in the here and now.

"What's on your mind?" he said.

And for some reason, she told him. "I'm trying to focus on what's absolutely central in the here and now."

"Which would be finding Mia and bringing her home safe, right?" Harvey said.

"That's part of it."

"Only part?"

"Or maybe all. Maybe I'll get lucky and the rest will come automatically."

"You're losing me, LeAnne."

The truth was she'd sort of lost herself. For a moment or two she also lost all sense of where she was, or why. Her life stood on nothing solid, stood on nothing at all, like a magician's trick. Poof and gone. Poof was a kind of explosion, of course, so it couldn't have fit better.

And then — poof! — she got past the kiss and had a clear memory of Marci by the cherry blossom fountain, vivid all the way down to the taste of the apple brown betty liqueur. *What's her future if something happens to me? That's my biggest worry.*

And just like that, everything made sense, as though LeAnne had been following a script the whole time, the magic rules of life.

"I can feel you thinking," Harvey said.

Chapter Twenty-Three

LeAnne didn't explain herself to him. The point was how clearly she saw that finding Mia was all that mattered now. She hadn't understood anything so completely since . . . since before everything went bad. And maybe even before then: how well had she understood Katie, to take one example? But she didn't want to think about Katie, or all the doubts Stallings had tried to plant in her mind, or those six girls, or IEDs under the pole-vault pads. What could she do about any of that?

"Can I ask you something?" Harvey said. "None of my business, so if you want me to fuck right off, just say so."

LeAnne twisted around so she could see him. Would everything important always be happening on her blind side for the rest of her life? *However long that might be?*

" 'However long that might be?' " Harvey said. "I don't understand."

What the hell? She'd spoken that thought aloud? "Nothing. Forget it. I —" She paused, sniffed the air. "What smells in here?" Which was way off track — the track being all about finding Mia, thank God she had a firm grip on that — but her head hadn't stopped hurting since that whistle of Harvey's, and with the windows so steamed up she was feeling closed in; and now this smell on top of everything.

"Wet dog," Harvey said. "You don't seem to be a dog person."

"That's what you wanted to ask me about — the dog?"

"No. Well, yes, that too, as long as I don't forfeit the other question."

LeAnne twisted around even more so she could take a good long look at him. His nose was actually perfect, in a strange way.

He smiled. "You're scaring me a bit — like you've got X-ray eyes."

"Ha," said LeAnne, and she looked away. "The dog's a stray who's somehow become my responsibility. No one's claimed her, and her chances at the shelter are not too good. In the market for a dog, Harvey?"

"This isn't a good time," Harvey said. "I'm considering a job offer out of state, starting September."

"Where?"

"California — in the Anderson Valley, to be specific. Ever been there?"

"No."

"Heaven on earth."

LeAnne tried to get rid of the windshield condensation with the back of her hand, but all she did was make everything streaky. Through the streaks appeared a distorted world. "Marci had this theory about Iraq, all about hell being under the surface and sometimes popping through."

"And those pops are the IEDs?"

LeAnne nodded. Then came a silence, and when she looked at him again, there were tears on his cheeks. Too bad for him, but worse for Marci.

"Let's have your question," she said.

Harvey wiped his face on the sleeve of his rain jacket, only making everything wetter. "It's not really my place to —" There was a beep. He took a phone from his pocket, checked the screen, his attention turning outward right away. "They may have found something." Harvey zipped up his jacket and reached for the door handle.

"Where are you going?"

Harvey pointed with his chin at a pickup across the street, somehow missed by Le-Anne although it was right in front of Coreen's house. "My ride," he said.

"I'll take you," said LeAnne.

"There's my school," Harvey said after they'd turned off Apple Street and gone a few blocks east, meaning back toward the river. "That monkey bar set?" Harvey said. "Built and paid for by volunteers." He cleared his throat. "I designed it."

"Yeah?" Maybe it would have been polite to slow down for a good look, but LeAnne didn't think of that till they were past it.

"Well, not from scratch — I adapted something I saw on the internet."

LeAnne almost smiled. There was something about his tone — a combination of making fun of himself and pride — that she didn't recall hearing before from anybody.

"Does Mia play on it?" she said.

"She does, as a matter of fact. Mia's an athletic kid, goalie on the eight-year-old soccer team, runs like a deer. She used to do flips off the top bar until the principal stepped in."

"She's got athletic genes."

"On both sides, actually." The fun, or liveliness, or just plain pleasure in talking went out of Harvey's voice.

"Max — what's his last name again?"

"Skelly."

"— was an athlete, too?"

"Back in the day," Harvey said. He glanced over at her. "Max is ten or twelve years older."

"Older than who?"

"Me and Marci. Ten or twelve years older than Marci *was.* We were only twenty when we got married — kind of ridiculous, in retrospect."

"Why?"

"A little on the young side, don't you think?" Harvey said.

"That depends."

"On what?"

"On how long you end up living," LeAnne said. She didn't know what to make of Harvey: he seemed not in possession of some important facts about life, but she kind of liked him anyway.

"I hadn't thought of it that way," Harvey said. "I must seem stupid."

"Why do you say that?"

"Or maybe innocent is a better word, at least in contrast to you."

"How do you mean?"

"That's sort of in the territory of the question I was gearing up to ask," Harvey said. "You've obviously been through a lot."

"Obviously?" she said.

They came to a stop sign. LeAnne turned to face him. He looked afraid. That was good. "Obviously, like how?"

"Poor choice of words," he said. "I didn't mean obviously. I —"

LeAnne reached up to her right eye, her movement slow and deliberate, and then even more slowly and deliberately, she tapped it with the tip of her fingernail three times, making three hard clicks. "Obviously like this?" she said.

She'd come to the end of kind of liking Harvey, was swinging the other way and fast, but he surprised her. Harvey didn't flinch. He stopped looking afraid. Neither did he look shocked or disgusted. What was the best descriptor? Solemn? Something like that. He simply faced her right back in a solemn, homely way. "What can I do to help?" he said.

"I don't want any help," LeAnne said.

"Then that's what I'll do," Harvey said.

Had he meant that as a joke? Whether or not he had, LeAnne came close to smiling again. How was that possible? LeAnne had no idea. Someone honked behind her, a soft, small town kind of honk. The rain stopped falling. LeAnne drove on. She settled down inside.

They crossed the bridge to the hilly side of town. Down below, LeAnne saw some ducks gliding along with the current. She checked the rearview mirror: the dog, no longer asleep, was sitting up and looking in the same direction — down at the river, for sure — and in her alert mode.

Harvey turned toward the backseat and quietly, like he didn't want to disturb LeAnne, said. "Hey, big girl, what are you growling about?"

"She has a thing about ducks," said LeAnne.

Harvey gazed at the river. "She can see them from here? I didn't think dog vision was very good."

"She can see ducks. She can probably smell them, too, and God knows what else. She's living in a different world." LeAnne realized the truth of that last thought as she spoke it.

"Maybe you are a dog person after all," Harvey said.

"Definitely not," LeAnne said.

She followed Harvey's directions — across Main Street and into the nicest part of town she'd seen so far, but in no way fancy, instead similar to Coreen's neighborhood only with bigger houses and lots, and more trees. LeAnne spent the time trying to organize everything Coreen and Harvey had told her into some sort of neat arrangement, got pretty much nowhere. "Coreen says Mia has nightmares."

"First I've heard of that," said Harvey.

"And that she'd got a good imagination."

"For sure. I have the kids write a story every two weeks — no less than a page, no more than three — and hers are always the best."

"What are they about?" LeAnne said.

"Ghosts, mostly."

LeAnne stopped at a red light, thought about ghosts and Mia. After some time, Harvey said, "It's green." She drove through.

"How about the custody thing? I can't remember what you told me."

"The custody of Mia?" said Harvey. "I don't think we discussed it. But interesting that you'd bring it up."

"Why?" LeAnne said. But hadn't the subject of custody come up already? Maybe with Coreen? She wasn't sure. How could she organize what she couldn't remember?

"First of all," Harvey said, "Marci had full custody from the very beginning, meaning after their divorce."

"Was that what Max wanted?"

"I don't know. It never came up. Marci made sure of that. Plus Max had no visitation rights. Anything in that regard was at her discretion, and she allowed it hardly ever, and only with her present. None of that really mattered after Marci enlisted because she and Mia weren't around. I doubt Max has seen Mia in two years, maybe more."

"I don't get it."

"Which part?"

"The part about how Marci made sure of having her way."

"For that, you'd have to know something about their marriage. I actually wasn't aware of this myself until recently, but the fact is —"

"You're talking about the abuse?"

"Coreen told you?"

"Yes." LeAnne was sure of that. Abuse, and not just once but three times: she started getting angry.

"That's how I found out, too," Harvey said. "Marci managed to record the last incident on her phone — plus she took pictures of her face right after. Enough evidence to get Max in trouble with the law, but Marci couldn't bear going public. Instead, she held it over him and took Mia out of his life for good." He shook his head. "Marci — the one and only."

They came to a small, boarded-up train station. Beyond it, where the tracks had run, there was now a paved bike path.

"I'm getting the impression you forgave her," LeAnne said.

"For cheating on me?" said Harvey. "Oh, yes — years ago, in my heart. At the time, of course, I wasn't so cool about it. There's cheating in the abstract, which you can rationalize in all sorts of ways, and then there's how it goes down in your own life. For example, you've got to confront the specific issue of who the new person is. Kind of reflects on you." He pointed ahead. "Pull in there, beside the sheriff."

LeAnne parked beside a patrol car, directly opposite one of the station's boarded-up windows. A Missing Child poster was stapled to the plywood, the pigtailed girl now showing some resemblance to Marci, although the picture hadn't changed. LeAnne opened the door, intent on asking Harvey exactly what about Max reflected on him. Or had she missed his meaning? Before she could get any further with that, the dog leaped over the seat and out her door.

"Stop!" LeAnne jumped out of the car and shouted, "Come back here right now, you son of a bitch!"

The dog neither stopped nor came back, instead taking off down the bike path and disappearing around a bend.

" 'Son of a bitch' isn't quite right," Harvey said. He put his finger and thumb in his mouth, sucked in a deep breath. LeAnne held up her hand in the stop sign.

"But it worked the last time," Harvey said.

"Just don't."

LeAnne grabbed the leash, and she and Harvey headed down the bike path. On one side lay backyards, some of them semirural, with chickens pecking around and a goat or two. The other side was a dense head-high tangle of thorny scrub and undergrowth, sloping down to a marsh; mist hung in the lowest hollows.

"Who has custody now?" LeAnne said.

"Coreen. The lawyer wrote all that up before Marci got posted overseas."

"Isn't she a little old for a commitment like that?" LeAnne said.

"What choice is there?" Harvey kicked a stone off the path and into the scrub. "I wish the trains were still running," he said.

They rounded the bend where the dog had disappeared. Up ahead a tall, narrow pine rose on the scrubby side of the path, and under it stood three men with a dog sitting at their feet. Even at a distance LeAnne could see it wasn't her dog, putting it that way — *her dog* — just for convenience. This dog — similar in size, but lighter-colored and with a normal tail — wore a K-9 vest and had a sitting posture that spoke of training, obedience, being good. The men — two of whom had Sheriff's Department on the backs of their rain jackets — were all big, the biggest being the man in the unmarked jacket, who was really kind of enormous.

"Christ," Harvey said.

"Something wrong?" said LeAnne.

Harvey didn't answer. They walked up to the three men, each muddy from the knees down. One of them turned out to be the officer LeAnne had first seen coming out of Coreen's house. LeAnne didn't recognize the second officer, but hadn't she already seen the real big, round-faced guy with the shock of jet-black hair hanging over his forehead? She thought at once of Wakil Razaq Salam, kind of crazy since he was dead and hadn't looked at all like this man.

"Hey, Harvey," said the first officer.

"Hi, Sheriff," Harvey said. "What's up?"

"Not totally sure," the sheriff said, then turned to LeAnne and paused.

"This is LeAnne, a friend of Marci's from the army," Harvey said. "LeAnne, meet Sheriff Cosgrove and Deputy Lima." Harvey turned to the big man, looked up at him with no expression on his face. "And this gentleman is Max Skelly."

The big man's gaze — all their gazes, excepting Harvey's — were locked on her bad side. He said, "Pleasure," and nodded toward LeAnne in a proper sort of way.

Chapter Twenty-Four

Harvey wasn't a big guy and didn't look at all like the aggressive type, so LeAnne was surprised when he moved a little closer to Max and said, "What are you doing here, if you don't mind me asking?" Heavy on the sarcasm, that last part, almost like a dare.

"Drove up to help with the search," Max said, showing no sign of taking offense. "Mia is still my daughter, after all."

"Technically," Harvey said.

"I won't argue," Max said. "Arguing wastes time and in situations like this, time is critical, isn't that true, Sheriff?"

"Guys," said Sheriff Cosgrove. "Whatever this is, don't drag me in. The reason I called you, Harvey, is that you asked me to get in touch if anything came up."

"And?" Harvey said.

Deputy Lima spoke up. "Champ here might of picked up a scent."

"Mia's scent?" Harvey said.

The deputy nodded and took a plastic baggie from an inner pocket. Inside was a gym sock with a small hole in the toe. "This was on the floor in Mia's room. Champ gets a sniff or two every morning to keep her memory fresh. She alerted as soon as we started this sector today. Something's got her goin' down there." The deputy pointed to the scrubby side and on down to the marsh.

"But whatever it is, we can't find it," the sheriff said.

"Is Champ reliable?" Harvey said.

"As they come," Deputy Lima said.

"Then let's try again," Harvey said, moving into the undergrowth and getting his foot caught in a nest of brambles right away.

"Best to follow Champ," the deputy said. "She always knows the easiest —"

Something was moving in the scrub, partway down the slope to the marsh.

"Mia?" Harvey called. "Mia?"

But whatever was down there was bigger than a kid. The sheriff and the deputy both put their hands on the butts of their sidearms. Then came more noise and a furious sort of crashing around like big things were getting ripped apart, and a moment or two after that her dog — the expression LeAnne had adopted just for convenience — burst through the densest and spiniest thicket in the underbrush, just a few feet from an almost bare section that would have been a lot easier. She seemed to be headed on up the path, even took a few running steps that way, before noticing Champ.

LeAnne knew little about what was going on in the minds of dogs, but it was clear that her dog took an instant dislike to Champ. Her dog snarled — something soft and black falling from her mouth — and charged Champ, teeth bared, spittle flying. Champ was the same size or maybe even bigger, but she immediately lay down and rolled over, exposing her throat. LeAnne's dog stood over Champ in a nasty and bullying way. Champ made no move to defend herself. Her eyes rolled weirdly around in their sockets.

"What the hell?" said Deputy Lima, drawing his revolver.

"Whoa," said LeAnne, her parade ground voice there when she needed it. The men all turned to her, the deputy lowering his weapon. She ignored them, moved toward the dog, clapping her hands once, good and hard, like thunder. "Come!"

The dog trotted right over and sat beside her, on the right, even nudging LeAnne's leg with her head, like maybe she wanted some petting.

"I don't get it," Sheriff Cosgrove said. "This your dog?"

LeAnne nodded.

"Champ submitted?" the sheriff said. "Wow."

The deputy didn't seem happy about it. "An animal like that belongs on a leash at all goddamn times."

LeAnne held it up. "She got away." Was an apology expected? They'd come to the wrong woman.

"What's her name?" the sheriff said.

LeAnne considered the question. "Goody," she said at last. Goody: it didn't fit and was perfect at the same time.

"Christ," said the deputy.

LeAnne clipped the leash to Goody's collar. Goody, still sitting, swept her strange tail back and forth over the wet pavement. Meanwhile, Harvey took a few steps up the path and picked up the soft, small object Goody had dropped and brought it back.

"What's that?" the sheriff said.

"Black armband," Harvey said.

"McCutcheon's gives them out, don't they?" said the sheriff.

"What's McCutcheon's?" LeAnne said.

"The funeral home," said Harvey. "They hand these to the families of the deceased."

Sheriff Cosgrove snapped on plastic gloves, took the armband from Harvey, and turned it inside out, exposing a printed label: McCutcheon Funeral Home, Bellville WA.

"So who got one?" the sheriff said. "Supposing for the moment that this isn't from some other funeral."

"I didn't notice at the time," Harvey said. He looked over at Max. Max was gazing at the armband, no expression on his face. The sheriff slipped the armband into an evidence bag, then got on his phone, moved away.

"Up, Champ, for Christ sake," the deputy said. Champ wriggled around on her back, eyes on Goody. "Up!" Champ rose. LeAnne felt Goody stiffening and got hold of the leash with both hands. Champ took a few quick steps over to the deputy's side — actually kind of behind him — and stood still, panting slightly.

The sheriff returned, pocketing his phone. "McCutcheon's distributed three armbands at Marci's funeral — one to Mrs. Cummings, one to her sister, and one to the girl."

"Mrs. Cummings is at home," Harvey said. "And her sister's back in Boise. Meanwhile, I'm guessing you'll want my fingerprints, Sheriff."

"Why would that be?"

Harvey looked surprised. "For the forensics people — I just handled a piece of evidence."

The sheriff had a bushy mustache, still wet from the rain. When he spoke it made wriggling movements that LeAnne found slightly nauseating. "Let's not get ahead of ourselves, Harvey," he said.

"What do you mean?" Harvey said.

"Don't want to jump to conclusions," said Max.

Harvey glared at him, but the sheriff said, "Exactly right. No telling where this particular armband came from, like I said." He turned to LeAnne. "You're a friend of Marci's? Did I get that right?"

"Yes."

"You served with her overseas?"

"No."

"Stateside?"

LeAnne nodded.

"Whereabouts in particular?" Sheriff Cosgrove said.

"Walter Reed."

There was a silence, a silence in which her bad side once again served as a magnet for all their gazes, excepting Harvey's.

"I'm getting confused," the sheriff said.

"I don't see why, Sheriff," Harvey said. "She's a friend of Marci's from the army, and she came here to pay her respects."

"But she wasn't at the funeral," Deputy Lima said.

"I'm right here," LeAnne told him. "You can talk to me."

"Okay," the deputy said. "How come you weren't at the funeral?"

"George?" said the sheriff. "I'll handle this, if you don't mind." A blood vessel throbbed in the deputy's neck. The sheriff turned to LeAnne.

"How come you weren't at the funeral?" Exact same words that Deputy Lima had used, but Cosgrove had a more sympathetic way, and they ended up sounding different.

"I didn't get here in time," LeAnne said.

"Where'd you come from?"

"Herat Province."

"Where the hell is that?" said the deputy.

"I believe LeAnne here is having a little fun with us," Sheriff Cosgrove said.

"I'm not having fun," LeAnne said. "I'm helping with the search."

The sheriff nodded. "Appreciate that." He glanced at Goody, sitting at LeAnne's side and in mid-yawn at that moment. "And maybe, since you're the helping kind, you can help me solve a little puzzle. Supposing, for the sake of argument, forensics — or maybe McCutcheon's — determines that the armband here was the one the kid wore. How come of all the objects your dog might find down in the swamp, that's what she brings back?"

LeAnne could barely follow that, still less come up with a scientific answer. But were they maligning Goody in some way? That was unacceptable. "Maybe she's better at this kind of thing," LeAnne said.

"Better?" said the sheriff. "I don't get it."

"Better than your dog," she told him. Rubbing it in: she'd hardly ever done that in her life, maybe never. It felt pretty good!

"Goddamn it," Lima said, moving toward her. LeAnne knew how to formulate plans quickly in situations like this. The plan she had now began with snatching that .38 right out the deputy's holster.

Cosgrove stepped in between them. "Let's everybody calm down."

"But did you hear what she just said?" Lima's voice rose. "Champ's the best in the whole state!"

"Not anymore," LeAnne said. True for sure, but this time the rubbing it in part didn't feel as good.

"Jesus Christ!" said the deputy. "You gonna let her get away with that?"

Cosgrove raised both hands. "Harvey? How about you take your friend out for coffee? Nothing more to do here till we nail down the facts on the armband. I'll call you soon as we hear."

"Fair enough," Harvey said, putting his hand lightly on LeAnne's back. She jerked away from his touch and started back down the path by herself. Not quite by herself: Goody was with her, on the blind side as always, dragging her leash, which LeAnne realized she had dropped, possibly step one in the gun-snatching plan.

"You did good," she told the dog.

"She sure did," said Harvey, trailing behind; she hadn't realized he was there, within hearing range, and said no more the rest of the way to the car. The dog growled once or twice. "Maybe she hates compliments," Harvey said.

LeAnne opened one of the rear doors. Goody hopped in and snatched up something from the floor.

"She's got a dog of her own?" said Harvey.

LeAnne saw that Goody had the toy dog in her mouth; Mia's toy dog, in fact.

"There's your answer," she said.

"My answer to what?"

For a moment LeAnne didn't know where she'd been heading. Then her mind caught up with itself, if that made any sense. "That armband was Mia's, one hundred percent guaranteed."

"I don't get it," Harvey said.

"I'll explain on the way back."

"The way back where?"

LeAnne couldn't think of the answer to that.

Harvey shot a quick glance at her, then lowered his gaze. "How about that coffee?" he said. "I know a place."

"I don't want coffee."

"Tea, maybe?"

"I don't drink tea."

"No? Marci loved it."

"She did?"

"Green, especially."

LeAnne drove away from the old train station — Harvey up front, Goody in back — and was turning onto Main Street when the rain started up again. "Okay," she said.

"Okay what?" said Harvey.

"To tea," LeAnne said. "I'll try green tea."

The Bitterroot Café had four or five tables and a nice view of the river out the back slider. From their table LeAnne could also see the Honda, parked in the alley beside the café, with Goody sitting up straight in the backseat, gazing at a nearby brick wall.

At first, green tea did nothing for her; then

it was not bad; and after that, nice. LeAnne realized this was the first conscious moment since that last mission where the word *nice* applied; all the different aches in her head were gone.

"Something to eat?" Harvey said.

That sounded good. LeAnne ordered fried chicken, a cheeseburger, a tuna sandwich, and a few sides. Harvey showed no reaction to that; he had soup.

"I keep thinking about the custody situation," LeAnne said.

"Regarding Max, specifically?"

She took a close look at Harvey.

"What?" he said. "What? That X-ray thing scares me."

"You're a liar," LeAnne said. "But yes — regarding Max, specifically. You're obviously way ahead of me."

Harvey spooned up some soup, blew lightly on it.

"Have you ever had a mustache?" she said.

He paused. "That's a funny question."

What was wrong with her? Somehow the image of the sheriff's nauseating mustache had gotten mixed up with the sight of Harvey's clean-shaved upper lip, quite pleasant to her eye. "Sorry." A headache came back, very faint, like an electric guitarist tuning up before plugging in. She put down her cheeseburger, half-eaten.

"No big deal," Harvey said, sipping soup and patting his mouth with a napkin. "I did try a mustache once. Marci hated it. I grew it again after the split — what a statement, huh? — but one day I saw it as others did, thank God. As for Max, I called the sheriff as soon as I heard about Mia, meaning the morning after the funeral. I explained how Max had irrevocably renounced all claims to custody. Cosgrove's not stupid. He filled in the rest of the theory himself — the news of Marci's death reawakening the whole thing in Max's mind, all the self-justification that would accompany taking action, him being the girl's only parent, Coreen too old for this, et cetera. You were thinking along those lines?"

"What do you teach?" LeAnne said.

"Huh?"

"You said you were a teacher. What do you teach?"

"Third grade. Mia's in my class — didn't I mention that?"

LeAnne needed more time to remember, but she never seemed to get it. Who wouldn't be angry? "What subjects? I meant what subjects do you teach?"

Harvey sat back. "Third grade subjects. Spelling, reading, arithmetic — the usual."

LeAnne didn't care about that. She'd been going in a different direction. All she'd really wanted to do was to tell him she guessed he'd be a good teacher. Instead, she'd landed them in a snarl. LeAnne sat back, too, and folded her arms across her chest.

Harvey glanced around the table, taking in the sight of all her uneaten food. Now would come some bothersome question about cooking quality or lack of appetite. Except it did not. Instead, Harvey smiled at her.

"What's funny?"

"Nothing. I'm just smiling."

"Why?"

Harvey shrugged. "Funny thing about happiness," he said. "Sometimes it just bubbles up — kind of like Marci's IED image, only in reverse."

LeAnne understood what he was talking about, remembered when she'd been that way herself. But now she had to be realistic. The best she could hope for would be to stay on track, get from A to B. "Did Cosgrove do anything with your information?"

Harvey nodded. "Cosgrove's known to be a pretty straight-up guy. He went down to Seattle and interviewed Max right away."

"Max lives in Seattle?"

"Moved there five or six years ago. Had a

chance to buy into a lumber business and now he owns it. Max alibied out — he was at some conference on Bainbridge Island the day of the funeral, was seen by multiple people in the bar that night and then again at breakfast."

"What was his reaction to being questioned?"

"He wasn't offended or anything like that, according to the sheriff — just worried about Mia."

"Is he married?"

Harvey shook his head. "I think there's been a girlfriend or two. He's been off my radar for a long time."

So: a dead end. LeAnne stared into her tea mug. She got the strange sense that Marci's face was about to appear on the green surface of the tea, that Marci would soon be showing her the way. But before any miracles could happen, barking started up outside in the alley, muffled barking but plenty audible. LeAnne looked up. Goody was in the front passenger seat, barking furiously and pawing at the windshield.

LeAnne rose and hurried outside. "Goody! Calm down, for Christ sake." She opened the car door. Goody leaped out, bolted down the alley and straight back, then just stood beside LeAnne and barked at the car. The barking was so loud that LeAnne barely heard the ringing of a phone — a ringing inside her car, beyond doubt, even though she had no phone.

LeAnne got into the car, followed the ringing sound. It was coming from under the driver's seat. She fished around, felt the ringing phone, pulled it out: a red phone. LeAnne had seen this red phone before — the phone that Captain Stallings, G-2, had tried to foist on her outside her tent at 2241 Lost Hills Road, and that she had refused — but it was like an object from another life.

LeAnne pressed the talk button and the ringing stopped. Goody went silent.

"Hello?" LeAnne said.

Chapter Twenty-Five

"Hi, LeAnne." She recognized the soft voice of the speaker at once. "Stallings, here, G-2. Thanks for picking up — you're not easy to reach."

Silence from LeAnne's end.

"LeAnne? Are you there? Can you hear me?"

"You said you wouldn't bother me again."

"Can you speak up? I didn't copy that."

LeAnne said it again, a lot louder this time. She got out of the car, stood beside it. Goody was looking up at her, an intense expression in those coal-black eyes, like she was paying close attention to the conversation.

"And I meant it at the time," Stallings said. "Which is the best I've ever been able to do in this life, don't know about you. But how are you? You sound a lot better."

"How did you do this?" LeAnne tried to bring back the details of their last meeting and some of them returned, but on the question of how Stallings had gotten the phone into the car, her mind came up blank. That was doubly infuriating: her shortcomings on top of what he'd done.

"Definitely better than the last time I saw you," Stallings said, and then after a pause added, "in Arizona."

Her voice rose. "I know where it was. You didn't answer my question."

"Does it really matter now?" Stallings said. "I take it you're up in Washington."

"You've been tracking me with this phone?"

"Not in any surreptitious way."

"What the hell are you talking about?"

"Maybe surreptitious is the wrong word," Stallings said. "I meant sneaky."

"You're not tracking me in a sneaky way? Because . . ." Facts came together in her mind. ". . . because you told my mother I was in Oregon the other day? That makes it on the up and up?"

"Technically, you're still in the army, LeAnne."

"What are you going to do? Throw me in the stockade?"

"The optics of that would be very bad."

"Optics, huh?" LeAnne said. "You're an asshole."

"I didn't mean it that way, as I'm sure you know," Stallings said.

"The plain meaning was bad enough."

"Sometimes that can't be avoided, but plain meaning helps when there's a mission to accomplish, which is where I am at the moment. What's that noise?"

LeAnne realized that Goody was growling again.

"Sounds like some kind of motor."

LeAnne gave Goody a nod, meaning *keep it up.* Instead, the growling stopped at once. Goody came closer, pressed against LeAnne's legs, possibly with affection except she was pressing so hard that LeAnne was jammed against the car.

"Whew, now it's gone," Stallings said. "What's the attraction in Washington?"

"The rain."

There was a silence. Then Stallings said, "I hope you realize your mother's worried about you. She seems like a very fine person."

"You called to tell me that?"

"Partly," Stallings said, his voice for the first time hardening a bit. "But mainly I need your help — not for long, just a day or two, three tops."

"What kind of help?"

"I'd rather discuss that in person."

"And if I say no, you'll just show up here?"

"Oh, I wasn't suggesting that. No reason to invade your personal space. I'll get you on a plane headed my way."

"Where is that?"

"I'm in Kabul."

Through the phone came a sound LeAnne took for the desiccating Afghan wind.

"Forget it," she said. "And don't call me ever again."

"Hear me out, LeAnne. You wouldn't want it said that —"

She clicked off, tossed the red phone back in the car. The hand that had held it was shaking and wouldn't stop.

Harvey came out of the café, pocketing his wallet.

"Some problem?" he said.

"No."

He crouched down, took Goody's head in both hands. "You just don't like being all on your lonesome, is that it, big girl?"

Goody's weird tail swung back and forth; not weird, LeAnne reminded herself, but mutilated.

"The sheriff called." Harvey didn't look up at LeAnne, kept his gaze on Goody. "They're still waiting on a fingerprint match, but you were right — McCutcheon's is sure the armband was Mia's."

"How did they know?"

"Because of the size, extra small. It was their last one — they had to reorder. A search party's headed back down to the bike trail."

"Let's go."

"A little problem with that," Harvey said. "Cosgrove, for the time being, would prefer if you didn't . . . well, help out right now."

"Fuck him."

"I agree. And just after I told you about his straight-up rep. You never know people until you see them in action."

"Not your fault," LeAnne said. "He doesn't have the balls to stand up to his own deputy. That's all it's about — I've seen shit like this many times. Hop in."

Harvey rose. He raised his hand, as though to lay it on her shoulder, and then thought better of it. "The thing is, LeAnne, he was pretty adamant."

"So what?" She was halfway in the car, and Goody was already totally inside, on the backseat, up and alert.

"Just that if you come, there'll be a scene," Harvey said.

"So what?" she said again.

"A scene that will end up being a distraction," he went on. "And I don't see how that helps find Mia."

LeAnne gazed at him. "Are you the kind who doesn't step up, Harvey? Is that what really happened with you and Marci? You didn't put up a fight?"

Harvey's cheeks went bright red, like she'd slapped them good and hard.

"Get in," she said. "Don't worry — I'm not coming. I'll just take you to your car."

LeAnne drove Harvey back to his pickup, parked outside Coreen's house. There was no talk until Harvey opened the door to get out.

"I'll try to patch things up with Cosgrove," he said.

"In a nice way, I'm sure."

"What do you mean by that?"

"Forget it."

"No," Harvey said. "Finish what you have to say."

"Sometimes you've got to fight," LeAnne told him.

"I'm starting to think it's your default position." Harvey didn't slam the door, also didn't close it extra-softly; just did it in the normal way. That puzzled her. Harvey was angry. Angry men slammed doors. Clever angry men closed them extra-softly. LeAnne couldn't take it further than that.

Harvey drove away, hadn't gone more than

fifty feet before Goody crawled over and . . . took possession of the front passenger seat; there was no other way to put it.

"The back's not good enough?" Easy to check on Goody in the back through the rearview mirror. "How come you always have to be where I can't see you?" From her right came sounds of Goody settling in, getting comfortable. LeAnne drove for a while, going nowhere in particular, just trying to calm down inside, trying to make her headache go away, both without success. Then she felt Goody's paw on her leg, pressing down way too hard to be comforting, the tips of her claws digging in. "What the hell?" LeAnne twisted around. Goody was sitting up now, her huge head only inches away, teeth exposed. "You're hungry? Thirsty? What?" Goody dug in harder.

LeAnne turned into a drive-through, ordered a burger with no bun, parked in the lot. She took the burger from the paper bag, held it out. "Here. Eat." Goody's head snapped forward and she grabbed the whole thing, chomped it down in less than a second. LeAnne's headache vanished. She gazed at the dog. The dog gazed back. LeAnne got the feeling Goody wanted to do the whole thing again, and at the same time realized she was hungry herself. But hadn't she just eaten? She went back over the lunch at the Bitterroot Café, remembered she'd left most of her order untouched. LeAnne started the car and was about enter the drive-through lane again, when she noticed the sign on the white-columned building across the street: McCutcheon's Funeral Home.

LeAnne cracked Goody's window open an inch, no more — Goody's window, Christ, what was happening to her? "You're staying here. You're lying down. You're getting with the program." Goody did not lie down, but she made no move to follow when LeAnne got out of the car.

The front door at McCutcheon's was unlocked. LeAnne went inside. She was in a broad hall with a high ceiling and a thick, pale carpet on the floor. The light was silvery, the air still, sounds hushed. It reminded her of heaven in some movie she'd seen, but if heaven was like this, it was a deathly sort of place. LeAnne came close to turning around and walking right back out.

But she was on a mission. Not Midnight Special — *a ginormous fuckin' freight train, barrelin' through to hell and gone* — but something . . . quieter. She was in her own country, after all.

LeAnne kept going, past an empty chapel, an empty office, and an urn full of small white flowers with a smell that brought back her father's funeral in every detail if she wanted to go over them, which she did not. A step or two past the urn, she picked up the sound of a song she knew: "Rip This Joint." LeAnne followed the sound around a corner to the open door of another office, this one smaller than the first and full of technical equipment. A white-haired man with his back to her was working at a screen displaying a smiling photo of Marci with a baseball cap tilted back on her head. He tapped at a keyboard and the music stopped, then resumed again earlier in the song, right at the beginning of the saxophone solo. LeAnne knocked on the door.

The man turned to her, touching a key and pausing the music at the same time. He had pale skin and dark shadows under his eyes. His gaze went right to her bad side, but then very quickly switched to a head-on look. Maybe there was something to be learned about people by how speedily they got that done; she had a lifetime to find out. However long that might be.

"Hi," he said. "Can I help you?"

LeAnne told him her name. "I was a

friend of Marci's," she said, gesturing with her chin at the picture on the screen.

"In the service?" he said.

"How did you guess?"

That embarrassed him, probably not easy to do with someone in his business. LeAnne felt kind of proud of that. "Uh, sorry," he said, "no real reason. Just that I know most of her friends from around here and —"

"Not a problem," LeAnne said, the pride turning to something like shame, and she fell into a tongue-tied state of uncertainty.

"My name's McCutcheon, by the way. Fred to everyone up in this part of the state. I don't remember seeing you at Marci's service."

"I got here too late."

"That's a pity," McCutcheon said. "You can watch it if you like."

"Watch it?"

"Well, not the whole thing." He jabbed his thumb at the screen. "Won't be complete for a day or two more — still in the editing process."

"You're making a video of Marci's funeral? Like a wedding video?"

"A lot like that, actually, in a technical sense and even spiritually, if I may say so. There's a surprising level of demand, and maybe not even that surprising, taking the long view of life's mileposts, and all."

"Yeah," LeAnne said. "I'd like to see it."

McCutcheon drew over a roll chair with his foot. "Have a seat."

LeAnne sat down — on McCutcheon's left, but there was no room on the other side. He smelled like the white flowers in the hall.

"I like to start with a sort of video collage of the person's life," McCutcheon said. "Collage being maybe too hoity-toity. Basically I use whatever I can get, boiling it down to two minutes — two thirty, tops — before I segue to the service. Here's Marci."

The image of smiling Marci in the baseball cap dissolved into a grainy video of baby Marci shaking the bars of her playpen; followed by birthday girl Marci blowing out candles — a still photo that lingered on the screen long enough for LeAnne to count the candles: seven. After that came some teenage Marci: at the beach with Coreen; at the edge of the Grand Canyon with her arms spread, as though preparing for take-off; having happy times with various friends; Marci pinning a boy on the wrestling mat. That was followed by a few seconds of blank screen —

"Oops," said Mr. McCutcheon, "how in heck did that happen?"

— and the next picture was Marci's wedding photo, the same one LeAnne had seen on Coreen's sunroom wall — Marci in her low-cut wedding gown and Harvey adoring her.

"Love that shot," said McCutcheon, in a very soft voice, possibly to himself.

LeAnne nodded. Meanwhile, the video collage seemed to speed up, as though McCutcheon had started worrying about his time limit. Marci in uniform, Marci on the deck of a submarine, Marci holding baby Mia high in the air, Marci and Mia — looking about her age in the Missing Child poster — at the edge of the Grand Canyon.

"Here comes the second dissolve," said McCutcheon. "Second and last — some of my competitors get a little dissolve-happy, in my opinion."

Out of the dissolve came a snatch of video. Marci was sitting on the edge of . . . a fountain? A fountain beside a cherry tree? And she wore the prosthetic leg?

"What is this?" LeAnne said, perhaps quite loudly.

"Coreen struck up a relationship with one of the nurses when she visited Walter Reed. The nurse caught this on a lunch break. Sent it in just yesterday, in fact."

There was another woman in the scene, a

dark-haired woman facing away from the camera. She also was sitting on the edge of the fountain, somewhat rigidly, and perhaps aggressively, too; the tendons at the back of her neck stood out. Just from the way she carried herself you could tell that this was not a pleasant woman, no one you'd want to know.

Marci's lips moved like she was saying something. Then she watched the other woman. The other woman must have replied, a reply that Marci liked, because she laughed. Actually threw back her head and laughed — and in that moment looked young and happy and carefree. Sunshine gleamed on the silvery parts of her prosthetic leg.

"Says so much about her, if you ask me," McCutcheon said. LeAnne felt him glance her way. Tears were flowing, but only from her real eye, so maybe he didn't see. He seemed about to say something, seemed to change his mind. Now the photo of Marci in the baseball cap was back on the screen. "So much for the collage," said McCutcheon. "Now we get to the service, if you're still interested."

LeAnne nodded.

"Still just a rough cut, bear in mind," McCutcheon said. "Plus I went to a three-camera operation last month, so things have gotten a little complicated. Not to mention the music issue. A lot of folks have a favorite song that needs to be included — and we've dealt with an amazing variety — but maybe nothing as discordant as this one."

" 'Rip This Joint'?"

"You're familiar with it?"

"Marci knew every word."

"Quite a feat, right there. I've heard it maybe ten times now and I still don't have a clue what it's about. Drugs, do you think?" He hit a key or two and the image on the screen changed to rows of chapel pews, seen from above.

"More like a party," LeAnne said. "A traveling American party."

"Yeah?" said McCutcheon. "What a country!" He pointed to the screen. "This is the footage I'm using from the balcony cam, just for the ending — which was when the song started playing, but I'm not happy with the live feed." He fiddled with the controls of another machine, blinking above the screen. "You want it to be right."

The balcony cam scene started up. The three essential parts were the pastor at the podium, the mourners in the pews, and the coffin separating parts one and two, a coffin covered with the Stars and Stripes. The pastor was talking about how we hadn't lost Marci since we knew where she already was, looking down as he spoke — the same old comforting shit LeAnne had heard many times, and now tuned out as the camera slowly zoomed in closer on the front row of pews. She recognized a few people: Coreen, Harvey, and Mia. Mia sat next to another little girl, smaller than she was. Mia wasn't crying, but her eyes were open wide and had an expression of horror in them. Without looking, the other girl reached over and took Mia's hand. Their heads moved, almost imperceptibly, closer together.

McCutcheon pointed to the screen. "Mia, Marci's daughter, the one who disappeared. You heard?"

"What do you think happened?"

"Can't say," said McCutcheon. "But we had something similar a few years back. They found the kid in a treehouse on an abandoned lot where he'd lived as a toddler. Simply up and run away to a sort of sanctuary, as least in his mind."

"Alive?"

"Yes, so no harm done. Let's pray for something similar in this case."

LeAnne was not in a prayerful mood. "Who's the other girl?" she said.

"With Mia?" said McCutcheon. "That's

my granddaughter Belinda Jane, but everyone calls her B.J."

"They're friends, Mia and B.J.?"

McCutcheon nodded. "More so this year, I think. They're in the same class at school."

"Harvey Wald's class?"

"Correct." McCutcheon glanced her way. "For a newcomer, you're on top of things in our little burg."

The camera panned over toward the podium, where the pastor seemed to be wrapping up. "Rip This Joint" began to play, the sound not very good, as McCutcheon had said, murky and bass heavy. The mourners began to move out of range, Mia and B.J. trailing, and talking now, their heads again very close. Or rather it was Mia talking and B.J. listening, and whatever Mia was saying seemed to bring an astonished look to B.J.'s face. At least it appeared that way, but the moment was short, a fraction of a second, and then the girls passed from sight.

"Can you back that up?" LeAnne said.

"Say when."

"When." The tiny moment went by once more. A strange interaction, or was she reading too much into it? "What do you think they're talking about?"

"Girls have themselves some serious conversations in a way boys just don't," Mc-

Cutcheon said. "That's one thing that hasn't changed over the years."

LeAnne wasn't buying that. She'd heard many boys of eighteen, nineteen, twenty, boys she'd served with, in conversation. The style, syntax, vocabulary, and volume were very different, but the talk was just as serious.

"Were you in the military, Fred?"

"Not me." He went quiet and turned back to the controls, mixing in the good version of "Rip This Joint."

"Is today a school day?" LeAnne said. "I've lost track."

McCutcheon shook his head. "Spring vacation."

"What do the local kids do on spring vacation? B.J., for example."

He checked his watch. "Right about now she'll be at gymnastics."

"Yeah?"

"Just a bitty thing, but the coach says she has promise."

"Bitty things are what they're looking for in gymnastics."

"Really? You know something about it?"

"A little," LeAnne said. Then, just when she'd been on a purposeful sort of roll, she dead-ended. Hadn't she been headed in some direction, following some idea? She squeezed her eyes shut, like a kid thinking her very hardest. Both eyes, meaning at least in this one task the bad one was pitching in. LeAnne got lucky. "Where's the class?" she said.

Chapter Twenty-Six

Goody was asleep when LeAnne got back to the car, sprawled across both front seats although mostly in LeAnne's. Her tail, with its uneven end, rose once and fell with a thump; if not asleep, then at least her eyes were closed.

"Move it."

Goody didn't budge.

"We don't have time for this shit." LeAnne had a real bad feeling, unfamiliar and at first unplaceable. Then she got it: she was afraid. But of what? Something specific? Or a general sort of dread?

Goody's eyes opened. She gazed at LeAnne with one of her coal-black looks, the meaning of which, if any, was not evident. LeAnne gave Goody's haunches a push. Goody swung her head around and growled, her inner ferocity beyond doubt. The next thing LeAnne knew was that she'd raised her fist and was about to . . . She caught herself in time and lowered that too-quick hand. Goody rose in a deliberate way — which, in a human, LeAnne would have called dignified — and shifted over to the passenger side, revealing that she'd been lying on her toy.

LeAnne picked up the stuffed dog, slightly slimy with Goody's saliva. The stuffed dog had only one eye? When had that happened? This development stunned LeAnne. There had to be some meaning in it, but what? She turned the dog over in her hands, a floppy-eared kind of dog, white with brown patches, a somewhat familiar type, maybe a popular breed. She squeezed it, feeling for anything that might be hidden inside, and was checking for an opening, like a tiny pouch or zippered pocket — and finding none — when Goody leaned over and snatched the thing away.

Initial Evaluation for Post-Traumatic Stress Disorder:
Integrated Summary and Conclusions:

5. If possible, state prognosis for improvement of psychiatric condition and impairments in functional status:

▪ ▪ ▪ ▪

A Missing Child poster was thumbtacked to a message board outside Just Tumblin' Around Gymnastics, a low, flat-roofed building with a circular drive. LeAnne stopped in front of it, studying Mia's face in the hope of somehow seeing inside her, and then drove around and back out onto the street, where she parked and waited. Every mission was based on a plan. At the moment, she had none. Winging it was usually fatal in her combat experience. Carefully conceived plans could also be fatal. All that was on the negative side. On the plus side was the fact that the twisting and shearing behind her fake eye had gone dormant and she had no pain; and also — no leaving this out — she had the feel of Goody's tail resting on her knee. Crazy that that was a positive, or even factored in at all, but it was true.

Cars began rolling into the circular drive. The door to Just Tumblin' Around Gymnastics opened, and girls from about eight through ten years old in sweats and tights began coming out and climbing into the cars. Soon all the cars were gone and only one girl remained, a bitty little thing — B.J.

She sat down on a bench out front and got busy checking her hair for split ends. LeAnne was struck by something she'd missed on the video, namely the resemblance of B.J. to Tasha, the bitty little best friend from her own gymnastics days. Same sturdy body type, same short, squarish feet, even some facial similarities, especially the peaches-and-cream complexion. LeAnne looked over at Goody.

"Is this the kind of thing you'll help or hinder?"

Goody clutched the toy dog firmly in her mouth.

"Lots of kids are crazy about dogs. Dogs in general. But what about this particular girl and you specifically?" LeAnne took another look at B.J., still busy with the split ends, her eyes crossed. "Girls in gymnastics don't scare easily, right? Isn't that a given?" LeAnne clipped the leash to Goody's collar. "Don't fuck up. That means dropping your little buddy, for starters."

Goody let go of the toy.

"You understood? Or just a coincidence?"

Goody gave her a coal-black stare. LeAnne opened the door and they got out, LeAnne first and not even having to fight for the privilege. They crossed the half-moon-shaped island of lawn separating the street from the circular driveway, Goody on her right, but not straining at the leash, instead walking at exactly LeAnne's pace, like a well-trained dog. B.J. heard them coming and looked up, smoothing down her hair on both sides.

"Hi," LeAnne said. "Don't worry about Goody, here. She's pretty big, all right, but harmless. Relatively."

"I like dogs," B.J. said. She smoothed down her hair again. "Can I pet her?"

"Don't see why not, myself," LeAnne said, moving closer, Goody right with her. They stopped in front of the bench. B.J. extended a small squarish hand and gave Goody a tentative pat or two on the top of her huge head. "She likes that," LeAnne said.

"Her tail's not wagging," said B.J.

"She's funny that way. Try scratching between her ears."

B.J. scratched between Goody's ears. Goody went very still. LeAnne shortened her grip on the leash and held tight, but there was nothing to worry about; Goody was just falling into one of her trances.

"It's still not wagging," B.J. said, turning to LeAnne — and catching sight of her bad side for the first time. She looked away, real fast, and shrank back a little, her hands clasped together in her lap.

LeAnne felt dizzy. She fought it off, tried to smile, tried to find something funny to say about Goody, but all that came out was, "Don't be afraid. It . . . it looks worse than it is, believe it or not, much worse."

"Sorry," said B.J. "I didn't mean —"

"You didn't do anything wrong," LeAnne said. "My name's LeAnne. I was a friend of Mia's mom." The girl's eyes shifted, like she was having some sort of thought. "From the army," LeAnne added, in case B.J. was trying to figure out the relationship. "Mind if I sit down?"

"Yes," said B.J. "I mean no. Um, like, sit down."

LeAnne laughed, a laugh that sounded weak and distant. "That's a tough one." She sat down, keeping B.J. on her left, and the dizziness began to fade. Goody tried to shift over to LeAnne's right, got herself tangled in the leash. LeAnne started straightening that out, felt B.J. watching her. "How was gymnastics?" she said.

"Okay," said B.J.

"What skill were you working on?"

"Back walkover on the beam."

"How's it going?"

"Not too great."

"How about on the mat?"

"My back walkover? One of my best! Not

that I'm any good, really."

"Don't be too quick to criticize yourself," LeAnne said. "I struggled with that one for the longest time."

"The back walkover?"

"On the beam. Fell so many times I must've thought I was a bird."

B.J. laughed a tiny laugh. "You did gymnastics?"

"I was pretty average. But I had a friend who ended up being very good — looked a lot like you, in fact — and she gave me a tip that helped big-time."

"Yeah?"

"Just before you raise that front-foot heel, my friend Tasha always put her hands just so."

"Like she was praying?"

"Exactly. She said it made her narrow, like the beam itself."

"Hey!"

"Try it next time."

"I'm gonna," said B.J. "Do you say a prayer, too?"

"I didn't myself, but it can't hurt. Just make it short."

B.J. nodded her head in a very serious way, possibly committing the short-prayer tip to memory. LeAnne counted silently to thirty. B.J. started smoothing the sides of her hair once more.

"I missed the funeral," LeAnne said, "but I'm sure they had prayers."

"Lots."

"You must be worried about Mia."

B.J. nodded again. "My dad's out on the search — that's why he's late."

"What about your mom?"

"She's at work."

"Here's a good short prayer for gymnastics, in case you decide to go that route," LeAnne said. " 'Please make this fun.' "

" 'Please make this fun.' Thanks."

"You're welcome. Did you know your grandfather is making a video of the service?"

"No."

"I saw some of it, mostly the ending. It looked like you were a big help to Mia."

"Really?"

"I did notice that as you were leaving, she said something that seemed to surprise you." LeAnne felt B.J. turning toward her, also felt the girl tensing up, but she herself remained facing forward, bad side hidden. "I couldn't help wondering what that was about."

"Did — did anyone else notice?"

"Oh, I'm sure not."

There was a long pause. Goody was lying

down now, eyes closed, snoring softly. Le-Anne got the weird feeling she was actively helping in her own way.

"You're from the army?" B.J. said.

"I am."

B.J. lowered her voice. "Are you part of the mission?"

"It depends what mission you're talking about."

B.J. lowered her voice even more. "The secret mission."

"I have clearance," LeAnne said.

"So . . . so you know about it?"

"There are lots of secret missions. Remind me."

"Her mom's secret mission," B.J. said, now just a whisper.

"Ah," said LeAnne, lowering her own voice.

"It's true, isn't it?"

"Depends on what you've heard."

Now LeAnne turned to B.J. The kid suddenly looked even younger than she actually was, almost like her kindergarten self. "That she's alive," B.J. said. "On a secret mission. But no one can know or she'll die."

The dizziness returned, worse than before. LeAnne might have fainted if she'd been standing. "Mia knows?"

"Her mom sent for her. So Mia wouldn't

be upset. It worked."

"What do you mean?"

"That's how I noticed. At first she cried all the time. And then it stopped. So I was like, how come. And she told me."

LeAnne took a deep breath, pushing back the dizziness. "Told you that her mom was alive?"

"And wanted to see her. It's true, isn't it?"

"Of course, her mom wanted to see her," LeAnne said, like some politician picking every word very carefully; which made her feel sick inside but didn't stop her.

"I swore not to tell. But if you already know —"

"Exactly right. The only unclear part is how Mia found out about this."

"There was a message from the army," B.J. said.

"A message from the army?"

"The night before the funeral. One of those commandos came to her window."

"Commandos?"

"With his face all painted camo."

"This is sounding so strange."

B.J. nodded. "Like a dream. That's what I said — are you sure it wasn't a dream?"

"And what was Mia's answer?"

"To the dream thing? It made her cry, so I

didn't ask again."

A van with the words Bellville Growers Supply and Services painted on the panel door pulled into the circle, the driver tapping the horn. Goody awoke and was on her feet in an instant. The driver glanced out, a man of about LeAnne's age who looked like a younger, less-content version of Fred McCutcheon. His gaze went to B.J., LeAnne, Goody, and back to LeAnne.

"You won't tell?" B.J. said.

"No."

B.J. ran around the van and jumped in. The van drove off. Goody ambled over to where the van had stood, then squatted, and pissed right there.

Fred McCutcheon was just descending the front steps of the funeral home, a golf club bag over his shoulder and one of those white flowers in his blazer lapel, when LeAnne drove up. She got out of the car, told Goody, "This'll be quick," and approached him. Goody, left in the car, started making a murmuring sound in her throat, low in volume but in no way positive.

McCutcheon paused on the bottom step. "You're back," he said.

"I've got kind of an odd question."

"Do you?"

LeAnne started to sense a change in his attitude. Was he late for his tee time? Something else? Who cared? "Yeah, I do. It's about Marci. Simply put — I told you it was odd — did you actually see her body?"

McCutcheon gazed down at her. "Yes, odd for sure. Plus rude and impertinent and nasty. And the same words apply to your behavior in general. I don't know what you're up to, but I don't take to being pumped, and I really don't take to strangers coming up here and accosting my granddaughter."

"Accosting?"

"My son just called me. I don't know what you said to B.J. — she just turned nine, for heaven's sake — but whatever it was, she doesn't want to talk about it, and that's not how we operate in this family. You had no right."

"I don't care how you operate," LeAnne said, imagining McCutcheon's son starting in on B.J. just from the sight of the bad side. "All I want to know is did you see Marci's body, yes or no?"

McCutcheon had one of those naturally sympathetic faces, but all that was gone now. "Contemptible," he said. He stepped carefully around her and walked toward his car.

"Answer me, you asshole!"

McCutcheon got in his car and drove away. The whole town seemed to go silent, except for Goody, front paws against the passenger-side window and barking her head off.

Back in cabin six at Shady Grove, LeAnne's head was pounding, the pain makers behind the crater back at full strength. Where were her pills? She searched around, couldn't find them. Didn't she have pills? Ibuprofen, at least? Hadn't she picked up ibuprofen somewhere along the way? She sat down on the bed, trying to hold all the pieces of her life together in her mind. The trashed, post-pill-search interior of the cabin was a pretty good material rendering of what was going on inside.

"Christ, help me."

There was nothing to be done until dark. She lay down. Goody stood by the door, watching with her coal-black eyes.

She awoke. She was full of pain and drugs for pain, different parts of her body hooked to different machines.

"Or maybe the same machine."

"What's that, sweetheart? I didn't quite catch it."

The light was dim. Maybe because her eyes were closed. She opened them. In fact, opened only one. The other eye didn't seem to want to open. The light was still dim. Was something pressing on the uncooperative eye? She tried to raise a hand to explore, but her hands would not be raised. A figure loomed closer. Her mother? Yes. Her mother was leaning over her.

"What the fuck? I told them no. No! No! No! How can they do this to me?"

"It's all right. Don't fuss. Just try to relax. We'll get through this."

"You, maybe."

Coal-black night, starless and moonless, but not raining. LeAnne turned on the bedside light. Goody was still standing by the door, still watching her — or possibly just facing in the right direction and in one of her trances. LeAnne went into the bathroom and splashed cold water on her face; her scars shone like war paint in the mirror. Behind her, Goody slurped up water from the toilet bowl.

"There's no barking tonight," LeAnne said. She took the flashlight out of the desk drawer. "No noise, no fucking up."

They left the cabin, headed up the white crushed-stone path, got into the car. Le-

Anne drove south, turning onto a dirt lane that ran by the cemetery. After a hundred yards or so, she pulled over and parked under a tall tree. LeAnne switched on the flashlight, popped the trunk, and took out the long-handled spade she'd bought at the camping store in Arizona. Then they walked to Marci's grave, Goody unleashed and silent on LeAnne's right.

LeAnne shone the light on the round bronze marker, the flowers — some of them new — and Marci's stone. *Daughter, Mother, Patriot. She gave all.* LeAnne turned to Goody. "We have to know for absolute sure." She propped up the flashlight on a tree root and got it properly aligned. Not only Marci, maybe not Marci at all: LeAnne had to know even just one thing for absolute sure. Dread was all around, the night heavy with it, moving right through her, like she was immaterial. She tipped over Marci's stone, rolled up the strip of newly-laid sod, and began digging.

LeAnne wasn't close to being at full strength, but the soil had been freshly dug and didn't resist the spade at all, almost like the earth itself wanted to cooperate. She found the right kind of rhythm — scoop, turn, dump; easy, like marching — and the hole deepened. Goody sat at the edge, her eyes gold in the reflection from the flashlight.

"*We* have to know? I fuckin' said *we?*"

LeAnne dug. Six feet under was what you heard, but at a depth of no more than two feet the spade struck something hard. She bent down, brushed away dirt, and saw she'd come to the outer casket, made of fiberglass, plain white. LeAnne cleared around the sides, then bent again and raised the lid. Inside was the coffin, also white, but made of wood, with carved flowers at one end. Dust swirled in the flashlight beam. LeAnne's hands got unsteady and even though the inner coffin wasn't locked or fastened shut in any way — what would be the point? — it took her some time to get a good grip under the lid and raise it.

And there was Marci, with a nice haircut and wearing a pretty summer dress. Her eyes were closed and her face was frozen in an expression of nothing. Therefore what? Did her final facial expression even matter? Not to Marci. She didn't care. Where she'd gone, you got to not care, with the bonus of a nice 'do and fine duds. LeAnne knelt in the dirt.

"Wake fuckin' up."

She leaned forward to kiss that frozen face. Before she could do that, Marci's lips moved. Just the tiniest bit, but LeAnne saw clearly, possibly with her bad eye. She closed the good one. Yes, for absolute sure, a sight for the bad eye alone. Then came Marci's voice.

"What if something happens to me?"

"I know," LeAnne said.

Goody bit down hard on the back of LeAnne's jacket collar and pulled her away. She got going on a low, menacing, dangerous growl that didn't stop until LeAnne had the hole filled in, the sod relaid, the stone standing back in place, and the flowers properly arrayed. All as before except for the night air, which now smelled faintly of death; maybe not so faint to Goody. As for the realm where you got to not care: it didn't exist.

Chapter Twenty-Seven

LeAnne awoke to the deathly graveyard smell. She opened her eyes and found herself on her bed, dressed in last night's dirty clothes. Cabin six was full of late-morning light, and Goody lay with her back to the door. LeAnne took a hot shower, scrubbing off the smell. But then, drying herself, she realized that one small part was already dead, so maybe the smell came from her. How was she supposed to go on like that? She wiped steam off the mirror and studied that dead part, her fake eye. Perhaps it was just some trick of the light, or leftover mist on the mirror, but the fake eye did not seem completely dead. How could that be possible? LeAnne had no clue, but the fake eye had changed overnight and was no longer the polar opposite of the good eye. Much less lively, yes, and also different in other ways: more grounded? more mature? Somehow the fake was stepping up.

"I'm going crazy." She went into the bedroom. Goody lay supine, all four paws in the air. "I can't think. Help me think." Goody began wriggling around on her back, mouth open, tongue hanging out. A plan began taking shape in LeAnne's mind.

"A map of the town?" said Dot, opening a drawer in her office. She handed LeAnne a glossy tourist brochure. LeAnne unfolded it and found a multicolor souvenir–style map with no indication of scale, elevation, topography.

"I'm looking for something more detailed," LeAnne said.

"Is this for the search? The sheriff must have good maps."

"You'd think."

"Ha! Problems with authority, huh?"

"I wouldn't —"

"Don't worry about it — I'm the same way myself." Dot rose, went into the back room, returned with a large three-ring binder. "They resurveyed the town ten years ago, just before they upped the tax rate."

LeAnne sat down, started paging through. Goody stood beside her, on the right.

"Dog's comin' around, huh?"

"Don't know about that. But she does have a name now."

"What's that?"

"Goody."

"Cool," said Dot. "One of those ironic names. Should we stop looking for takers?"

LeAnne turned to glance down at Goody, who'd begun gnawing at the rug, but not in a sneaky way. "I'll think about it." She followed the bike trail from page to page, studying the slope down to the swamp, the swamp itself, and the country on the other side — hilly at first and later, well beyond the town limits, rising up into mountains with steep grades, ten degrees or more — and tried to picture how the terrain would look in life, tried to commit it all to memory, like a prospective battlefield. "What's out here?" LeAnne said. "To the east."

"National forest," said Dot. "Beautiful country — cross-country skiing in the winter, mountain biking in summer, hunting in the fall."

"Hunters wear camo," LeAnne said.

"Uh, sure, sometimes."

"Or it could be some sort of retired veteran. Or a dream."

Dot tilted her head to one side. "You're losing me, the teensiest bit."

"I'm just babbling."

"You don't strike me as the babbling

kind," Dot said. "Get enough sleep last night?"

"All I needed," LeAnne said.

"I've got extra sleeping pills, if you're interested," Dot went on. "No charge."

Sleeping pills: something to remember. As for Dot's maps — and LeAnne had memorized hundreds, maybe even thousands of maps — her mind had retained the look of their small, tidy hand-lettering, and that was about all.

"Can I borrow these?"

LeAnne drove east out of town, found an overgrown and rutted track marked "former logging road 31N" on the map, and followed it up into some wooded hills. "Or a dream — can't forget that possibility," she said, glancing over at the dog. Goody was asleep on the passenger seat, the toy dog under one of her paws. "But if Mia believed it was real . . ." That was as far as LeAnne could take it. Her brain just wouldn't do the work.

LeAnne rounded a bend and came to a spot with a lookout on the left. She stopped the car. Beyond the edge of the lookout, the ground sloped down, lightly treed, all the way to the swamp. On the far side of the swamp, at the foot of the upland that rose to the bike trail, tiny Day-Glo dots were moving around. That would be the search party, about two miles away.

"Up and at 'em." LeAnne opened the door. "Let's see what you can do." Goody's eyelids rose. She yawned, got out of the car, stretched, and then just stood there. "How come you're not sniffing around? You're here to sniff around." Goody stayed how she was, if not in one of her trances, then in some sort of neutral state. LeAnne reached inside for the toy, brought it to Goody, held it a few inches from her nose. Goody turned away. "What the hell? I need you to perform." Goody crossed over to the other side of the track and sat in a patch of sunshine by the nearest tree.

LeAnne studied the swamp. There was open water, glinting in the sun; there were boggy parts, low and brown; and also strips of solid ground, green, with bushes tall enough to cast shadows. Could you somehow thread your way right through the swamp on the solid bits? Not that LeAnne saw, but she'd need binoculars to be sure. And where were they? She thought all the way back to January seventeenth and the ride in from the abandoned gas pumps to the five-building compound and that crowded dwelling where the addition of

Katie and her had made sixteen people; way too many for the space. LeAnne also remembered the two chickens, and all the civilian feet shod in homey, woven slippers or sandals. And then that hairy hand, out from under the burqa. LeAnne tried to get back to the problem of the binoculars, but her mind was stuck on the hairy hand. Time passed. She finally grew aware she was letting her body slump horribly, like some undisciplined loser.

LeAnne straightened right up. "It doesn't fucking matter." What mattered was . . .

She tried to frame the issue, at first getting nowhere, and then finally realizing — or remembering — that the issue was Mia. Mia had been parted from her black armband either on the far slope or in the swamp itself. Had she tried to get across? If she'd tried and failed, the Day-Glo dots would find what remained. If she'd succeeded, she would have ended up on this old logging road. LeAnne moved onto it, checked the other side: rough, upsloping country, dense with trees, mostly evergreens, and thick undergrowth. So why go up there when you had this easy road? LeAnne began walking along it, heading north. She saw no signs of anyone's recent presence: no footprints, no tire tread marks, no bits of paper or plastic:

perhaps one of those places where nature was still in charge, a creepy place to be for an eight-year-old girl at night. LeAnne's daddy had had no patience with night fears: *Gonna fold up on account of you don't see so good?*

Don't see so good? "Daddy was way ahead of the game, big girl," LeAnne said aloud. But then she realized she wasn't sensing Goody at her side. She looked back down the logging road. The dog hadn't budged, still sat in the patch of sunshine near the car. "Hey!"

Goody turned her head slowly, even insolently, the kind of move that would have ended with her doing push-ups by the dozen in some alternate world.

"Get the hell over here!"

The dog stood up, stretched, and came down the logging road, in no hurry. Just before reaching LeAnne, she paused, one forepaw raised. At that moment her demeanor changed, suddenly all business. She went into a brisk trot, right past LeAnne and on down the road. LeAnne hurried after her, was just about to catch up, maybe fifty yards or so farther on, when Goody suddenly darted to her right, sprang high over a rotting stump without the slightest seeming effort, and disappeared in the trees.

LeAnne broke into a run — huffing and puffing almost at once, so pathetic — and came to the stump. No sign of Goody. All LeAnne saw were tree trunks, shadows, rocks, the ground slanting up sharply. She grabbed a branch, swung herself forward, scrambled into the woods.

Had she run up grades as steep as this, as wooded and rough? Yes, many times. But not now. It wasn't a case of the mind still knowing how and the body not delivering: both parts were impaired. She filed that thought away for future reference, which she'd probably forget when the time came. That was pretty funny in a way, and LeAnne was smiling as she squeezed between two big rocks, their tops touching as though they'd rolled into each other, and reached a small clearing, a quarter of an acre or a little less, almost flat. Goody was sniffing her way around the forested edges of the clearing, in a quick trot, her tail standing straight up.

LeAnne called to her in a low voice. "Goody?"

There was a moment of deep silence, and then Max Skelly stepped out of the woods, smoking a cigarette, binoculars around his neck. He grinned, like this was a pleasant surprise. "LeAnne, right? Marci's friend from the army?"

Her pulse, which has sped up a bit, ramped back down. "That's right."

"The sheriff banished you, too?"

LeAnne nodded.

"Don't know what he's expecting to achieve," Max said. He reached into the pouch pocket of his hoodie, which read Skelly Lumber across the front, and held out a pack of cigarettes. "Smoke?"

"No."

"You'd think he'd want all hands on deck at a time like this — especially folks like you, who know their way around in rough country."

"What makes you think I know my way around in rough country?" LeAnne said.

"I didn't hear you coming. The dog neither. That's a sure sign."

LeAnne realized that Goody was back beside her, pressing against her right leg. "What are you doing up here?" she said.

"Same as you, I expect." Max took a drag on the cigarette. "If there's anything to this whole armband idea, then maybe Mia made it up to the road."

"Right," said LeAnne. "But you're not on the road."

"Already walked it twice — not even three miles long, start to finish, state highway on both ends. State highways with traffic —

meaning she would have been seen, most likely."

LeAnne nodded. It made sense, especially if you knew about the road and its limits, which she should have learned from the map, but somehow had not.

"So I moseyed on up here," Max went on. "It's the only open spot you could get to at night, especially for a kid. And it's really a dead end." He jerked his head at the forest rising behind him. "The next two miles or so are pretty much impassable."

"You know the terrain."

"Loved the outdoors as a kid. Roamed all over the woods, the mountains, everywhere." Max dropped his cigarette butt, ground it under the heel of his boot: a heavy, combat-style boot, a shitkicker.

"Nice binoculars," LeAnne said. They looked like Steiners, far better than the binoculars she'd lost. Max's were camo coated. "Ever in the military?"

His gaze went to her bad side. "No."

"Marci was."

"I'm aware of that."

"On account of you."

He still had a slight smile on his face, but now it changed, as though losing its inner support. For a moment, LeAnne expected some sort of outburst; she was mistaken.

Instead, Max turned away. "I won't argue," he said. "I'm sorry for what I did back then, not that it does any good. I was a different person."

"Sorry for beating Marci up?" LeAnne said, in no mood for him to sound reasonable or to be apologetic. "Is that what you're talking about?"

He nodded. LeAnne waited for some excuse, like Marci had asked for it, or egged him on, but there was none of that. She felt a strong urge to double down, to push him harder, and was trying to think of the most hard-hitting way, when Goody suddenly moved forward and began sniffing at Max, starting at his boots and moving higher.

"Hey, pal," Max said, "what's up?" He tried to pat Goody's head. Goody twisted her head away and kept sniffing. "I know what you're smelling." He pulled a baggie from his back pocket, took out a sandwich. "Ham and cheese," he said. "Okay for her to have it?"

"Yeah."

Max held out the sandwich. Goody ignored it, continued sniffing him. Max laughed. Goody kept sniffing him. Max's laughter faded away. At that point, Goody went still, then grabbed the sandwich and trotted off to eat it by herself. Max laughed again. "Big personality," he said. "What's her name?"

"Goody."

"Cool." Max lit another cigarette, licking his thumb and forefinger and pinching out the match tip flame. "I never really got the details on what happened to Marci," he said.

"What difference does it make to you?" LeAnne said.

He glanced at her, then looked away. "You're a tough customer," he said. Then, his voice lower and softer: "No reason a beautiful woman can't be tough, too. Just takes some getting used to, at least for a country boy such as myself." He took a deep drag and exhaled slowly, his face momentarily vanishing behind a cloud of smoke.

Beautiful woman? Had she heard right? A combination of that and the sound of Max's voice in this lower register shifted something inside LeAnne, and she felt Max's sexual presence.

The smoke cloud blew away. He seemed to have moved closer, was gazing down at her. He had dark eyes, eyes hard to look away from at that moment. Max touched her shoulder. His hand felt good — there was no denying that: one of those men who knew a thing or two.

"Hungry?" he said. "We could grab a bite

somewhere."

The possibility of pleasure — temporary or even fleeting, but still pleasure — was suddenly on the table. LeAnne didn't know what to say. Then she remembered Mr. Adelson: *morons make the same mistake twice, and smart people make new ones.* Kind of confusing because Max had been Marci's mistake, not hers, but somehow it applied. At that moment came another memory, this one of Marci herself: *I'd like a do-over on that decision — let's leave it there.* Here was an opportunity so rare in life: a do-over — in this case to make Marci's life right, which maybe made no logical sense and yet still felt right. LeAnne twisted her shoulder away and Max's hand slid off her.

"Marci had her leg blown off in an IED explosion," she said. "Then in the hospital she threw a clot in her lung and drowned in her own blood. That is what happened to Marci."

Something changed in Max's eyes. Was it the temperature going down? Or actually heating way up? LeAnne didn't know. Max smiled a very small smile, kind of boyish. "I asked and you told me," he said. "Thank you."

LeAnne nodded.

"She didn't deserve it," Max said.

"We can agree on that."

"A positive note," Max said. He glanced around. "Are we out of here?"

LeAnne didn't see why not. The clearing showed no signs of recent human presence other than Max's cigarette butt and was hemmed in everywhere except for the entry point. "Let's go, Goody."

Goody trotted over, licking her muzzle. They made their way out of the clearing and back down, Max first, cigarette dangling from his lips, his movements quick and sure.

"I'm parked thataway," Max said, pointing north on the logging road. He held out his hand. LeAnne shook it — an enormous hand, warmer than hers, demonstrating just a hint of its squeezing strength for a split second. *She fell for one of those macho men.* And who could blame her?

Max started walking north. LeAnne watched him, and after he'd gone twenty yards or so, she called, "Max?"

He stopped and faced her.

"Did she have any enemies?" LeAnne said.

He shaded his eyes with his hand, as though warding off a glare, even though the clouds above were dark and thick. "Excuse me?"

"Mia. Was she being bullied, maybe, or

anything like that?"

"You're asking the wrong person," Max said, lowering his hand. "What do I know about her life? I got cut out."

"Poor you," said LeAnne.

Max gave her a long look. Then he turned and walked away. LeAnne headed in the other direction. When she reached her car, she looked back. He was gone. She gazed across the swamp and saw the Day-Glo dots, now a little closer.

LeAnne drove back down former logging road N31, Goody sitting up and panting on the passenger seat, and swung west on the state highway, headed back into Bellville. She'd gone about half a mile when blue lights flashed in the rearview mirror and Sheriff Cosgrove pulled her over.

Chapter Twenty-Eight

The sheriff came to the side of the car. Was it possible he was the bearer of good news? LeAnne slid down the window. He hunched down, peered inside like some run-of-the-mill cop looking for run-of-the-mill drugs or some other stupid shit.

"That dog under control?" he said.

She'd forgotten about his bushy mustache, how it wriggled around like a hairy crawler when he spoke, capturing all her attention and nauseating her at the same time. "What the hell?" she said. "That's why you pulled me over? To check on the dog? What about Mia?"

"What about her?" said Cosgrove.

"Have you found her, for Christ sake?"

"No. Have you?"

"Have I? What's that supposed to mean?"

"Step out of the car, please."

Goody was panting harder now, drool trickling off her tongue.

"Why?" LeAnne said. "I wasn't speeding."

"Step out of the car."

"Are you arresting me?"

"That depends. Step out of the car. Don't make this difficult."

LeAnne grabbed the wheel with both hands. "Arresting me for what?"

Cosgrove gazed down at her, not speaking, but his mustache still seemed to be wriggling around. She was going to puke unless she stood up right away. LeAnne opened the door and got out, quickly closing the door in case Goody had a mind to follow. But Goody stayed where she was, still panting. If she was having any thoughts, they were elsewhere.

LeAnne took a deep breath, felt a little better. She took a good look at Cosgrove, a medium-built man maybe two inches taller than she was, with a soft middle. "What do you want?"

"What the law wants," Cosgrove said, "is any information you may be concealing on the whereabouts of the child."

"Are you insane?"

Cosgrove's face reddened, but his voice stayed calm, maybe in a slightly exaggerated way. "How about starting with your own whereabouts, specifically on the night of the funeral, meaning the ninth of this month."

LeAnne laughed in his face. "I'm a suspect? You're insane or stupid or both. Why would I do anything to harm Mia?"

"I'm not suggesting you intended to harm her. And I don't know anything about your motivation firsthand. But this morning I spoke to someone who does."

"Someone who knows about my motivation? What the fuck are you talking about?"

"His name is . . ." Cosgrove took a notebook from the chest pocket of his shirt and flipped it open. ". . . Machado. Dr. Ernest Machado, assistant director of psychiatric services at Walter Reed Army Medical Center." He glanced up. "Ring a bell?"

LeAnne went lightheaded. For a moment or two, she lacked the strength to look anywhere but at his mustache, as though her vision was narrowing into one tiny circle, like an editing trick in a silent movie. She leaned over and vomited on the road.

The sheriff stepped back quickly, keeping his shoes clean. LeAnne reached out for the car, steadied herself against it.

"Dr. Machado says you left the hospital without authorization," Cosgrove continued, voice strengthening, like momentum was now his. "Furthermore, that such authorization would not have been forthcoming on account of your mental state, which he described as . . ." He checked the notebook again and read from it. ". . . severely unstable. Dr. Machado believes you and Marci Cummings formed a short-lived but intense and mentally — or is it mutually? Can't read my own damn writing — destructive relationship and that when she died, you suffered a psychotic break." He looked up. "Meaning you snapped. When I asked whether in your state of mind you might glom onto Marci's daughter, the doc said it was entirely possible. Now comes some story from McCutcheon's granddaughter about a scary-looking commando outside Mia's window. So I ask you again — where were you on the night of the funeral?"

Scary-looking? Had he really said that? Or was it her imagination? LeAnne turned away from the car and peered at him, trying to make up her mind. "What did you say?"

"You heard me. Where were you the night of the funeral?"

"Before that — about B.J."

"Planning on attacking the credibility of a kid? See that all the time, but it's still kind of low, if you ask me. B.J. McCutcheon says Mia told her she saw a commando outside her window the night of —"

"What kind of commando?"

"Huh?"

"You heard *me."*

The sheriff's eyes shifted for a moment. Then his chin tilted up in an aggressive way. "Scary-looking."

LeAnne punched Cosgrove in the mouth with all the strength she had. He staggered and almost went down, one hand going to his face, the other fumbling for his sidearm. LeAnne made a move for it, but the damaged version of her was too slow; so slow that this pudgy provincial lawman not only held on to his revolver, but also got in a pretty good backhand whack with the barrel, raking it across her bad side, a blow she didn't see coming. Inside the car, Goody started bashing around and barking at top volume.

LeAnne's head got strange inside, sort of molten. She went down on one knee, tried to steady herself but could not, and slumped to the ground. The chances of rising on her own anytime soon seemed pretty slim, but then, right through the ground, she felt the force of what Goody was doing in the car. LeAnne rose. She raised her hands. She made them into fists.

Cosgrove stepped back and pointed the revolver at her head. Blood seeped from his mouth, reddening the tips of his mustache.

"Don't force me to defend myself," he said. The look in his eyes said the opposite.

"Meaning you'll shoot me."

"That I will," Cosgrove said.

LeAnne came close to saying, *Be my guest.* But the car was actually rocking now. She glanced over at Goody — Goody beside herself — and said, "Easy, there," much too quietly to be heard. Goody went still.

"Hands behind your head." Cosgrove made a little motion with his weapon.

"No way," LeAnne said. She kept her hands where they were, still squared for combat. He glared at her. She glared right back. The violent urge that had taken hold of her shrank down to something manageable. LeAnne lowered her hands. "I had nothing to do with Mia's disappearance. I wasn't even here that night."

"Prove it."

That was maddening. Prove it? How? Some details of her trip — like the gingerbread men with the mint-green eyes — were very clear, but there was no orderly arrangement, or even complete attendance, no matter how disorderly, of all the wheres and whens.

"Maybe you'll think better in a cell," Cosgrove said. "Nice and quiet. Meanwhile, you're under arrest for assault against an officer of the law. I need you to turn around and place your hands on top of the vehicle."

LeAnne stayed the way she was. Cosgrove spoke into the transmitter on his collar. Calling for backup? LeAnne wasn't really listening; she was watching Goody. Goody was watching her. One of her paws rested on the red phone, sitting in the cup holder.

"What's the point of making this difficult?" Cosgrove said. With the back of his free hand, he wiped the side of his mouth and saw the blood. His voice rose. "I'm taking you in, one way or another."

LeAnne gazed at him and said nothing. Should she have been scared? She wondered about that. Had he bloodied her face, tit for tat? She didn't give him the satisfaction of seeing her check. Siren sounds rose in the west, getting louder.

"Here and now's your one chance to make a deal," Cosgrove said. "I'll drop the assault charge. Just tell me where Mia is."

"You're embarrassing yourself," LeAnne said. "But let's keep that between us."

"What the hell are you talking about?"

"I can prove I had nothing to do with Mia's disappearance."

"Out of the blue? What changed?"

"Sure, out of the blue. You win." LeAnne waited, but not for long.

"Go on," he said.

"I need to make one call."

Cosgrove thought that over. LeAnne could feel him doing some sort of careerist arithmetic. He took out his own phone.

LeAnne shook her head. "Has to be my phone." She pointed inside the car. He came closer, keeping the gun on her, and took a look. "In the cup holder," she said.

He nodded. "You got a weapon in there, too?"

"No."

"How are you planning on getting the phone without that animal jumping out and attacking me?" the sheriff said.

"Don't call her an animal," LeAnne said.

"Because I'll shoot her if she does."

Which would be your last act on earth. LeAnne opened the door, said, "Stay," reached past Goody, took the phone, closed the door. Goody didn't move once. LeAnne had the crazy thought that she was in control, not just of Goody — in fact, not of Goody — but of everything else. Cosgrove made another gesture with the gun, this one meaning *make the call;* he was like an orchestra conductor with a .38 instead of a baton. LeAnne was almost smiling when she hit the call back number.

"Good to hear from you," Stallings said.

"You know where I was the night of the ninth."

"Is that a statement or a question?"

"Both. Neither. Just tell me."

"Mind saying why?"

"A sheriff here is asking."

There was a silence. "And it would be good if you weren't in his county that night?"

"Exactly."

"Ninth of this month?"

"Yes. Let's have it."

Another silence. "Got an idea," Stallings said. "I'll come over there and tell him in person."

"What are you talking about? I'll put him on right now."

"In person is always best, in my experience."

"Then we'll settle for second best. I can't wait."

"Can't wait an hour?"

"An hour? You're not in Kabul?"

Stallings clicked off.

Cosgrove checked his watch. "Fifty-eight minutes," he said. By that time two more squad cars and an ambulance had joined them out on the state highway just west of the intersection of former logging road

N31. The EMTs, the sheriff, and one of the cops stood in a little group by the Honda; LeAnne leaned against it; Deputy Lima stayed in his cruiser, his face trying on a series of unpleasant expressions. Champ sat beside him, eyes on Goody, who remained in the Honda, gazing right back at Champ.

Goody's ears went up. A moment after that, LeAnne heard a faint *whap whap* coming out of the west. Then Champ's ears rose. And finally the other humans heard it, too. A small dark green helicopter — a Kiowa, with its jutting lower jaw; LeAnne had ridden in them many times — came skimming over the treetops, banked, slowed, then landed on level ground by the roadside and shut down. Captain Stallings, dressed for some reason like a hot-shot pilot in a leather flight jacket over his blues — the actual pilot was wearing jeans and a flannel shirt — jumped down and approached. He had a bounce in his stride, like there was no containing his good mood.

"Hi there, everybody," he said, giving LeAnne a quick nod. "My name's Stallings, US Army Intelligence. Who's in charge?"

The sheriff stepped forward.

"Sheriff Cosgrove?" Stallings said.

"That's right."

"How about we walk and talk a moment

or two?" Stallings put his hand on Cosgrove's back, herded him across the road, showed him ID and a document or two. LeAnne couldn't hear what was being said, but could see that Stallings did most of the talking. Then came nods of agreement and the sheriff, the other cop, and the EMTs got into their vehicles, although they didn't drive away. Stallings walked over to LeAnne. He looked at her bad side, cleaned up by the EMTs, and said, "Good God. They got rough?"

LeAnne waved that away with the back of her hand. "Did you tell him?"

"Tell him what?"

"What you're here for. To clear this up. You know where I was that night from the GPS."

"Just west of San Jacinto, Nevada. You either slept in the car or paid cash for a room somewhere. I've actually got closed-circuit TV of you in a coffee shop at eight thirty-two that evening." He took out his phone and showed her a still photo. A frontal shot, taken from above. She seemed to be talking to someone out of camera range, and she was in an angry mood; her ruined side actually came off as the saner of the two. But that wasn't the point. The point was the time and date stamp in the top right corner.

"So," LeAnne said, "you showed this to the sheriff? We're done?"

"Not quite exactly done," Stallings said. "Although very close. It'll give me real pleasure to wrap this up, get you out of this ridiculous situation, but first I'd like it if you'd do one little thing for me."

"You son of a bitch."

Stallings smiled, not one of those weaponized smiles, but a sincere one, and gentle. Which only demonstrated to her that gentle people could be dickheads, too. "I don't blame you for being miffed," he said.

"Miffed?"

"Or something else much stronger. But this is the kind of situation that calls for a realistic approach — realpolitik, if you will."

LeAnne held up her hand to stop all his bullshit. "What do you want?"

"Your presence for seventy-two hours, tops. Just say yes and I'll march myself right over to your sheriff buddy and show him the whole shebang."

"And suppose I say no."

Stallings looked sad. "Then whatever happens will be under the purview of our sheriff here."

"He wants to put me in a cell."

"So I heard."

LeAnne tried to think, could come up with nothing better than "What if I double-cross you?"

Stallings shook his head. "I've seen your record. You're incapable of doing something like that. And not just because you've behaved heroically. That was only an expression of what you are inside."

"What a load of crap," LeAnne said.

Stallings shrugged his shoulders; maybe he was an odd two-layered type, gentle on the outside, icy within. "Believe what you want," he said.

What did she want to believe? Only impossible things. "Seventy-two hours," LeAnne said. "Tops." Maybe some people had the kind of brain that could come up with another way, but not her, not now. Locked up? Behind bars? She couldn't allow that, not even overnight, or for an hour, or a single minute.

Stallings made a little bow. "Thank you."

"Where are we going?"

"I'd prefer to discuss that en route."

"Of course, you would." LeAnne didn't push him. She was pretty sure she already knew.

Stallings laughed, went over to Cosgrove and did what he'd said he'd do. It took maybe two minutes. That left only the question of Goody. She looked down. Goody was beside her, on the blind side, looking back with those coal-black eyes. She wanted Goody with her, but what was right?

"Find me a number for Harvey Wald," LeAnne said.

"Yes, ma'am."

Harvey lived in a little white house at the end of a cul-de-sac on the flat side of town. He was waiting outside when they drove up, Goody in the passenger seat and Stallings in the back.

"Harvey Wald," LeAnne said. "Captain Stallings."

The men shook hands.

"I'm not sure what's going on," Harvey said.

"Didn't LeAnne explain?" said Stallings. "I'm borrowing her for seventy-two hours. You're taking care of the pooch."

"I got that part," Harvey said.

LeAnne noticed Harvey's posture, erect like a soldier, but relaxed at the same time. "Let's get Goody inside," she said. And to Stallings: "Mind waiting here?"

Stallings checked his watch. "We've got a plane to catch."

"Will it leave without us? Come on,

Goody."

Goody jumped out of the car and ran to Harvey's door, like she was somehow way ahead of them. Harvey opened up and they went inside.

"This is interesting," LeAnne said.

"I took down all the walls," Harvey told her. "Well, except for the bedroom and the bathroom."

She gazed at a black-and-white photo of a dark thunderhead split by a lightning bolt. "You took this?"

"I fool around with photography a bit."

He went into the kitchen area, filled a bowl with water, and laid it on the floor. "Here, Goody."

Goody, who'd been sniffing around, immediately went to LeAnne and sat on her foot.

"She prefers to drink from the toilet."

"I'll act accordingly."

"She eats kibble twice a day. Plus snacks. She likes walks. Here's her leash."

She gave Harvey the leash. Their hands touched.

"I'm hearing strange things," Harvey said. "Like about you being a suspect."

"That's old news, Harvey."

"Totally false, of course."

"What do you think?"

"Totally false. But I don't get why you're leaving all of a sudden. I thought you were . . . involved in all this."

"I am," LeAnne said. "But I made a deal."

"What kind of deal?"

"The deal part doesn't really matter. It's army business."

"Army business that has to do with Marci?" Harvey said.

"No."

"Then with what?"

With what? With Jamie. With the whole team. With protection. With herself and her whole goddamn life.

"You're not going to tell me?"

LeAnne gazed at Harvey. She had a crazy thought: that photo of the thunderhead was too much like what went on inside her and would have to go. Meanwhile, how was she going to answer his question on the subject of her army business? LeAnne found a simple way. She patted the damaged part of her face.

Harvey gazed back at her. Slowly, leaving plenty of time for LeAnne to stop him, he leaned forward and kissed the bad side.

"Why did you do that?"

"Because anything I said would be, quote, easy for me to say."

"Like — time to put it behind me, move

on with life, all that shit?"

Harvey shook his head. "Your face looks good to me," he said. "That's all."

Chapter Twenty-Nine

The Kiowa had two-by-two seating. LeAnne rode in back, Stallings up front with the pilot. It was too noisy to talk, unless you were wearing a communication headset, which LeAnne was not. The noise bothered her and so did the rotor tips flashing by at the top of her field of vision, over and over, a dizzying visual static against the blue sky. She spent most of the flight hunched over, her head almost between her knees, like some totally boot newbie on day one.

Death was good. A new thought, somewhat surprising but true. Mighty engines droned on and on, taking her closer and closer. One side of her face seemed to have a hot iron pressing on it, but her face happened to be far away and so there was no pain. All she felt was a kind of shifting around in her head, a crumbling, like after an earthquake, also not painful. She couldn't see a thing.

Perhaps she was sleeping.

She heard a voice she knew: "How much longer?"

Another voice, new to her, said something about headwinds and the Alps. The first speaker — a woman — wasn't happy to hear that. "Why in hell did they transfer her so soon?"

"Her only chance — wasn't going to make it otherwise."

A hand took hers. She remembered that hand, so similar to hers in size, strength, and power.

"Hang in there," said Colonel Bright. "I'm not letting you go."

A city appeared to the east: low skyline, mountains beyond — had to be Spokane. The helo tilted, banked in a long curve, and landed on a pad at Fairchild AFB. Stallings picked up his briefcase, and LeAnne followed him out of the helicopter to a runway a few hundred yards distant. They mounted roll-up stairs and entered the hold of a C-17, which could accommodate fifty-four soldiers in the sidewall seats but today had none. Only two of the seats were locked down in the sitting position. LeAnne and Stallings sat. The rest of the cargo was ASVs, six of them, all brand new.

Stallings gazed at them. "Eight hundred grand apiece," he said. "It never ends."

"Right," said LeAnne.

He turned to her. "I didn't mean that personally, regarding your . . . your sacrifice or anything like that. I was just referring to this conflict in general."

"I don't really care," LeAnne said. "Just say what you've got to say."

Stallings nodded. "What galls me more than anything is that someone of your brains and capability got taken off the board."

LeAnne snorted.

Stallings's face went pink; for a moment he looked like some teenager's embarrassed uncle. "Sorry if I'm off on the wrong foot here," he said. "If you've been thinking about this at all, you're probably aware that my assignment is to unpack the events of January seventeen, find out exactly what went wrong with Operation Midnight Special, separate the bad actors from the good."

"Why bother, if it never ends?" LeAnne said.

"Way above my pay grade, questions like that," Stallings said. "The point is that six on our side — including Captain Cray — were killed on that mission, and let's not leave out what happened to you. Why not do everything in our power to make sure it doesn't happen again?"

LeAnne didn't answer. She was stuck on *let's not leave out what happened to you.* Like there was a choice, and it could have gone the other way; and maybe in the long run it would go the other way, probably more comfortable all around.

"So what I'd like to nail down first," Stallings resumed, "is your take on the terp's behavior that night, in fact her behavior in general."

"Katie? Haven't we already gone over this?"

"We've only touched on it. I need you to remember everything she did."

Everything? That was impossible. Also she didn't want to remember any of it.

"By the way," Stallings said, taking an envelope from inside his flight jacket, "I've secured some funding for this."

"What are you talking about?"

"Research. It's a line item in my budget. There's three grand in here, all yours."

"I don't want it."

"You're still active in a technical sense — I could order you to take it." Stallings laid the envelope in the space between them. "Let's start with a terp's duty, which is predicated on being directly at the side of his or her military counterpart at all times during a mission. From the fact that Katie was completely unharmed in an attack involving the detonation of two M67s in a small, mostly enclosed space, we can infer that she was derelict."

LeAnne searched her memory. At first, all that would come was Katie's BBC accent and how she used it to mock the Afghani men. But then from out of nowhere LeAnne caught a whiff of the sweet and sour fruity smell of Jolly Ranchers, and a clear image of the muttering boy in that crowded dwelling on the night of January seventeen rose in her mind, quivered a bit, and then stabilized itself: a runny-nosed boy who seemed very nervous, although you couldn't be sure about things like that on account of cultural differences, and she'd asked Katie what he was saying. To which there'd been no response. And she'd looked for Katie. And Katie wasn't there.

"I don't see it," LeAnne said.

"Meaning what?"

"She loved American things. Like learning our slang — shitkickers, for example."

"Did you know she prayed five times a day?"

That seemed a bit familiar. But so what? "I had grunts under me who did the same thing," LeAnne said.

"Yeah?"

"Well, one."

"Was he any good?"

"Average."

"But still," Stallings said, "that's the most encouraging thing I've heard in a long time. As for Katie and her motivations —" He reached again inside the flight jacket, this time producing a photograph. Was this particular photo familiar or was it the actual subject — a man in a President Karzai–style karakul hat, narrow-faced with prominent ears and deep-set eyes, dark and highly intelligent?

"Who's this?"

"Never seen him before?"

"Are you saying I have?"

"Nothing like that," Stallings said. "Just gathering information. His name — real name, although there was some question about that at first — is Gulab Yar-Muhammad. He works for Taliban intelligence — we'd probably call him assistant to the director, or something like that. He's also Katie's uncle."

LeAnne looked into this image of the eyes of Gulab Yar-Muhammad. She wanted no part of anything they projected. "How . . . how did this happen?"

"Meaning how did this get missed in

Katie's vetting process?"

LeAnne's voice rose. "Yes, for Christ sake, exactly that."

"We're looking into it," Stallings said.

"Who is? You, specifically?"

"No, not me, specifically. Although that will obviously change if our little plan bears fruit." Stallings rubbed his soft hands together like he couldn't wait.

"What little plan are you talking about?"

"This one right here," Stallings said, patting his briefcase. "Involving you." He held up two fingers. Every little thing he did was starting to bother her. "Two objectives. One — determine whether Katie set you up — not just you, of course, but . . . well, us. And two — use her to get to her uncle. No need to explain how valuable an asset he would be. Agreed?"

LeAnne shrugged. Almost right away she forgot what she was supposed to be agreeing to, and instead found herself picturing the six Afghan girls, standing shyly by the jumping pit. Their names wouldn't come to her, not one. The only names she could recall were Mia and B.J.

"Here's where we stand at the moment," Stallings was saying. "We've taken Katie in, and we're holding her at a safe house in Kabul. She denies having any foreknowledge whatsoever of the attack. She claims that she did not leave your side, while also claiming she was stunned by the explosion and has no memory of what happened, a self-contradicting position to my way of thinking, but we can't budge her off it." He opened his briefcase, went through some papers. LeAnne liked the leathery smell of the briefcase. Stallings's own smell — some sort of limey deodorant overlaid on nervous sweat — was unpleasant. The combination twisted around itself in a way that was hard to describe. Was she having a Goody-type experience? She realized she was missing Goody already. Meanwhile, Stallings was looking at her in an expectant way, as though awaiting a reply.

"What?" LeAnne said. "What do you want?"

Stallings sat back. Had she spoken at high volume? Hard to tell, especially since the four turbofans of the C-17 were starting to rev.

"I just wanted to make sure you realize we're headed for Kabul," Stallings said.

LeAnne nodded.

"Okay, then." Stallings patted the briefcase. "Same page. We're good."

The C-17 taxied down the runway. LeAnne wished there'd been a window, wanted badly to see out. She had a strong premonition that she wasn't coming back.

Meanwhile, Stallings was shooting her a sidelong look, back in the uneasy uncle role again.

"Spit it out," LeAnne said.

The C-17 shuddered slightly and lifted off.

"This might be a little awkward," Stallings said. "Please don't take it personally. But I can't help noticing . . . maybe that's not the way to put it. What I'm trying to say is they've done a great job with your new eye. So realistic, if you don't mind my saying so."

"What can I take personally?" LeAnne said.

"Touché," said Stallings. "And, of course, in civilian life I wouldn't dream of going . . . where I'm going. But it concerns the mission."

"What does?"

"Your new . . . your prosthetic eye. Is it removable?"

"Huh? Of course, it's removable."

"Is it easy to take out and put back in?"

LeAnne shrugged. "I guess so. Why?"

Stallings rubbed his hands together again. "Did you know Katie was a big admirer of yours? Or at least purports to be?"

"We got along all right."

"For her, you're the model of . . . how to put it? American womanhood? Something like that. You made a huge impression on her. Which was probably why she was so relieved when we told her that you hadn't been badly hurt in the attack."

LeAnne tried to rise, but she'd forgotten about the seat belt and it kept her in place. "What did you just say?"

"Concussed, yes, and there'd been some concern, even worry, for a while, but the stateside docs were able to save your eye and you were pretty much as good as new, no, uh, scarring or anything of that nature."

LeAnne tried to unbuckle herself. Her fingers just couldn't do it.

"She actually fell to her knees and thanked God — well, Allah — when we told her," Stallings went on. "That's why we think the sudden, unannounced appearance of the real, present you will shock the truth right out of her. It'll be a stunner, if you see what I mean, psychologically speaking."

LeAnne's voice seemed to come to her from far away. "And you want me to take my eye out first?"

"Thank you for saying that. It was going to be an awkward request."

LeAnne felt her face blushing bright red

— at least the undamaged side, the right side now beyond blushing — like she was deeply embarrassed about something. But wasn't it Stallings who should have been blushing? His color was that of your ordinary office worker on an ordinary day. At last the buckle opened. LeAnne thrust the seat belt aside and stood right up.

"Sorry if I didn't prepare you better," Stallings said.

LeAnne didn't even look at him. She marched herself aft, past the six ASVs, snapped the very last seat into place, and sat down. LeAnne folded her arms across her chest and after that remained completely still. Inside was turmoil beyond comprehension, at least to her.

"Is it illegal?" LeAnne said.

"Illegal under the law, no," said Katie. "But taboo. Taboo is stronger than the law, as maybe you don't know in America."

"I actually don't know that," LeAnne said.

"Pah," said Katie. "Laws can be changed. That is the difference."

"Uh-huh," LeAnne said. "Tuck your pant legs into your socks."

"Why ever would I want to do that?"

"So you don't get caught in the chain and go ass over teakettle." LeAnne rolled the bike next to Katie, sized things up, took a wrench, and lowered the seat as far as it would go.

"Ass over teakettle? I don't understand."

"Sure you do."

"But why teakettle?"

"It's just what we say."

"The expression is vulgar," Katie said. She tucked the hems of her slacks — black, of nice-looking fabric and cut — into the tops of her socks. Per LeAnne's orders, she was wearing sneakers — the first time LeAnne had seen her in anything other than heels or city-type boots. The sneakers, white on white, looked like they'd just come out of the box.

"Hands on the grips," LeAnne said, keeping the bike steady. "Swing your leg over. Sit."

"This is not comfortable."

"Feet on the pedals. Not like that."

"My feet are on the pedals."

"Balls of your feet."

"Balls of my feet. You are very dictatorial, you realize, in fact reminiscent of . . ."

"Of who?"

Katie shook her head.

"Out with it," said LeAnne. "When I'm insulted I like to hear the payoff."

"Of . . . of certain family members."

"You're talking about members of your family?"

"But who on this earth has a perfect family?" Katie said. "Now will you give me a push?"

LeAnne gave Katie a push. She wobbled forward.

"Faster! Pedal faster."

Katie peddled faster, got the wobbling under control. She rode across the hard-packed dirt of the compound as far as the razor-wire-topped wall, turned unsteadily, and came back, picking up speed — actually much too much speed.

"I am riding! I am riding!"

The droning died away to a silence of the muffled, cottony type, all vibration gone but the sensation of gliding still there.

"Sorry to wake you."

LeAnne looked up. Stallings stood in front of her, a garment bag folded over one arm, a cooler in his free hand.

"What do you want?" she said.

"Brought you this." Stallings held out the garment bag. LeAnne didn't take it. He laid it beside her, set the cooler on the floor.

"Where are we?"

"Lajes — pit stop. We'll be airborne again in fifteen minutes. Anything else I can get you? Any questions?"

"Yeah, I've got a question. Does Colonel Bright know about this?"

"You're referring to our mission?"

"What else?"

"I haven't actually had the pleasure of meeting the colonel, although, of course, I've heard all about her. But the short answer is no. We all operate in our own silos."

"How's that working out?"

"I hear you."

Stallings returned to the front of the aircraft. LeAnne noticed one of the doors, just behind the starboard wing, was open. She rose, walked over to it, and stood in the moonlight. Mountain silhouettes rose in the distance. She heard music.

LeAnne had always been good at sleeping during down times, like before a mission, but sleep wouldn't come for the rest of the flight. Somewhere over the Mediterranean, she took the garment bag into the head and opened it up. Inside hung a new combat uniform with "Hogan" on the right side of the chest. LeAnne stripped down, changed into the uniform, regarded herself in the mirror. Then she took it off, rehung it neatly in the garment bag. When she got off the plane at Kabul International Airport, she was wearing what she'd started with: jeans, T-shirt, a light jacket, and Marci's red sneaks. She was half a world away from where she should have been. LeAnne stood up straight and followed Stallings toward a waiting Growler, idling on the runway.

The driver jumped down and ran toward them. It was Corporal Crannack, looking completely unchanged. He was grinning, a grin that expanded with every step. He ignored Stallings completely, drew up in front of LeAnne, and saluted.

"Welcome back, Sarge. You're a sight for fuckin' sore eyes, that's for goddamn sure."

"Hey, Luke," she said, then paused, and somehow the right thing came to her, for the first time in way too long. "Lookin' pretty good yourself." She started in on a fist bump, but he swept past, grabbed her, hugged her, raised her off the ground. He pounded her on the back until it hurt and she wanted him to never stop. She was home.

Chapter Thirty

The setup was familiar to LeAnne from movies and TV, but she hadn't thought about — or missed completely — its essential creepiness. She and Stallings sat at a desk in a darkened room before a two-way mirror. On the desk lay a pad of paper and a pen for each of them. Beyond the two-way mirror was another room, more brightly lit, where three people sat at a table. The two on the near side of the table — a big man and a big woman, both in uniform — had their backs to the mirror. The third person, on the far side of the table and facing the mirror — was Katie.

She didn't look good, seemed to have lost weight, for one thing, and she'd been trim to begin with. There were dark patches under her eyes, almost like bruises; the eyes themselves now the dominating feature by far, almost black and somehow much more liquid than solid. But what caught LeAnne's attention most were Katie's eyebrows. She'd always attended to them scrupulously, even obsessively, but now they were neglected, thick, prominent, even coming close to making her look like someone else.

Sound came through a speaker somewhere out of sight.

"How about we circle back a bit?" said the female interrogator.

"Circle back" was the kind of expression that interested Katie, but she showed not the slightest reaction. In fact, for a tiny moment, her eyelids appeared to get heavy, as though about to close.

LeAnne wrote on her pad: "Can we talk?" And turned it so Stallings could see.

He wrote on his pad: "V. quietly."

Then why hadn't he answered aloud? Some kind of humor? Was Stallings having fun? She twisted around to see him, but he'd sat down first, on her bad side, and she didn't get a good look. She spoke in a low voice. "Have they drugged her?"

Stallings replied even more softly. "No mistreatment whatsoever," he said. "By the book and then some."

Meanwhile, the male interrogator was speaking. "Don't see the point myself. All we've been doing is going in goddamn circles."

"Katie?" said the woman. "How do you respond to that?"

Silence. Was Katie thinking? LeAnne couldn't tell. Katie sat motionless. Nothing moved in the interrogation room except the play of light in Katie's eyes.

"Other than a touch of sleep deprivation," Stallings said, again very softly.

That made LeAnne angry. But why? If Katie had done — meaning done to her, namely ruined her life — what Stallings and the army believed she'd done, then her anger, and way, way more than anger, should have been directed at Katie. But it wasn't. What the hell was wrong with her?

"Katie?" the woman said. "Response? I'm trying to be nice to you here."

Katie nodded, an almost imperceptible movement. "What do wish to know?"

"What we wish to know, you stupid lying cunt," said the man, "is exactly what you did on the night of January seventeenth and who told you to do it."

LeAnne's head snapped back, as though the male interrogator had just slapped her face. Katie showed no reaction. Katie did not like vulgarity — except when used sparingly in an aristocratic sort of way — and would normally have made that very clear, even in a situation like this, but she showed no reaction. LeAnne knew right then, and all her anger started redirecting itself in the proper way.

"I have told you and told you so many times already," Katie said. "I knew nothing of the attack."

"Then how the hell —"

The female interrogator silenced the man with a raised hand, although perhaps he went silent just a hair too soon; still, LeAnne could tell that they were very good.

"What we need to understand," the woman said, "is why, given that your assignment was to stick to Sergeant Hogan like glue and that she was wounded, there wasn't a scratch on you?"

"But not badly wounded," Katie said.

"Excuse me?" said the woman.

"LeAnne — Sergeant Hogan, I mean — it is my understanding her wounds were not serious."

"Your point?" said the man.

"It's true, is it not?" Katie said. "About her wounds?"

"So?" said the man.

"We don't see what difference it makes," the woman said.

For the first time, Katie seemed animated. "Well, but it's obvious. If she was barely affected, doesn't it mean she was some distance from the detonation? And I was standing with her but on the other side, if you see, meaning even still more distant. And so therefore."

"So therefore what?" said the woman. "I'm not quite following."

"So therefore unscathed," Katie said.

"That's your explanation?" the woman said.

Katie nodded.

"Complete bullshit," said the man.

No reaction from Katie.

"More of a mixture, I'd say," said the woman. "Mostly bullshit but some truth. What was your impression of Sergeant Hogan?"

"My impression?"

"What did you think of her?"

Katie's look turned inward. What seemed to LeAnne like a full minute passed before she spoke. "Sergeant Hogan was my ideal."

"Then why would you put her at risk?" said the woman.

"But I did not. I have told you and told you."

"When will you realize we're not buying it?" the woman said. The interrogators rose. "Think up something new."

The interrogators headed for a door on the far side of the room. As they went out, the man turned.

"Don't even dream of putting your head down. I come back and your head's on that table, I knock it off your skinny fucking neck."

They left. The door closed. Katie took a deep breath. She leaned forward, put her elbows on the table, resting her head in her hands. Her eyelids closed, and she started to slump forward. The door in the far wall flew open. The male interrogator stormed in, grabbed Katie by the hair, and sat her up straight. She didn't make a sound. The man left without saying a word. Katie sat, eyes open, hair askew on one side.

"Okeydoke," said Stallings.

LeAnne followed him out of the darkened room, along a cinderblock corridor, past a small office where the interrogators were busy with their phones — the woman drinking coffee, the man with his free hand in a bag of Doritos — and came to a closed door. Stallings pushed it open, revealing a tiny bathroom.

"Made sure it was cleaned and cleaned again," he said. "Should be good to go for your preparations."

"Preparations?"

"With your eye situation, and so forth."

LeAnne went into the bathroom. Yes,

almost certainly the cleanest bathroom she'd seen in this country. The mirror shone. Wasn't there a shining mirror in some fairy tale? She tried to remember. *Christ, help me.*

LeAnne washed her hands with a fresh bar of floral-scented soap, dried them on a fluffy white towel with a *W* logo. She leaned closer to the mirror and removed her prosthetic eye. LeAnne hadn't taken a good look at what lay behind for some time. She did so now and did her best not to be shocked, or sickened, or repelled, or even affected at all. She wrapped the eye — a beautiful object, in a way — in a tissue from a conveniently placed pop-up box, and went into the corridor. Stallings glanced at her and nodded. They rounded a corner, came to a door. Stallings nodded again. LeAnne opened the door and went in.

She was in the interrogation room. Katie sat at the table, her back to LeAnne, facing what seemed like an ordinary mirror on the opposite wall. Had Katie heard her, and just assumed her interrogators were back? Or was she unaware? Marci's sneaks moved in a very quiet and squeakless way, ideal for sneaking up on people. LeAnne picked up Katie's smell — a mixture of fear and needing a shower — and walked around the table, into Katie's line of sight.

Could you kill someone with nothing more than a vision? Katie's whole face seemed to fall apart, as though under attack by some hate-filled portrait painter. Blood rushed into her head, drained out, rushed back in. Katie's eyebrows, now so thick, twisted into strange, spiky shapes, and her hands rose toward her face, clawlike. Her mouth opened wide enough for LeAnne to see for the first time that she was missing teeth in the back, and she screamed, first silently and then in a horrible rising wail. Katie got up, her whole body trembling, moved around to LeAnne and fell at her feet.

LeAnne went stony inside.

Katie looked up, tears flowing down her face. "Forgive me, I beg you."

"Why should I?"

"Oh, LeAnne, I would rather hurt myself than you. All I told him was your method. Not a solitary fact more. Just that one tiny thing!"

"I don't understand you."

"Why, the footwear. The shitkickers. No more, I swear! That one tiny, tiny thing. He promised me no harm would come to you — nothing, complete and total nothing!"

LeAnne gazed down at Katie, giving her a

good long look at this nothing.

Katie sobbed. "He would have killed me for certain. He kills so easily."

"Who?"

"How could I bring forward this relationship in the vetting? You would never hire me. I wanted the job so badly. And the visa at the end, yes, that."

"Who?"

"My uncle," Katie said. "Gulab Yar-Muhammad." She peered up at LeAnne, stifled a sob. "Does it hurt you? I hope not. I will pray for you not to hurt every single day for the rest of my life."

"What about Jamie?" LeAnne said. "Did he get included in the promise?"

Katie looked away and was silent.

"Get up," LeAnne said.

Katie rose and stood before her, a small, slight woman with tears and snot mixed together on her face. LeAnne knew she could kill Katie with her bare hands, then and there. She had the strength and the skill, and no one was going to stop her, even if it wasn't in the plans.

Katie reached out, slow and tentative, and touched LeAnne's arm. She inched in closer, rested her head against LeAnne's shoulder. LeAnne just stood there. Then, for no particular reason, she thought of

Goody. She put her arms around Katie, did not hug her or hold her tight or anything like that. It was more than enough already.

The door opened and Stallings entered.

"Thank you, Sergeant," he said.

"Feel like I been in a goddamn firefight," said Corporal Crannack. He and LeAnne were alone in the office where the interrogators had taken their break. "And that's just from hearing what went down."

LeAnne didn't agree. There was a surge of exhilaration after firefights — if none of your people got hurt — before exhaustion and numbness took over, and nothing was surging in her now. After a minute or two of silence, Crannack got restless, grabbed two beer cans from a shelf-top icebox, cracked them open, and handed one to LeAnne.

"No, thanks." But LeAnne took the beer, sipped, then sipped some more. "Know anything about dogs?"

"Dogs? Had 'em all my life. News to me that you're a dog person." He clinked his beer can against hers.

"I'm not," LeAnne said. "At least, I wasn't. But now I've sort of got this dog."

"What kind?"

Someone knowledgeable had covered this ground. Dot, maybe? LeAnne couldn't remember the details. "A mix. She's pretty big. And her head is huge."

"Cool. What's her name?"

"Well, Goody, but someone else gave it to her."

"Yeah? I had a pit bull name of Baddie one time."

"You didn't."

"Short for Badass. Took no prisoners. Once he even got a bear to back off."

"What kind of bear?"

"It was written on the cage, but I don't remember. One ginormous son of a bitch, that's for sure."

"The bear was in a cage?"

"A nice one. At the zoo."

"Baddie made a caged bear back off?"

"Shoulda seen him. Cage or no cage, woulda made no difference."

LeAnne laughed. They clinked beer cans again. "Maybe —" he began, but then Stallings entered. Crannack rose and saluted.

"At ease, Corporal."

"Care for something frosty, sir?"

"I'll take a rain check," Stallings said. He turned to LeAnne. "We've got a deal. She delivers the uncle. We cough up the stateside visa. You good with that?"

"What was her choice?" LeAnne said.

"That or we hand her over to the Afghan authority."

"A no-brainer," said Crannack. "Sir. Favorite brainer type of the entire Crannack family, going back generations."

Stallings blinked in a baffled way, as though Crannack were speaking another language. "LeAnne?" he said.

"Yes. I'm good with it."

"Then that's that — job well done. Corporal, you will convey Sergeant Hogan to the airport. We've got her on a flight departing in —" He checked his watch. "One hour and thirty-three minutes."

"Yes, sir."

Stallings went out. Crannack drained his beer. "Sarge?" he said.

"Uh-huh."

"That's a new eye you got, correct?"

"Yeah."

"Does it work?"

"What the fuck's wrong with you, Luke?"

"Looks good, is all I'm saying. So it kind of works, right?" He raised his empty beer can in salute.

LeAnne followed Crannack down several flights of cement stairs — the smell of piss growing stronger all the way — and out to an alley. A dusty Growler was idling a few steps away, a driver at the wheel. Fifty feet ahead an ASV was also waiting, almost blocking the alley completely. A door in the same block of crumbling mid-rises opened, and two soldiers hustled out, one in front of Katie — now wearing a white head scarf — and one behind, both like giants next to her. LeAnne paused, one foot on the narrow running board, waiting to see if Katie looked her way. And Katie's head did start to turn in her direction, but at that moment LeAnne heard a crack from up above, and a thin red jet shot straight out the top of Katie's head. Katie slumped into the arms of the soldier behind her, the white scarf turning red very fast.

LeAnne only caught a glimpse of that very last part with the scarf, because Crannack shoved her into the back of the Growler and flung his body over hers, as though she were nothing but a civilian. After that came things she only heard — shouting, running, calls for backup, the loading of ammo into weapons big and small, the *whap-whap* of arriving helicopters — but there were no more shots from above, and neither was there any return fire, meaning the target had not been found. LeAnne felt the beating of Luke's heart, first pounding wildly, slowly settling down to an approximation of normal.

Chapter Thirty-One

Someone had been talking about do-overs, but who? In the middle of the night, five miles above the ocean, LeAnne remembered: Marci. *I'd like a do-over on that decision — let's leave it there.* Now LeAnne wanted a do-over of her own. But what could she have done differently? She tried out various strategies, all of them petering out in different futile ways. Would you be a better person if you assumed that whoever you were dealing with was going to have her head blown off by the end of day? She was lost in a dark mental warren when the names popped into her head. LeAnne had a pen but no paper; she wrote on her hand so she wouldn't lose them: *Wrashmin, Durkhani, Hila, Muska, Laila (2).*

Harvey met her outside arrivals at Sea-Tac. He'd had a haircut, maybe a bit too short, and looked younger.

"Welcome back," he said, reaching for her duffel. LeAnne held on to it. There was nothing she could do about being a civilian, but she could carry her own stuff. "How did it go?" he said.

"I don't know what to tell you."

"No rush," he said. He leaned forward and kissed her, not smooth in action or timing, a kiss on the lips but meant to be quick. It turned into something else, something much more passionate, taking LeAnne by surprise. They held each other tight. She felt his body in her arms, kind of soft compared to men like Jamie or Luke, and wanted him anyway, despite of or because of that softness. It didn't matter. The decision had been made. LeAnne got her hands on Harvey's chest and gave him a little push.

"I reek," she said.

"Not to me."

"Don't be such a saint, Harvey."

"Why not?" said Harvey.

LeAnne pulled him back, gave him another kiss, this time of the pecking kind. They entered a parking garage, rode an elevator, stepped out, walked toward Harvey's pickup at the end of a row. In the passenger seat, a huge head rose up to window level. Barking started up immediately, plus thumping, scratching, clawing. Harvey ran over and opened the door. Goody flew past him, bounded to LeAnne, stood straight up, her paws digging into LeAnne's shoulders and licked her face in a frantic way.

"Hey, there," LeAnne said. And "easy now." Plus "that's enough, you can stop." But she loved it. Goody finally stopped, raced down to the end of the row, tore back to LeAnne, and went through her whole welcome home routine all over again.

Five minutes later, Goody was asleep in the backseat, her toy dog tucked between her front paws, and they were on their way to Bellville.

"You haven't asked me about Mia," Harvey said.

"I assumed if there was news you'd tell me."

"Sorry," Harvey said. "I wanted to see how you were first."

"So there is news? What?" All at once, LeAnne could hardly breathe, as though death had come smothering in from all sides.

"Good news, actually — Mia's been found."

"Alive?"

"Oh, yes. And unharmed."

"Thank God." Here, in some way, was her do-over, after all. She took a deep breath, felt light and strong at the same time, the way she'd always used to feel. "What happened?"

"Max found her, actually. He decided that the distance from Coreen's house to the bike path — three miles by the shortest route — was beyond the capability of an eight-year-old at night. Instead, he searched within a half-mile radius of Coreen's. Mia was in a shed on the property of an older couple who spend the winter in Hawaii."

"But," LeAnne said, immediately back to feeling like her new, lesser self. There was more than one "but." She tried to line them up.

"What did she eat?" Harvey said.

"Yeah."

"Turns out the old guy uses the shed as an office. He had bottled water in there, plus snacks — peanut butter, crackers, chips, stuff like that."

"And . . . and . . ." It came to her. "The armband?" LeAnne said.

"Nothing definitive on that," Harvey said. "She thinks she went to bed wearing it but doesn't remember what happened after she went out the window. The sheriff believes she lost it wandering around, and it's possible that an animal or bird carried it to the swamp."

"For Christ sake."

"Or that McCutcheon got things wrong, and the armband was from some previous funeral. The point is she's safe and sound."

"And the commando? Marci's mission? All that?"

"Now Mia thinks it must have been a nightmare. And it sure sounds more like a nightmare than a real event to me."

"What was she planning to do once she was in this shed?"

Harvey shook his head. "Apparently she mostly slept, the poor kid."

"How long are we talking about?"

"Why, since the funeral."

LeAnne's voice rose. "In days, Harvey."

He glanced at her. "Eight."

That was all? LeAnne gazed out the window. Rain was falling, not hard. Goody made soft snoring sounds. It was peaceful in Harvey's pickup. "Is she in the hospital?"

"They checked her out right away, but she's in good health. So now she's back home."

"With Coreen?"

"That's right," Harvey said. "Although not just with Coreen."

"I don't understand."

"Max is staying there, too. For the time being."

LeAnne sat up straight. Then came movement in the back, and Goody, too, was sitting up straight. "Why?" she said.

"It's what Mia wants." Harvey cleared his throat. "There's talk of some sort of shared custody, Mia spending maybe the school years in Seattle and the summers with Coreen." He glanced her way again, expecting who knew what.

The miles went by, ten, twenty, more. LeAnne began to see her whole life in three missions, the first two — Midnight Special and the interrogation of Katie — as complete failures. That left mission number three, last chance to get it right: *What's her future if something happens to me?*

"I want to see that shed," LeAnne said.

Harvey sighed. "Is that a good idea? Mia's fine, and that's what counts. Plus Max is her father, when all is said and done."

"I hate that expression," LeAnne said. "Just drop me off at Shady Grove."

The rain fell harder. Harvey bumped the wipers up to maximum speed. "I'll take you to the shed."

Harvey drove down a cul-de-sac with a vineyard at the end, the vines all in blossom, as though a dusting of snow had just come down. The last house stood at the end of a long driveway. Harvey parked in front of it.

"They don't come home till June," he said.

LeAnne knew he was talking about the old couple in Hawaii. What she was unsure of was the current month. She got out of the truck. "Goody? Let's go."

Goody, her toy still between her paws, looked up but didn't move.

"Goody?" This wasn't like her. "Has she been acting strange?"

"Well, yeah," said Harvey, "but in her normal way."

"Goody. Now."

Goody rose, yawned, stepped outside, and stretched. Harvey led them around the house, across a wide lawn — very green but not manicured in the suburban way — to a low shingled building, more like a cottage than a shed. LeAnne peered through a window into a pleasant-looking room with hardwood floors, a desk, an easy chair, and a small fridge and hot plate in one corner.

"How did she get in?" LeAnne said.

"The door. Apparently the old guy often forgot to lock up."

"Who says?"

"That's what his wife told the sheriff on the phone." Harvey pointed to the vineyard. "Up that slope and down the other side and you come out at the end of Coreen's street."

LeAnne had already gotten that part — half-mile radius, an eight-year-old at night, Max's theory — and didn't feel like giving it any more thought. She glanced down for Goody, expecting her in her usual place on the bad side, but Goody wasn't there, instead she lay on her back, halfway across the lawn, paws in the air.

"Goody! Come here!"

Goody ambled over, sat on LeAnne's foot, yawned again, then got busy scratching behind her ear.

"I've seen enough," LeAnne said.

"Doing anything for dinner tonight?" said Harvey, pulling into Shady Grove.

A normal, everyday question, but it seemed to come from an unfamiliar world.

"Or maybe you just want to catch up on sleep," he said, after what might have been an uncomfortable silence.

LeAnne glanced at him and nodded. "How about another time?" She patted his knee, resting her hand there for an extra moment. They looked at each other.

"Sure," Harvey said. "Anything you want."

LeAnne shouldered her duffel, walked up the white-gravel path, opened the door to cabin six. Goody, toy in her mouth, burst past her and leaped onto the bed, wriggled around, got comfortable. LeAnne went into the bathroom, stripped off the clothes she'd been wearing for way too long, turned the shower lever to hot, and stepped in. Too late she thought of the names on her hand. She looked: they were all blurred, and now they washed away.

LeAnne got into bed.

"Move over."

Goody did not move over. LeAnne didn't have the strength to do anything about it.

A hand touched hers. It felt familiar. A woman spoke. "I'm here, angel."

The voice, too, was familiar. LeAnne put these impressions together, made the right guess.

"I told them not to let you in."

"It's all right. I'm here to help."

"Help? How the fuck?"

Her mother stroked her hand. "Whatever you want. Just say."

What did she want? Nothing but impossible things, nothing but miracles. "Gingerbread men," she said, the only realistic want that came to mind.

LeAnne awoke to the sound of Goody slurping up water from the toilet. Nighttime. She checked the clock. Zero one forty, meaning she'd slept with no interruption since . . . she didn't know exactly, just remembered that it had still been daylight. LeAnne rose, rummaged through her duffel, got dressed. Goody bolted past her on the way out the door, and moments later was sitting up straight in the Honda, all business.

A crescent moon shone in the sky, about halfway to the horizon. LeAnne didn't like moonlight on a mission, but this thin little moon wasn't so bad. It gleamed on the wet patches in the swamp to LeAnne's left as she drove up former logging road N31, making lots of tiny earthbound crescents. She leaned forward, watching for that squat, rotten stump on the hilly side, her depth perception so poor. After a few minutes, Goody went tense, her head jutting forward in an aggressive way. The stump appeared at the limit of her headlight beams a moment or two later. LeAnne pulled over.

She took the flashlight from the glove box, and they got out of the car. "No barking, no noise, no bullshit." LeAnne switched on the light, and they made their way past the stump and started up the steep, overgrown slope. LeAnne had been slow on this same climb by daylight, and was slower now, but

Goody seemed even speedier than before. She bolted beyond flashlight range and disappeared. "And no running ahead," LeAnne added, way too late and pretty much talking to herself.

She squeezed through the space between the two big rocks, which looked strangely insubstantial in the flashlight beam, and entered the small clearing where they'd found Max smoking a cigarette. LeAnne swept the beam from left to right, found Goody on the far side, her tail standing straight up. She crossed the clearing, followed Goody's gaze, saw nothing but massive tree trunks growing closely together, the spaces between them dense with vines and brambles, all of it overhung by a heavy, pressing darkness. Goody lowered her head, sniffed a bit, and then moved forward, slowly now, at a pace LeAnne could keep up with. No easy or even possible route appeared in the cone of light, but that didn't seem to matter. All she had to do was stick to Goody.

They climbed over a fallen tree and went up a sharp rise, LeAnne forced to use her hands once or twice, holding the flashlight in her mouth. At the top, she paused to remove a thorny vine that had attached itself to her sleeve. She took a look around, shining the light here and there, and saw they'd actually come upon a trail. Very narrow, overgrown, almost disappearing in places, but: a trail. There was something she needed to remember. She stood there and waited. After a few moments, Goody growled and made a sort of jabbing motion with her head, getting impatient.

"Shut up."

And then it came to her. Max in the clearing down below: *The next two miles or so are pretty much impassable.* But they'd gone nothing like two miles, maybe not even a quarter of a mile, and here was a path. The fog that had dwelled in her mind since the night of January seventeenth lifted a bit.

LeAnne studied the trail, pretty much level in both directions. Through the treetops, she found the North Star, to the left of the moon and higher in the sky. The trail, at least on this stretch, ran east to west. East, deeper into the mountains, had to be right. She started walking east, saw that Goody had made the same decision for reasons of her own and was already rounding a bend about fifty yards ahead.

Past the bend, the trail began climbing the mountainside in a series of switchbacks. There was no sign of Goody, but LeAnne could hear her, ignoring the switchbacks and taking a straight line, up and up. She could also hear flowing water to her left, and soon she came to a simple bridge, just two thick planks stretched over a narrow stream. Goody was drinking down below, moonlight in her eyes and in the drops of water falling off her tongue. The dog seemed to be watching her. The strange, chopped-off tail wagged back and forth. Goody hopped up onto the bridge, with no sign of effort, and pressed against LeAnne's leg. LeAnne scratched between Goody's ears, just the way she liked. Goody pressed harder, hard enough to knock LeAnne right off the bridge if she hadn't braced herself. LeAnne got the feeling that Goody would have been happy to simply stay like this forever, and envied her.

They crossed to the other side of the stream, climbed another rise, went by some man-high boulders. Through the trees to the left, LeAnne spotted a dark, squared-off silhouette. She shone her light in that direction, saw a small, rough-hewn wooden cabin with a stovepipe poking through the roof. Her fog-free mind came through with exactly what she needed: *The third time — this was out in an old hunting cabin of his family's, always too much boozing in a place like that — she left.*

But it probably wouldn't have mattered. Goody was zigzagging toward the cabin, nose to the ground, cutting back and forth so powerfully that LeAnne could hear her claws tearing at the soil. Goody raced around the cabin, stopped at the door, and rose up to her full height against it, pawing and pawing.

LeAnne went to a window, shone her light inside. No one there, but she knew that already. She saw a room with a woodstove, and in the back another room with two bunk beds. The door to the bedroom was open, but there was a key in the lock: on the outside. LeAnne walked around the cabin until she found the window to the bedroom. There were bars on the window, a grid of steel with spaces of no more than four inches. She peered through, saw a blanket on the lower bunk of one bed, and the upper bunk of the second. Kids liked that upper bunk.

Goody squeezed against her, also peered in, tail wagging so hard LeAnne felt the breeze.

"Good girl."

CHAPTER THIRTY-TWO

The crescent moon sank from view, and the North Star and all the other stars faded away. LeAnne was parked on Apple Street, four houses down from 136, Goody sleeping beside her, partly in the passenger seat, partly stretched across the center console, her heavy head on LeAnne's leg. LeAnne straightened up and rubbed her eyes, which was kind of weird: why rub the fake? But it felt right.

A car went slowly by, rolled-up newspapers getting flung into driveways and onto lawns from the driver's-side window, almost like they were ejecting themselves. It was a beautiful sight and somehow fragile in a way she couldn't explain. She was starting to think that she was understanding less and less about life as it went on, when the door to 136 opened and Max came out. He wore a blazer and blue jeans, carried a large envelope, was maybe on his way to work.

Something about lumber? Max got into an expensive-looking sports car, not small although it had seemed that way with him standing alongside, and drove up the street, meaning toward her. LeAnne sat motionless. Max passed by, gaze straight ahead and intense, the engine of his car throbbing, low and powerful. Goody raised her head.

"Best if you stay here," LeAnne said. Goody thumped her tail on the seat. "Won't be long." LeAnne opened the door. Goody sprang past her, out onto the street.

They walked to 136. "Don't fuck up." LeAnne knocked on the door. Goody, on her right side, started panting. LeAnne knocked again, and Coreen opened the door.

"Why, LeAnne," she said, fastening the top snap of her housecoat, "this is a surprise."

"Where's Mia?"

"Asleep in her room. Did . . . did you want to meet her? I'm sure that can be arranged. Why don't you —"

"We need to talk. You and me."

Coreen glanced past her, down the street. Her hair was unbrushed, and she looked older than before.

"When's he coming back?" LeAnne said.

"I'm not sure."

"Where did he go?"

"To see his — well, our — lawyer, I believe."

"About what?"

Coreen drew back. "Family business."

"That's exactly what I want to talk about."

"My goodness," Coreen said. "I appreciate your friendship with Marci, very much. But I really don't see —"

"Is it about changing the custody arrangement?"

"We're still discussing the ins and outs, if you must know. But he really does seem like a changed man to me. And he is her father, after all. Blood is thicker than water."

"Don't tell me about blood." LeAnne pushed past Coreen and entered the house. Goody hurried by, got in front.

"Just a damn minute," Coreen said. "You can't just walk in here and —"

LeAnne whirled around. "This is nothing compared to what I can do. Close the door."

Coreen, eyes wide, closed the door.

"Let's go into the kitchen," LeAnne said.

They went into the kitchen.

"Sit."

Coreen sat at the table. LeAnne went to the counter, filled two mugs with coffee from a pot that smelled fresh brewed. She handed one to Coreen.

"I like a little cream," Coreen said.

LeAnne fetched cream from the fridge. She sat opposite Coreen, aware that the morning light from the window was shining directly on her bad side, and glad of it.

"Thank you," Coreen said.

LeAnne nodded. She felt Goody getting comfortable under the table. "Do you remember what you said last time I was here?"

"I'm not sure what you mean."

"You said . . ." But it was gone. Sitting in the car, waiting for dawn, LeAnne had not only remembered the phrase but had also gone over and over it in her mind. It was the whole fucking key to getting to Coreen to open up.

Coreen's eyes narrowed. Down below, Goody pressed against LeAnne's foot.

"You . . . you . . ." Then she had it! "You asked me to tell you what kind of a mother and grandmother you were, for not doing better. Remember that?"

Coreen's eyes filled with tears. Her mouth opened in a lopsided way, like some kind of breakdown was coming.

"Save the waterworks," LeAnne said. "There's no time. This is your one chance to be the very best kind of mother and grandmother. Is that what you want?"

The tears overflowed, but Coreen made

no sound.

LeAnne poured more cream in Coreen's mug. Creamy coffee slopped over the rim. "Did Max know she was prone to nightmares?"

"Yes."

"How?"

"That was Marci, letting him know in no uncertain terms. She blamed the nightmares on . . . on how Max had treated her."

"Are you saying Mia witnessed the beatings?"

Coreen looked down. "Maybe once. But when she was very little."

"And now Mia wants to live with him?"

"At least some of the time. As I mentioned, he seems quite changed and —"

"Spare me. Here's what you need to know. Mia was never in that shed on the other side of the vineyard, not for a single goddamn minute. Max had her in a cabin east of the swamp from night one."

Coreen put hand to her chest. "Those old hunting cabins? They're all condemned."

LeAnne waved that aside. "And Mia did not dream up the secret mission. She heard about it through her window the night of the funeral, just as she said. Do you understand, Coreen? He's got her believing Marci's coming home someday, but only if she doesn't breathe a word."

Coreen stopped crying. Reddish patches appeared on her face, a mottled combination of confusion, humiliation, anger.

LeAnne rose. "Don't interfere."

LeAnne walked down the hall, Goody behind and then in front. Goody stopped at the first door and stood there, highly alert. LeAnne turned the knob, glanced down at Goody, and gave her the quiet sign, finger across her lips — which made no sense, since she hadn't taught Goody any signs, plus Goody probably couldn't or wouldn't learn them — and opened the door.

The room was dark, and at first LeAnne couldn't see a thing. Her eye seemed slow to adjust, maybe just worn out from having to do all the work alone. Standing blindly in a backlit doorway to a darkened room was a bad move, made you an easy target: a faceless silhouette in a frame. But this wasn't that kind of mission. LeAnne was about to step forward when she heard a soft sound, like movement beneath bed covers, followed by silence, although not the silence of nothing going on — this was an intent kind of silence.

Then came a child's voice: "Mom?"

LeAnne felt along the wall, found a switch,

flicked it on. A pigtailed girl was sitting up in bed, squinting against the light, looking thinner than in the Missing Child poster.

"My name's LeAnne. Your mom and I were friends in the army."

Mia squeezed her eyes shut, opened them, took her first good look at LeAnne. She shrank back.

"Your grandma's in the kitchen. She knows I'm here."

"I want her."

"In a minute. She's pretty upset right now."

Mia shrank back a little more.

"On account of how you've been treated," LeAnne went on. She took a step into the room but left the door open.

Mia raised her hands. "Don't hurt me."

"That would never happen. I look bad, but you shouldn't be afraid. I got wounded in the war, that's all."

Mia turned from the sight of LeAnne's face, and her gaze fell on Goody.

"This is Goody," LeAnne said. "She's friendly, in her own way."

"She's big."

The hair rose on the back of Goody's neck. She sniffed once or twice, then headed straight for Mia. LeAnne was just about to grab her when Goody paused, one paw still raised. The hair on her neck flattened back, and she rested her chin on the covers of Mia's bed, coal-black eyes soft and almost docile.

"You can pet her if you like."

Mia reached out, slow and tentative, and gave Goody one light pat on the nose. Goody made a sound LeAnne had never heard from her, almost a purr. LeAnne crossed the room and sat on the edge of the bed, her unruined profile angled Mia's way. LeAnne raised her feet so Mia could see.

"These are your mom's shoes. She gave them to me in the hospital." Was that strictly true? LeAnne knew she didn't quite have the facts on that episode. Did it matter? "War's a nightmare," LeAnne said. Her voice cracked. She took a deep breath, got hold of herself. "Not the dreaming kind, but real. You're in one of those real nightmares right now. We're going to make it stop. Don't you want that?"

Mia shook her head.

LeAnne saw where one of Mia's knees pressed against the covers and rested her hand there, very lightly.

"There is no secret mission. Your mom was very strong and brave, but she died in the hospital. All the rest of this is just your father making trouble."

Mia tilted up her chin, a miniature expression of Marci-like defiance. "That's what he said they'd say."

"They?"

"Anybody who found out."

"Found out what?"

"About . . . about the mission." Mia shifted her knee away, out from under LeAnne's hand. "The coffin's full of rocks."

LeAnne gazed at Mia, anger rising inside. But letting it out would be the worst thing she could do. "Didn't your mom tell you to comb those pigtails out at night?"

"All the time." Mia started to cry.

LeAnne reached out to console her, but Mia still shrank away once more. "Get dressed. We're going for a ride."

"Where?"

"To see the proof. Don't you want to know for sure?"

Mia started getting out of bed. LeAnne thought she heard soft, retreating steps in the hall.

Mia sat in the passenger seat, Goody in back. After a few minutes, Mia noticed the stuffed dog, lying on the console. She picked it up. "How did Ruben get here?"

"A long story," LeAnne said. "But Ruben has your smell on him — that's how Goody knows you were in that hunting cabin."

Mia gazed down at Ruben, touched the little hole where his missing eye had been.

"The commando outside your window was your father. Don't you get that by now?"

Mia didn't answer. LeAnne turned into the gravel parking lot at the cemetery.

"Did this commando say your father would be taking care of you until your mom came back? And then you'd all be together?"

No reply. Goody rose up over the seat back. She snatched Ruben out of Mia's hand and withdrew. LeAnne parked the car, got out, took the spade from the trunk.

Cpl. Marci Cummings.
Daughter, Mother, Patriot.
She gave all.

LeAnne and Mia stood before the stone. Goody lay in a flowerbed nearby, on her back with all paws raised, tranced out.

"You'll have to brace yourself for this," LeAnne said, although she had no intention of doing any actual digging: wouldn't her willingness to do it be enough to get the message across?

"What do you mean?" Mia said.

"Make yourself strong inside."

"How?"

"Good question," LeAnne said. She tipped over Marci's stone. It fell with a thump on the soft grass. Mia flinched. LeAnne rolled up the strip of new sod for the second time. "Won't take long," she said. "The coffin's not even two feet down."

"How do you know?"

LeAnne turned to her. "Because I did this already."

And that information should have done it. Mia looked at LeAnne and at the tipped-over stone. She didn't say a word. LeAnne waited and waited, then finally dug up a small spadeful of dirt. Down at the bottom of the hole she'd made lay a fat worm. It wriggled around.

"Stop," Mia said.

LeAnne gazed at Mia. The expression on the kid's face reminded her of soldiers she'd known, in shock after their first firefight. She scooped up the little dirt pile and dropped it back in the hole. It was a windy day, clouds racing across the sky like things were running late.

"Help me get it all back together," LeAnne said.

Mia came forward, a bit like a sleepwalker. She unrolled the strip of sod and patted it into place with her hands. Then the two of them lifted the stone and walked it back into its setting.

"How about we have a thought for her?" LeAnne said.

They got down on their knees. LeAnne found she actually couldn't think about Marci at that moment, so she just watched the cloud shadows hurrying across the graveyard. Then they rose and walked back to the car, Goody on her right as usual. For the first time — and maybe late in the game — LeAnne wondered if Goody was intentionally protecting her blind side. She glanced down at Goody's face, found no answer. Meanwhile, over on the left, Mia wiped her eyes on the back of her forearm and took LeAnne's hand.

In the parking lot, LeAnne got Mia into the front of the Honda, Goody in back with Ruben, and was putting the spade in the trunk when the expensive-looking sports car came barreling up. It squealed to a fishtailing stop, and Max sprang out and marched toward her, jaw jutting out and red in the face.

"What the fuck do you think you're doing?" he said.

"It's done," said LeAnne. "Get lost."

"Out of my way. That's my daughter."

Max strode around toward the side of the

car. LeAnne got there first, blocked his path, holding the spade in both hands. A spade was not a good weapon, but LeAnne raised it horizontally like a pugil stick, metal end on her left.

"I'll shove that down your throat," Max said.

Inside the car Mia started to scream, and Goody went crazy, barking and howling and clawing at the glass. Max came at LeAnne, huge and very strong; even at her best she would have been no match for him in any fight that was all about strength. But fights never ended up being only or even mostly about strength — her face was living proof. Max grabbed for the spade. LeAnne faked left, once, twice, fakes Max bought both times, jerking his head away from the blade, meaning that after the second fake his momentum was in the direction that she was dealing from for real, dealing with the end of the wooden handle. It cracked hard against his temple, like sounded punctuation, and he staggered back. That was when LeAnne drove the blade into his chest, right under the breastbone, but not with all her power. She refused to let herself kill him, no matter how much she wanted to. She was all through with that. Max let out a whoosh of air and sat down hard, in pain and showing it. Things quieted down in the car.

LeAnne stood over Max, hefting the spade, maybe not such a bad weapon after all. He looked up, clutching his chest. "Don't," he said.

A huge, powerful guy, but essentially soft — a familiar type. The truth was that her own daddy, although a much nicer man, also belonged in that category. LeAnne tapped the blade on Max's head, a nice firm tap.

"How'd you swing the alibi?"

His eyes shifted; he didn't answer.

She tapped his head again, now with some force. Max cringed as the blade came down and cried out when it struck.

"The night after the funeral," LeAnne said, glancing at the sports car. "You drove that baby up from Seattle, got Mia in the cabin, raced back in time to be seen at breakfast?"

She raised the blade high.

He looked up at her, saw what she was capable of, and nodded. "Something like that," he said.

"Not perfect," said LeAnne, lowering her weapon. "But good enough for the sheriff."

"I think I'm bleeding inside," Max said.

"I doubt it." LeAnne was wondering

about Sheriff Cosgrove. Any point in calling him, getting the law involved? Probably, except she didn't feel like it. At the moment, in this parking lot, she was the law, and why not?

LeAnne turned her back on Max, tossed the spade in the trunk, climbed behind the wheel, and drove away. Somehow Goody was now in the front passenger seat with Mia squeezed in on the console between them. "I'm sorry you had to see that," LeAnne said.

"I mostly just heard it," Mia said.

"Goody was in the way?"

Mia nodded.

LeAnne patted her knee. "You good?"

"No."

"Better, at least?"

"I don't know."

"Think about it," LeAnne said. "But not too much. The whole scheme was all about him and his needs, not you and yours. Now you've got to put him out of your mind."

"How?" said Mia.

LeAnne nodded. "Maybe that's pushing it."

Chapter Thirty-Three

LeAnne was on a bit of a high after all that, a feeling she'd almost forgotten existed, at least for her. Harvey took her to dinner at the Bitterroot Café. They drank apple martinis made with local apples and white wine from local grapes. Between the main course — crab legs for LeAnne, pork chops for Harvey — and dessert, Harvey handed her a small gift-wrapped box.

LeAnne opened it up. Inside lay pearl earrings.

"They're beautiful," she said. "But you shouldn't have." Not least because it was a little on the early side.

Harvey beamed. "Aren't you going to put them on?"

LeAnne went into the bathroom, tried on the earrings. Because of something about the light or the mirror, the earrings seemed to turn the damaged part of her face pearly. She returned to the table.

“Wow,” said Harvey. “I hope you like them.”

“I do.”

The waiter poured the last of the wine. Harvey raised his glass. They clinked.

“Here’s to jewelry,” he said.

LeAnne laughed.

“The truth is I’ve been saving them.”

“Oh?”

“For the right occasion,” Harvey said. “Even if I didn’t know it consciously.”

“What do you mean?”

“They were for Marci, originally. Her birthday. But she left before . . . but the separation intervened.” His eyes opened wider, like he’d just been struck by a thought. “You don’t mind that, do you?”

LeAnne shook her head. “I’m proud to wear them.”

Harvey drove her back to cabin six at Shady Grove. She invited him in. Goody went into the bathroom, slurped water from the toilet, and didn’t come out.

LeAnne started feeling nervous, and Harvey seemed nervous, too. She poured vodka from a bottle she’d bought somewhere, sometime. Soon she turned down the lights, and later, just before they got into bed, switched them off completely. Darkness was the only way for this, at least in the beginning.

Harvey started out just right — cautious, gentle, attentive. In fact, amazingly attentive, as though he knew exactly what was going on inside her. And to her surprise, there was a lot going on inside her. LeAnne pulled Harvey on top, drew him in, felt all kinds of passionate feeling rising and rising in him. He was proving to be a deeply emotional man, and as this encounter went on — and blissfully on — she got swept up in deep emotions herself, until he finally came, murmuring, "Oh, Marci."

Not long after that, he fell asleep, perhaps unaware of what he'd done. But LeAnne was glad it had happened, and later in the night, when he got up to leave — the next day being a school day — she kissed him good-bye.

LeAnne packed up, laced on her red shoes, got Goody walked, watered and fed, and checked out of Shady Grove. Then she called on Coreen, leaving Goody in the car.

"I'm moving on," she said.

"I thought you might be staying," said Coreen.

"Nope," said LeAnne. "I hope I can trust you."

Coreen stepped back. "With Mia? What an insulting thing to say!"

"Glad to hear it," LeAnne said. "Where is she?"

"At school."

"Give her these, maybe when she's older." She handed Coreen the pearl earrings. "I'll send you a card when I'm settled somewhere."

Coreen walked her to the door. "Oh goodness, almost forgot," she said. "This came special delivery." She handed LeAnne an envelope with the Walter Reed return address in the top left corner.

LeAnne opened it when she got outside: a letter from Dr. Machado. He was glad to hear she was doing all right — even had a dog, a good idea in his opinion — and asked her to drop by when she returned for her scheduled six-month checkup. "A reminder that you report to X-ray," he wrote. "Normal protocol in these shrapnel remnant situations — watchful waiting, as I'm sure the surgeons explained."

Shrapnel? Surgeons? Scheduled six-month checkup? She'd forgotten. And with any luck, would soon forget again. It was trash collection day in Bellville, and Coreen's barrel stood at the end of the driveway. LeAnne crumpled up Dr. Machado's letter and dropped it inside.

"All set?" she said, getting into the car. Goody lay on her back, paws in the air, tongue hanging out. She made no response that LeAnne was aware of. LeAnne drove down Apple Street, crossed the bridge, turned north on Main, headed for Canada.

After five or six miles, there was no one else on the road, a narrow, winding road through rolling country, sun and wind somehow changing the color of the forests, from yellow through all the shades of green to blue, and back again. On a short, straight stretch she came to a single-bar gate and stopped: Canada. Open 9:00 a.m. to 5:00 p.m.

A uniformed customs and immigration officer came out of a small gatehouse.

"Be good," LeAnne said. Goody, now sitting up, licked her muzzle. LeAnne lowered the window.

"Hello," the officer said. "Destination?"

"Canada."

"Somewhere specific?"

"We're just driving around."

He looked past her at Goody. "Vaccinations up to date?"

"As far as I know."

"As far as you know?"

"Yes."

"Passport."

Passport. Hers was the red military kind. She remembered seeing it somewhere. LeAnne opened the glove box. Stuff fell out. She fished around in the glove box, found the passport, handed it to him.

"Military," he said.

"Yes."

"Meaning you're traveling under orders. Orders to just drive around?"

LeAnne said nothing. Goody yawned one of her huge yawns. Did that mean she felt totally unthreatened? That was good to know.

Now the officer was examining her passport photo. "Turn to me, please."

She turned her face to him. He saw what there was to see, hardly reacted at all. Then he looked past her again and pointed. "What's that?"

The Bronze Star was hanging from the open glove box.

"A medal."

"Can I see?"

LeAnne handed him the Bronze Star.

"What's it for?"

LeAnne didn't answer.

The officer turned the medal over and read aloud the inscription on the back.

" 'Heroic or Meritorious Achievement.' "
He handed her the passport and medal, tapped the roof, and said, "Enjoy your visit."

LeAnne drove north from the border.

"Dr. Machado thinks you're a good idea."

Goody hung a paw over the edge of the seat, got more comfortable. They hadn't gone a mile before the names came to Le-Anne, unbidden and insistent: Wrashmin, Durkhani, Hila, Muska, Laila (times 2).

ACKNOWLEDGMENTS

I am very grateful to two US Army veterans who read and critiqued the manuscript for this novel. To First Sergeant Chris Hochstetler, USA, retired, and to Anthony Saffier: many, many thanks. Any errors in the book are mine alone.

ABOUT THE AUTHOR

Spencer Quinn is the #1 *New York Times* bestselling author of the ongoing Chet and Bernie mystery series, as well as the bestselling Bowser and Birdie series for middle-grade readers. Keep up with him by visiting spencequinn.com or his blog chetthedog.com. Spencer Quinn (pen name for Peter Abrahams) lives on Cape Cod with his wife, Diana, and their dogs Audrey and Pearl.

The employees of Thorndike Press hope you have enjoyed this Large Print book. All our Thorndike, Wheeler, and Kennebec Large Print titles are designed for easy reading, and all our books are made to last. Other Thorndike Press Large Print books are available at your library, through selected bookstores, or directly from us.

For information about titles, please call:
(800) 223-1244

or visit our website at:
gale.com/thorndike

To share your comments, please write:

Publisher
Thorndike Press
10 Water St., Suite 310
Waterville, ME 04901